TWO TIME

CHRIS KNOPF

TWO TIME

 RANDOM HOUSE CANADA

www.randomhouse.ca

Random House Canada and colophon are trademarks

Library and Archives Canada Cataloguing in Publication

Knopf, Chris
          Two time / Chris Knopf.

ISBN-13: 978-0-679-31450-9
ISBN-10: 0-679-31450-4

          I. Title.

PS3611.N66T96 2006   813'.6   C2006-901999-1

Text design: CS Richardson

Printed and bound in the United States of America

10 9 8 7 6 5 4 3 2 1

TWO TIME

ONE

SOMETIMES AT SUNSET over the East End of Long Island God plays artist, spraying pinky red paint all over the sky. If your timing is right, and you're sitting on the deck of the Windsong Restaurant in East Hampton, you can catch the whole glitzy performance.

I'd already ordered an Absolut on the rocks and was settling in to watch. Jackie Swaitkowski hadn't shown up yet, which was no surprise. She was never on time for anything. She lived by an Einsteinian concept of space-time. It was all relative. I didn't care. As far as I was concerned, she could do what she wanted. She was a pal.

Two stories below the deck was a small parking lot where cars could line up along the edge of the lagoon. It served the restaurant and a small marina catering to big sport cruisers and a handful of fishing scows owned by the tattered remains of the local Bayman population. On the opposite shore of the lagoon was a small scrub-covered island with a single two-story house perched precariously over a short sandy cliff. Beyond that was Gardiner's Bay, named for a family who'd owned a big island out there since the middle of the seventeenth century. Until recently, one old Gardiner had it more or less to himself. I don't like that many people, but I think I'd be lonely living on a huge island all by myself. Maybe not if Jackie showed up once in a while. Wouldn't have to be on time.

There were four other people on the deck with me. A freshly scrubbed pair of young fluffs were leaning across a table vamping at each other. He wore yellow cotton pants, a green sweater and tasseled loafers without socks. None of which fazed his date. The delusion of perfect happiness floated freely across her pale blue eyes. The other two were a pair of hags from somewhere up island—faces stretched by surgery into metallic masks, nails hard as epoxy and hair like lacquered teak. One wore a white cotton top embroidered with sequins that matched her slip-ons and something sparkly painted on her eyelids. The other smoked a cigarette held at the outermost tips of her fingers, like you'd hold a splinter with a pair of tweezers. Neither could pronounce the letter R. They said things like "Don't I know it" and "I mean, honestly." They didn't seem to notice me. I wasn't offended.

The waitress came out every ten minutes to check on us, but didn't catch a lot of action. We were all nursing our drinks. I'd planned on working on a single Absolut until Jackie showed up. I never used to care how many drinks I had or when I had them, but I was on a program of self-improvement. I lit a Camel to preserve the program's transitional character.

A black Lexus pulled into the parking lot down below. Nothing happened for a few minutes, then the door opened and out shot a scruffy miniature French poodle chasing a ball thrown by the driver. He looked sharp and held together in a pure white band-collar shirt and pants the color of his car. His hair, also black, was cut close to the scalp, and his moustache clipped straight above his lip. His white shirt was professionally laundered and neatly tucked. His shoes were the kind of expensive black leather slip-ons that looked effeminate in store windows, but au courant on some people's feet. Definitely not mine.

The poodle conserved nothing in his pursuit of the ball. He captured it on the fly between his legs, then scooped it up in his mouth. It was almost too big to carry, but by holding up his head he could peel back at nearly a full run.

"I don't know what Michael's been doing lately," the woman with the sparkling eyelids was telling her friend, "but it's not working."

"Doing?"

"With his life."

"Oh, that."

"It's ludicrous, the whole Rolfing thing."

"I don't know what that is."

"Rolfing. It's like massage only deeper. More penetrating. They penetrate your muscles."

"Michael's penetrating his muscles?"

"Not his. Other people's."

"This can't be good."

"I don't even know what that means. Rolfing somebody."

"Sounds intestinal to me."

"It's not. It's like massage. I don't know."

"Would you like Michael penetrating your muscles? I don't think so."

"My daughter says it used to be huge in Europe. In Scandinavia."

"They go swimming in the winter. Break the ice."

"I don't understand any of it."

"For this, Michael leaves a perfectly good marriage."

"Not if you ask his wife."

"Exactly."

On her next pass I let the waitress bring me another vodka. Jackie was in deep schedule denial. It happened.

The poodle showed no signs of tiring. The guy had been throwing grounders, but now switched to the long ball. It gave him more time to stand at the edge of the dock and look up at the big boats. Or maybe at the sunset, it was hard to tell. When he wasn't throwing the ball he kept his hands in his pockets, clinking change and car keys. You could tell he was in good shape by the tight wedge formed by his shoulders and waist. Measuring a man's latent physical ability, even from a distance, was a fighter's habit. My father taught it to me, unconsciously. This one would be hardheaded, but inexperienced. No marks on him, no signs of wear. But never underestimate people, my old man would always tell me.

The poodle ran up on a blur of dirty white legs. The guy took the ball from its mouth and lobbed it past a pair of wooden dinghies and into the water. The dog listened for the splash and then without hesitation leaped between the boats into the oily dock water.

As the sunset faded the artificial light from incandescents around the parking lot began to alter the color and mood of the deck. It was early May, and the angle of the earth kept the sun up in the sky well into the evening. What little breeze we had from the lagoon fell off to a whisper, though it still brought in the scent of low tide and the caterwaul of seagulls circling casually over the Baymen's fleet.

The young swell in the yellow pants left the table and went inside the restaurant. He was thick around the middle and his feet were badly pronated. Would go down in half a second. The girl watched him leave, her eyes ready to make instant contact should he look back. He didn't. As soon as the door swung shut she turned her head toward the lagoon, as if caught without a focus, a legitimate reason for looking at anything at all. Or to avoid looking at me, who was flagrantly staring at her. She turned her head back suddenly and caught me in the act. I winked. She smiled stupidly and tried to look interested in the remains of her tuna salad. Her feet were hooked together under the chair the way my daughter would do when she was sitting at the tiny tea table I'd built for her. It made me want to protect the girl from bad choices in life. Another old fighter's habit.

A cell phone twilled impatiently. The sound was momentarily untraceable. One of the women from the East Side stopped talking and looked in her purse. Then it happened again and the guy on the docks looked toward his car. Yellow Pants came back out on the deck, moving chairs to clear his path, masking the sound of the cell phone's next ring. But the man on the dock heard it, and walked a few steps to the passenger-side door, opened it and dropped into the seat. He left the door open and sat with his feet outside on the gravel surface. He held the phone in his hand as it repeated the persistent chirping. He punched at the keys, but with no apparent effect. The two women started talking again, complaining about the coffee, comparing it unfavorably to the cappuccino they'd recently had at a trattoria off the Piazza del Duomo.

"Firenze. That's what they call that town over there. I keep telling you. Fur-en-zee."

"Doesn't sound anything like Florence to me."

"I always thought she was a queen or something."

"Before they had democracy."

"Nothing they say sounds like anything I recognize. My sister's husband's family—they're Italian."

"I always wondered what the hell this woman Florence had to do with anything. And I was there for, what, a week?"

The guy with the Lexus pulled his feet inside the car and shut the door. I caught sight of the poodle. His nose was just above the crest of the water, the ball in his mouth slowing his progress. A little wake formed behind him in the greasy seawater. I mourned the expensive upholstery inside the Lexus.

The first boom was almost subterranean—too low for the human ear. The girl with Yellow Pants whipped her head around like a startled herbivore. The inside of the Lexus was filling up with beautiful orange-red blossoms, a turbulence of roiling flame that broke like a wave against the tinted rear window. The car began to rock back and forth. The rear window splintered into a jagged web woven by a drunken spider.

I heard someone yell something. It came from the stairs that ran along the side of the deck. It was a familiar voice. The poodle stopped swimming and looked up at the car. The girl with Yellow Pants reached for her white wine. Disorientation swept the deck.

There was something about the color of the flame. I ran to the edge of the deck to get a closer look. Yellow Pants huffed at me as I shoved his chair out of the way.

I heard Jackie Swaitkowski again, yelling my name. By then I knew what was going on with the flame. I thought I was probably out of time, but there was nothing left to do but leap over the railing above the stairwell, almost landing on Jackie, who was down there staring at the car, pressed against the wall with the back of her hand stuck to her mouth. I grabbed a handful of her shirtfront. She yanked back involuntarily.

"Move."

When she saw it was me, she stopped resisting. I pulled her up the staircase, shouldered open the main entrance to the restaurant, and slammed into the cigarette machine that filled the vestibule just inside the door. The air began to glow a soft, flickering yellow.

"Sam?"

I pulled her around the pay phone and rack of brochures that also clogged the vestibule and shoved her inside. The place was almost empty. A man with a thin black moustache was behind a glass counter standing in front of an old-fashioned cash register. Below were rows of breath mints and kid-sized candy bars. He was staring at the brilliant, fuzzy glow from outside that was flooding the interior of the restaurant, one hand feeling around the top of the counter for the telephone.

We plowed over a sign that said "Please Seat Yourself" and made for the back of the room. The path was blocked by a table filled with Happy Hour hors d'oeuvres and crudités. Jackie tried to pull away from me.

"What the hell are you doing?"

I tightened my grip on her shirt and threw her over the table. She slid across the surface through buckets of buffalo-style chicken wings and big glass bowls filled with green peppers and celery sticks. I put my hands under the table and flipped the whole thing over on its side. A big fist of air punched from behind, and a glittering spray of glass that felt like electric sleet washed my back as I vaulted the overturned pine-slab table.

It was heavy enough to save us from being flayed alive by the hurricane of pressure-treated beams and floor joists, window frames, Cinzano umbrellas, ashtrays and Long Islanders that blew in from the Windsong deck.

—

Some time after that a small woman with short cropped black hair was pulling at my fingers. They were woven together behind Jackie's head, which I was holding off the ground. The woman was speaking only to me, since Jackie had her eyes closed. Or one eye for sure. The other was too mashed up to tell.

The woman said something to me, but I couldn't hear her. I shook my head.

"It would be helpful if you let me examine her, sir," she shouted.

The big slab table had saved our lives, but hadn't stopped the blast debris from swirling down on top of us. A piece of something, maybe the big glass salad bowl from the appetizer table, had slammed into the side of Jackie's face. I didn't see it happen, but I saw the result. When the short woman found us, I was telling her why baseball was never the same after the advent of free agency, and checking her breathing periodically by putting my cheek down next to her nose.

I let the short woman move her hands down under Jackie's head as I moved mine under her neck. She used her thumb to pull open Jackie's good eye, into which she shot the beam of a tiny flashlight. When she was done she poked around Jackie's chest with a stethoscope. While she was doing that another medic ran up with an elaborate-looking plastic thing in tow that he threw on the ground with a clattery smack. Without looking up, the short woman shot out an order that caused the guy to turn on his heel and run off.

"What about the others?" I asked, but she didn't answer me, and I didn't want to ask her again until she was ready.

She eventually looked at me.

"Sorry?" she asked.

"The others. On the deck. What about them?"

"How many were there?"

"I don't know. Five?"

She went back to Jackie, gently folding her hands down by her sides and configuring the plastic thing into the brace it was obviously meant to be.

"I'll tell the recovery people. Locate parts for five," she said.

"Parts?"

"I really need you to let me work, sir."

She put her soft little hands on my wrists and I let go. That's when I realized I was listening to my breathing from inside my head, and the sound of a little dog barking frantically in the distance.

I lay back and looked up at the sky, still a lovely pale blue, with a faint hint of pink and purple from the sunset over on the western horizon and the flickering remains of the fire on the edge of the docks, seagulls drifting into view, wondering what all the commotion was about.

TWO

JOE SULLIVAN WAS the kind of guy directors always cast as a cop—thick around the middle, bullet-shaped head upholstered in blond crew-cut hair and dotted with small, close-set eyes. That he was, in fact, a cop didn't help. Always wore a cynical, half-bored, half-suspicious expression to match the big Ford patrol car and tough cop sunglasses. Smith & Wesson short-barrel .38 and a walkie-talkie on his belt. Starched shirts and spit-polished shoes. Natural defenses.

I was up on a ladder when he pulled into my driveway. It was mid-afternoon and the sun was parked directly over the Little Peconic Bay. There was just enough haze in the air to diffuse the light and contain the fuzzy summer heat. A seasonal southwesterly was blowing hard enough to move the leaves on the trees along the back of the property, but not enough to dry off sweat or clear the air. Eddie, the mutt that shared the house with me, was curled up under the scraggly rhododendron that flanked the side porch. I was in a white

T-shirt and cut-offs, work boots and white socks. The tool belt and nail apron cinched around my waist dragged the cut-offs uncomfortably down on my hips. I had a framing square in one hand and a hammer in the other. I was trying to grow a third hand to hold a level when I heard Sullivan's car crunching up the gravel drive. I'd already set the ridge beam, now secured by two temporary sixteen-foot two-by's. At least I hoped I had. The top angle on the first rafter seemed right, but there was something wrong with the bird's mouth notch where it joined the plate. So maybe the top angle really wasn't as good as I thought it was.

"Yo, Sam," Sullivan called from below. "What're you doing?"

I took the two framing nails out of my mouth.

"Raising high the roof beams."

Eddie staggered out from under the rhododendron to say hello. Normally he'd have hopped up to a visitor with a sort of sideways, wagging bounce, but the heat had undermined his social skills. Sullivan squatted down to scratch his ears.

"Those ain't beams," he yelled up to me. "Beams're horizontal. Those're rafters."

"Take that up with Seymour."

"Who's Seymour?"

"Seymour Glass."

"Don't know him."

"Hell of a carpenter."

"Work alone, does he?" Sullivan asked.

"In a manner of speaking."

"Maybe he could help."

"This is the only hard part."

"What, framing the house?"

"Setting the ridge plate. Confounds even the most subtle minds."

"Not the guys I used to work with. Dumber'n shit. Could still set a ridge plate."

I tapped the side of the rafter into perfect position with the ridge and checked it with the framing square. The joint at the plate still had a big ugly gap.

"Done some building?" I asked Sullivan.

"All over the Island. Set a lot of ridge plates. Never did it by myself."

"It's simple engineering. It's all in the numbers. A few calculations and about a hundred years of fiddling around and she's in there, dead nuts."

"I'd come up there and help you but I'm on duty."

"Sure, hide behind the badge."

"You wouldn't let me anyway."

"Probably not."

"Too pigheaded."

"There's beer in the refrigerator."

"I can help you with that."

"On duty?"

"They encourage it."

He disappeared into the original part of the cottage. I was working on an addition off the back. Improving my place in the world. I'd drawn it up, and so far had done all the work myself, shy of pouring the concrete. My father had dug the hole for the original building with a pick and shovel and laid up the foundation out of cinder block. It was more necessity than heroics. He had very little money. Made up for it with grim determination.

"I got you one," Sullivan called up from just outside the rear door.

I slid the hammer into the holster on my tool belt and lowered the unraised rafter down to the floor deck. Maybe the whole roof system would work itself out while I was having a beer with Sullivan. Sometimes lumber would do that if you left it alone long enough.

"What's it gonna be?" Sullivan asked me as I was climbing down the ladder.

"What?"

"That." He pointed with the neck of the beer. "What're you building?"

"Bedroom. Bath. Little storage upstairs. More shop room in the basement."

He took a long drink.

"Why don't you plow the whole thing under and build a new house?" His gaze wandered out on the bay as he wiped his mouth on his sleeve. "You gotta great lot here."

"How's that beer?"

"Cold."

I unbuckled the tool belt and let it drop to the ground. It was an electrician's belt, but I liked it for carpentry, too. Lots of clever little pockets and a sturdy, built-in hammer holster. I took off a separate nail apron and pulled up my terry cloth sweatband so I could wipe the bottle across my forehead. The heavy wet heat made it a bad day to toss around Douglas fir and dimensional calculations. Sullivan, Eddie and I walked over to the two handmade Adirondack chairs I kept under a leafy Norway maple. Eddie spread himself out on the grass. Sullivan and I took the chairs.

I liked all the seasons here at the edge of the Little Peconic, but the extremes of summer and winter were a little less likable. In dead winter you had howling, salt-filled winds blowing through secret cracks in the walls and down the front of your foul-weather gear. In deep summer the air would often come to a dead stop, letting all that drippy, cottony heat glob up your cardiovascular system and dull your mental functions.

"How's your ass?" he asked me.

"Beg pardon?"

"I heard they pulled about a hundred glass splinters out of your ass."

"Less than fifty. Out of my back. Nothing in the gluteus."

"So no big sweat."

"All the little cuts are sealed over, but I'm still sleeping on my stomach. Got back seventy percent in my right ear, eighty percent in my left. Jackie's right came all the way back. Her left is gone forever. Funny break."

Sullivan still wore a smirk, but it slipped a little.

"Yeah. Luck's an odd thing. You're lucky you're alive."

"Don't get metaphysical."

"No problem there. You're not my type."

I tried to keep part of my mind calculating the rafter cuts, but it wasn't happening. I stared up at the precariously placed ridge plate and waited for inspiration.

"Don't you ever wonder why?" Sullivan asked.

"All the time."

He nodded like I'd just won him a private bet.

A windsurfer came into view. He was long and muscular, wearing a small blue tank suit and gripping the boom with a lanky confidence. His hair, long enough to fall down his back, was pressed wetly between his shoulder blades. There wasn't nearly enough wind to give the guy much of a ride. I wondered what my father would think of windsurfing and jet skis and parasailing and the other modes of modern recreation that flew by on the bay. Not that he ever paid much attention to all the salt water sitting there outside his front door. Except for the occasional trip out to catch bluefish for dinner, he was a land guy—all grease, earth and dust.

"They're not getting anywhere," said Sullivan.

"I figured."

"Not what they're telling everybody, of course. They're calling it an ongoing investigation, which means they got squat. I ran into the lead guy over at Bobby Van's. Having dinner with his wife. She didn't want him talking shop, but you could tell he was fed up with the whole thing. He used to think it was a ticket to Hollywood. Big high-profile thing. Now two months later it's an embarrassment. Even I'm embarrassed for him."

"You're an empathetic guy, Joe."

"Embarrassed, empathetic, it's all the same to me. Adds up to nothin' for the prosecutor, nothin' for the press. Nothin' for the grieving widow."

"Nothin' for the innocent bystanders."

"Yeah," he said, "that, too. Not a happy place."

He seemed pensive. Almost philosophical. Even empathetic.

"So, you got a deadline on this thing?" Sullivan asked, looking up at the addition.

"What do you mean?"

"You work on it every day?"

"When I'm not working for Frank."

"A lot of work doing a whole addition. Especially doing it yourself. Lotta work."

"Yup."

"I know. I've done it. It's tough."

"Definitely."

"Hard work."

"Yeah."

We sat in silence for a while, then Sullivan let out a noisy sigh to fill the dead air.

"Of course, I'm the only one officially working," he said.

"And drinking on the job."

"Long as we're not out of beer."

He dragged himself out of the Adirondack and lumbered into the house. While he was gone I busied myself thinking about the geometry and load distribution of roof rafters. And my high school girlfriend Sylvia Granata's jawline, which I'd always admired as one of God's acts of architectural perfection. Sullivan rolled back across the lawn and flopped into the chair, disrupting the image I'd almost formed in my mind. He handed me a Sam Adams and kept the microbrew from a case my friend Burton Lewis gave me the last time he was over. Sullivan never let his working class roots drag down his finer sensibilities. Especially when I was buying.

"What do you know about the guy that was blown up?" he asked.

"Papers said he was some sort of securities broker. Up island."

"Close."

He dug a small notepad out of his back pocket. It was covered in a cramped but orderly script.

"Investment adviser. With a broker's license. Had one office, in Riverhead. Spent part of the time there, the rest on the road. Specialized in high tech. IPOs. LBOs. SOBs, that kinda stuff." He looked over at me. "Typical smart young prick, like we got out here a dime a dozen."

"Along with all the smart old pricks."

"BMWs and cigars. Usually with a nitwit model or nose job JAP."

"Sometimes both."

"Only this guy was married. And local, too, if you think about it."

"Riverhead. Close enough."

"Yeah, right."

Sullivan pulled himself to the edge of the chair so he could lean into his story.

"That's all there is on this guy. There's nothing else to say about him. Had a little shit office, traveled all over hell checking out high techs and start-ups. Worked through cell phones and fax and email—basically a one-man money machine with zippo overhead, and zippo contact with the rest of humanity."

"Tech's had its ups and downs."

"Not an issue for this guy, from what they tell me. Up, down, middle, didn't matter. Got paid comin' or goin'."

"No friends or family?"

"No friends that they know about. Mother's in a home in Riverhead. Off her rocker. Been there forever. A brother in Southampton. Some hippie artist. Can't find the father, presumed dead. No other relatives. No record, no arrests, no press clips. No nothing. Very low profile."

"Pretty interesting."

"You think so?" he asked.

"Well, yeah. An invisible guy somebody thought interesting enough to blow to smithereens."

"Yeah, totally. Nothing left. They said the car was wired with more explosives than that suicide thing in DC that killed, like what, thirty people? Dug a deeper crater."

"Hamptons are always topping everybody."

"Made the national news."

The windsurfer flipped up over a wave made by the wake of a big sport cruiser and landed with the sail flat on the surface of the water. I watched until I saw the guy pop back up again with his hand on the boom. Wind filled out the sheet and shoved him off in another direction—out of harm's way.

"Well, who knows," I said, looking back at Sullivan. "The wrong advice from a broker, or an adviser, can lose you a lot of money. Can piss people off."

"Like how much? I mean, like how much can you lose?"

"Well, geez, I don't know. Millions. Jillions."

"That's what I keep telling these guys in East Hampton. They don't get the dimensions of this thing."

"Aren't there State and Federal people mixed up in this?"

"There were—two months ago when it happened. I think the FBI interviewed his clients. Didn't come up with anything they liked. The Staties gave a lot of forensic help and stuff, but they're too busy setting speed traps and polishing their holsters."

"Sounds like Smokey envy."

The second beer killed whatever carpentry ambition the sun hadn't already baked out of me. I took a bigger swig and leaned back in the chair, closed my eyes and tried to redraw Sylvia's jaw in my imagination.

"At least it's not your headache," I said to him.

"Well, it's not like it's anybody's headache, exactly. It's like our job."

"East Hampton's."

"Well, not really. Now that it's all screwed up everybody's got a piece of it."

I opened my eyes again and saw him staring down the neck of his beer. Sullivan wasn't always the easiest guy to read. Probably because he often concealed what he was actually thinking. When he actually knew what he was thinking in the first place.

"Things have been sort of slow for some reason," said Sullivan. "Even with all the summer people pulling their usual crazy shit. Ross got us all together this morning and handed out copies of the file—had witness interviews, including yours, and the names of State and Federal people who're still officially assigned. Who'll be happy to have somebody else to blame for turning up a big goose egg."

"Should keep you out of trouble," I said, lofting my beer.

The bottle felt cool in my right hand, and I thought I felt a little breeze coming in off the bay. I slumped down deeper in my seat and put my head back against the wooden slats of the Adirondack. Trying to achieve a momentary state of perfect relaxation.

The windsurfer took a sharp turn to the left in the freshening breeze and headed straight toward the big gray-green buoy I'd been watching bob around out there for the last fifty years. I hoped he knew it was there. He wouldn't be the first gentleman sportsman to plaster himself all over its battleship-grade plate steel hull.

"So, Sam, how busy're you with that thing?" said Sullivan. "You got a deadline or anything?"

"What thing?"

He pointed at the addition.

"That thing. What you're building."

"I don't know. Close it in before winter, maybe."

"Yeah. You gotta do that."

"Get the roof on."

"Yeah. Sure."

"Windows, siding."

"Still have plenty of time to go talk to the guy's wife," he said to me, offhand.

"The guy's wife?"

"The dead guy. The guy that got blown up."

"I'm talking to his wife?"

"Well, somebody's got to. They took her testimony, or whatever you call it. But they didn't get shit out of her. She's a doctor, but not the medical kind, some kind of PhD. Ed Lotane, the lead guy in East Hampton, told me she was loony, couldn't go out of the house. Acra-phobic or something like that. Afraid of the whole freaking world."

"Agoraphobic."

"That's it. Plus, she's kind of skinny and sickly, and has a big house, so naturally the cops think she's got some heavy juice. Even though she only lives in Riverhead, and was married to a local guy, for Christ's sakes, which shouldn't bother those yokels in East Hampton. But, for whatever reason, this broad's statement is about half a paragraph, and made'a nothing."

"What has this got to do with me?"

"Aw, geez."

He tossed an imaginary object to the ground and stood up. His blue polyester uniform strained at the midriff, revealing a T-shirt at his belly button. Two shirts and a leather harness. Just the thing for July.

"What's the big deal?" he asked. "You just go up there and talk to her. I'll tell you what I need to know. It's no big deal."

"What're you talking about? That's probably not even legal. Even if I wanted to do it, which I don't."

"You don't care if the people who busted up Jackie's face just get away with it? You said you were curious."

"Sullivan, you're the cop here. This is your job. I'm a private citizen. What's the problem with talking to his wife, anyway?"

I raised my voice so he could hear me as he walked away, heading toward the Little Peconic. "Aw, Christ," I said to myself, before getting up to follow him.

Eddie and I caught up with him at the edge of my backyard. Beyond that was about thirty feet of polished beach pebbles, and after that, the blue-green Little Peconic Bay. A thrity-eight-foot Catalina was sliding by just outside the green buoy that marked the Oak Point channel. By reflex I checked the tide. It was low. If he'd passed inside the buoy his keel would have dug a nice furrow in the sea bottom.

"What," I said.

"Forget about it."

Eddie hopped down off the breakwater that defined the line between my yard and the beach. He liked to keep tabs on things at water's edge, ever watchful for maritime threats, like beach balls and lobster buoys.

"What do you think Ross would say if he knew I was interviewing your witnesses?"

"She's not a witness. She's just his wife. You find out what you find out, I'll just go back and ask the same questions, and that's it. Never stopped you before."

"That was different. I had an interest in that."

"You don't got an interest in this? You got your ass tattooed with glass, your ears blown out and your friend's walkin' around with half a face. Not to mention all the dead people." Sullivan's voice had started to move up a notch in volume, but he caught himself.

"Anyway," he said. "You're a nosy bastard, everybody knows that. There's no statute that says you can't pay a call on somebody. It's a free country."

"Interfering with an ongoing investigation."

"What interfering? You're just talking to her."

"I don't get it, Joe. What's the hang-up?"

Sullivan found a small rock in the grass and tossed it across the beach and into the bay.

"Two years is all I got," he said.

"Two years?"

"Of college. Two years at the community college. Studied beer mostly."

"We had that at MIT."

"Exactly my point. You went to MIT. You been around, you did some things. You got the education. The problem with those boys in East Hampton is they don't even know what questions to ask. Fuckin' PhDs, financial analysts, all that shit, it's like, you know, inhibiting."

"Not for you."

He put a meaty fist up on his hip just behind the black leather holster that held his .38.

"That's right. I'll talk to anybody. But I need an angle," he said. "Something they haven't thought of yet. Something to chase down. You might come up with it, you might not. Plus, I'll owe you a favor. That's got to have some appeal."

I made him look me in the face.

"I can't afford to go messing with anything more controversial than breathing Southampton air. The Chief frowns every time he sees me."

"That's just Ross. He's suspicious of his own mother. Assuming he's got one."

"His mother wasn't a murder suspect."

"That case is closed," said Sullivan. "Over and done."

"I need to keep my head down."

"Right," he said, "and I need you to go talk to this lady and tell me what you find out."

He turned away from the bay and slapped my shoulder as he walked by on the way back to his car.

"This is entirely fucked up," I called to him.

"Just let me know how it goes."

"I don't even know who she is."

He turned around and walked backward as he spoke.

"I left the name and address on your kitchen table. And phone number. And a list of questions. And a summary of the case I got from East Hampton. Burn it all when you can. Ross finds out I gave it to you he'll can me in half a New York minute."

After he left, I went up the ladder to set the two rafters that formed the addition's south gable. First I measured the dimensions with my lucky twenty-five-inch tape. Then I recut the angles at both the ridge and the top plate to suit the measurements instead of the math I'd been using before. The rafters fit perfectly. I checked it all with the framing square, then re-checked all the elevations with the transit. For added insurance, I scabbed a few Techo gussets at the joints and tacked the sixteen-foot two-by supports to the floor deck.

Then I went inside and got another beer, which I drank out at the edge of my lawn, waiting for the first signs of sunset to form over the top of the North Fork and looking for errant sailors and windsurfers to come crashing into my private coast, and yet again mess up the layout of a life that always worked better by eye than formal calculations.

THREE

I'D MOVED OUT HERE after an act of self-immolation cleared out the preceding thirty years of my life. My parents were dead, leaving me the cottage where I'd been raised. It stood at the tip of Oak Point, a scrubby peninsula that juts fearlessly into the Little Peconic Bay on the northwest border of the Town of Southampton, Long Island. My father was an old-school mechanic, so it wasn't surprising that his cottage expressed the character and refinement of a '55 Chevy. Sturdy, sure-footed and unadorned. My mother had tried to introduce a little gentility after he died, but the effort withered on the vine. Since I moved in, I hadn't done much to improve the situation. With few friends or family, no job or any other meaningful pursuit beyond drinking vodka and watching the sun sizzle down behind the green mounds of the North Fork, home improvement seemed pointless.

I don't know why I started building anyway. Probably some newfound professional enthusiasm. Every kid who grew up on the East End of Long Island worked in construction at least part of the time. The booms and busts would parallel the fortunes of Wall Street, though I could always get some kind of work, even in the slow times. The weather never stopped chewing up all the big wooden houses over in the estate section. And there were always a lot of rich people who were richer than everybody else, no matter what the economy was doing, and most of them had a house out here. I worked for them—or rather, I worked for the carpenters and contractors who lived off the trade.

I liked to work for a guy named Frank Entwhistle, who'd hired me thirty-five years before. His son, Frank Junior, now ran the crews. He needed a finish carpenter and cabinetmaker. Not an easy hire, now that most of the tradesmen, and for that matter waitresses, store clerks and bartenders, came from up island.

The only affordable housing locally was held like family heirlooms, and passed along to anyone bound to the dream of lost possibilities. I'd grown up with these people, and I recognized them around Town, going in and out of the hardware store or in the checkout line at the food market, but I didn't know most of them anymore.

I worked for Frank more or less when I felt like it, and occasionally helped maintain his fleet of pickups and light-duty earthmovers.

Luckily he hadn't asked me to set any ridge plates.

The cottage my father built had a big screened-in porch that faced the water, a living room of sorts with an over-sized woodstove, a kitchen, a bathroom and two ten-by-ten bedrooms. I lived out on the porch most of the year so I could keep an eye on the Little Peconic Bay. After five years, it was still there, so the vigilance must be paying off. I kept a round table, a few chairs and a cot out there so I could eat and sleep and entertain a select guest list. People like Jackie Swaitkowski and Joe Sullivan. Maybe an occasional Jehovah's Witness or a neighborhood dog Eddie'd bring home to share water and biscuits. A little hospitality to prove to God I wasn't completely disillusioned with His creations.

The cottage was never the center of Oak Point social life. At least not when my father was around. People shied away, and my mother tucked herself into a corner of the living room with her knitting when she wasn't waging a losing war on the sand and salty damp air that clung to the walls and soaked through cereal boxes and bed linens. My father wasn't much with people, especially the ones who lived in the house he built. He ran almost entirely on momentum and the acid gas of a nearly uncontrollable fury. I never knew why he was the way he was. I never thought about it until he was gone. I do know how he died. Beaten to death in the smelly men's room at the back of a dusky, threadbare bar in the Bronx. It was down the street from his weekday apartment. They never learned who did it. They never really tried. There were no witnesses, even though a half-dozen barflies and the bartender were there at the time. The police figured it was a pair of junior-grade wise guys passing through the neighborhood under their customary cloak of invincibility. They assumed it was provoked. They knew my father.

While I was growing up he spent most of his time in the City, working on cars and oil burners while my mother, sister and I were in Southampton at the cottage on Oak Point. In those days the peninsula was a working class neighborhood, on the whole, made up of guys from the Bronx like my father and local service people and unheated, do-it-yourself summer retreats. But it was wooded and filled with East End light, and under the beneficence of the Little Peconic Bay, and, most of the time, free of my father's corrosive wrath.

———

After making and breaking my share of good and bad habits over the years, I decided to stick with those already established, for better or worse. One of them was running along the sandy roads that thread their way along the bay coast and connect several North Sea neighborhoods. The day after Sullivan came to see me, Eddie and I were up early and moving west at a brisk pace. In the summer this was only possible in the morning. Later on the heat was too much. At least for a fifty-three-year-old guy with a full set of bad habits to counterbalance the benefits of regular exercise. Eddie might've stood it, but not happily.

An atomized mist had been sprayed around the scrub pines and oaks. A smooth cloud cover hung above the treetops. The sun had a few hours to burn it all off. Enough time for me to make it all the way to the Hawk Pond Marina where my friend Paul Hodges lived on his boat. My T-shirt was already getting soaked and I had to occasionally wipe off the sweat that slipped through my terry cloth headband. The chirping bugs from the wetlands were quiet now, having exhausted themselves during the night, but their diurnal relatives were up and about, buzzing around the forest and sticking themselves to my arms and legs. Eddie stopped a few times to pick a critter or two out of his fur. We shared some water from a bottle Velcroed to my waist and soldiered on.

"You burning some of that for me?" I asked Hodges as we approached down a slender swayback dock.

"I knew the smell of food would turn you up," he said, standing in a cloud of smoke coming from the rusty Weber grill he'd set up on the dock next to a short mahogany gang-plank. Some of the smoke was caught under the market umbrella that shaded a white plastic table and two canvas director chairs. Hodges was somewhere in his mid-sixties, big around the middle and heavy shouldered, with short, gnarly legs. His arms were formed out of thick bunches of twisted cable. He'd seen forty years of fishing boats and construction crews, which had turned his skin into the working side of a catcher's mitt. Under the best of circumstances you wouldn't have called Hodges a good-looking man. He looked more like a superannuated frog. The gray-white hair that burst out in lunatic clumps from his head and chin didn't help.

Hodges had a pair of Shih Tzus he'd inherited from his wife. They treated Eddie like he was some sort of rock star, skittering up to him, all sharp-edged noise and wiggling fur. Eddie was magnanimous.

"Canadian bacon on the grill. Scrambled-up shit in the skillet. Season to taste. Want a beer with that?"

"Coffee's fine."

"Not if you're drinking mine."

He dumped our breakfast out on paper plates and went below for beverages and sesame seed bagels. The swan couple who freeloaded around the marina glided up to the side of the boat, hoping to get in on the action, which provoked Eddie and the Shih Tzus to go berserk. The swans floated away, deciding it wasn't worth the trouble.

"And don't come back," Hodges called to them as he came through the companionway.

"I thought you were a bird lover."

"In the sky or on the grill, exclusively."

We ate and drank coffee under the big umbrella and watched the colorless sky turn blue overhead.

Hodges ran a bar and grill out of a dilapidated boathouse on the grounds of a commercial marina up in Sag Harbor. Most of the trade were professional fishermen or men and women who crewed on the charter boats during the season. The place was called the Pequot and it had a rickety deck out back where Hodges and his daughter Dotty, who helped him run the restaurant, ate most of their meals. At least until one afternoon when the deck collapsed while Hodges was finishing off a plate of the house special—baked, stuffed whitefish of unknown origin.

"How's the rib cage?" I asked him.

"Almost healed. Give's new meaning to breathing easier."

"And the neck?"

"Good as it's gonna get."

"Can still make breakfast."

"They want me to do more rehabilitation."

"Some people are beyond that."

"That's what I tell 'em. How's your butt?"

"My back. It was my back."

"We're a pair of sorry chewed-up fuckers, aren't we. More eggs?"

I was still hot, but the breeze coming off the bay had started cooling me down. Hodges's cuisine was sitting surprisingly well in my belly. All of which was eroding the desire to run back home. Hodges sat back in his chair with his coffee and looked at me intently. Something he rarely did.

"What?"

"I saw a friend of yours in Town yesterday. Jackie What's-her-name."

"Swaitkowski," I told him.

"Looked like crap."

"I know."

"She said you'd been around."

"I saw her before she went in for another round of surgery."

"She's not telling you," said Hodges.

"Telling me what?"

"She's not doing too good, but she won't tell you."

Jackie's moods had always flown around the room like a drunken sparrow. But since all this she had trouble getting anything off the ground.

"I can't do anything about that," I told him.

Hodges grunted and looked up at the sky. The sun had done its work on the low clouds. The bay water reflected the color of the sky and the languid disposition of a midsummer's day.

"Ross Semple's got the Southampton cops working on the case," I told him.

"Joe Sullivan to the rescue."

"I guess. It's sort of out of his league."

"At least he'll work the crap out of it," said Hodges.

"He wants me to talk to the guy's wife. The guy who got blown up."

Hodges seemed to like that.

"Excellent. Get the old team back in action."

"Sullivan and I are not a team. Not remotely."

Hodges scraped a few spoonfuls of some indeterminate fried stuff up against the side of the pan and hovered over my plate.

"More?" he asked.

"Nah. No sense pushing my luck."

He shrugged and served it to himself.

"You are full of shit, you know," said Hodges.

"Just full, thanks."

"You're dying to stick your nose into this thing."

"No, I'm not. I'm really not. I want to work on my addition, put up a little crown molding and make a few cabinets for Frank Entwhistle, and stay out of trouble. Stay about a million miles away from anything that even remotely looks, sounds or smells like trouble. For the rest of my damn life."

"I guess that's what Jackie'd want you to do. Stay out of trouble."

"She's alive."

"That's right."

"Aw, Christ."

"All you have to do is go talk to the guy's wife," he said, and folded his arms.

Eddie and the Shih Tzus clattered down the dock and jumped into the cockpit of Hodges's boat, looking at us like we were supposed to provide the next segment of entertainment.

"One thing I can do," I told Hodges.

"What's that?"

"Have a little more of that coffee."

Hodges went below deck to retrieve whatever was left in the antique pot. He poured us both a cup. I took a sip and looked up at the sea gulls cruising in random patterns, cool white marks of brilliance against the deep blue background.

"Fucking hell," I told Hodges while I tried to drink the sludge from off the bottom of his crappy old percolator.

FOUR

IT WAS GRAY AGAIN the next morning. Warm, wet air was stuffed in all the enclosed spaces, and my skin stuck to everything it touched.

My car was a '67 Pontiac Grand Prix with a modified 400-cubic-inch V8 and a four-speed manual transmission that my father and I had installed at great cost to the harmony of our already disharmonious household. A car this old and poorly conceived took a lot of effort to keep running, but replacing it seemed pointless. The body was free of rust or Bondo, though I needed to add a coat of paint over the gray-brown primer. The interior still smelled of leather, or at least I imagined it did. Maybe moldy leather.

That morning I built myself an extra-large mug of Belgian chocolate nut coffee from beans I'd bought at the corner coffee place in the Village. I liked it a little better than French vanilla or caramel classic, my other favorites. I poured it into an enormous insulated travel mug with a New York Yankees logo printed on the side.

I was wearing an off-white linen suit, last cleaned and pressed in the middle of the prior decade. It was still wrinkle-free, but a little musty. I was counting on natural forces to air it out. I put it together with a striped tie and an Egyptian pima cotton shirt that cost my ex-wife Abby a hundred dollars twenty years ago. It felt like liquid silk.

It was too hot to leave Eddie in the car, so I had to lock him up in the house. I felt like a rat, but I knew I wouldn't be able to concentrate if I was worrying about him asphyxiating in the backseat of the car.

I left the radio on for him. Morning jazz on WLIU. Plus a full bowl of fresh water and a few Big Dog biscuits, even though he was officially more of a medium-sized dog. I still felt like a rat.

The linen suit, insulated Yankees mug and I climbed into the car and spun out of the driveway. The Grand Prix was an extreme example of an absurd era of automotive engineering. Heavy as a bulldozer, powered like a jetfighter and roomy as the penthouse suite at the Waldorf Astoria. Strictly mid-twentieth-century technology gone psychotic. A good car for my father. People in the Hamptons just averted their eyes.

I don't know why my father bought the car in the first place. He didn't have much money and was hardly much of a sport. I don't remember ever seeing him laugh out loud, or express a materialistic desire for anything, mechanical or otherwise. He just showed up one day driving the thing. It looked almost new, unsullied and legally registered. My mother was suspicious.

When I was the head of R&D at one of the big hydro-carbon conglomerates, I drove a string of serenely perfect European sedans. They were better cars than the Grand Prix, but none of them had a center console big enough to stow a huge mug of Belgian chocolate nut coffee.

I dug a piece of paper with the directions Sullivan gave me out of my breast pocket and spread it out on the passenger seat. I wouldn't have to look at it until I was in Riverhead, the tired old mill town at the crotch of the North and South Forks of Eastern Long Island. I knew how to get there, but I didn't know much about the place. It used to be where local people could shop affordably for things like groceries and Barcaloungers, but strip development up island and general prosperity had eroded that role. Now it was just a little urban barge afloat on an ocean of wealth and aspiration. Not a likely place to lodge a high-tech financial consultant.

To get there, you had to go west from Southampton, cross the Shinnecock Canal and head up Route 24, past an enormous stucco duck and through Flanders, another raggedy old town that looked like it had wandered away from somewhere in rural Alabama. When I hit town the directions sent me up an incongruous four-lane divided highway toward Long Island Sound. As I crossed the river that named the town, I looked east toward Southampton but saw only gray translucence enveloping the Great Peconic Bay.

To either side of me were flat open fields. Huge irrigation machines were spraying geysers over the crops. Banged-up pickup trunks were out there, too, throwing up dusty contrails. Before I turned off the highway I noticed it was a sod farm. But not like the ones in Oklahoma. They were growing instant lawns. Just cut it up, haul it off to Biffy and Foo-Foo's, roll it out and the automatic sprinklers do the rest. I wondered if they also harvested cappuccino or BMW convertibles somewhere in the area.

In a few more turns I was on her street. It was an arid subdivision, sparsely developed. The curbs and asphalt were fresh, but the common areas were weedy and poorly graded. The lots had all been clear-cut, realtor signs providing the only visual relief. I felt like I'd just toured the United States and ended up on the outskirts of Des Moines. I hoped the Grand Prix didn't frighten the neighborhood kids.

Her house was a huge white two-story colonial with black shutters, a two-car garage and a professionally manicured lawn, cut to the length of a putting green. I waited a long time for someone to answer the doorbell. I rang it twice to make sure it was working.

The door opened a crack.

"Yes."

"Mrs. Eldridge?"

"No."

"Is she home?"

"Who's this?"

"My name's Sam Acquillo. I'm here about her husband's death."

"She know you?"

"No."

"You have to call the attorney."

"I'm with the police."

It was quiet for a moment.

"You have to call the attorney."

The door shut softly and latched with a barely audible click. I rang the doorbell again. A few minutes later, the door opened.

"Yes."

"What's the attorney's name?"

"Gabriel Szwit. S-z-w-i-t."

"Here in Riverhead?"

"In the phone book. That's why I spelled it."

The door closed again. I spun on my heel and walked back to the Grand Prix with an air of cool self-possession. I didn't want the neighbors to see me sweat. That's okay, Mrs. Big Shot Widow. Just wait. I'll be back.

I drove to a phone booth on a far corner of a gas station in Flanders and called information. Mr. Szwit was in Southampton Village. I called Sullivan.

"What do you mean call the attorney?"

"That's what she said, Joe."

"Well, you don't gotta do that. You're the police. All you got to do is say you want to talk to her."

"I'm not the police, Joe. You're the police."

"Jesus Christ. Nothin's easy."

"Call Szwit. Have him tell her to expect a guy named Sam Acquillo. Then call me back. I'll wait here."

"He might want to be there."

"Great."

"No big deal."

"Don't take too long. It's hot."

The station sold a brand of gasoline I didn't recognize. A small crowd of young black kids were hanging out front, mumbling to each other and watching a skinny gray dog peel a wad of gum up off the hot tarmac. Their clothes poured down off their bodies and curled around their feet. They drank diet soda from liter bottles and stayed clear of the wiry little white guy manning the full-service pumps. Everyone was smoking cigarettes despite the pervasive gasoline vapors. So I lit a Camel. Solidarity.

The phone rang.

"Go on over. But go slow. The lady's some kind of dipsoid."

"What kind of dipsoid?"

"I told you. Some sort of phobiac. Afraid of the outside or some shit."

"Agoraphobic."

"Yeah. I think we covered this."

"Szwit isn't coming?"

"My wife's afraid of birds. Scare the shit out of her. We never get to eat on the patio at the Driver's Seat. She thinks they're gonna get caught in the umbrellas, panic and dive into her ears."

"Her ears?"

"Yeah. She thinks birds want to fly in her ears. This has never happened, to my knowledge, to anybody, but this is what she thinks."

"Otherwise, a pretty normal gal."

"Outside of marrying me."

"So he won't be there."

"Who?"

"Szwit."

"He's on his way."

"Okay."

"Let me know how it goes."

The kids had melted off under the late morning sun. I looked for little puddles of denim and nylon. I bought a liter bottle of Fresca and climbed back into the Grand Prix. I was starting to lose whatever enthusiasm I'd stirred up for this whole thing. I thought about my roof rafters and tool belt. I lit another Camel and turned on WLIU to distract the whiny little voice inside my head.

It took even longer to get the door open this time. After I rang the doorbell I caught a little curtain movement from a second floor window. I was getting her attention.

The same woman's voice came from the crack in the door. "Yes?"

"My office called Mr. Szwit. My name is Acquillo."

"Identification."

Oh, Christ.

I flipped open my wallet and slid my driver's license behind the yellowy plastic window. I stuck it up to the crack in the door for about half a second.

"Just a moment."

The door closed again and I waited again. I was starting to get to know the door knocker. It was Colonial, like the house. Plate steel, painted flat black, with scallops cut into the surface to simulate hand forging. The kind of thing my parents wouldn't even know how to describe.

The door swung all the way open. A short, obese woman peered around the edge and watched me enter the foyer. Her dress was a cotton sack printed with something and cinched up around an area approximating her waist. She wore an apron, stubby heels and an angry black scowl. Warren Sapp would have a tough time knocking her down.

"Wait here," she said, then heaved herself up the stairs. Alone again.

The foyer was done in shades of off-white. The natural wood banister was the only point of relief. I strolled forward to catch a glimpse of the living room to the right. It featured the same palette, except for the love seat and a pair of high-backed stuffed chairs, which were upholstered in a muted floral pattern. It looked like everything in the house could float away on a stiff breeze. A set of louvered doors blocked the view to the kitchen. I heard voices. Then the fat lady came back downstairs. She waved at the living room.

"Go on, sit in there. Mrs. Eldridge'll be down in a sec."

I sat on the chair that faced the stairway so I could see her come down. The air-conditioning was set low, maybe sixty-seven degrees. I warmed my hands with my breath. I wanted another cup of coffee. Something really hot in a doubled-up paper cup.

Mrs. Eldridge glided down the stairs and swept across the carpet with a soft, leggy delicacy, and before I had a chance to stand, slid into the opposing high-backed chair, where she perched like an oversized cat, her stocking feet tucked up under her butt, her hands folded prayerfully in her lap. She wore a white cashmere sweater buttoned up to her throat and black cotton slacks. Her hair was too perfectly arranged, as if fresh from the hairdresser. And black. Too black, even for a woman her age, which I guessed to be late thirties. She was like her living room. Not much color, except for the eyes, which were the most brilliant, frigid icy blue I'd ever seen.

"Well," she said, neither a question nor a statement.

I stood up and leaned over to offer my hand.

"I'm Sam Acquillo. I was there when it happened."

Her nails, long and perfect like her hair, were painted a deep maroon. A tangle of blue veins crazed across her wrist and the back of her hand. When I shook her hand, bony and cool-dry, I was afraid I might crush it like a piece of ceramic, but her grip was blunt and to the point.

"Appolonia Eldridge. I was here."

I retreated back to my chair.

"I'm sorry for your loss."

"You knew Jonathan?"

"No. I was just having a drink. Waiting for a friend."

"Yes. Of course."

She looked away, toward the shrouded bay windows, as if the conversation had just concluded. I felt myself disappearing, until she returned her gaze, then I was back in the room.

"The retired engineer. And the young lady lawyer. Jacqueline Swaitkowski. She was badly injured, but you saved her life. And your own."

"You read the report."

A suggestion of a smile teased her face.

"You feel I shouldn't have?"

"No. Of course not. I'd have memorized it by now."

"You look too young to be retired."

"Didn't retire."

The blocky woman who'd opened the door came plodding into the room holding a silver tray and tea service. Appolonia looked a little startled. The woman thrust the tray under her nose.

"It's your tea, girl. You haven't had it yet."

Appolonia looked at me with mild exasperation.

"Honestly, Belinda."

Appolonia was forced into the ritual of pouring the tea into a cup, dropping in sugar and squeezing the lemon. It seemed to take about four hours.

"We haven't offered Mr. Acquillo any tea?" Appolonia asked.

Belinda looked over at me like I'd just broken into the house. I held up my hand.

"I'm all set, thanks."

"Not a tea drinker, I surmise."

"Coffee. And vodka. Not usually at the same time."

Belinda plodded out of the room with the tea tray. The room struggled to regain its state of repose.

"I'm at a bit of a loss," Appolonia said over the lip of her teacup.

"On why I'm here."

"Yes."

"Me, too."

"So maybe we should start with that," she said, helpfully.

One of the trainers who helped teach me to box used to say fights were won with the legs, not the fists. Balance and movement put you where you were supposed to be, or kept you away from where you weren't, like that killing zone between the inside clutch and the full extension of the other guy's reach. But sometimes, for no reason at all, the canvas felt like it was full of bumps and ridges, and ripples that undulated and shifted and screwed up your balance. Your feet got all tangled up and you lost your sense of where you were supposed to be. I'd been feeling that way ever since I'd driven up Mrs. Eldridge's street.

"They're afraid of you."

She cocked her head and widened those crystal blue eyes. "Who?"

"The cops. They don't know how to talk to you. They aren't used to this kind of thing. They spend ninety percent of their time with dumb hard cases, or routine stuff that's safe and predictable, and that's how they like it. This is all way too weird for them."

"As am I. Way too weird."

"Not what I meant."

"Well, you said they were afraid of me. That's awfully silly, if you think about it."

"I agree. Any ideas?"

"Ideas?"

"About who killed your husband?"

She smiled at me.

"Ah, this is why they sent you. Your diplomacy."

"Sorry."

"What exactly did you retire, or whatever you did, from?"

"R&D. Hydrocarbon processing."

"Jonathan wanted to be a scientist." She sipped her tea. "No. No ideas."

"I know this is hard."

"It's all right. How's your hearing?"

"Most of it came back. Jackie's not so lucky."

"Jonathan had to sleep with a sound machine. It was set for crickets and rain. He said the house was too quiet. He had ears like a spaniel."

That reminded me.

"What was the poodle's name?"

"Pierre. He's fine. They fished him out of the water. Belinda knows where he is. I didn't like him. I'm sorry. Jonathan was the dog person."

Her dead husband was right. The house was too quiet. No clocks, no creaks. No sound intruding from outside. It was clenched within a white, funereal stillness. A busy little poodle would have been like the sound machine—a little blast of chaos, a connection with the living.

"He wanted to be a scientist, but became an investment adviser," I said.

"It's no less intricate than the hard sciences, but the money's better."

"He did pretty well?"

"It would appear that way from the proceeds of the will."

She looked down at her hands.

"Mr. Acquillo."

"Yeah?"

"Jonathan lived his own life. I knew very little about his business or the people he worked with. We never discussed those sorts of things. Never, not one single, solitary word. We never entertained or traveled together. That would have been impossible. He wanted to leave his job back at the office, and find some relief from it all here. With me. He was gone at least half the time. He traveled all over the country, all over the world, visiting companies his clients might have an interest in. That was one of his specialties, fieldwork. Few advisers ever bother to visit the companies they recommend, but he believed it was the reason for his success. They were technology companies, applied science. So science did find its way into his career. And that, sir, is the sum total of everything I know about Jonathan's work life."

"How long have you had it?"

"What?"

"Agoraphobia."

Her shoulders slumped a little, but she still looked stiffly amused.

"It's an anxiety disorder. I don't know if agoraphobia is exactly the right term. And I don't relish discussing it, I'm afraid."

"Sorry. I'm just thinking it must be difficult."

"It's a bitch, Mr. Acquillo. That doesn't make me one."

"'Course not."

"Or some terrifying creature."

I jerked my head toward the back of the house where we could hear Belinda rattling around.

"You're not the one I'm afraid of," I said.

That loosened her up a little, or so I imagined from an almost imperceptible shift in the way she sat in her chair.

"It isn't much of a life, you know, but it was infinitely better knowing that, at least some of the time, it could be spent with Jonathan. We would sit, right here in this room, and chat. About just about everything. I read the newspaper every day, and watch a little CNN—you have to be careful not to watch too much, it's habit forming. And I have a group on the computer with whom I converse. And Belinda, she's out and about a bit. You can keep up very well if you try a little. And, of course, Jonathan lived in the whole world. He knew so much. But then, you know, we didn't just discuss current affairs. He really wasn't the big stiff people thought he was. If you knew him as I did. You can't imagine what it means to me to have him taken away."

"I can. I can imagine, but that's all. I've lost a lot of people, but not like that."

Her composure began to waver. She put her teacup down on the tray as if the weight of it was suddenly impossible to bear.

"I still can't quite understand why you're here."

I shrugged.

"One of the cops investigating the case asked me to talk to you."

"Very curious."

"He's actually a friend of mine. Since I was there when it happened, he thought maybe you'd be more likely to talk to me."

"I have nothing to hide. I've told them everything."

"So, no theories."

"No. And I don't care."

"Pardon?"

Having regained her strength, she scooped the teacup off the table. She looked right at me.

"It's absolutely immaterial to me. He's gone, and nothing will change that."

"With all due respect—"

"Please, Mr. Acquillo, understand. There's nothing I can do about this. I'm here, in this house. Jonathan left me enough to live on—my God, enough for me to live a thousand years. But I'm hardly up to a crusade. I can barely imagine a trip to the grocery store, so how am I to hunt down my husband's killers? Isn't that for the police? Foolish me, I always thought that's what they did. Not send over retired engineers. With all due respect."

She looked over my shoulder. When I turned around I saw Belinda standing in the foyer.

"I changed my mind," I told her. "I'll have some of that tea after all."

Belinda looked over at Appolonia for permission.

"Please, Belinda," said Appolonia. "It's quite good."

Belinda spun on her heel and left abruptly enough to stir the air.

"She's really a doll once you know her," said Mrs. Eldridge.

A few hundred comebacks leapt to mind, but I managed to shove them back down.

"You'd like my friend, too. Joe Sullivan. The cop who asked me to talk to you. He's new on the case. He'd be here himself, but he thought it'd be too much for you."

"I'm sturdier than I look, Mr. Acquillo."

"Sam."

"Okay. Sam."

"I believe that."

"Because of your powers of perception?"

"Yeah. Engineers are big on deductive reasoning."

"I've heard that. I studied abnormal psychology. Surprise, surprise."

"Doctorate."

"Boston University."

I pointed to myself.

"MIT. Just across the river. Though I once lived in a BU frat house. In the attic with the mice."

"This is why your friend thought I'd speak with you? You'd know the secret handshake?"

"Must've been tough to go to class."

"I was better then. But yes. It was."

"And Jonathan was at Harvard Business School. When you met him."

"You must have quite a file."

"Just guessing, based on the dates."

"That's right. I trust you aren't interested in the exact circumstances."

"Maybe a little. If I'm not prying."

She smiled and looked toward the window, which was shrouded in tissue-thin, translucent sheers. Her skin was very pale in the diffused light, though you could see tiny wrinkle lines around her eyes and at the corners of her mouth. It was the kind of face that wouldn't age well. Too undernourished.

"That's all you're doing," she said, then after a bit of a pause, "We met when Jonathan was in a clinical study. Nothing exotic, I can't even remember the point of the research. I was helping verify the data with follow-up interviews. The sort of statistical drudgery advisers delight in visiting on graduate students. But, luckily, the subjects came to me. At my house. I lived with my parents." She added, anticipating the question, "I grew up in Boston. Brookline."

"So did my ex-wife. Newton, actually."

"Jonathan grew up out here."

"Me, too."

"Curious."

"But irrelevant?" I asked.

"Possibly."

"Wow. Too subtle for me."

"I thought you were the subtle one. Subtle enough to talk to the crazy lady."

"Or crazy enough."

She saluted me with her cup of tea.

"Touché."

"Not trying to cross swords, Mrs. Eldridge."

"Appolonia."

"Just trying to learn more about your husband."

"Ever consider there are some things you can never know?"

"Sure."

"Though you know a lot already, don't you."

"Not really."

"More than you admit."

"Engineers are trained empiricists. You only know what you see."

"At least you know how to duck."

"Learned that from Rene Ruiz."

"Engineer?"

"Prizefighter."

"Explains the nose."

"Courtesy of Rene."

"So you didn't duck in time."

"That's what I learned from Rene. Timing is everything."

"Like when you jumped behind the big table."

"So you got a file of your own."

"It didn't say."

"What?"

"Why you jumped behind the table."

"To keep from getting blown up."

"At that point it was just a fire. It didn't say why you jumped behind the table. No theories?"

"No theories. Certainties."

"Really?"

"I wouldn't think you'd want to know."

"If I'm asking, I want to know. Rest assured."

I shrugged.

"Oxygen," I said.

"Now who's being subtle."

"You can tell how much oxygen a flame's getting from its color. And how hot it is. And the balance between the two. The flame inside the car was starved of oxygen, but very hot. All the windows were shut, but the heat was great enough to melt glass, which would suddenly let in a lot of air. That would cause a rapid acceleration of combustion.

Rapid enough to be, for all intents and purposes, an explosion. I didn't know about the C-4. I might've tried to get further away."

"So he went quickly."

"Yeah. Quick enough."

She looked away from me, and might have been ready to
tear up, but the doorbell rang. Saved.

Belinda let in a short guy with thinning, slicked hair and
glasses. He wore a gray suit and held a worn leather briefcase
tightly under his arm like he was afraid one of us might try
to snatch it. Belinda looked like she was mad at him. For
showing up, or not showing up sooner, or on general princi-
ple, hard to tell.

He walked right up to me and stuck out his hand.

"Gabriel Szwit."

"Sam Acquillo."

He was one of those jumpy, fidgety kinds of guys who
gravitate toward professions like accounting and law so
they'll have an official stereotype to justify their social inse-
curities.

Appolonia also shook his hand and got Belinda to bring
him a glass of water. He sat on the sofa facing us with his
briefcase held upright in his lap. Maybe he had lead weights
in there to keep him anchored to the ground.

"So, can somebody catch me up?"

"Nothing to catch, Gabe," said Appolonia. "We're just
chatting."

He looked confused.

"The police said you had some information that might
interest Mrs. Eldridge."

"They did?" I asked.

Gabe looked over at Appolonia for a little help. She looked
at me for the same thing.

"An officer Sullivan called and said you wanted to share a piece of information that hadn't been included in the original report. I agreed to you coming on that basis, though I'd thought Mrs. Eldridge might have waited for me to get here before engaging you in conversation."

Mrs. Eldridge didn't seem to notice the reproach.

"Oh, yeah," I said. "I guess we were so engaged I lost track."

"I see," said Szwit. "Perhaps now that your memory's been refreshed."

Appolonia looked over at me, calmly composed, as if I had the next month and a half to cough up the goods. Szwit took the other tack.

"Otherwise," he said, looking at his watch.

"The phone, of course," I said, as if relieved by the return of my short-term memory.

"Of course," said Appolonia. "To be fair, Gabe, Mr. Acquillo mentioned early on that he knew something about the phone."

Her delivery was so deadpan I couldn't tell whose leg in the room was being pulled, or even if that was what she was doing. The undercurrents flowing through that silent house were powerful enough to dislodge it from its foundation.

"You know that Jonathan got a call on his cell minutes before the explosion," I said.

Neither of them nodded, but I pressed on anyway.

"It wasn't his phone," I said.

I sat back in my chair and took a sip of my tea, shrugged my shoulders and asked, "Which raises the question, whose was it?"

Szwit shook his head.

"I'm sorry, you're saying the cell phone on which Jonathan received that last call did not belong to him? How could you possibly have known that? Did you speak with him? That certainly wasn't in the report."

It wasn't in the report because I hadn't said anything about it when they grilled me. For some reason it just hadn't registered until that moment sitting in Appolonia's living room.

"I was watching him," I said. "Killing time waiting for my friend. I watched him try to answer the call. He pecked at the keys, hunting for the right one. You don't do that with your own phone."

"It might have been a new one," said Appolonia. "I certainly wouldn't have known," she added, for Gabe's benefit, I thought.

"Might've been," I said. "Easy enough to check out."

"You could ask Alena."

"Mrs. Eldridge," said Gabe, "I don't think this conversation should extend to Ms. Zapata."

"Don't you love lawyers?" she asked me. "Is 'no' the only word they know?"

"You should meet Jackie Swaitkowski. Full of surprises."

"I should."

"This is your piece of vital information?" Szwit asked, simultaneously suggesting it was neither vital nor information.

"Yeah, " I said. "You explain it."

"Jonathan had trouble answering his cell phone? It means nothing. Everybody struggles with those phones."

"A guy who ran a multi-million-dollar consultancy through his computer, and spent half his life on the road, couldn't answer his own cell phone?"

"If it was new," Appolonia repeated, trying to steer me toward a safe harbor.

"Should be easy enough to find out."

She looked over at Gabe.

"Any objections?" she asked, as if to say, don't even try.

"Hell, no. I was just hoping for something more substantial. Something that went somewhere."

I was hoping the same thing, but at that point I was more concerned with getting out of there before the lawyer, or Belinda, made a leap for my jugular.

"You should talk to Jonathan's assistant. Alena Zapata," said Appolonia. "She's still working for his business, tidying things up. Though not for much longer. I have the number and address."

She rose with little effort and went to get a piece of paper out of a small fold-down desk. She stood with her weight on one leg while she wrote down the information. I noticed for the first time that she had a little shape around the chest and hips, despite her thin arms and legs. She actually was, or could have been, very attractive, if you like your women in black and white. I wondered if Jonathan liked having her all to himself. She'd always be there whenever he came home. To sit and engage him in witty, sophisticated repartee. Fragile and desperately in need of protection. To be indulged, and coddled. His own alone. No one else to see or hear. A world unto themselves. Refined, yet profoundly isolated. Until it collided with several pounds of high-grade plastic explosive.

She walked over and handed me the slip of paper.

"I do have one thing to tell you, though you'll find it of no use whatsoever."

"Sure. Can't hurt."

She was now close enough for me to smell her. It was a flower smell, sweet and fresh. Like Easter Sunday. Or something you'd get from Crabtree & Evelyn. She seemed to be unsure about telling me what she wanted to tell me.

"Go ahead."

She pursed her lips and nodded. She went back and sat down in her yellow chair. The flowers lingered in the air. I waited until she was ready.

"Have you ever looked over at the person you're closest to, and thought, just for an instant, that you have no idea who they really are?"

"Yes."

"I never felt that way about Jonathan Eldridge. Some people are just so completely who they are. I don't believe he knew he would be killed, because I would have certainly known it, too."

She didn't expect me to respond, so I didn't. I just finished my tea, thanked her for her time, shook Gabe's hand and made for the door, one eye peeled for Belinda. Before I could grab the doorknob, Appolonia called to me.

"Mr. Acquillo."

I stepped back so I could see her in her high-backed chair. "Yeah."

"Jonathan was everything to me. I can't imagine going on without him. I don't know why I bother."

Belinda finally came from wherever she was lurking and made a grab for the door, hoping to propel me out of the house. I held my ground.

"Maybe you're more curious than you think," I said to Appolonia. "About how it happened."

She nodded, a faint, indifferent little nod.

"Perhaps. Some perverted form of curiosity."

"Hey, people have lived for less," I said, backing out of the door and into the color-drenched heat where I belonged, where I could take a few big gulps of air and re-establish my bearings.

But the day had turned cooler, for no reason I could divine. The weather in the Hamptons is like that. It can fool you all the time. You might think it's a metaphor for human nature, but that'd be presumptuous. A truly pathetic fallacy. Nature as a whole never did, and never will, care all that much about the contradictions of human behavior. The zigs and zags between philanthropy and betrayal, adoration and deceit.

FIVE

J ACKIE O'DWYER MADE THE MISTAKE of marrying the
first guy she slept with after graduating from law school and
moving back to her hometown of Bridgehampton. A mistake
rectified when Bobby Swaitkowski inserted his brand new
Porsche Carrera into the trunk of a two-hundred-year-old
oak tree that was protected by the Historical Society, and
therefore allowed to define the inside of a very tight curve
along a back road connecting Bridgehampton and Sag
Harbor. The Highway Department moved to clear the hazard—an impulse not unlike shooting a trained bear that's
attacked a tourist—but were immediately thwarted by members of the Society who pointed out that Bobby's Porsche hit
the tree about twelve feet off the ground, which, extrapolat-
ing from an abrupt rise in the road some distance away,
meant his forward velocity was in the neighborhood of a
hundred and ten miles an hour. You could hardly blame the
tree for being in the wrong place at the wrong time. The

chairman of the Society even asserted that Bobby's estate should cover the cost of a tree surgeon. Bobby's widow, being a lawyer, advised the chairman and others of like opinion that any payment from her would coincide with a cold day in hell. It was a painful way to launch her legal career, but indicative of the type of law you practiced out on the East End of Long Island.

Bobby left her a house he'd built himself on a heavily wooded flag lot about a half-mile down the road from the old oak tree. He wasn't much of a carpenter, so Jackie didn't end up with much of a house. It was a 3,500-square-foot box sheathed in vertical rough-hewn batten and board cedar that was supposed to turn a weathered gray, but by now was mostly mildewy black. There was no trim on the casement windows, or exterior architectural detail of any kind. Jackie still drove Bobby's Toyota pickup with oversized wheels and big lumber racks welded to the frame. I parked the Grand Prix next to it in the driveway and rang her doorbell.

It usually took her about half a second to answer, so it felt funny standing there waiting. Maybe my doorbell karma wasn't what it used to be. Years of misanthropy catching up. When the door opened, it was a crack.

"Hello out there."

"Jackie, it's Sam."

She swung the door open like she did in the old days, with authority.

"Sam. A sight for."

"Sore eyes?"

"Yeah. Especially this one," she said, pointing to the massive bandage on her head.

Since I'd seen her the week before they'd done some more work on her. She was wearing something new, kind of a white helmet with a cap and chin strap that covered most of the left side of her face. The right side was black and blue, which she'd tried to soften with face powder. Jackie's proudest feature was a mane of wild, tightly curled strawberry-blond hair. Now contained, it made her face seem small and strangely defenseless. There was an opening in the bandage at the back of her neck that set free a shock of blazing frizz, but all that did was call attention to its overall absence, advertising the tragedy.

We stood in her doorway looking at each other until I had the sense to realize she was crying. The kind of thing I was always late to see.

"Ah, Sam," she said, and fell forward into my arms. I held her with my hand resting on the back of her head, letting her cry into my shirt. I didn't know exactly what else to do, so I just stood there with her in the doorway and waited it out.

"So you're doin' great, huh?" I said, when the sobbing slowed down.

"Couldn't be better," she mumbled into my chest. "Top o' the world."

"Nice to hear. Wanna sit down? Lie down? Curl in a ball?"

"You hate this, don't you. Having to act like you're sympathetic."

"Not a lot of practice."

"I know. I'm so damn dumb."

"No, you're chatty. Dumb means mute. Wordless, silent. At best reticent, laconic and taciturn. You're none of those things."

She pulled back and wiped off her good eye with the back of her hand. She picked at the bandage.

"I'm getting this thing all soggy. What do you think?"

"It's a look."

She turned and took my hand and pulled me into her chaotic mess of a living room. We had to pick our way around gigantic piles of magazines and God knows what else, and a collection of engorged cardboard boxes that might have been storage, or might have been furniture. Eventually we reached the massive white sofas that anchored the center of the room, and dropped down into the cushions.

"Wow. That was great," she said. "Should've done that a while ago."

"I always love a good cry."

"You've never cried in your life, you thug."

"Yeah, but I'd love it if I did."

She worried at her bandage.

"They say this'll take a few more weeks to get right. You gotta heal between surgeries. I feel like I been storing my face in a Veg-O-Matic," she said, slumping deeper into the floppy, marshmallow cushions.

Jackie was one of those people who threw more energy out into the world than the atmosphere was able to absorb. It caused her to ping-pong around through life. You thought you knew where she was heading, and then suddenly, zing, she'd be off in some other direction.

"Hodges said he saw you in Town. Steppin' out."

"At the grocery store. First time. I like Hodges, but he always looks at my tits when he talks to me."

"He sent me around to check on you."

"Not necessary. I'm a brick."

"So, you're okay."

She stopped picking at her bandage and started picking at her shirtfront.

"No, I'm not. I'm all fucked up."

"So let's unfuck you up."

"How're you going to do that?"

"By getting you out of the house."

"I've been to the grocery store."

"No, like out and around."

"Not like this. The stares."

"Let's fix that."

"Oh, sure."

I took her into the master bathroom and sat her on the john. I studied the bandage for a while, then went through her closet and vanity for supplies.

"You gotta talk to the doctor," she said.

"What do they know about it?"

She saw me with her big hair-trimming scissors in my hand.

"Jesus, Sam, what the hell are you doing?"

"Just stay still."

First I cut a line from the knit of her brow to the back of her head, right above the little dent everybody has at the back of their heads. Then I cut away most of the helmet. I had her hold the important part of the bandage against the wound while I reconfigured the chin strap into a single piece over the right side, secured below by a gauze choker. The net result freed her mass of hair so that it covered most of the damage and exposed the uninjured, though black and blue, side of her face. I tied things off with some yarn that I could string through her hair, and fooled around with her coif until she almost looked normal, for a girl with a stoved-in face.

I made her stand in front of the mirror.

"How did you do that?"

"I'm a design engineer. The doc took a more expedient, less cosmetic approach. This'll work just as well."

"It still looks pretty bad."

"Way less bad. Got anything to drink in this house?"

It took about a hour for her to shower, shave her legs and put an inch of makeup on her face, but eventually I got her out of the house. She hadn't worked around to thanking me yet, but at least she'd stopped sighing and moaning. By the time we were in the Grand Prix it was late morning. The sun was all the way out and the sky all the way blue. The air was dry and clean, so I kept the windows rolled down to air things out. The wind tossed around some empty coffee cups and messed up Jackie's hair a little, but she didn't seem to mind. Liberation.

This time of year I never drove on Montauk Highway, the main artery on this part of the Island. It was filled day and night with summer people. But you had most of the secondary routes to yourself because the summer people were mostly from Manhattan, and were afraid to deviate from established routes. They'd all seen *Deliverance*.

Hodges once told me the East End of Long Island had a different kind of light from the rest of the country. He'd learned this in the 1950s from one of the artists who'd set up shop out in Springs, then a homey little enclave in east East Hampton. He compared it to the light of Florence—bright on a sunny day, but with all the edges burnished off, as if filtered through a diffusion screen. Hodges told me it was caused by the way the big river of weather coming out of Pennsylvania and North Jersey would clip the Boroughs, then push up over Long Island Sound into Connecticut, leaving the East End in its wake, covered by a thinned-out trail of cloud cover. I don't think any of this was scientifically valid, but I knew he was right about the way the light looked because I saw how it composed shadows and drenched the leaves and potato fields with an oversaturated blue-green and cast dollops of chiaroscuro under the spreading boughs of red oak and silvery elm. As you moved from forest to fields, the landscape was recast and the light embraced the whole, claiming the separateness of this narrow, peninsular world.

I decided we'd go to Riverhead by way of Shelter Island, the chunk of wooded landmass caught between the jaws of the North and South Forks. It was less direct as the crow flies, but you got to catch little ferries on and off the island. There was usually a nice breeze and some sea spray over each of the narrow channels and I thought Jackie could use the extra oxygen.

"How's work?" I asked her after we'd been underway a while.

"S'okay. I handed off most of my cases. No client complaints."

"Except for me."

"No, you're a keeper. Especially since you never ask me to do anything."

The South Ferry was doing a brisk business. The guys directing the boarding cars sandwiched the Grand Prix between a Land Rover and a tradesman's step van. Jackie and I squeezed out into the air so we could stand by the gunwale and watch the cormorants dive-bomb into the chop. Jackie's hair unfurled against the wind. I held her around the waist so I could give her an occasional squeeze.

"You never ask me to do anything and you never tell me anything," she said.

"It's the law. Discovery is part of the process."

She was quiet the rest of the way to Riverhead, so I just smoked and listened to afternoon jazz on WLIU and thought about how to gang cut the rest of the rafters for my addition. Jackie's mood still threatened to breed gloom within the capacious cabin of the Grand Prix, but the light that continued to flow down through the abundant Shelter Island foliage was undaunted and unrestrained.

SIX

Jonathan Eldridge's office was on the second floor of a two-story building cobbed on to the end of a row of storefronts on Main Street in Riverhead. Downtown extended a few blocks in either direction, and was decorated by the retail iconography of mid-twentieth-century America. In other words, it was thoroughly beat up and godforsaken. We parked in the back and walked up a rear outdoor stairway to the separate entrance.

"It's open," a woman yelled from inside after we pushed the buzzer.

Eldridge hadn't overextended himself on office appointments. It was basically a single room carved up by waist-high cubicle dividers into a loose arrangement of workstations, each with at least one computer terminal and keyboard. Sitting at a command post at the center of the room was a young woman identified by an enormous nameplate mounted to the front of her desk. It said she was Alena

Zapata, Jonathan Eldridge's assistant, though the visual evidence was less persuasive.

Her hair was a rooster shock of brilliant magenta, or maybe a light purple, depending on the way the light hit it. The color confusion was exacerbated by her brilliant red lipstick and the pale, bluefish tint of her complexion. She had a huge mole on her gaunt right cheek, what I thought was a Marilyn Monroe beauty mark, but discovered later was a tiny tattoo of Eve Ensler.

Jackie had already staggered back a few steps as the overall effect hit her, so when the purple-haired woman said, "Holy cow, what happened to you?" I couldn't see her reaction.

"Are you Alena?" I asked.

"'At's what the sign says."

She crammed a rounded O into the word "sign."

"I'm Sam, this is Jackie. Did the Southampton police tell you we were coming?"

"Yeah, but it doesn't matter. I got an open door policy. Sit down where you want."

I dug a pair of chairs out of the other workstations and sat us in front of her desk.

"So, what can I do you for? Sorry about the reaction," she said to Jackie, without taking a breath. "It was, like, a shock and all."

"Shocks all around."

"I know you've already told the police everything," I said, jumping in, "so I hope you don't mind going over the same stuff."

She shook her purple plume.

"Nah, not at all. What else I gotta do? I'm all caught up here. You want coffee or something? I don't get a lotta company. The FedEx guy, the mail guy. The deli downstairs delivers. You had lunch? It's cheap."

"We're all set. Coffee sounds great. Black for me. A little milk for Jackie."

Standing, she had to be about five-ten, excluding heels. She poured the coffee from a slimy old Krups coffeemaker, but it wasn't bad if you had a wide tolerance.

"So, it was just you and Jonathan?" I asked.

"Yeah," she said, stirring in Jackie's milk, "when he was here, which wasn't all that much. Maybe a third of the time. He was always outta town."

"Doing fieldwork."

"Yeah, that's what he called it. Are you a cop?"

"An investigator," I said, and then immediately felt deceptive and asinine. "Kind of. Just a friend of a cop who asked for some help."

"Just a co-victim of a vicious, wanton act of murderous cruelty," said Jackie.

"Yeah, don't I know it. Co-victim?"

"We were the only survivors," said Jackie. "That's where, like, the face came from. It was, like, blown up and shit."

I shifted in my chair so I could take Jackie's hand. I gave it a hard squeeze.

"Wow. That's intense," said Alena.

"How was Jonathan to work for? Good boss?" I asked.

"Oh, yeah. A peach. I really did like the guy. He was very good to me. Very generous and polite. It sorta made up for being, like, in solitary confinement all the time."

"So, you handle the administrative stuff."

"I got a broker's license, buddy. Series 7. I handled whatever Jonathan wanted me to handle."

"You just dissed her, Sam."

"Sorry. Did you buy and sell? I thought Jonathan was strictly analysis."

"Well, yeah, sort of," said Alena, a little defensively, "but we did trades, too. I cleared them through a broker in the City. We're full service. Coulda traded a lot more, if Jonathan wanted to. He liked the straight fee approach. Percent on assets. Said it was less stress. He didn't like stress."

She shook her head, remembering.

"Was he tense a lot?" I asked.

"No, never. That's the point. He used to say that people ought to ascertain their personal level of stress tolerance, then engineer their whole lives around staying right there, right below what they can take. It was a theory of his. Only, he could afford to live pretty good and stay clear of his personal best, stress-wise. To stay that calm I'd have to, like, not work and lie around in bed all day, and eventually starve, which can be pretty stressful in its own right."

Alena sat back in her office chair, which gave into a partial recline. She tapped her nails on the armrests.

"You mind if I smoke?" she asked us, looking at Jackie, who was already smoldering a bit herself. I pulled out my lighter and lit her cigarette and one for myself.

"Jonathan never woulda let me smoke in here in a million years. I suppose I still shouldn't, in honor and all, but there's not much else to do."

"When do you leave?"

"End of the week. I got a gig in the City. No biggie. It was time for me to head out anyway. This is just a really shitty way to terminate employment."

It was stuffy in the office, even with a window AC unit running on high. The smoke didn't help. The ceiling was drop-acoustic panels and fluorescent lights. The carpet a smudged beige, indifferently vacuumed. Only the PCs looked new and alert, at the ready. Plugged directly into Jonathan's lifeblood, the hemorrhage of information available off the Web. If it wasn't for the communal impulse wired into most people's genes, maybe everyone would run their careers like Jonathan's. Separate, but jacked-in. Efficient, lucrative and stress free.

"So, no ideas?" asked Jackie, hackles still firmly in place.

"Beg pardon?"

"About the bombing. Your boss. The sweetheart."

"Not my sweetheart, sweetheart. Strictly business. Anyway, I called him a peach. Not a sweetheart. Not that there's a difference, semantically speaking."

Alena glowered at Jackie over the top of her CRT. The situation took me back to running a huge corporate enterprise, where so much precious time was wasted mediating a particular flavor of institutional conflict my friend Jason Fligh, the president of the University of Chicago, privately characterized as bitch shit.

"You're a smart young woman," I said to Alena, bracing for Jackie's snort. "You probably have a theory on what happened to Jonathan. Few knew him better. Nobody better, if you're talking about his business."

Alena pulled her eyes off Jackie and refocused on me. Approvingly, as if to say, now we all know who the sensitive one is in *this* team. Erroneously. She sat back and touched the outer crust of her purple hair.

"To me, the business here is basically research. We research companies people might want to invest in. We sell opinions. That's really what this is all about. Opinions, not proclamations. Jonathan wasn't a theater critic, he just told people what he could figure out about a company. That's it. Sure, I bet some of the companies weren't too happy about what he said, but that was their fault. And mostly, I think, the companies should all feel okay about him, because he was such a straight shooter. He told it like it was, which most of the time was pretty good for those guys. Frankly, I think he

CHRIS KNOPF

was overall pretty optimistic, and if you look at his record, you know, how these companies ended up performing, it was pretty much the way he had it scored. Where's the beef in that?"

I was sitting there feeling some sort of odd warmth for Alena's simple loyalty and frank appraisal of her boss when Jackie went and spoiled the mood.

"Bullshit."

"Excuse me?"

"Bullshit," she repeated. "Jonathan Eldridge was a financial adviser of the first rank. Specializing in high tech, the most volatile and capricious market segment. Billions of dollars could be made or lost through decisions based on his analysis. You talk about it like he ran a local beauty pageant."

Alena looked at me.

"Is she with you?"

"You bet, toots," said Jackie. "Actually, he's with me."

"What my colleague means," I said, as I draped an arm over Jackie's shoulders, "is there must have been occasional disappointments felt by Jonathan's clients when certain recommendations inevitably missed the mark. Some people might've had some serious losses, which might've caused a little rancor."

"He means thoroughly pissed off," said Jackie, helpfully.

"I know what he means. Yeah, sure, not everybody loved everything we did. Though only a couple had a beef. People like Ivor Fleming."

"Ivor Fleming?"

"Investor. Nasty stubby little jerk from up island. Made it in scrap metal, for Chrissakes. Pissed off at the world, I think. Anyway, only guy Jonathan ever fired. You know, stopped working for. Said he caused too much stress. You got that right."

68

"Lost money on Jonathan's recommendations?" I asked.

Alena looked down at her CRT, then off toward the one lonely, dirty window in the lightless office.

"Yeah, though I couldn't entirely hundred percent tell you why. I managed the office stuff, ran the trades, made nice nice to clients when Jonathan was out of town, did research online. I said I handled everything, but there were things Jonathan did on his own. He didn't exactly report to me on every conversation. I usually knew what was what, but I wasn't always privy."

Which hurt her feelings, obviously. Even Jackie let a little sound of sympathy escape her lips.

"Anyway," she said, rebounding, "he did his shit, I did mine, everybody was happy. Hard to believe, maybe, seeing this dump, but we were, you know, actually happy here in our little world."

The canned air in the office sat heavily for a few moments, then Jackie struck out on a new tack.

"Are all his records still here?" she asked.

Alena looked around the room, as if for an answer.

"No, I don't think so. After he got blown up the cops, serious cops in suits and earphones, came in here and swept everything away. All I got is the same administrative stuff I always had."

"Names of clients?"

"I still got that. Names, addresses and phone numbers. I copied it all for the cops. Everything I had. Including stuff on Ivor, though they never asked me about him. They spent a lot of time messing with my computer, but finally gave it back to me. Good thing, since it's all I had to settle everything out."

"Can you copy that for me?" I asked. "The names, addresses, phone numbers?"

69

"And email addresses? You bet. Why the hell not."

Jackie jerked her head toward the other computers in the room.

"What about those?"

Alena shrugged.

"If you want to anchor your boat, or need a doorstop. Cops took out the hard drives. You can knock, but nobody's home."

"For good?" asked Jackie.

"I don't know. Ask the cops. I'm heading for the City. You can take it from here." Alena's attention was back on to her computer screen. "Where should I send the information?"

Jackie slid her business card across Alena's desk. She knew I didn't have a computer.

"What about phone records?" I asked, suddenly remembering my ostensible purpose for the visit. "Cell phone records? Calls to and from?"

"Fascinating," said Alena.

"Really."

"Yeah. Nobody ever asked me for Jonathan's personal phone records. I kept expecting it. You'd think."

"Probably didn't need to. Get everything directly from the phone company."

"Probably," said Alena, unconvinced.

She opened a deep drawer and pulled out a stack of phone bills.

"Good old paper. All in chronological order, of course, cross-tabbed to accounts payable and the general ledger. Just like Jonathan wanted them."

She used the stack of bills to point to a copier machine in a far corner. Jackie took the hint and went to make copies. While the machine whirred I sat there wondering whether to admire or be depressed by the drab orderliness of Jonathan

Eldridge's office, his profession and his life. I respected any-one who had a zeal for research and analysis—like Appolonia said, engineering and finance weren't all that different when you thought about it. Lots of data, fundamental formulas, tricky little puzzles. Though never entirely controllable, both ultimately manageable pursuits. Maybe that was what trou-bled me about Jonathan. It seemed as if control was the prime objective. Financial analysis was merely the medium, the vehicle.

I always knew my edge as an engineer was a taste for chaos, for the unruly aspects of problem solving, a prejudice toward intuition over methodology. I knew how to crunch numbers. I just didn't like it very much. Made me edgy, irritable.

"If you could sort those client names by friendly and unfriendly, it'd help," said Jackie.

Alena looked at me as if to validate the request. I nodded. She nodded back. Transaction complete. Jackie sighed.

"That'll take a little longer, but it'll be in your email when you get back to the office," said Alena. I sensed in her an air of poised competence. I wondered how Jonathan regarded the obvious. I wondered what he thought looking at her across the broad desktops. Did he recognize that appearance was irrelevant in a world run on email and voice messaging?

"How'd Jonathan get along with his wife?" I asked, as abruptly as the question occurred to be. Alena pulled her eyes away from her screen.

"Mad about her. Just mad. Never said one word to me on the subject, mind you, but you could tell when he talked to her on the phone. Friendly, nice, not all gooshy, but kind. That's really what I always thought. Kind. Not like you'd normally describe a lovesick couple. But it was there. Real grown-ups."

She turned her head back to the computer.

"I don't like to think about it," she said.

"Sorry. Had to ask."

"I know. Co-victims and all that."

Jackie had already thanked her and was gathering to leave the office when I had one more thought.

"Do you know the names of the cops who took the hard drives? Feds, Staties?"

She spun around in her chair and pulled open the top drawer of the adjoining desk. She took out a business card and handed it to Jackie.

"Take it. I already wrote down the info. In case I need it again. In my next reiteration."

"If you think of anything else," Jackie started to say.

"I know," said Alena. "Heard it all before. Will do. No prob. Even if you aren't the nicest co-victim I ever met. No offense," she added, looking at me.

"Sorry," said Jackie. She pointed to her head. "Brain damage."

"No prob," said Alena, again, though by now she was engrossed in whatever was playing across her computer screen. Back swimming in the stream of data, negotiating currents, shooting the rapids. I escorted Jackie out the door while the fragile peace was still intact.

"Sorry, Sam," said Jackie when we got outside. "I don't know what got into me."

"A little of the old Irish fire, by my accounting."

"Old Irish idiot."

She swung open the Grand Prix's gigantic door and dropped into the passenger seat. Wet heat poured out of the car and washed over me. I was glad I'd left Eddie home again, though I feared it was starting to piss him off. Hard to explain the dynamics of heat exhaustion to a gung ho mutt like Eddie. Maybe if I showed him a video.

"All right. But you feel better for it. Admit it."

"Picking a fight is good therapy? You'd think that."

"As long as you win the fight."

"You're a peach, Sam."

"So what'd we learn?"

"We're ridiculously over our heads and have no business prying into this investigation."

"That's what I told Sullivan."

"It's one thing to chat with people like Ms. Fright Wig in there, or poor Mrs. Eldridge, it's another to search through the guy's client records for material evidence, or ask the FBI to share the fun with us. They'll think you're a dangerous lunatic and try to get me disbarred."

"Both propositions have been advanced before to little effect."

The big tangle of kinky hair I'd freed from the bandage was twirling around her head from the wind gushing into the Grand Prix. It looked good on her. Reckless and unkempt.

"I'm not kidding, Sam. Sullivan should never have involved you."

"So you're going to go through everything Alena sends you and see if anything interesting pops out."

She shook her head and snorted.

"You're not even listening."

"You're a peach, Jackie," I told her, but she was busy staring out the open window, wind in her injured face, O-2 in her lungs and the first hint of renewal sneaking into her consciousness.

SEVEN

Eddie was so glad to get outside he circled the house at a full run, then drank a little water and did it again. I opted for a gin and tonic, which I brought out to the weatherbeaten Adirondacks, which I'd pulled out from under the maples and set up just a few feet from the breakwater. When Eddie'd had his fill of tearing around, he lay down in front of me with his tongue hanging out of the corner of his mouth. I looked in his eyes for signs of reproach, but only saw the resident look of gleeful anticipation.

I'd pulled a stack of mail out of the mailbox when I got there. Tucked between an electric bill from LIPA and a slippery, full-color promotional flyer from a home center store up island was a photograph from my daughter of a dentist in the 1920s straddling a patient and extracting a tooth with a pair of pliers. She was a graphic artist, with full access to every conceivable image to capture and reformulate into a postcard. This was the communication channel we'd settled on. I didn't have a computer, so her preferred approach, email, was out of the question. I also hated talking on the phone, especially with her. Way too many pregnant pauses that formed after some offhand comment of mine, without the benefit of visual contact to clue me in on whatever offense I'd just committed. Years ago, at the advice of one of Abby's friends, I tried to restrict myself to simple declarative sentences and one- or two-word questions whenever I had to speak to my daughter on the phone. With little success. I had a gift for provocation, especially with people I didn't want to provoke. Somehow, though, brevity became the stylistic conceit of our correspondence, best expressed within the two-by-two hole of the standard postcard:

> Hot water's out, sup's pissed. Boss a dick,
> hours late. Mom freaked, calls too much.
> City, zing. Tom, yum.
>
> —Allison

They should study the genetic composition of provocation. I could supply the data.

I dug a chewed-up pencil out of my back pocket and found a field of white paper on the back of another utility bill.

> Peconic calm, surly sky. Cash is cool, ham-
> mers fly. Back's healed, ear, huh? Status quo,
> oh, no. Eddie misses you. You can tell by the
> way he drools on your pillow.
>
> —the Dad

I had a backlog of these epistolary haikus scattered around the cottage written on whatever paper was handy.

If I didn't hear from her for a while I'd transfer one to a post-card and send it off. Past experience taught me to mete them out discretely. It took over four years to get to this stage, and I was grateful, but careful.

I wondered how I'd explain to her what I was actually up to besides swinging a hammer. I wondered if I could explain it to myself. Maybe if I sat there and drank for a while I'd be able to get in touch with my feelings. Clarify my priorities. Figure out just what the hell I was doing.

"What the hell am I doing?" I asked Eddie.

Part of me knew Hodges was right. I had a heretofore repressed impulse to stick my nose into this thing. Especially now that the official investigation had crapped out. At least, that's what it looked like. Hard to tell these days if they were actually stymied or had it all solved, but for some reason had to keep quiet. Not enough evidence, political pressure, inter-departmental turf wars, all the stuff that would piss me off so much I'd probably pop a cranial artery. Which was reason enough to stay the hell out of it.

"Rule one. Don't go looking for trouble," I said to Eddie.

On the other hand, somebody tried to kill Jackie and me, albeit indirectly. Along with a bunch of innocent people. To say nothing of Jonathan Eldridge, who may or may not have been innocent, but probably didn't deserve to be blown to smithereens.

The ugly blind brutality of a car bomb is impossible to appreciate until you're up close to one of them. I hadn't been able to sleep through the night for two months after it hap-pened. And I still woke up a lot, freaked at little night sounds. It made me feel helpless and foolish. Powerless. And furious.

A big tern glided gracefully down to perch on the edge of the breakwater. Eddie looked at it like, man, you gotta be kidding me. He gave the bird a second to settle in before launching an attack across the lawn. The tern took flight with as much dignity as haste would allow.

I watched Eddie cut across the bay frontage, then make an unexpected right turn to leap over the rosebush and picket-fence border between my property and the house next door. It was a gray and white bungalow that shared the tip of Oak Point with me. An old lady named Regina Broadhurst used to live there. It had been empty since she died the year before, so it gave me a jolt to see a gray Audi A4 parked in the driveway. Or maybe the jolt was because I knew who owned the Audi.

So did Eddie, which is why he was there barking at the side door. It was opened by a woman in a white silk dressing gown and bare feet. She had long, thick auburn hair that matched the dark reddish brown of her complexion. When she bent down to pet Eddie's head her gown opened up, revealing enough breast to identify a tan line, even from a few hundred feet. She scratched his ears, then tossed him a treat of some kind. He caught it, did a quick spin, then ran back over to me. The woman followed him with her eyes until she saw me sitting in the Adirondack. Then she backed slowly into the house and shut the door.

Eddie ran up to me with a Big Dog biscuit in his mouth, his favorite. He dropped down in front of me to eat, showing off the prize. As he crunched away I had a chance to get in touch with feelings of another sort.

"Goddammit," I said, in the direction of Regina's house.

EIGHT

THE NEXT MORNING I wasn't working on my addition like I'd sworn I would. I was driving back over to see Appolonia Eldridge and her lawyer. Earlier I'd reached Joe Sullivan on his cell phone.

"So you really didn't learn shit," he said after I relayed what I learned.

"I don't remember seeing Ivor Fleming in any of the reports."

"The Feds said they checked out all his customers."

"You don't think we should talk to him?"

"You'll need a good reason to go back at a money guy like Fleming."

"That's what I'm trying to do. Get a reason."

"What?"

"Not sure yet. I'll let you know."

"Talk to me."

"I want to try something out on Mrs. Eldridge. Just let me do it without all the explanations."

"Don't fuck me up."

"Never on purpose."

He wanted more, but I'd rushed him off the phone. It was like that with Sullivan. Too much information was rarely a good thing. He was better with faits accomplis.

After Sullivan I'd called Gabe Szwit, whom I thought would be a hard sell, but after I gave him my idea he surprised me.

"Let me call Appolonia," he told me, "and see if we can meet again at her house."

So I was in the Grand Prix heading over to Riverhead again. Only this time I had Eddie in the backseat where he belonged. It was cooler, and I just couldn't leave him in the house again. Dogs have to be out in the air. Or the wind, in Eddie's case, his head stuck out the window, ears swept back, tongue flapping out the corner of his mouth.

"If you catch anything, it counts against dinner," I told him.

When I got to Appolonia's I rolled the windows up just enough to discourage him from jumping out of the car.

"Try to keep a low profile," I told him as I walked away from my inconspicuous '67 Pontiac Grand Prix.

A pair of kids in hockey gear watched from the street. A mailman hopped from mailbox to mailbox down the perfect, flat black asphalt. Two doors down a woman was trying to adjust her sprinkler without getting wet, unsuccessfully. I listened for other dogs that could set off Eddie, but all I heard was the distant sound of a powerful motorboat starting a run across the Great Peconic Bay.

Belinda answered the door. As friendly and welcoming as always. Appolonia and Szwit were waiting in the living room, equipped with tea and a pot of coffee for me. I felt like one of the gang.

"Hello, Mr. Acquillo."

"Thanks for seeing me again."

Appolonia was dressed in a men's oxford-cloth shirt and gray slacks. She looked like a starving arctic bird. Gabe was still in a suit, but felt secure enough to leave his briefcase on the floor. Progress.

"I filled Mrs. Eldridge in on your idea as well as I could," he said. "I thought it had merit."

"I thought it did, too," said Appolonia. "But why don't you go through it again."

"Okay. I don't think I can learn any more about your husband's murder than the cops, the Staties, the FBI, Homeland Security, etcetera. But I can't see how it'll hurt if I poke around a little. Only thing is, I'm just a guy. An unofficial guy. I can't, I won't, go around pretending to be a cop or a PI. That feels stupid, and looks stupid when I'm exposed. I need some official reason to be talking to people."

"Your police friend Officer Sullivan seems to think you're official enough."

"He shouldn't. I need genuine cred."

"Cred?" said Appolonia.

"He means credentials. Street patois," said Gabe, looking at me like, hey man, I know some shit, too.

"Which you can give me," I said to Appolonia.

"Me?"

"Yeah. You own a business. Might be a business now in name only, but it's still a legal LLC, with assets and liabilities."

"The liabilities are trivial. And Jonathan was the only asset."

"Not really. There's a client list I bet other guys like Jonathan would love to get their hands on." I didn't mention that Alena had already handed it over to me with hardly a thought. "Took him years to develop, and by definition, every name is a prospect."

Appolonia blanched a little at the implication of that, but nodded thoughtfully.

"Sam thought he could be assigned the task of assessing the quality of the list—this is the part that appeals to me— as a means of putting a value on the operation as a whole. We might be able to sell the company, Appolonia, not simply liquidate."

"I have plenty of money, Gabe."

"I know, but why leave anything on the table? I want you to have all you can out of this terrible tragedy."

He said it like he really meant it. It struck me that Gabe had more than a professional interest in his client. Which was okay with me. I wanted the best for her, too.

"So, what do we need to do?" she asked.

"Simple," I said. "Hire me as a consultant. You don't have to pay me, just confirm I'm working for you if anyone calls. Tell them I'm transitioning Jonathan's business. That's the kind of thing consultants do. Transition things."

"I also like the part where we don't pay him," said Gabe, attempting a little joke.

"Okay?" I asked.

Appolonia looked at me in that calm but studied way she had.

"You don't think you'll learn anything about Jonathan's death. But you want to try, is that right? It's not about financial gain for any of us."

"Don't forget they almost killed me, too. And messed up my friend Jackie. If I don't try I'll feel like a bum. That's all."

"I wouldn't want you to feel like a bum."

"Good. So that's it. Gabe'll handle the paperwork. I'll let you know what I find out, either way."

"I don't suppose there's any harm in it."

"So it's settled," said Gabe, reaching for his briefcase to pull out some forms for me to sign. Johnny-on-the-spot.

"Just one question for you, Sam," said Appolonia.

"Sure."

"Why so long? This happened months ago. Why the new interest?"

I didn't have a good answer for that, but I tried to answer truthfully, the best I could.

"I've had some trouble in my life. I don't need any more. In fact, avoiding trouble has become my life's vocation. Then this thing happened. I guess I tried to pretend it didn't matter, but it does."

"A knight errant."

"Oh, no. Don't make me into a nice person. I'm not. I'm doing this for my own reasons."

"I could say the same thing about myself."

"Good, then we're square."

"We're square," said Appolonia as she rose from her chair and floated out of the room, leaving me with Gabriel Szwit, who watched her with the eager hope I'd seen in the eyes of devoted retrievers. I felt sorry for him. He didn't know how hopeless it was for him.

Not yet, anyway.

———

I spent the rest of that day cutting bird's mouths into rafters to finish framing out the roof of the addition. It was warm, but a cloud cover held back the worst of the sun. I drank a lot of water and worked at a steady, deliberate pace. Eddie hunkered down under the grandiflora hydrangea by the breakwater and kept watch. I tried to clear my mind of everything but dimensions and construction theory, but it was hard to do. Jonathan Eldridge had a way of creeping onto the site and slowing progress.

I was about to go down the ladder to get a beer when Jackie Swaitkowski pulled into the driveway. She was in Bobby's claptrap Toyota pickup. She got out and waved at me with a manila envelope.

"I got your message about the client list," she said as I led her to the chairs and beer cooler. "It's all here. Alena divided it into hostile and non-hostile, an easy task since there're only three hostiles listed."

We sat down, and after digging out Heinekens for both of us, I read through the papers. There was a name, address, email and dates of engagement for each client. Only eighteen of them. That surprised me.

"Me, too," said Jackie, reading my mind. "Pretty exclusive club. Smells like big money, not just investors, but PE types."

"PE?"

"Private equity. Large individual investors. Guys looking for unconventional opportunities, large positions, start-ups, that stuff. I emailed Alena, who said as much. Jonathan was paid a fee, a percentage of assets invested, to uncover opportunities and vet companies clients might already be looking at. Sounds like fun."

"You'd hate it."

"Probably."

"So, Ivor Fleming's a hostile. And a woman. Joyce Whithers."

"Owns a restaurant in Watermill. Alena just said 'rhymes with rich.'"

"And a guy named Butch Ellington."

"Jonathan's brother."

"Ellington?"

"Real name's Arthur Eldridge. Changed it just to piss off

his brother, according to Alena. A play on Butch Cassidy and his mother's maiden name. For reasons unknown."

"But he was a client."

"As Alena put it, 'blood and water and all that.' They managed his retirement account. She said Butch had plenty of money. Successful artist. But pretty whacked out, which I guess goes with the territory. Nothing like Jonathan."

"The wonder of genetics."

"Ivor Fleming's got a house out here, in Sagaponack. Alena gave me an address and a phone number."

"Have you tried to reach the Fed who took all the computer files?"

"Warming up to it. Need a good shtick."

I told her I'd been retained to valuate Jonathan's business. She could play my lawyer.

"I thought I was your lawyer."

"My financial consultant lawyer."

"It'll take about a half a second for him to tag us as the only survivors of the bomb blast. He won't like it."

"Then show him a little tit. That always works."

"Okay. Good idea."

We drank our beers for a while in silence, watching the sailboats out on the Peconic try to make some headway in the turgid summer air. Then Jackie noticed the gray Audi A4 parked in Regina's driveway.

"Hey, somebody move in?"

"I hope not."

"That's neighborly."

"Hate crowds."

"That looks like Amanda's car."

"It is."

"Oh, yeah. It's her house now. Actually, it's her peninsula. And the peninsula next door and all parts in between."

"Not this part."

"You knew this could happen."

"Happen?"

"That house has the best view in the area, except for yours. She can live anywhere she wants now that she's divorced Roy. Him defrauding her providing adequate grounds, I guess. Not that you need anything like that in New York."

"How's that beer?"

"You're not going to talk about it. You'll never talk about it."

"I want to talk about Ivor Fleming."

"Man, you're a pigheaded bastard."

I had Ivor's file open in my lap.

"So Fleming's an alchemist," I said.

"Huh?"

"Scrap-metal baron. Turns iron into gold."

"Apparently, at least from what Alena said. Came from Brooklyn. Has a big processing plant up island. Sells recycled steel, mostly to car manufacturers, here and overseas. That's all I know till I do some research."

"Tough business. All rust, heat and sharp edges."

"My guess is Ivor's no pussycat."

"Don't mention cats around Eddie. Gets him worked up."

Jackie hung around with me for another beer, then left me to finish up the rest of the rafters. She didn't press me about Amanda, my new next-door neighbor, for which I was grateful. Like I told Appolonia, I'd been trying hard to avoid trouble in any form, and there was nothing about Amanda Battiston that didn't feel like trouble.

NINE

Sagaponack is a sprawling billionaire preserve along the ocean in the Town of Southampton. A lot of stupid big houses were built there in the eighties and nineties, and development was still going strong in the new century. When I was a kid I used to ride through the area on my bike. Then it was mostly farmland with an occasional summer bungalow, but I'd long since given up those associations, as if my childhood had taken place in another part of the universe.

I was driving over to Ivor Fleming's house with the windows down to mix some air in with the cigarette smoke and smell of Viennese cinnamon from the coffee place on the corner in the Village. I missed having Eddie to run back and forth between the two rear windows searching for ground threats, like summer people walking miniature purebreds, but it was still too hot to leave him in the car. I'd actually snuck out the basement hatch so I wouldn't have to endure him looking at me with that what-the-fuck look on his face.

Not surprisingly, Ivor's house was oversized and foolishly conceived in the fashionable dormer-ridden, cedar-shaked, postmodern vernacular of the times. It had a full length porch along the front of the house and a big circular driveway to allow maximum display area for indigenous and foreign luxury cars.

It was Saturday, so I thought the chances were good I'd catch him at the house. I parked behind a shimmering black Mercedes, climbed the porch steps and rang the doorbell.

A Doberman answered the door. Or, at least tried to knock it down from the other side. I looked back over my shoulder to plot an escape route. Then a woman's voice, speaking urgently in Spanish, quieted the dog. I was glad I'd left Eddie at home. He'd scratch the hell out of the Grand Prix trying to defend my honor. Doberman or not.

"'Ello?" said the little Spanish woman who opened the door.

I held up the letter Gabe had drafted for me.

"Is Mr. Fleming home?"

"He know you coming here?"

I shook the letter.

"I just need to ask him a few questions. He'll want to see me."

"He not tell me you're here."

I slipped Gabe's letter through the door opening.

"I'll wait."

The door closed and I could hear the woman drag the Doberman across the tile floor. A lot of time went by, so I sat in one of Ivor's big white caned chairs. Victorian, with a high back. Not too comfortable, but sturdy. Creaked when you shifted around, which I did a lot while waiting for Ivor.

"I already talked to the police," a man's voice said through the closed screen door. I stood up.

"I'm not the police. I represent the firm."

"The firm?"

"Jonathan Eldridge Consultants. His company."

The door opened and out stepped a pasty little guy in a slippery nylon shirt two sizes smaller than him, which was an accomplishment. The color was indefinable. Maybe shiny rust, or diluted magenta. His hair was too thin to completely cover his head, but what was left was died black and smeared over his skull from ear to ear. He wore heavy black-framed glasses that exaggerated his bony little face. He looked at least part Asian. Maybe Filipino or Indonesian.

"You're talking about this at my house?"

"Sorry. Just trying to expedite."

He was reading the letter I'd shoved at the Spanish lady. Like me, he probably had trouble understanding Gabe Szwit's legalese.

"I don't understand."

"I'm doing a valuation on the firm." I pointed to the part of the letter I thought might have the relevant language. "Not easy with a closely held entity. Lots of intangibles."

Ivor looked up at me like he was having trouble believing his ears.

"This has got nothing to do with me."

The Spanish lady who'd answered the door popped out on the porch and asked him something in Spanish. I tried to follow it, but the words zipped by too quickly. She had an eye on me while she talked, gauging my reaction.

"Si, si," said Ivor and shooed her off with the letter. Then he flicked it at me. "Sit down."

I sat.

"I'm sorry the man's dead," said Ivor, joining me in the adjacent porch chair. "But I don't have anything to say about him or his business. This is what I told the people who investigated this thing. We did business over the phone. I hardly knew him."

"Good will is a big part of a valuation. I'm interested in assessing his client relationships. How was yours?"

Ivor looked out over his soulless acreage as if seeking divine guidance. It let me get a better look at his face. He'd had cosmetic surgery—you could tell from the stretched translucent skin around his eyes. Explained the Ferdinand Marcos grimace.

He looked back down at Gabe's letter.

"What the hell are you talking about? There's nothing to value. Just this one guy giving investment advice. Who's dead."

"So you're probably unaware of the methodologies Mr. Eldridge used in assessing investment potential. His proprietary tools."

Ivor looked neither surprised nor impressed.

"For what, losing money? I can do that all on my own."

"So things didn't work out that well with Jonathan's advice."

"Not so good, but that's the game. I hire guys like Eldridge all the time. Some of 'em hit it, others don't. I don't know why I bother. Odds're about as good at the casino."

"Most of Jonathan's clients seemed satisfied."

"Suckers. Rather lose their shirts than admit stupidity."

Ivor sat back in the big white wicker chair and slid down like a teenager watching TV, his dark little body almost disappearing into the floral cushion meant to soften the hard wicker surface.

"Look, uh," he checked the letter again, "Mr. Aquo."

"Acquillo."

"Aquo. It's the weekend. My time off. This here," he waved his hands around, "is my weekend house. Where I come to get away. I don't see people here, and I sure don't talk business here with people I don't know who turn up on my doorstep. With letters." He shook it at me.

I didn't have a good response, mostly because I sympathized with his position. I didn't like people turning up uninvited at my house either. Messes up my balance, which is what I had in mind for Ivor.

"So," he said to me, getting up from his chair, "you want anything? Iced tea? Beer?"

"Iced tea's okay," I said, caught by surprise. I thought about the beer for a second. Too early, even for me.

When he went inside he let out the Doberman. It was a black-and-tan mass of coiled springs and dead-eyed menace. Big, especially for a female, maybe eighty pounds. Her long claws tapped across the wood floor over to my chair, where she turned and sat down, pressing up against the armrest to make it easy for me to stroke her smooth, rock-hard shoulders.

"Wait'll Eddie smells you. Will take some explaining."

Didn't faze the Doberman. She just sat there and soaked up the attention. I scratched up under her ears. She lifted her head and pushed it into my hand. Big old baby. Just looked scary.

"*Perrito, que pasa contigo? Hay que chula eres!*" mewed the Spanish lady at the Doberman when she came out on the porch with my iced tea. "*Que tienes, Pobrecita? Quieres un beso?*"

The Doberman stood partway up and shoved her long snout into the woman's leg as she put down the tray.

"Scratch her ears. She digs that," I suggested, but the Spanish lady ignored me. I searched around my long-dead memory for a translation, but she left before I could embarrass myself with an attempt.

"Portate bien y sientate alla con ese caballero," she called back from inside the house.

The Doberman sat back down so I could continue ministrations.

"Perrito?" I said to her. *"*More like *caballo grande."*

Ivor came out with a beer and handed me an iced tea. I immediately regretted my decision.

"So, you met Cleo."

"Big girl. Likes her ears scratched."

Ivor had put on a pair of oversized sunglasses, rendering the Marcos imitation nearly complete. He got back in his chair and took a long pull on his beer. He snapped his fingers at Cleo.

"Ven aca."

She shot over to his chair and took up her usual spot next to the arm.

"Dogs're smarter than people, sometimes I think," said Ivor.

"I know one that won't dispute that."

"'Course you were smart enough not to get out of your chair with Cleo wanting you to stay."

"Hadn't indicated that."

"Didn't have to. You stayed put. I just wanted to get my beer before concluding our conversation."

I toasted him with my iced tea.

"Gracias."

"De nada. So you understand. I have nothing to say about Jonathan Eldridge or his business. The entire subject is as dead as he is. Though I'm puzzled about this valuation. I'm not an expert in the investment adviser business, as you could tell if you looked at my investments. But to my knowledge there's nothing there to sell. And why you'd come here to talk to me about this on a Saturday, that's puzzling, too. The whole thing is puzzling."

He looked like he was grappling with the puzzle, then he snapped his fingers.

"Unless," he said, "you were thinking I'd be interested in buying something from *you*. That this is some sort of a roundabout sales pitch. Is that what this is?" He directed the question to Cleo. She didn't give it up.

"I guess that's what I'm trying to figure out," I told him. "If there's anything of value here. For the estate. Mrs. Eldridge."

Ivor was stroking Cleo's side, but otherwise sitting very still in his chair. I assumed he was looking at me closely, but I couldn't tell with his sunglasses on. Though I was more interested in Cleo's stare, which was fixed steadily in my direction. I guessed at the distance between me and the Grand Prix. No way.

I had a little bit of iced tea left, so I took my time finishing it. I finally set it down on the wicker side table and was about to experiment with leaving when I heard a truck pull into the driveway. A black pickup, with a deep bed and a double rear axel. Diesel. It pulled up behind the Grand Prix and two guys got out. One really meaty guy in a blue nylon warm-up jacket and dirty bone-colored polyester pants. And a much skinnier guy, some kind of white and African-American mix, though with the same taste in couture. They both looked to be in their early forties, but were probably younger. Hair salon haircuts. Bad skin. Hard lives.

"What do you know, more company," said Ivor, sitting back in his chair. "And I thought it'd just be another quiet Saturday morning."

The two bounded up onto the porch. Cleo never looked away from me. I had the feeling she and the meatballs had already met.

"Hello, Mr. Fleming," said the skinny guy. "How is everything?"

"It's about to get better. Mr. Aquo here was just planning to leave."

"If it's cool with Cleo," I said.

Ivor snapped his fingers and pointed to the floor. She dropped down on her belly, but her haunches were still bunched up, ready to launch.

"Thanks for stopping by," said Ivor, though the sentiment lacked sincerity.

On the way to the Grand Prix I realized I had an escort.

"Gonna be another hot one," I said to the big guy, who fell in on my right. "What do you think?" I asked his partner, now on my left.

"Hotter'n shit's my guess," he said.

They walked me over to my car and watched me get in. Then went back to their truck. I snuck around the Mercedes and rounded the parking circle. The pickup had gone the other way on the circle and gotten ahead of me, so I followed them out to the road. There was a white gate at the entrance of the driveway made to look like the ones at the old estates over where my friend Burton lived. It had been open when I came in, but now it was closed. The pickup stopped and the two guys jumped out and came back to my car. The skinny guy leaned down to look in my window.

"Get out a minute, would ya?"

"Needed to stretch my legs, anyway," I said. "Long driveway."

I swung the Pontiac's gigantic door wide enough to force him to move back a few paces. The big guy leaned against the pickup's tailgate and started picking his teeth with a wooden match. All style, these guys.

"Mr. Fleming probably explained to you that he doesn't appreciate being disturbed at his weekend house. During the weekend," said the skinny guy.

"Probably okay during the week. When he's not here."

"That's right. You can see that when shit like this happens it makes him feel," he searched around for the right word, "concerned."

The skinny guy didn't look like he was carrying anything he could use to hit me over the head. Or shoot me. So I had to assume his job was to scare me to death with talk, and the other guy, who'd thus far remained eloquently silent, was there to provide a physical component if necessary. So I started looking him over.

Heavy arms, but mostly fat. Face clear, pockmarks aside. Hadn't given or taken much in any actual fistfight. Probably specialized in baseball bats and kicks to the gut. Snubby gun barrels crammed up under the chin. Though at the moment the biggest challenge these guys presented was their black pickup truck.

"So, you're going to kill me," I said to the skinny guy.

He jerked back his head and smirked.

"Kill you? What the hell for?"

"Well, it's either that or beat me up. But, if you beat me up, you'll have to kill me."

The skinny guy didn't like where this was going. He was thinking we'd have more foreplay, ramp up to the scary stuff about killing and maiming.

"Connie won't kill you unless I tell him to."

"Connie?"

The meaty guy stopped picking his teeth and looked at me like he'd heard that plenty of times before.

"Short for Constantine. My grandfather's name. From Hungary."

"Oh, sure. They're still talking about him in Budapest."

The skinny guy struggled to get control of the conversation.

"You're a talker," he told me.

"Design engineer. Even worse."

"So you understand what I'm sayin'."

I hated it when I said things to myself like, "there was a time," but that's what I was thinking standing there, leaning against the Grand Prix's ten-ton driver's side door, sizing up Jack Sprat and his fat friend. I'd been coming around to the realization that fifty-three-year-old guys aren't as resilient as they used to be. I could probably drop both of them, but there was a real danger somebody'd get a shot in on the way down, and they told me at the hospital that I was one shot short of my life's allotment.

"Yeah, you're gonna have to kill me. Because if all you do is beat the shit out of me, you'll only mess up my brain. It'll make me crazy, and then I'll have to hunt you both down and kill *you*."

Then I shrugged, like it was all out of my hands.

The skinny guy ran a long finger down his hollowed out cheek and squinted at me.

"I think maybe you're already crazy. We're just talking here."

"That's a relief. I got a lot of things to do today. You just got to let me out so I can get at it."

I made a show of climbing back into the Grand Prix. I stuck my head out the window.

"You gotta get that tank out of the way. This thing's too big to squeeze around."

Then I lit a cigarette to give the meatballs time to gather themselves up enough to open the gate and move the pickup truck. Which they did, slowly, like it was their idea, or to buy time to figure out what had just happened. I cruised casually out of the driveway, but gave the Grand Prix a good kick once I was looking down a clear stretch of pavement.

Like Satchel Paige, I resisted the urge to look back until I'd made it out of Sagaponack, up through Bridgehampton and on to Sag Harbor and the Pequot, where I could get Hodges's daughter Dotty to give me a midmorning glass of vodka to counter the nerve-unsettling effects of all that iced tea.

TEN

I never tire of the smell of fresh-cut Douglas fir. I guess I would if I smelled it all the time, but I didn't have to because Frank Entwhistle let me work more or less when I felt like it. Though he was definitely glad to hear from me when I called, the day after I'd been to see Ivor Fleming.

"I need a guy to do finish at the Melinda McCarthy job. Actually, tomorrow would be a good time to start. All the rock's up and the floor's in. She's sort of eager to get in while there's still a little season left. She's on me pretty hard."

"Timing is everything."

"I'm ahead of what I told her, but she doesn't remember."

"I can only go so fast."

"Not your problem. The pool's almost finished. That'll cool her off."

"Good way to focus the crew."

"Don't hammer any fingers."

I didn't call Sullivan or Gabe Szwit or anyone else that week. I didn't want to think about Jonathan Eldridge or Jackie's face. I wanted to earn a little money and chew on my meeting with Ivor Fleming without having to share every little detail with people who'd have more questions than I was ready to answer. I thought about Ivor's meatballs, wondering what would have happened if anything had actually happened. It made me a little nauseated to think about. I've had too much of that kind of thing in my life. It's not like exercise, where repetition builds up your strength. It's the other way around. The more you get, the less you can withstand.

Not that I got hit as much as other people during my brief boxing career. I wanted to hit harder, I was just better at avoiding than delivering a punch. I was fast and athletic, but lacked the pile-driver power real fighters brought to the pursuit. I usually made up for it with a kind of blind, reckless fury.

But I got hit enough. In and out of the ring. And now, at this age, intimations of mental deterioration were stealthily eating at what was left of my indifference to consequences.

So instead of thinking about all the stuff I didn't want to think about I spent the next two weeks putting trim, baseboards and crown moldings in Melinda McCarthy's new house. She'd picked some fairly simple molded poplar, easy to work with and destined for paint, so it wasn't a hard job. The painters were right behind me, plugging holes, caulking and sanding over my lapses in concentration. They were Spanish guys. Central American, as were most of the Spanish people moving into the hard labor jobs on Long Island. Worked like bastards. Kept their heads down, trying to be invisible to administrative threats. Friendly enough, amused by my mangled Spanish. I thought about asking them how to say "be a good Doberman and go bite your little shit of an owner" but never got around to it.

When I was done with the job I took part of my pay and invested it in a case of Absolut and a harvest of fresh fruits and vegetables from the fancy green grocer in the Village. Countervailing forces. I was just settling into one of my rotting Adirondack chairs with a plateful of celery and the first vodka of the evening when I caught some movement over at the place next door. Eddie was already trotting across the lawn in that direction.

The evening was warm, but a fresh westerly was doing a good job of sweeping the languid haze of the day off the beach so the magic-hour light of the sun could saturate the dune grass and hydrangea growing along the breakwater. It looked good on Amanda, too, as she strode across her lawn to meet Eddie and toss him another Big Dog biscuit. She had the type of skin that looked slightly tanned even in the dead of winter. But it was July, and she was a deep reddish brown, contrasting sharply with her pale yellow dress. I couldn't see her eyes behind her sunglasses, but I could tell she was looking at me. I was about to look away when she waved. I waved back. No self control.

"I have a nicely chilled bottle of white," she called to me, holding it aloft. "But I could use a place to sit."

While I was working on a response she crossed her yard, stepped carefully over Regina's wildflower garden and the collapsed split-rail fence that divided the properties, and completed the trip to my Adirondacks. She usually had a way of hiding behind her thick auburn hair, but the freshening breeze off the water was brushing it aside, bathing her face in the evening light. Up close, the dress looked like some kind of rayon that flowed around her legs and painted itself across her midriff and breasts. She stood in front of my chair holding the wine bottle by the neck, tapping it distractedly against her thigh.

"And a glass," she said.

"And a corkscrew. Unless you're planning to use your teeth."

"And an invitation would be nice."

"You're already here."

She used the bottle to point to the other chair.

"To sit. You could say, 'Have a seat.'"

I stood up and took the wine bottle out of her hand and brought it into the house. I pulled the cork and brought the bottle back with a wineglass. It was meant for red wine, but it was all I had. When I got there Amanda was in my chair, legs crossed with an espadrille dangling from her toe. Overall, you'd have to say Amanda was a beautiful woman, but her legs, now mostly on display, could stop your heart. She tapped on the arm of the other chair.

"Here, take a load off."

I poured her wine and lit a cigarette. She took a sip and leaned her head back in the Adirondack. I was grateful she didn't want to clink glasses. Instead we just sat there and worked on our drinks for a few minutes, pretending to be hypnotized by the restless splendor of the Little Peconic Bay.

"I have to admit I was a little surprised you never wanted to talk to me again," Amanda finally said, easing right up to the crux of the matter.

I was grateful to have the Peconic to look at, though I'd have been happier if a distraction like the Loch Ness monster or a flying saucer had suddenly presented itself. Instead I had to be content with the coming sunset lighting up the edges of the miniature bay waves, throwing off a warm glint in contrast with the cool blue of the troughs in between.

"Didn't have that much to talk about."

"Takes a lot of reticence to fill up eight months."

"You had a lot to work out."

"Alone, as it turned out. It's common knowledge that women love to go through wrenching personal experiences on their own, with no help or support from people they thought cared about them. It's a female characteristic. Steely resolve to go it alone. Take it like a man, so to speak."

"I told you I always end in disappointment."

"You did. And you never lied to me," she said.

"I never did."

"But I lied to you," she said. "That's what you're saying."

"It's not what I'm saying. Though you did lie to me, since you mention it."

She had been looking at me, but now got distracted by the Little Peconic Bay.

"The last time I saw you was in the courtroom," she said. "Roy was giving his statement. He kept looking over the prosecutor's shoulder, at the back of the room. I followed his eyes and saw you."

Roy Battiston was Amanda's ex-husband. He'd tried to scam her out of her inheritance, among other things, but I got in his way. Amanda might have been mixed up in those other things, I never worked it all out. Roy would have given her up, probably, but the deal I cut with him made that impossible. I don't know why I played it that way, exactly. I never worked that one out either.

"I had nothing else to do that day," I told her. "Too much time on my hands. That's why I started working for Frank Entwhistle. That and no money."

"You left without a word. I waited outside the courthouse for an hour, thinking you'd just gone off to buy a pack of cigarettes and you'd be back."

I couldn't help my eyes from drifting over to her bare ankle, which was connected to an agreeably fashioned calf and long muscular thigh, and then on up to her face, still partially concealed behind a pair of wraparound sunglasses.

"You look good."

She tore herself away from the Peconic and shook her head at me.

"I'm trying to talk to you about the most difficult and painful things imaginable and you tell me I look good. You never told me that before."

"I didn't. But I thought it. So that's kind of like a lie. A lie of omission."

"It's my nice yellow dress."

"The dress is doing its part," I agreed.

"That's why I bought it."

"Good choice. Fashion standards are high out here on Oak Point."

"You're avoiding and deflecting. Again."

"I think the grandiflora's almost all the way in bloom. Early this year."

I whistled to Eddie, who was out on the breakwater asserting dominance over the local waterfowl. He trotted over and sat down in front of Amanda, looking expectantly.

"Your fault," I said to her.

"Must be love."

"Stomach love."

He stood and wriggled up close to put his head in her lap, challenging further the capacity of the yellow dress to conceal the tops of her thighs.

"Hay que perro tan bueno," I said to him.

Amanda mussed around with his ears.

"I tried to reach you at the hospital after they blew you up. But they said you didn't want any calls."

"I wasn't blown up. Just blown around a little."

"You and your lady friend."

"Jackie Swaitkowski's her name and she's my lawyer."

"I thought Burton was your lawyer."

"He's my friend. Jackie's my friend and my lawyer. Come to think of it, Burton's your lawyer."

"Only because of you. To get me through the divorce and estate settlement. You can imagine how complicated that was. He did it because you wanted him to look after me."

"I never told him to."

Eddie caught sight of something moving out on the pebble beach and bolted after it. Amanda got up and followed him, bringing along her wineglass. I stayed put so I could watch the way the breeze brushed her thick hair all the way to one side and messed around with her dress. I remembered the first time I saw her walk across a beach, coming toward me against the wind. It was the first time I saw her whole face. Something about it dislodged a critical component inside in my brain. My better judgment, maybe, but that's what happens when your brain dislodges.

"I'm a fool for coming here," she said, back from the breakwater and standing in front of me.

"Too late for that."

"Too late?"

"Regret and self-incrimination. They're disallowed. Oak Point regulations. You're permitted to avoid and deflect. Even lie by omission. But you're not allowed to come out here, looking like that, and move in like you own the place, even if you do, and start angling for sympathy and understanding with idiotic throwaway lines like that."

She whipped the last mouthful of wine on the ground and pointed the glass at me, anger gathering around her eyes.

"Can I refill that for you?" I asked before she could say what she was about to say. She stood frozen for a few moments, then relented. I picked up the bottle as she held out her glass.

"It's easy to see why people stay clear of you," she said.

"I'm working on that. Trying a little self-improvement."

"Let me know if it takes," she said, sipping her wine and slowly lowering herself back into the Adirondack.

We put our heads back and silently watched the evening settle like a velvet blanket over the bay. The conversation from there was blessedly superficial and free of disturbing undertones, and the drinks blunted whatever ambition either of us had to journey into more treacherous territory, so when the sun finally dropped below the horizon she went back to her house and I went into mine to get some sleep, however tortured with remorse and tangled in conflicting impulses it would have to be.

ELEVEN

WHEN I HEADED UP research and development for one of the world's largest industrial companies, I took some adolescent comfort in knowing I could kick the ass of any other division head. To say nothing of senior management and the board of directors, with the possible exception of Jason Fligh, who like many brilliant black people my age had gained access to opportunity playing college football. He'd been a running back at Penn and was almost as fit in his current job as president of the University of Chicago. He told me if I met his faculty I'd understand why.

I never had a chance to test my inflated self-regard with the divisional VPs, though I did break the chief corporate counsel's nose, thereby abruptly truncating what had been a relatively seamless rise through the corporate matrix. I don't remember actually popping him one, though I know I did it from the sting on my knuckles and the subsequent commotion.

That one episode notwithstanding, I far preferred engineering to boxing. Though I never lost the habit of going to the gym and jumping rope, sparring and hitting the bag. A habit that had once developed into a near obsession, leading me to spend hours during the week and big chunks of the weekend at a boxing gym in New Rochelle.

In retrospect it's easy to understand why. Gave me a place to go that wasn't my house or office. And a way to exhaust some of the toxic wastes thrown off by my nervous system and accreted around my heart during the day.

Soon after moving into my parents' cottage I found a crappy little boxing gym just inside the charred pine barrens north of Westhampton Beach. There weren't any real fighters out of there, it was only a workout joint, though a few of the young Shinnecock Indians looked capable of getting serious if there'd been anyone to teach them how. The other guys were mostly municipal types—cops, road crews and volunteer firemen. I was the only one who actually knew how to work a bag or even throw a proper punch. Most of them would break their wrists before they had a chance to do any real damage. Not that I let anyone try on me. I never sparred with amateurs without serious supervision from the corners. Too easy to get out of hand, for tempers to ignite when the poor dopes realize they keep getting socked and never seem to land one of their own.

The gym was called Sonny's and it was started by an ex-cop named Ronny who thought the area needed a place for poor African-American and Shinnecock kids to hang out and have a legal way to beat the crap out of each other, and occasionally get a shot at a cop outside his patrol car, stripped of ordnance and imperial invincibility. Which is more or less how it worked out, to Ronny's credit. Or Sonny's, whoever he was.

Sonny's was up in the woods above West Hampton, on the periphery of the pine barrens, just inside the area caught in a huge fire a few years ago. Never a pretty looking place, the pale green cinder block building now stuck out against the charred pines and bright green second growth like a post-apocalyptic architectural fantasy. Not that it would threaten the aesthetic sensibilities of the clientele.

Sullivan often worked out there in the morning, so I forced myself out of the house in time to pick up a cup of hazelnut at the coffee place in the Village and still get there before he staggered into the showers.

I found him bludgeoning the sandbag with little effect.

"You ought to keep your elbow a little higher with that right hand," I told him. "It'll put more shoulder into the jab."

"Not interested in any of that Marcus of Queensberry shit."

"Tough talk with Marcus out of town."

"Stinkin' French."

"Some of my best friends have been French."

"Yeah? Who?"

"Three out of four grandparents. Though to be fair I only met my old man's mother once or twice. Hard woman. Could have shown Marcus a thing or two."

Sullivan stopped slogging at the bag and held it with both gloved hands, steadying himself.

"You want to crap all over the Irish for a few minutes so we can call it even?"

"I want to talk about Jonathan Eldridge. After I get a little time on the bag. Now that you got it softened up."

"Have at it."

I caught up with him about an hour later at a diner on Montauk Highway in Hampton Bays. When I was growing up it was open twenty-four hours, making it a prime late-hour destination, a way station for teenagers and husbands to sober up a little before sneaking into the house. Now it was going the way of all local joints within striking distance of the beach, serving Belgian waffles with strawberries along with the standard greasy eggs and ham. I mostly went for the French roast coffee served in a china cup and saucer.

"I wondered when you were going to turn up," said Sullivan, squeezing himself into the booth.

"Frank asked me to do some trim work. But I talked to some people before that."

"Yeah? What do you think?"

The waitress came by so I had to wait while he ordered a few tons of carbohydrates with a side of ham.

"Be still my heart."

"All that bag work, man. Gotta feed the engine. So, what do you think?"

"I think we'll never know who killed Jonathan Eldridge."

"There's the old can-do spirit."

"Jackie told me we were in way over our heads. She's right. The best investigators in the world were on this thing when it was still hot. They got nowhere and now it's ice cold. The whole thing has the stink of professionalism."

"In your educated opinion," said Sullivan.

"Yeah, actually. All the reports you gave me said it was a car bomb. That's what your people concluded. Unless the Feds and Staties are blowing smoke up Ross's ass, that's what they think, too."

"Tell me what I'm missin' here, but I think a car actually blew up. With plastic explosives."

"Much later. Maybe twenty, thirty seconds after the fire."

"What fire?"

"Read my witness report. First there was a fire inside the car. A very hot fire. Explosive, though not all the way to the boom stage. That's a very difficult thing to achieve, even in a controlled environment, like an industrial furnace or kiln."

"You told 'em that?"

"I thought the explosion was caused by whatever started the fire, after the windows gave out and a flood of oxygen was introduced. I didn't know about the C-4 until I read the files. Makes a lot more sense, given the force of the blast."

"I'm already confused."

"Jonathan gets in his car and shuts the door. A fire erupts inside the car that instantly reaches super-hot temperatures. Consumes all the oxygen in the passenger cabin, feeds off whatever air the subsequent vacuum sucks in through the ventilation system, gets hotter, finally hot enough to melt the glass in the windows, causing a burst of flames that sets off the C-4. At least that's what it looked like to me."

"You know this from looking?"

"You really want the technical version?"

Sullivan used both hands to ward off the thought.

"No, that's okay. Science shit is your deal."

"This is very sophisticated stuff. Not beyond the forensic capabilities of the FBI, but unless they're holding something back, I don't think they found evidence of anything beyond the C-4, which leaves a pretty distinct marker. Or they just ignored my statement. Who the hell am I."

"You talked to his wife. The whack job."

"Appolonia. And it's an anxiety disorder. Your instincts were right. You shouldn't bother her. I'm in there for now, but I'm on thin ice. She's not opening up to any cop. Or any kind of authority."

"Guilty conscience?"

"Fear. Lots and lots of it. More than you can imagine. But she did agree to let me pose as a guy valuating Jonathan's business. For estate purposes. Gives me an excuse to bother people."

Sullivan sat back in the booth so the waitress could drop a small mountain of eggs, toast and hash browns in front of him. Then she poured a glob of their regular burnt-bean coffee on top of my French roast. And they tell you service isn't what it used to be.

"Never needed an excuse before," said Sullivan.

I was never very good at getting along with people. At least not according to ordinary rules of engagement. I used to tell myself I was too busy to attend to the relentless clamor and clatter of human interaction. To indulge the compulsive infantilism of the emotionally needy, the indignation of the disenfranchised, the crafty connivers and brainless bullies. Or even the sainted ones, the selfless and thoughtful. I only wanted to know the people I already knew. Those I loved. Loved so completely no surplus attention was available to divert to other purposes.

You can't call it a philosophy because the word implies forethought, deliberation. It was just the way I was, which I didn't understand entirely until it all tumbled and fell. Or, more accurately, disintegrated before my eyes.

"How those eggs going down?" I asked him.

"Like butter through a goose."

"Good. Keep chewing so I can tell you what else I'm thinking."

He took another mouthful and nodded.

"One of Jonathan's clients was Ivor Fleming." Sullivan's eyes registered the name, but I kept talking. "For whatever reason, it looks like he's only one of two clients unhappy with Jonathan's investment advice. Unless you count his brother, though that's a different kind of thing."

"Fleming's got a lot of juice, or so they say. Never had a twitch out of him since he moved into Sagaponack. You'd never know he was there. Not that guys like that are big on high profiles. I can find out easy enough from the boys up island. Who's the other unhappy one?"

"Joyce Whithers."

"Well, there's a big surprise. Owns the Silver Spoon, which makes sense since she was born with one crammed up her ass. I heard she called 911 over a guy bucking his check. Has to replace all the waiters and bartenders every season. Nobody'll work for her. Pays cash for everything 'cause she's stiffed every supplier from here to Brooklyn. I never understood why the ones who got it all can just stick it to somebody who's actually working for a living. Shit like that really works me up."

"Have another bite of eggs. Cholesterol has a calming effect."

"Yeah? Never knew that. What about the brother?"

"I don't know. I've only talked to Fleming."

"And?"

I told him about my visit to Fleming's house in Sagaponack. The only thing I left out was the iced tea. Too damaging to my credibility.

"Shit, Sam, should we be liking this guy?"

"Maybe. I don't put a lot of stock in reputations. Just because he's got some dumb punks working for him. I knew a lot people like that in the Bronx. Liked to play the part, push people around. Makes it easier to get a table at the Knuckle Buster Bistro on Saturday night. The real ones you don't know about unless you're inside. But I wonder about him."

"I'll see what they say up island. Not a lot about him in the case files."

"Yeah. I read that—air-tight alibi. Which is one reason I wonder about him. You wanted an angle on Mrs. Eldridge, but I think you're better looking at Fleming. He seemed to think I was trying to peddle him something. I thought at the time he meant Jonathan's business. But maybe there's something else. You could apply a little heat, see what cooks."

"I like that. Gives me something."

"Just *tenga cuidado*."

"Huh?"

"That's Spanish for watch your ass. Don't underestimate him, or his meatballs."

"Nobody's stupid enough to mess with a cop."

"Right. And keep your elbow up with that right. You're just tiring yourself out without really hurting the other guy."

Sullivan sopped up the rest of his grease-sodden eggs with the crust of a piece of toast and stuck it in his mouth. Then he made a gesture most people even outside of New York would understand.

"Yeah, and this is Irish for who gives a fuck."

—

"I want to start over," said Amanda, speaking through the screen door and looking down at Eddie, who was trying to push it open with his nose. I let her in and poured her a cup of coffee and one for myself while she scrunched around with Eddie's ears. It was late morning and I was just back from helping Frank estimate a new job. She was wearing an oversized men's dress shirt over a white bikini. I could smell freshly applied suntan lotion.

"Okay," I said, and led her out to the screened-in porch. The day was warming up quickly, but at least on the porch we'd have a fighting chance at a little breeze.

"I have a proposal," she said, blowing across the top of her coffee mug. "Let's say we just met. I've recently moved in next door. I used to work in a bank, but now I don't have to, so I'm just hanging around trying to figure out what to do next."

Eddie jumped up on the daybed where Amanda had settled with her coffee. He wanted her to do that thing again with his ears. I was at the beat-up pine table in the corner where I could keep an eye on her and the Little Peconic at the same time.

"That's an Oak Point tradition."

"Exactly. After getting settled in, I managed to strike up a conversation with my reclusive next-door neighbor. They say he's a hard case, but he talks to me. So we get to hang out a little, keep each other company. Almost like we've know each other for a few years."

"And you're bribing his dog."

"Not a difficult task."

"Okay," I said. "So what do we talk about?"

"Whatever we want. As long as it isn't emotionally challenging."

"Like the pennant race," I offered.

"Or the collapse of the stock market."

"You're asking a lot," I said. "You know how much I love to dwell on painful recollections."

"I know that. But there's so much else we can talk about."

"Like car bombings?"

"That's entirely up to you," she said.

She looked at me expectantly. I didn't know if I really wanted to tell her anything, but I found myself telling her anyway. I always had trouble shutting up around Amanda. Maybe she knew that.

"I have been giving it some thought," I said.

"Get out of here."

"You might be curious yourself," I said.

"I am. I want to know who blew up that man."

"Jonathan Eldridge. Plus four customers, a waitress and a guy counting the till."

Eddie had enough with the ear thing. He shook his head and jumped off the daybed. She gave him a little pat on the rump to send him off.

"Any theories?" she asked.

"None they're sharing with me."

"Not them. You. What are your theories? And don't insult me by saying you don't have any."

"I think it's one of his clients. The whole market's taken a dive. Have to blame somebody. Why not your investment adviser? Especially a solo operator like Eldridge. Unobscured by a big organization. Makes it more personal."

"But a car bomb? Seems like overkill. Literally."

"When you kill to make a point, you want the point unambiguous. We've certainly learned that by now."

Amanda thought about it for a minute.

"So it should be easy," she said. "Just grill all his clients."

"You working the case?"

"No. Are you?"

I laughed. I couldn't help it.

"Don't try to Dan Rather me, Mrs. Battiston."

"Miss Anselma as of two weeks ago. Mr. Acquillo."

I took another sip of my coffee to buy time. For over twenty years I'd have conversations with Abby that always left me feeling hollow and unfulfilled. I think because she never quite understood what I was talking about. Or she'd leap to interpretations that had no basis in what I was trying to say.

So after a while, I just gave it up. Somehow after that I lost the facility for communicating with other people, especially women. I thought forever, until I met Amanda. Now there she was, back sitting on my screened-in porch, raising new questions about natural affinities, affection and trust.

"Yes," I heard myself saying, "it should be easy to figure out, but it's not. Anyone capable of a hit that flagrant, and sophisticated, probably knew it was completely untraceable."

"You know this?"

"Just a guess. But I do wonder about one of the clients. You might know him."

"From the bank?

"From the bank. Ivor Fleming."

"Don't know him from the bank. Heard of him from my real-estate buddies. Overpaid for a place in Sagaponack."

"Overpaid?"

"I sound like a gossip."

"Overpaid how?"

"The rap was he wanted to keep a low profile. No disputes, no ripples. Just walked in, plunked down the cash and moved in."

"The rap?"

"Real-estate talk," she said, cocking her head at me in the condescending way you do with a child. Or a tourist.

"The house is tucked well out of view. Flag lot," I said.

"Right. Low profile."

"Does the gossip say why?"

"He's a gangster."

"Of course."

"Has a business, buying old junk cars or something. Right. Pure front. Has to be a gangster."

"You've thought about this."

"I didn't know he was Eldridge's client. Anyway, you asked."

"I did. Maybe you know another client. Butch Ellington."

She'd been leaning out from the wall as we talked about Ivor Fleming. Now she dropped back and shooed me away with her hand.

"Oh, Butch. Absolutely. Love Butch."

"Love Butch?"

"He's a hoot. Crazy artist. The definition thereof."

"From the bank?"

"Definitely from the bank. I was Dione's personal banker."

"Dione's the wife?"

"And business manager, I guess you'd say. Handled all the money, of which there was a nice amount, though I shouldn't say how much for the sake of confidentiality. Even though I'm not with the bank anymore."

"He's Eldridge's brother."

She looked at me, slightly jolted.

"No, sir. His brother?"

"So I'm told."

"Ellington?"

"Crazy artist. Changed his name. Used to be Arthur."

"He never said anything about a brother."

"They weren't close."

"Probably embarrassed about it. Butch hated everything to do with money. Though he tried not to go on too much around me, given my job and all. Dione had me over a few times. I like her. We still talk pretty often. She looked in on me a lot after the thing with Roy happened. One of the few."

Her voice dropped off and she created a distraction by jumping up to go pour herself another cup of coffee. When she came back she dropped into the other kitchen chair at the pine table, pulling up one leg and holding it in place with her knee tucked inside the crook of her right arm.

"How about that," she said, "Arthur. You'd think Dione would have said something."

"Like you say, probably embarrassed."

"Probably."

"I'd like to ask her."

"Ask her?"

"About her brother-in-law. Ask her why she thinks some-body blew him up."

"Really funny she never said anything. I probably never gave her the chance. Me being so completely focused on me."

"No self-flagellation."

"Another Oak Point regulation?"

I didn't know what she wanted, or why. I didn't know any of those things myself. I'd been sorry to see her show up at Regina's, but now that she was there, I bought her argument. We could just pick up from a point somewhere back in the past, before a lot of things had happened. I'd told her a while ago I was a big fan of avoidance and denial. Wouldn't be much of a life strategy if I couldn't put it into practice.

So I toasted her with my coffee mug and gave up the fight.

TWELVE

IT WAS SATURDAY MORNING when I found an invitation to a fundraising event that night in Southampton Village taped to my screen door. It was actually addressed to Amanda, but she'd written a note to me on the envelope.

"Butch Ellington will be there auctioning some paintings. You're my date. Don't give me an argument. I've already bought your ticket. Amanda, your former personal banker."

When Saturday came, I didn't see her during the day, which made it easier to work on my addition. I'd used up some more of my pay from Frank on framing material, which the lumberyard had left stacked in my driveway. I wanted to get as much into place as possible and nailed in before the wet fir started to warp, which it does a lot easier these days than it used to. It felt good to swing at big common nails after all the finish work at Melinda McCarthy's, shooting what amounted to galvanized needles into three-quarter-inch poplar with a pneumatic nail gun. A power nailer would have been just as effective on my addition's frame, but advanced construction techniques didn't square with the cottage's general disposition.

I filled in all the rafters and finished the framing detail on both gable ends before calling it a day. Hot, sore, sweaty and covered in sawdust, I felt justified bringing an aluminum tumbler full of ice and vodka with me into the outdoor shower. A frozen bite on the tongue, steaming water on my shoulders, dust and grit circling down the drain.

My mood adequately fortified, I was able to face the question of what to wear to the fundraiser. I still had a few clothes left over from my marriage, in which my wife Abby held full command of wardrobe selection and acquisition. Fortunately for me, she had reasonable taste, combined with an abhorrence for discount pricing, which was not so fortunate.

"Why pay less" is what I usually said looking at the price tags, though she never heard, distracted by her scrutiny of how the fabric fell, or absorbed by where the item might fit into her master sartorial strategy.

I thought I could redeploy the linen suit I'd worn to go see Appolonia Eldridge, but I'd used up my only dress shirt. I dug around some cardboard boxes I'd dumped in the closet when I moved in and came across a light blue silk T-shirt.

"Dimwitted Pretense Wear from a men's store exclusively serving the asshole in every man," I told Eddie, who was watching disinterestedly from the bed. It was surprising the T-shirt had made its way into the boxes; even Abby's relentless hectoring wouldn't have got me into that thing.

Though it wouldn't hurt to try it on.

"Not a word," I warned Eddie.

I wasn't sure. I either looked like Don Johnson's idiot goombah cousin or one of my own idiot goombah cousins trying to look like Don Johnson. Eddie was noncommittal.

I figured what the hell, I didn't have anything else to wear and there was a chance fundraisers and benefactors would find it idiotic enough to stay clear.

I walked my indecisions over to Amanda's house and rang the bell.

"My. Don Johnson or Al Pacino. Which is it?"

"Jesus Christ."

Amanda, on the other hand, didn't look like anybody but herself at her best. She was wearing what my daughter called an LBD—Little Black Dress. Made of a material that managed to define her form without giving everything away. The straps were the kind that invited a scissor snip, and helped delineate a neckline that resolved itself in distant proximity to her neck. The lower skirt part I think was simple and trim, but I was distracted by the slit feature.

"I hope you're driving," she said, brushing past me and walking down her driveway toward the passenger side of her Audi A4. I caught up to her, took her arm and gently led her to the Grand Prix.

"Got more leg room," I told her.

The day had made the transition from late afternoon to evening and the air was just starting to shed some of the heat of the day. The sky over the Little Peconic was turning a shade of periwinkle above the shredded bands of magenta glowing along the horizon. Since it was late July the rangy oaks that named the peninsula were still green but had turned pale and lost much of their luster, their leaves curling brown at the edges. We drove through the Oak Point neighborhood and out to North Sea Road. I had the windows partway down to cloak the commingled residue of decaying leather, Camels and unwashed mixed-breed dogs. The artificial wind thundered in, making conversation difficult and messing up Amanda's hair, which she didn't seem to mind. She slipped off her shoes, which were just a few delicate straps of black leather, a sole and high heels. She laid her head back on the seat and I put on the jazz station to provide cover for both of us.

The fundraiser was at one of the really big houses in the estate section surrounding Agawam Lake, just south of Southampton Village. The word "house" didn't really describe it, though "mansion" seemed archaic, or overly abstract. It was more a collection of houses, aggregated into a loose assembly of forms, unified only by the capricious hand of its creator. You entered the grounds via First Neck Lane, following a driveway that seemed ten times longer than it looked from the road. The hedges in that part of the Village often had the effect of distorting perspective, disguising the trackless scale of the original estates, their acres of lawns, pools and tennis courts.

The driveway forked off a few hundred yards from the house. A young man who looked like he sang in the glee club, in white shirt, black pants and bow tie, directed us to a rise beside the lake where cars were clustering around a huge blue-and-white-striped tent.

"I think there's room for you over there to the left," he said. "About a square mile."

"I think he just dissed your car," said Amanda as we rumbled across the lawn.

"That's just envy talking."

"Well, this is an auction. Perhaps someone will make a bid."

The atmosphere under the tent was humid and laden with social complexity. A jazz quartet of bored black guys already plotting their routes back to Manhattan provided a soothing undercurrent of sound for bored old white guys pretending they were actually listening. Some of the couples stood in a glow of hearty beneficence, pleased to have survived long enough to share their good fortune, their faces open to any opportunity to bestow kindness and generosity. A few of the women wore the proud mark of cosmetic surgery, an oxymoron, unless you like sixty-year-old women with faces tighter than the head of a drum. Bony, undernourished things with an air of profound disappointment, scanning the crowd for someone to talk to who might be more advantageous to their status than the one already filling the role.

Most of the people there under forty were hawking trays of prosciutto-encased shrimp and endive slathered in cream cheese. The rest were either flush with fresh-faced excitement or standing around nervously, looking like newly minted social aspirants. Some even younger were there only through the coercion of parents or grandparents. Whippet thin, or softened by vestiges of baby fat, slack-jawed and heavy-lidded, the girls spoke to each other without making eye contact, and the boys, some looking as if they'd recently carried off a cruel practical joke, slouched in unconstructed Armanis and woven-leather slip-ons, consoled by the certainty of outliving their extortioners, but not their bank accounts.

A huge blond woman crammed into a bright red cartoon of a crinkly red dress suddenly burst out of nowhere and almost knocked us down trying to capture Amanda in an awkward embrace.

"Amanda, the black," she said. "Just to die."

"And look at you," said Amanda.

Which I did until I recognized her.

"Robin. Long time no see," I said, putting out my hand.

"Actually I saw you last, since you were unconscious at the time," she said, holding my hand longer than I needed her to.

"I never thanked you for driving me to the hospital."

"Laura drove. I mopped up blood. Same diff. You'd do the same, I'm sure."

Robin and her business partner Laura sold real estate. It had been a good few years for them, proven by her being at the fundraiser, the price of entry comparable to most people's monthly take home. She guessed I was looking around for Laura.

"She's home. Says she always gets drunk at these things and makes a fool of herself. In reality, hardly touches a drop. I think she means I make a fool of myself. But I don't care."

I'd never seen her under a bright light. The thick layer of makeup on her face smoothed out what excess weight hadn't already filled in. Her hair, rich blond in the dim light of a nightclub, looked almost green under the diffused glow beneath the tent. She had a glass of white wine in her hand that she used as a device for emphasizing the back half of every sentence, miraculously keeping most of the wine in the glass. Maybe because she'd braced herself with a tight grip on my coat sleeve. Abby would have noticed the patch of wrinkles left by her moist clenched hand.

"I bet there's a bar here somewhere," I said, gently pulling back from her grasp.

Amanda slid her hand under my arm and led me away.

"You know how he gets when he's thirsty," she called back to Robin.

"I don't, but that's okay. I know how I get."

The drink table was commanded by two Asian women with platinum blond hair and silver lipstick wearing bow ties and tuxedo jackets, sans tuxedo shirts. They looked like a pair of retro Playboy bunny, Japanese punk, off-planet archetypes, fitting into the tired old money ambience of the fundraiser about as well as a team of professional wrestlers. It made me feel a little better about my stupid T-shirt.

"The Pinot for me," said Amanda, "Absolut for him, on the rocks. A double. Keep him occupied for a few minutes."

I was grateful for the drink. It'd been so long since I'd been around any kind of a crowd, let alone this kind.

"It's not that bad," said Amanda, reading my mind. "Drink up. I'll drive."

Abby, my ex-wife, would have been intoxicated simply by the idea of the scene under the tent. It would have been her natural element, her aspiration and fulfillment, the consummation of all she held dear. If called upon, she could have parsed the whole gathering into specific social strata, the virtuous and venal alike, guided merely by the length of dangles on an earring, or the stitching on the placket of an oxford-cloth shirt.

"Which one is Butch Ellington?" I asked.

"You'll know."

Right then someone over in front of the jazz band called to her, and she let go of my arm and glided away. I dealt with the sudden trauma of abandonment by refilling my glass and heading toward the periphery of the event. This gave me a good perspective on the crowd, which eventually yielded results.

Even from a distance he stood out. Average height, but made taller by an unkempt ball of curly reddish brown hair, perfectly round plastic-rimmed glasses over tired eyes, decent shoulders but a tidy pot belly balled up above slender legs slid into old-fashioned boot-flared Levis. His T-shirt was bright white, and unlike mine made of regular T-shirt cotton. Like Robin, he was using his drink, something amber on the rocks, as a facilitator of conversation, but with even more animation. His target was a tall slender woman with straight, unnaturally black hair with shiny bangs cut straight across her forehead. She leaned back a little as if buffeted by his enthusiasm, but was holding her ground.

I didn't see much of Jonathan in him, but I expected that.

Back-to-back with Butch was a large woman, almost his height, with a round face and frizzy gray hair pulled into a ponytail. She wore a blousy native dress with lots of pleats and heavy embroidery that tried unsuccessfully to divert attention from her zaftig figure. She had rings on her toes and a massive necklace made of multiple strings of little wooden balls. I thought about rows of peasants turning them out on tiny little lathes. Like Butch, she was energetically engaged, in her case with a natty old guy in thin wire-rims and white patent-leather shoes.

Amanda must have caught sight of them at about the same time. I saw her working through the crowd in their direction. She got there several steps ahead of me.

"You probably know everything about coastal sand flow," I heard Butch say to her as she approached. "Amanda's lived here her whole life," he said, spotting me coming in on a separate tack. "Everybody thinks sand comes in from the ocean like the waves, only of course it doesn't, because even the waves are deceptions. The coast is actually just like a river, flowing parallel to the beach, the direction changing with the tides and winds, the intensity dependent on vast oceanic and subterranean forces nobody can even imagine much less control. These fools with their bulkheads and abatements. It makes you laugh. Everything they do makes it worse for themselves. Building castles made of sand, metaphorically speaking and then some, don't you think, Amanda? Man, you are a stunning thing. Isn't she, Dione?"

By this time he'd turned his back on the tall black-haired lady and was gathering Amanda into a much more fluidly executed hug than the one Robin had given her. Dione jumped into the action, wrapping her arms around the two of them. I kept a safe distance.

"I want you to meet someone," said Amanda in a muffled tone from somewhere inside the crush of affection. I waited for her to emerge.

"Butch Ellington and Dione O'Connor, this is Sam Acquillo."

"*Aquila*. You must be an eagle. An Italian eagle," said Butch, grabbing my hand in a sturdy handshake.

"It's Acquillo. Add a C, change the O to an A, then add another L. Probably means pigeon or something. Or 'stay clear of eagles.'"

Now that I was closer I saw Butch had the tuck of a scar on his upper lip that usually meant a cleft palate. I listened for the telltale in his diction, but didn't hear it. Or the words went by too fast to discern.

"I haven't actually lived here my whole life, Butch," said Amanda, "but I know the coast is like a river. I've actually swum in the Atlantic Ocean."

"So you're both Italians," said Butch, "you must be related."

"Only by neighborhood," I told him.

"Sam is really a Frenchman, he likes to say," said Amanda. "I think because the French are more likely to offend ordinary Americans."

"Then why aren't you Sam *Aigle*?"

"French Canadian," I said. "More likely to offend ordinary Frenchmen."

Standing with the Ellingtons made you feel like you'd just been dragged out of a theater audience for use as an onstage foil. Though more benign, innocent as they seemed in their unabashed gusto.

"I think Amanda is just a doll, don't you, Sam?" Dione asked me, smiling hugely.

"Her mother was a doll maker. Might explain it."

"Hey," said Butch to Amanda, "I was thinking of you the other day at the studio. We were talking about the Giant Finger Up the Ass of Authority and where in hell we're going to construct it. And Edgar said, what the hey, what about the WB building? Am I right? Aren't we talking, like, huge empty space, out of the weather? Sitting there doing nothing? And it's, like, yours now, right? Think how that'd make you feel, knowing you made it all possible."

He took hold of her by the shoulders, which caused her to stiffen slightly.

"Come on, Amanda, don't get all authoritarian on me."

"So a Giant Finger Up the Ass would be therapeutic?" she asked.

"It's a sculpture," said Dione for my benefit. "Plate steel. Gobs of rivets and welds. Thirty-seven feet high, Butch is thinking."

"It might be fine, Butch," said Amanda, "I just need to fig-ure things out."

Butch was already smiling, but the smile grew, stretching the shiny white crimp in his upper lip until you could almost see through the translucent scar tissue. He gripped both sides of Amanda's head and kissed her hard at the hairline. I took a step closer, out of habit.

"I love you, Amanda, have I told you that? You need some help figuring, I've got this guy who rehabs factory space in Brooklyn. I can give you his number. He buys our paintings, some of the big ones. He's cool. He's like this dharma pluto-crat. Like some Eastern European, Czech or something. Beautiful-looking guy, like sixty-five years old. Shaped like a bull. Loves to fuck. Women, I think, mostly. Hey, you want something to drink? What's that, wine? Gimme your glasses. Don't stop me, I'm foraging. Nobody move. Dione, talk to Sam. You know French."

He left before I could guide him on vodka selection. Dione beamed at us like an Irish-American Buddha in drag. Her face was broad and slightly freckled, contrasting nicely with her gray hair, threaded with streaks of dark brown. A light gleam of sweat had formed on her forehead and under her eyes. She wore no makeup, and doubtless no perfume, beyond the naturally occurring, which was easily discerned in the hot wet air beneath the tent.

"I don't speak French," I told her, "though I'm thinking of beefing up my Spanish. Coming up a lot lately."

"*Muchisimas personas Españolas pobres en el pueblo,*" said Dione.

"Give it a generation. We'll be working for them."

"I hate polyglots," said Amanda. "I always feel left out."

"Sam is more optimistic about the prospects for our locally exploited Hispanics than I am," Dione explained. "But it's a nice thought."

"I told Ling and Lo they could stay at the studio tonight if they wanted," said Butch, arriving with the drinks bunched precariously between his two hands. "They work out of Newark. I mean that's just nuts driving all the way back there. That's not their names, Ling and Lo. I made that up. Probably a grave insult. If their fathers heard me I'd have a Samurai sword up my ass."

"No improvement on a giant finger," I said, helping extract the vodka from the middle of the cluster.

"How about you, Sam, from out of the City?" he asked.

"North Sea. Shorter drive."

"I grew up in Shirley. I'm tempted to move back there just for the address. Shirley, New York. It's like a dumb joke. 'Where you from?' 'Shirley.' 'Who you calling Shirley?' I could never say Shirley without saying, 'Shirley you jest.'"

"Funny town."

"You haven't been here your whole life, though. I can tell from your accent. Sounds off-island. Connecticut?"

"Stamford."

"Butch is amazing with accents," said Dione, proudly.

"People have no idea how many American accents there are. Not as many as, say, sixty years ago, when elocutionists say we had, like what, five thousand. Now, I bet there're only, what, eight hundred. Half of them within a two-hundred-mile radius of New York. TV wrecked regional accents. But they keep popping up anyway. Not just geographic but demographic. Every twenty-something in the country now talks like a Valley Girl. The human impulse to distinguish ourselves by place of origin is irresistible. Explains all these new reference groups. Identify with the tribe. How long you live in Connecticut?"

"Twenty years, give or take."

"I figured. Not that Fairfield County is exactly Connecticut. More an appendage of Manhattan. New England doesn't start till north of New Haven. North of Fairfield County you'd think you're in Chicago, which makes no freaking sense at all. Pronounce car like 'care.'"

"On Oak Point we avoid the word altogether. Ride bikes."

He pulled back at that with a theatrical expression of astonishment. He pointed at me, then back at Amanda.

"Hey, I just got it. You're in Amanda's new principality. Sucking up to the princess, eh?"

"Butch, honestly," said Amanda.

"Nothing wrong with monarchical hierarchies, darling," he said, patting her cheek. "We're programmed for them, too. Christ, there's almost nothing we do that isn't totally programmed into our fucking DNA. If it wasn't for random mutations occurring at the quantum level, there wouldn't be any variation in behavior at all. We'd be like an ant colony. Who have queens, by the way, not sure about princesses. And generals and soldiers, and farmers, and naturally slaves. No artists, though, that's a cinch. Cause too much social agitation. Can't afford the hoi polloi witnessing perfect beauty and existential truth. First rule of mass control—kill the creators."

"But not the engineers," I said. "Somebody's got to build the little tunnels."

"Sam's an engineer," said Amanda, finally finding a spot to jump in.

"*Singing my days, singing the great achievements of the present, singing the strong, light works of engineers,*" said Butch. "Walt Whitman."

"Quite a singer."

"My favorite. Next to Caruso. And did I mention Albert Einstein?"

"Didn't know he could sing."

"No, but he was a great thinker."

"Though a lousy dresser."

"Einstein, Caruso, Picasso, Stravinsky and Joyce. They invented the twentieth century. Along with Conan Doyle."

"Mysterious choice."

"Read every story. Studied them. Highly underrated."

I volunteered to go get the next round of drinks, hoping to rest up for the next round of shagging conversational grounders. A good choice, since it turned out to be another hour before the fundraisers finally judged the donors oiled up enough to start the extraction process. After listening to the announcement over the PA, I used what energy I had left to ease up to a new topic.

"By the way, Butch," I said. "I'm sorry about what happened to Jonathan. Must have been hard."

The mention of his brother had a certain cooling effect on the repartee. Both Butch and Dione continued smiling, but for the first time seemed a little stuck for words.

"Whoa," said Dione, "bummer alert."

"Sorry," I said again. "Probably a painful subject."

Butch shook his disheveled head of curly hair.

"Not at all, man," he said. "It's totally cool. Thanks for the thought. Whole thing sucks big time. You knew him?"

"No, but I've met Appolonia since. I was there when it happened. Only surviving witness. Me and my friend Jackie Swaitkowski."

"His lawyer," said Amanda.

Butch's prevailing look of curious anticipation, sustained throughout the conversation, was now shaded with something more complicated. I felt a little bad for him.

"Look, I really am sorry," I said. "I just thought since I had this connection with Jonathan it was unfair not to bring it up."

"I said it's cool. Really, it's cool. I've been working it out. Jonathan and I weren't, like, best buds, but that was more my fault. Typical dickhead little brother. Always had to bust his balls. She's a creepy chick, though. Appolonia. Could never deal with that."

"I'm sorry, too," said Amanda, looking at Dione. "I would have said something before, but this is all news to me." The pitch of her delivery was a little brighter than the subject seemed to call for. It must have carried a sub rosa communication to the other woman.

"Without mystery, there'd be no revelation," said Dione, returning the serve.

I didn't exactly know where that exchange was heading, but I felt the need for a quick diversion.

"You ever talk to any of Jonathan's other clients? Joyce Whithers for example?" I asked Butch, looking at Dione to pull her attention back on me.

"Not unless you consider getting pissed on at the Silver

Spoon for daring to wear blue jeans," said Butch with an edge I hadn't heard before.

Dione took his arm.

"Forbearance, lover."

Butch smiled at her.

"When I was a kid I had a dog that loved everything and everybody on earth. People, squirrels, field mice, cats, other dogs, he just loved the crap out of everybody. Except for this one schnauzer. The little kind. Lived down the street. All my dog had to do was see this thing and he'd bust on over there and try to tear its heart out. And the feelings were entirely mutual. I don't know what these dogs ever did to piss each other off so much, but it was a hatred as unalloyed as anything I've ever seen. It taught me that our eternal universe is held in balance by these random binary units of perfectly harmonized hate. Balanced in turn by equally rare and capricious dualities of pure love. I feel blessed beyond words to have met my divine attraction in Dione."

She hugged him and beamed. He kissed her cheek.

"And doubly so for having sold Joyce Whithers a painting of this plucky little schnauzer sitting at a dinner table with a napkin tied around his neck, eagerly awaiting a bowl of soup with a great big silver spoon clutched in his cute little paw," said Dione.

"She couldn't believe the price," said Butch. "Bragged that she stole it. Venality is so predictable."

"How are you with Dobermans?" I asked him.

"Schnauzers, Dobermans, all Nazi dogs to me."

"This one's Latino. Ivor Fleming's."

I thought I'd finally done the impossible. Butch just stood there and stared at me, as if noticing for the first time there was an actual human being attached to the vodka and baby blue T-shirt.

"A client? Of Jonathan?" he asked me.

"Not real happily, given the results."

Butch shook his head.

"Jonathan worked for Ivor Fleming, and screwed it up?"

"According to Ivor."

Butch's frown deepened.

"These both friends of yours?" he asked.

I could feel Amanda stiffen. I took the cue.

"Farthest thing. Don't know 'em, don't want to. All I know is they're the only two people who didn't love your brother's advice."

"You know a lot," he said, his face softening again and the brilliant intensity of his eyes re-igniting.

"Not really. Just can't help being a little interested. Having been there and all."

"Survivor's guilt," said Dione, half as a question.

"I don't know about that stuff. Too deep for me."

We talked some more, and Butch's mood managed to swing all the way back by the time we heard the fundraiser people take over the PA system from the jazz band and announce the start of the auction. Though the opportunity to abandon the conversation was probably welcomed. He groped Amanda some more by way of farewell.

"Look, we're putting this thing together," he said to her, an inch or two from her face. "At the studio. All-day Council Rock on the Giant Finger at the Institute of the Consolidated Industrial Divine. Construction strategies and logistical permutations. No pressure on the dead factory space, I promise. Not another word. Just drinks, music, ritual and action fantasies. Productive delusions."

"Sam's an industrial designer," said Amanda, using my forearm to help extricate herself from his grasp. "I bet he knows something about rivets and welds."

"No shit. Beautiful. You come, too. Remember, though, no rules. No laws. Except the law of gravity. Only thing I give Newton credit for."

"I'm with you. Thermodynamics was a bust."

"Beautiful. Amanda, you know where we are."

Dione smiled at us beatifically as he led her away into the swirl of seersucker and chiffon. Their departure caused the soundproof enclosure that had formed around our conversation to disintegrate, and I suddenly felt exposed and threatened by the congregating mass of privilege and competitive fervor.

I looked around for a way out.

"We can go," said Amanda. "I already bought something in the silent auction. One of Butch's sculptures."

"I hope nothing anatomical," I said to her as I threaded a path out from under the tent and over to where I'd parked the Grand Prix. The big German sedans on either side had prudently allowed for the wide swing of the Pontiac's doors, one of which I opened for Amanda, giving her plenty of room to slide fluidly into the passenger seat. Nobody tried to stop us from leaving, so the auction must have been a good diversion. The young guy in the black bow tie saluted as we passed by. By now it was dusk, and street lamps lit our way out of the estate section and through the Village, its sidewalks filled with a parade of summer renters who looked like they were having a nice time, or at least willing to put up a brave front.

"I'm too dressed up to go home yet," said Amanda, after we'd cleared the estate section and it was safe to talk. "And not the Pequot, thank you."

So we compromised by heading for a nightspot housed in the dilapidated building that used to be the Hawk Pond Yacht Club. It was next door to the marina where Hodges kept his boat. It was too early in the evening for the regular swarm of clubgoers from out of the City, so after paying a confiscatory cover charge we easily found two stools at the bar.

"Home at last," I told the gangly African-American bartender as he mopped cocktail napkins and soggy dollar bills up off the bar in front of us.

"Welcome, son. What'll it be?"

Amanda ordered again for both of us, then slipped off the barstool for a trip to the ladies' room. Before leaving she stood behind my stool and put her arms around me, resting her head on my shoulder. There must have been an airborne narcotic mingled with the smell of her hair, because a single whiff almost gave me vertigo. I steadied myself by brushing her thick hair back from her face and kissing her forehead, much more gently than Butch Ellington had.

"I missed you, Sam," she said, from someplace far away. "I need you to forgive me."

"Nothing to forgive."

"Yes there is, and you know it," she said.

"We just met, remember?"

"I still need you to forgive me. You have to say the actual words."

"I forgive you. Trusting you is another matter."

She squeezed a little harder.

"Okay. I'll take that for now."

She took in a deep breath and sighed it out again. Then she went to the ladies' room, leaving me and the bartender to shrug at each other in commiseration.

"Tell me about it," he said, dropping the icy vodka down in front of me.

I'm not sure what all happened in the nightclub after that, except it involved more drinking and a few terrifying forays on to the dance floor, a place I'd only been once before in my life, with Amanda, coincidentally. This time, though, I got through the whole experience without causing a fistfight or unsettling disturbance of any kind, unless you count my dancing. When the place finally filled up with the usual slithery mass of sweaty hope and brainless expectation, Amanda agreed to make a run for it.

The velvet air outside almost felt cool after the heat of the crowded club. We walked over to the docks that shot out from the southeast shore of Hawk Pond. The moon was close to full, producing a pale illumination that added to the harder light from electric lanterns spaced evenly along the gangways. I picked out Hodges's boat, but his lights were out.

Amanda took my bicep with both hands and led me toward the waterfowl reserve directly adjacent to the club.

"Let's go this way. I know a good spot."

She slipped off her shoes when we reached the end of the docks, defined by the transition from wooden planks to a narrow sandy path. I followed her into the grassy foliage that grew along the banks of the pond. The glow of the moon slowly took over for the artificial lights of the marina, guiding our way over little dunes and through runoffs filled with rounded pebbles and slippery driftwood.

"Watch your step," she told me, taking my hand to steady herself.

About a hundred yards into the reserve the path led to a small clearing intended as an observation post, with a heavy teak park bench and a little Plexiglas-encased placard mounted on a stand meant to instruct people on the difference between ospreys and cormorants and how to spot Monarch butterflies on their way back from Mexico. It also had a great view of the pond, and the sparkle coming from little North Sea shacks lined up along the western shore, remnants of my father's time, ramshackle and relaxed.

I sat on the bench and lit a cigarette. Amanda dropped her shoes in the sand and walked out to the edge of the pond. You could hear the pulse of the subwoofers in the nightclub shouldering their way through the dune grass and scrubby plant life, laying down a low bass rhythm under the chatter of insects coming from the marshes surrounding us on three sides.

I watched Amanda, now just a silhouette against the dark waters of Hawk Pond, walk out to just above her knees where she scooped salt water up in her hands to splash on her face and run through her hair.

I must have lost track of her for a few minutes after that because I was surprised to see her suddenly back at the bench, standing in front of me with her hands on her hips.

"Not a bad location," I said to her.

"It'll do."

She reached down with crossed hands and gathered up the hem of her dress. Then she pulled the whole thing up and over her head and sat down on my lap, facing me, knees to either side of my legs. As we kissed she unbuckled my pants.

I slid my hands over her thighs and up her long, smooth back, meeting nothing but Amanda along the way.

"Don't say anything," she whispered in my ear.

I couldn't have anyway. Too absorbed, all the way gone.

———

I think we both fell asleep after that, at least for a little while, because I don't remember anything but awakening to a chilly breeze out of the north, the feel of goosebumps across her naked back and a dull glow in the east, harbingers of days to come, irredeemably altered.

THIRTEEN

WHEN WE GOT BACK to my house we found Joe Sullivan bleeding to death in my front yard. Or rather Eddie did. As I pulled into Amanda's driveway I could hear him inside the house barking furiously, something he rarely did. So I stopped the car and let him out. He shot past me and ran across the lawn, where he started barking again, swiftly circling the Adirondack chairs.

At first, in the dim light of dawn, all I saw was an indistinct form slightly slumped in one of the chairs. A pale shape, clothed in pale fabrics, made even more monotone by the tight-cropped band of blond hair that upholstered the top of his head. All of which was an effective backdrop for the big round blood stain that started on his right side and flowed down over his thigh. It wasn't until I felt his neck for a pulse that I got close enough to see it was Sullivan. Amanda ran up to me and I told her to run back to my house and call an ambulance.

I found a pulse buried under the jowly folds of his neck. I saw Amanda pop back out the door and I yelled to her to bring the flashlight hanging in the broom closet. While I waited for her I worked on quieting down Eddie. I wondered how long he'd been trying to get someone's attention. And what form of prescience had led me to lock him in for the night.

"Oh my God, it's Joe Sullivan. What happened?" cried Amanda as she ran up to the breakwater.

Even with the flashlight it wasn't clear exactly where the blood had come from. I unzipped his windbreaker and peeled it back to expose an even darker wet spot on his polo shirt directly below his right rib cage. I took off my jacket and made it into a pad that I slipped under his shirt and over the wound. I knelt down and braced myself against the chair so I could maintain pressure.

"I told you to watch your ass, you dumb shit," I said to him, though he wasn't up to answering.

Sullivan was a big man. I hoped he held a lot of blood.

———

Ross Semple, the Chief of Southampton Town police, looked a lot more like the junior engineers I'd hired to bench test new processes or perform field service for customers and the company's operating divisions. White short-sleeved polyester shirts, iridescent striped ties that changed color depending on the angle of observation and glasses with gigantic gray plastic frames that had gone in and out of fashion during a period roughly coinciding with the theatrical run of *Breakfast at Tiffany's*. A twitchy guy, all arms and legs that seemed to function somewhat outside central control. He never looked you all the way in the eye, and often had little side conversations going with himself, chuckling at private jokes clearly out of synch with the mood of the moment.

They'd just pulled Sullivan out of the ambulance and had raced him inside the hospital. Ross was there with two or three other cops looking ready to strip off their badges and mount a posse. He pulled out a crushed pack of Winstons and lit one up with the natural movement of unconscious habit.

"If you got an opinion on this, now'd be a good time to share it," he said to me.

I told him everything I knew about Ivor Fleming and why I knew it—beginning with his connection to Jonathan Eldridge, and maybe his murder, leading to the recent launch of my asset-salvage business courtesy of Appolonia Eldridge and Gabriel Szwit. I told him about my conversation with Joe Sullivan after the workout at Sonny's, though I left out Sullivan's earlier recruitment efforts, for both our sakes. Things were bad enough as it was.

Ross burned through two or three Winstons as he listened to my story, his eyes jumping around with the furtive vigilance of nocturnal prey. I don't know how much of what I told him he believed. It didn't really matter, as long as the story had a sturdy interior logic. Ross was professionally and temperamentally skeptical of everything and everybody, often with good reason. He just needed an excuse for why he shouldn't start fingerprinting and seeking an indictment at that immediate moment, assuming the inevitability of both would be realized in due course.

I left him with his Winstons and went into the ER to look for Sullivan. Just as I got to the right place a swarm of serious-looking people in baby blue polyester outfits pulled the curtain around his bed and basically told me to get lost. So I went upstairs to where I'd spent a few happy-go-lucky hours two months ago getting my back sewn up. I looked around for Dr. Markham Fairchild, the Jamaican GP who ran the recovery unit. At about six-seven and 350 pounds, Markham was a hard man to miss.

"Hey der, Mr. Ah-quillo. Back here on warranty?" I saw my hand disappear into his, which was about the size and consistency of an outfielder's glove.

"Hi, Doc. A friend of mine's downstairs with some kind of wound to the gut. They're working on him now. Any idea where he'll end up?"

"Trauma's our specialty here in Southampton. Unless he need fancy shenanigans up island. We know soon." Markham looked down at the clipboard he was carrying. "What's his name?"

"Joe Sullivan. He just got here about a half-hour ago."

He led me over to the nurses' station where he asked a tired but accommodating middle-aged woman in civilian clothes to look up Sullivan's status.

"Hey, I remember dat name. He was the fella I call for you last time you were here. What are you two, Bonnie and Clyde?"

"Yeah, I'm Clyde. If he gets up here, do me a favor and try to keep him breathing long enough to have a conversation. He's got some information I need."

"Like I wouldn't if you didn't ask me to."

The woman in front of the computer waved him over and pointed to the screen. Markham bent over to take a look.

"They move him upstairs. Not good, but not decided yet. Knife wound to the abdomen, blunt-force trauma to the head—probably got a concussion. Lost lots of blood. They know more once they get him washed up and into the OR."

"If that's all it is, I'll be back tomorrow."

Markham put his hand out and gripped my shoulder.

"Don't worry. We fix him up. And you too, next time he bring you in. Only satisfied customers here at Southampton Hospital."

———

I dodged Ross by ducking out a side entrance area near where I'd stashed the Grand Prix with Eddie, still somewhat freaked, curled up in the driver's seat. When I stopped for coffee at the corner place I bought us both croissants and bottled water, though I waited to pass out the goods until we drove over to the beach access next to Agawam Beach Club where we could look at the ocean while we ate.

The sun sat a few feet above the horizon, burning off the early morning haze. A young woman in black cycling shorts, white support bra and orange headband walked unhurried across the sand, cooling down or uninspired to run, it was hard to tell from a distance. A gaggle of seagulls, careering overhead, were dropping clams on the packed sand along the water line, and then diving in to squabble over the pulverized results. As I sipped my coffee and peeled off chunks of crois sant for Eddie, I noticed my hands were shaking. I had a full inventory of possible explanations, but I was too tired and brain-battered to delve. Or too afraid. Maybe that was the ultimate explanation. Fear of having to come up with one.

Instead I smoked a few cigarettes, finished the coffee and fed Eddie until he tired of French pastry and went to sleep, undaunted by the terrors of self-examination, happy to contend solely with threats apparent and unambiguous.

Watching him, a profound weariness suddenly descended on me and then, as if anointed by a blessed narcotic, I dropped like a stone into the deep well of sleep.

FOURTEEN

Jackie showed up at the end of the next day with a stringy, straight-faced kid in a black baseball hat, sunglasses and a dark gray suit. I was in the outdoor shower, or more precisely, just emerging while I toweled off my hair, so I didn't immediately know they were there.

"I've been seeing a lot of you lately," said Jackie. "More than I ever wanted to."

"That explain the bodyguard?" I asked, wrapping the towel around my middle.

"Sam, this is Agent Webster Ig."

The kid had been leaning over to pet Eddie's head. He stood up straight and offered me his hand.

"That's two letters," he said. "I and G. Ig."

"I called, but nobody answered," said Jackie. "Did you know you're the only person left on the planet without an answering machine? So don't blame me."

"Agent? For the government?"

"FBI. Nice dog," he said, yielding to Eddie's persistent attention. Jackie stood back slightly, rolling her eyes and pointing at the guy while mouthing the word "cute."

I let them follow me into the cottage so I could get dressed and put together my first drink of the day. I'd wanted to stay completely sober to hear that Sullivan was dead, but he didn't die. He was still unconscious, but Markham thought he'd come most of the way back.

"I told his boss to give it a few days, though, before he start bugging him," Markham had told me. "And not be surprised if he don' remember anyt'ing. That's usually the case with head trauma and blood loss."

Jackie and Agent Ig were out on the screened-in porch. Jackie was sprawled on the daybed and Ig sat stiffly at the shaky pine table where I ate most of my meals. His face was fresh as a baby's behind and the dark brown hair revealed when he took off his cap was just long enough to allow a precisely drawn part. You didn't always get the kind of law enforcement performance you might want from the FBI, but you couldn't fault the grooming.

"I need to tell you, as I did Miss Swaitkowski, that I can't discuss any details of the Eldridge bombing," said Ig, just to get the ball rolling.

"So you're just here for the view?"

"It's very nice, Mr. Acquillo."

"How 'bout a beer to go with it. Unless you're on duty."

"Two beers," said Jackie.

Once he had a beer in front of him, Agent Ig unbuttoned his jacket and sat back, crossing his legs. Discipline gone all to hell.

"But I can speak in generalities. And considering the two of you were the only witnesses, I suppose that's not entirely inappropriate."

Try as I might, I could never listen to stuff like that from people wearing business suits. There's something about official language when it's all dressed up. Though Ig looked earnest and open faced enough to get away with it. Like the top salesmen I used to know from our company's midwestern region.

"I told him generalities would be fine," said Jackie, pointedly.

"Absolutely. Engineers hate details. You know, like who did it."

Agent Ig started to speak, but Jackie cut him off.

"They don't know."

"But we're fairly certain who didn't," said Ig, taking a pull on his beer. "No terrorists, no foreign involvement of any kind. Nothing like that. The Bureau's determined it's a simple homicide."

"Not to the dead people."

"From a national security perspective," he said flatly.

"How old are you?" I asked him.

Jackie jumped to her feet.

"You got anything to munch on, Sam? Chips or anything?"

"Twenty-eight," said Ig, without hesitation. "Old enough to know the propriety of certain questions."

"Then you won't mind me asking why Ivor Fleming just tried to kill a cop."

"Sam?"

"Joe Sullivan. Stabbed in the gut. Knocked on the head. Left here in one of my Adirondack chairs. Another hour and he'd be dead."

Ig didn't flinch or hesitate. "That's a question for the local people," said Ig. "As is anything relating to Mr. Fleming. All of that was referred to the state and local levels."

"All of what?"

"Matters regarding Mr. Fleming uncovered in the investigation. All referred to local racketeering authorities. Nothing of interest at the federal level."

"I'm sure as hell interested."

Jackie stood in front of me so Ig couldn't see her face and scowled meaningfully.

"Come on, Sam. He's trying to help. You didn't tell me about Sullivan."

"I didn't want to."

"Why?"

"It's getting too dangerous. You said it yourself. We're way over our heads."

"He's certainly right about that, Miss Swaitkowski."

"Too late," she said. "You think it was Fleming?"

"Who else?" I told her about my conversation with Sullivan at the diner. And about Amanda's invitation to the fundraiser and meeting Jonathan's brother and sister-in-law. And how we found Sullivan on the lawn. I left out a few other details concerning Amanda, in the spirit of sticking to generalities.

"Holy cow, you actually went on a date," said Jackie. "Probably the first time in your life."

I looked at our agent.

"Any of this do anything for you, Web? Spark anything?"

"I sympathize with your situation. I do. As I said, any information we had that would help advance the cause we've already passed along. It's now in different hands."

"Then what're you doing here?"

"I asked him," said Jackie, gaily. "I wanted him to meet you."

"And what about the data on Jonathan's hard drives?"

"State's got everything," said Jackie. "And they aren't giving it up to me or you, or anybody else."

Agent Ig leaned forward so he could get in the middle of our conversation. He looked at me.

"I think you're giving too little significance to what I'm saying."

"Exactly," said Jackie.

"Exactly what?"

"The FBI thinks the whole thing is home grown," said Jackie. "We don't have to look anywhere else."

"We're not looking anywhere else."

She swatted me on the arm.

"Of course we're not, because it's all we have. But this confirms we're at least in the right neighborhood. I think it's very helpful," she added, smiling broadly at cute Agent Web.

"Jesus Christ."

"Just for clarification," said Agent Ig, jumping in again, "I'm not saying you should look anywhere. I think for your own safety you should stay as clear as possible from the whole matter."

"Well I can't do that now that I know it's a local thing," I told him. "I'm head of the neighborhood watch."

"Am I the only one who wants to eat?" asked Jackie.

"Good idea," I said. "Let's go."

"Not the damn Pequot."

"Come on, a little fish'll do you good. Web, you hungry?"

They followed me over to Sag Harbor in a mid-sized Ford that matched the color and ostentation of Ig's summer suit. Though I really liked seeing him in my rearview mirror. Comforting to know that if anybody tried to shoot me over dinner I had my own FBI agent along to shoot back.

"Dinner for four, Dot, counting Eddie," I said to Hodges's daughter when we got to the Pequot.

"Dorothy," she said, waving at a cluster of empty tables near the back of the restaurant without looking up from her book.

"Why it pays to be a regular," I said to my party.

"Nice place," said Agent Ig, admiring the sepulchral gloom that distinguished the Pequot's interior, accented by dirty brown natural-wood paneling, and dirtier brown tables and chairs, lit by wall-mounted fixtures shaded with red whorehouse globes and a few flickering fluorescents hanging above the bar.

Hodges came out from the kitchen to help get us settled. He wiped his hands on his apron before offering to shake.

"You look better," he said to Jackie.

"Thanks, I think."

"This is Webster Ig," I said, "friend of Jackie's."

"Two letters," Jackie told him. "An I and a G."

"Feel free to lose the tie, son," said Hodges. "Been a while since we had a dress code in here."

"And the fish of the day?" I asked.

"Cooked."

"Excellent. Cooked all around. And a burger for the pup."

I spent the rest of the night trying to squeeze more information out of the FBI, while giving up as little as possible to Jackie about my recent night out. The two of us never shared any kind of romantic life, which I think gave her the idea she could nose her way into mine. None of which right at that moment mattered a whit. All I cared about was that I was alive, eating at a friend's crappy little joint, watching another friend try to flirt through a layer of unhealed plastic surgery, feeling my little mutt pressed up against my leg and, for a moment anyway, not afraid for life, limb or soul.

FIFTEEN

I DIDN'T BOTHER with anything more elaborate than a polo shirt and pair of khakis to go see Joyce Whithers, assuming her to be impervious to the persuasive power of my sole surviving business suit.

The Silver Spoon was in a refurbished Italianate farmhouse set tight to the edge of a working potato farm about a half-mile north of the highway in Watermill. The approach to the two-story stucco building followed a long sandy drive that afforded an agreeable perspective on the old-world facade. The parking area was completely sheltered beneath a huge pergola on which grew a tangle of native vines meant to simulate Tuscan grapes and wisteria. In the evening a gang of hustling valets in bow ties and black sneakers fielded the flow of imported cars coming in for dinner, the only meal the place served. It was now the middle of the day so I had to park the Grand Prix on my own.

I'd called ahead this time, and brought Eddie for back-up, though I suspected the only creature on the premises approximating a Doberman was Joyce herself. On the phone she took the story of valuating Jonathan's business without much argument. She said she'd been considering a lawsuit against him to recover some of her losses, though her lawyers had advised her on the difficulty of suing a dead man. I guessed she saw my project as a possible way to pursue Jonathan into the hereafter.

"Are you empowered to discuss a settlement?" she asked, briskly.

"Valuation is the first step in that process," I told her.

"Then come," she said, and hung up.

Once inside the restaurant, she wasn't hard to find—in the middle of the reception area, struggling with a small tree planted in a big clay pot. She wore a pair of baggy denim shorts that fell just past her knees, an untucked men's dress shirt and tattered running shoes. Her glasses and a Bic pen were stuck up in a wad of thick dark gray hair that looked a month or two past the last brush with a beauty parlor.

I'd been told she was around Hodges's age, and also widowed, though some time ago. Maybe I could fix them up. They could swap notes on preparing whitefish and the trade-offs of keeping Slim Jims out on the bar or back near the cash register.

She probably didn't notice me standing there, but didn't flinch when I grabbed the lip of the pot to help her drag it into an open corner next to the maitre d' stand.

"Damnable thing," she said, standing back to appraise the situation.

"Looks good."

"Not yet. Needs something."

"A maitre d'?"

"Not likely. That fig tree has the greater wit." She finally looked at me. "And you are?"

"Sam Acquillo. Representing the Eldridge estate."

She took my hand.

"Whenever I think of the money that person cost me I could just spit. What's your part in this again?"

"I'm valuating the business for possible sale, or perpetuation under his widow's ownership."

"What on earth for?"

"To see if it has any value."

"It doesn't."

"To keep serving a list of happy clients?"

"Not all."

"So I understand. That's why I'm here."

"To see what kind of trouble I'll cause you."

"Just to talk."

She went back over to the little tree and starting fussing with the branches, snapping off delinquents with a deft twist of the hand. Then, without asking my help, she tried again, unsuccessfully, to swivel the heavy clay pot. She moved like a woman who'd been raised to use her hands to get things done. To build, configure and dominate her surroundings. Schooled to value things practical as well as cultural. In times of revolution, a woman prepared to man the artillery, to go down swinging the butt of an empty rifle, honor intact.

Two guys in white kitchen uniforms came in from the outside carrying plastic shopping bags. They looked straight ahead as they passed through the reception area and went through a door I assumed led to the kitchen. They ignored the gray-haired woman grappling with the clay pot and she ignored them.

I let her struggle with the pot until they were gone from view, then reached down and helped her rotate it about twenty degrees.

"It's not my department, ma'am, but I'm guessing the possibility of litigation would put a damper on plans to reformulate Jonathan's operation."

"Not your department?"

"I'm not a lawyer."

"My husband was, and he'd say you'd be an idiot to try to sell a one-man financial consultancy, especially if all it did was provide a target for people to sue, which he'd certainly take advantage of, as would I." She stood back to study the results of our latest effort.

"Let's give it another half a turn," she said, this time waiting for me to join her.

"Almost," she said.

"Did you ever talk to any of his other clients? Anyone else who had less than spectacular success?"

"Heavens no," she said, waving the question away like an annoying insect. She narrowed her eyes at me. I fought the urge to back away toward the door.

"You're asking because he was killed."

"Just gauging the mood of the clientele."

"You said you aren't a lawyer. Don't speak like one."

"Okay, bluntness it is. It's going to be very difficult to reconstitute, much less market, Jonathan's business given that it was solely dependent on him. Although he did have some proprietary analytical tools that could be marketed under his name or absorbed into some other operation. It's just the way he departed the scene that makes me question even that strategy. Not fair, maybe, but that's the irrational world of finance for you. I personally don't care one way or the other. I just want to learn what his clients are thinking so I can write my report and move on to the next goofed-up situation."

"That's better," she said. "Mercenaries I understand."

"So, any thoughts?"

"I didn't kill him, if that's what you mean. Not that I didn't mull it as an option, I was so angry. But I couldn't have, even if I had the means. Which I don't."

I tried my best to look embarrassed by the thought.

"No accusations, not at all. I'm just asking your opinion."

"The lesson learned is never do business with friends, or their children, and definitely not their idiot sons-in-law."

"Now I'm a little lost," I said.

She closed her eyes and slowly shook her head.

"I only got involved with him because of Appolonia, poor thing. Walter sat on the Boston Equity board with her father. Lovely people. Old Brookline."

An image of them all having dinner in Newton with Abby's parents leapt uninvited into my mind. Luckily Joyce picked that moment to stop torturing the fig tree and lead me over to one of the dining tables, freshly dressed in a bone-colored tablecloth and short vase stuffed with miniature red roses. A tall woman with a severely receding chin and straight, oily blond hair came out of the kitchen and handed Joyce a sheet of paper, I guessed a provisioning inventory. She stood immobile by the table while Joyce put on her glasses and looked it over. She handed the list back without comment, or even a look at the chinless young woman, who left as wordlessly as she arrived.

Joyce took off her glasses again and dropped them on the table, rubbing her tired eyes with the back of her hand. She let out a breath of exasperation.

"I know it's impossible," she said. "Even with her parents gone I really couldn't bring litigation. I know what I said, but

Walter would think it unforgivably vulgar to sue a friend's child. A mentally ill child at that. I'm just so angry about the whole thing. To be made such a fool of."

"So they must have left her pretty well taken care of, with or without Jonathan's portfolio."

"Oh my, yes. Greek shipping. You don't get any better taken care of than that. I always assumed her husband entered the investment field so he could manage her inheritance. Isn't that what all these opportunists do? I just hope he did a better job for her than he did for me, the insufferable little numbskull."

I thought I saw the faintest suggestion of a smirk momentarily pass over her face. I realized she'd caught herself amused by a private joke. A joke on herself. Then it was obvious. The loss for her wasn't financial. It was the damage to her sense of self-reliance. An affront to the posture of invincibility demanded by the people who bred her.

But I was even more taken aback when she reached across the table and touched my forearm with the tips of her dusty, calloused fingers.

"Give the girl a little advice for me, if you will," she said. "Let the husband's business die with the husband. It won't bring him back. Nothing will. Not that I don't sympathize with how she feels. If Walter wasn't already dead I'd kill him myself for leaving me."

Then she tapped my arm again and pulled her hand away.

"Now, if you'll excuse me," she said, though without any sign of getting up from her chair. So I thanked her for the help and left her mustering strength for another round with the fig tree, determined as she was to wrestle its leafy little being into utter submission, to better realize its role in her orchestrated existence, irretrievably disrupted by the unscheduled demise of Walter Whithers, for whom the same occasion was probably a blessed relief.

———

Belinda answered the phone.

"Not without the lawyer," she said.

"Aren't we past that?"

"His instructions. You remember the number."

I didn't, so I had to call information from the pay phone, as far as I knew the last one in Southampton, kept as a profit center in the basement of a burger joint on Job's Lane. Gabe was eager as always to drop whatever he was doing and run over to Appolonia's house. A half-hour after talking to him I met him just as he was getting out of a new black Jaguar.

"Quite the collectible," he said, trying to lean back far enough to take in the full scale of the Grand Prix.

I was going to straighten him out but decided it wasn't worth the effort. Anyway, he'd already headed into the house, which was good, since it kept something between me and Belinda.

She made us pause in the foyer, then herded us into the living room where Appolonia was already seated, complete with tea tray and a folded-over copy of the *Times*, exposing a half-completed crossword puzzle done in neat black ink. She wore a plain white cotton shirt with the collar pulled up, black Capri pants and sandals. The AC was turned so low I began to envy Gabe's suit jacket. Or maybe it was just the abiding chill within Appolonia's crystal enclosure.

She gently commanded Belinda to bring us both coffee before I had a chance to apologize for bothering her again.

"Not at all. It's nice to have a little company. The underlying purpose of which notwithstanding."

"You look well, Appolonia," said Gabe.

She nodded her thanks, but didn't return the compliment.

"So, Sam, what are you thinking about?" she asked.

"Boston," I said.

"My beloved city."

"Brookline, technically."

"Few realize it's a separate city, even those who live there. It must have been grand to grow up in Southampton."

"Grand wouldn't exactly describe my part of town, but it wasn't bad. Winters were kind of bleak, especially back when everything shut down after Labor Day and all the summer people went back to Manhattan. Half the lights went out and three-quarters of the stores disappeared. But we dug it anyway. Even the air changed. Like God had flicked a switch to send cool dry wind down from Canada."

"I think Jonathan was too busy to notice things like wind and air."

"Overachiever."

"I suppose."

"Married you. Some would call that a stretch."

She finally seemed to notice the tea tray by her elbow. I waited while she squirted lemon into the cup and took a sip.

"That can't be flattery, so you must have another point."

"Just came from a chat with Joyce Whithers."

I don't know what kind of rise I was trying to get, but all it did was give Appolonia a little smile.

"The restaurateur."

"And old family friend."

"The Silver Spoon. Said to be quite good. My parents' friend, not mine."

"You knew I'd find out eventually. Would have been easier to just tell me."

"Excuse me," said the lawyer, smelling a threat, "somebody catch me up."

"Later Gabe," said Appolonia, "I want to get to the heart of Sam's issue."

"Not an issue, just a curiosity."

"Everyone has parents, Sam."

"Not like yours."

"Jonathan took care of all the finances, and left me with much more than I originally entrusted him with. So, why does it matter how we started out? What's the relevance to your," she paused a moment, "enterprise?"

I fought an impulse to launch into a lecture on the importance of establishing every possible data point before attempting an analysis of a systems failure. Give her the same sensitivity training I gave recent chemical engineering graduates unlucky enough to be cast like frightened émigrés into my Technical Services and Support Division. Tell her about the catastrophic consequences that can accrue from the tiniest fractional quantities that go unnoticed in the statistical dust of an equation until suddenly complexity theory takes hold and before you know it there's a hole the size of infinity blown in your calculations. Which could mean a hole blown in the side of a gigantic pressure vessel, thereby causing the molecules that comprise other engineering graduates of various vintage to be intermingled with a stream of super-heated, partially deconstructed hydrocarbons.

Instead I took a breath, tried to remember an appropriate verse from the *I Ching* and asked if Belinda could bring me some more coffee. The sudden tension had pushed Gabe out to the edge of his seat, but when I sat back he joined me, though still unsettled.

"You're right," I said to Appolonia. "None of my business."

I was going to tell her about Joe Sullivan, but decided against it. I did bring up my chat with Ivor Fleming, but she said she'd never heard of him. Neither had Gabe.

"I also met Jonathan's brother, Butch, and his wife."

Appolonia covered her reaction by dropping her eyes to her lap.

"Ridiculous man, I'm sorry."

"Not a lot in common, the two of them. Butch and Jonathan."

"The closest I ever came to arguing with Jonathan was over Arthur. That's his real name. I never understood why Jonathan was so protective when all he received in return was ridicule and neglect."

"So not a lot of family get-togethers."

"Jonathan wanted to have him here for dinner, but I discouraged it. Too much for me. Imagine being in the company of a man who built his entire life in diametric opposition to all that I loved in his brother."

"Did as well though, financially. Tough to make it in the art game."

"No lack of brilliance in the Eldridge family. Only a difference in application."

Gabe had been listening attentively through all this, on the lookout for another sudden change in course. I asked him what he thought to get him back into the conversation.

"Never met the man. Jonathan retained me to help institutionalize their mother. That's how I came to know Appolonia," he added, looking over at her. She smiled a crooked little smile, but didn't return his look. "But I hear he goes in for society parties. Sounds like fun."

Appolonia gave a sound of contempt, subtle, but clear enough to make Gabe wish he'd kept his mouth shut.

"Artists and petty celebrities, people like Arthur, are kept around as court jesters," she said. "Given all the trappings of acceptance, but in reality they're little more than house pets. Jonathan could have steered him away from all that, but he couldn't be bothered with brotherly advice."

Growing up, all I had was an older sister who might have looked after me when I was little, I don't remember. We got along okay. There was rarely conflict or competition. We operated in separate orbits, unified only—along with our mother—in the common determination to stay clear of my father's random expulsions of noxious rage.

"The mother's still around," I said, as the recollection came to me. "In a home somewhere."

"Somewhere being here," said Appolonia. "The Sisters of Mercy home in Riverhead. But not terribly relevant to your inquiry, either, if you'll forgive me, since she's completely gone over to mental illness."

I knew the place. It was where my own mother died from Alzheimer's. Maybe they were roomies for a while. Mrs. Eldridge might have been the one who always stopped me in the hall to ask where she was and how she got there. Perplexed, but graciously polite every time. I would give her the best answer I could, which would satisfy her till the next time she saw me, when we'd do the whole thing all over again.

"It was always terrible for Jonathan to see her that way. I never met her, of course, but he'd try to give me an idea of what she used to be like. He said she often confused him with Arthur, which naturally irritated me no end. Arthur was his father's name, too, which didn't help. It's too cruel."

When I told her about my mother's Alzheimer's I wasn't trying to make a sympathetic connection, but that was the effect.

"Then you understand," she said softly.

Gabe spared us his own family history, thank God. My mood, always at risk around Appolonia, was sinking badly under the increasing heft of the conversation. I couldn't take much more.

"I think we've bothered you enough for one day," I told her, making a move to get out of my chair. Gabe looked at me as if to say, speak for yourself, pal.

"I said it wasn't a bother," said Appolonia, "but I won't keep you."

"I have a few things I should probably go over with you after Sam leaves," said Gabe, with a touch more officiousness than probably intended.

"Of course. And I have something to add before you go, if it's all right," she said to me.

I was partway out of the living room by this time, and about to give everyone an inane little wave before bolting for the door.

"Sure."

"I met Jonathan a year after my parents died. Were killed, actually, in a private plane en route to Martha's Vineyard, just like the young Kennedy son years later. A socially adroit departure, don't you think?"

I thought of my father in the men's room at the back of the bar in the Bronx, dying on the floor while his killers brushed off their polyester slacks and straightened their ties in the grungy mirror.

"I don't think they care on the other side."

"I was never a particularly courageous person, protected as I was, but to all appearances normal enough. Out and around in the world. Took the Green Line to the market, skied, once even rode a Ferris wheel. My circle considered me vivacious."

She pointed her index finger straight into the side of her head.

"Something switched off up here the instant I saw those two policemen at our front door, never to switch on again. If I find it hard to discuss my parents, I'm sorry. You seem to want to know everything, so there you have it. I'll leave the determination of relevance to you."

After the chilly atmosphere of Appolonia's house the air outside felt luxuriously thick with heat and humidity. Eddie was glad to see me, and seemed no worse for the wait.

I decided to spend the rest of the day and evening sitting in the one Adirondack chair not stained with Sullivan's blood, drinking vodka and letting Eddie retrieve tennis balls out of the bay. During that whole time nobody tried to punch me, lie to me, enthrall me or disrupt my powers of perception with clever illusions, so I guess I made the right decision.

SIXTEEN

AMANDA CALLED UP to me when I was just about to muscle a four-by-eight sheet of half-inch plywood up onto the rafters of the addition. All I could do was grunt back until the thing was laid down and tacked in place.

"Shouldn't you get some help?" she yelled.

"And miss all the exercise?"

"Sometimes doing everything yourself isn't manly, it's pigheaded."

The sun was almost directly overhead, so despite her sunglasses she had to shield her eyes when looking up. She wore a pair of denim shorts, a T-shirt and sneakers.

"So come on up and help."

"Me? I'm not a carpenter."

"Hands and back is all you need."

She was right. There's no simple way to handle a four-by-eight sheet of anything by yourself, especially plywood, especially suspended on ladders and scaffolding. Having her help made it possible to lay up one full side of subroof, from eave to ridge. The effort cost her a few splinters, while demonstrating the superior exercise value of genuine labor over the simulated health-club variety. As compensation I fed her beer from my dwindling stock of Burton's fancy imports and let her back-nail the subroof with a power nailer.

"So, does this mean the end of the hammer?" she asked.

"Gone the way of Peter, Paul and Mary."

"It's fun."

"Just don't aim it at anything unless you intend to shoot."

We worked until the daylight started to draw long hard shadows across the grass and the sun threatened the horizon with another evening of fireworks. I think she would have kept going despite her exhaustion—asserting her own version of manly pigheadedness—but quickly took my suggestion that we advance the construction schedule to the drinks-on-the-lawn phase.

We took what I guess you'd call an enhanced shower together in the outdoor stall. The experience was comparable to the other night, even stone sober in the full, though fading sunlight. I lent her a flannel shirt and pair of sweatpants to spare her the journey overland to retrieve clean clothes. I let her make a meal, enduring commentary on my kitchen organization, so we could eat something with our drinks out in the Adirondacks, which I'd bleached back to new, covered with cushions and dragged to the edge of the breakwater.

Amanda waited until the plates were empty and we were on our second round to broach the subject.

"We don't have to talk about it if you don't want," she said.

Of course there were any number of subjects that leaped to mind that I didn't want to talk about, though asking her which she meant might have been more perilous than just saying, "I don't mind."

I braced myself and said, "I don't mind."

"So how is he? Joe Sullivan."

"Awake, but not exactly alert. And like Markham said, doesn't remember a thing past the night before when he ate a hundred pounds of pasta at La Maricanto. He woke up thinking he'd just had a wicked case of food poisoning. It's a good thing they got him full of sedatives. Soon as he realizes somebody tried to whack him there'll be hell to pay."

"If he discovers who."

"I've got a pretty good idea who, and unless he's forgotten the last few weeks, he will, too. Proving it'll be the problem, particularly for Sullivan, being sworn to uphold the law and all."

"He'll want to skip the due process part."

"Though he won't, no matter what. His cop head is hard-wired. One of the things I like about him."

"You never said you liked anything about him."

This was exactly the kind of thing I was hoping we weren't going to talk about. But it could have been worse.

"He cares what happens to the people he's paid to look after. That's good enough for me. How're the hands?"

"Sore, but happy. So what are you going to do about it?"

"Band-Aids?"

"Joe Sullivan."

"Consult your lawyer."

"My lawyer?"

"Burton Lewis."

"I'm sure there's a connection."

"Everything connects to Burton one way or the other."

"And we're doing this when?"

"As soon as you decide if you want to change your clothes or go as you are."

"As if."

"When you're ready," I said, working my way deeper into the chair so I could catch the last act of the sunset, when the crimson orb dips below the line of hills over on the North Shore and shoots a fan of pink and lavender light back up into the sky. "I'll be waiting."

———

I first met Burton Lewis when he hauled me up into the cockpit of his forty-foot sailboat, moored in the middle of the congested harbor off Marblehead, Massachusetts. He'd just thrashed the entire New England racing fleet in a boat with the hailing port of New York City, NY, written across the transom. Whatever regional animosity this might have engendered, none was directed toward Burton, whose awkward good nature and unflagging civility made all forms of rancor seem ridiculous. In fact, Abby's family, who would have achieved a heroic shallowness were it not for the depth of their self-importance, fairly fell over one another to offer him obsequious congratulations. Which was maybe why, as the last guy to clamor over the coaming, and the only one announcing his yacht club allegiance as Yankee Stadium, I hit it off with the lanky young billionaire.

At the time Burton had a criminal law practice run out of a storefront in the Alphabet District on the Lower East Side. Like other very rich people who were rich through inheritance, he could have easily devoted his life to philanthropic ventures with little notice, but instead found a way to put time in at a law firm his grandfather had founded that specialized in corporate tax law, which under his subsequent management had became one of the largest practices in the world.

"You get bored defending indigents day in and day out,"

he'd tell me. "A person needs a little something different once in a while to stimulate the mind, stir the juices. Dashing off Schedule M-3s, petitioning for changes in capital structure, tasty audit-driven litigation and compliance hearings, that sort of thing."

Burton's house was built on a foundation that had supported the two previous Lewis mansions, built by his grandfather and father respectively. When Burton downsized from forty-six to twenty-four rooms he retained the original footprint, so the building tended to flow across the grounds in a disorienting sprawl that made you grateful for the people assigned to guide your way.

Amanda and I drew Isabella, a Cuban refugee and Burton's chief of staff, who'd been on the job since her husband dropped dead while serving subpoenas on behalf of Burton's criminal practice. Burton had only meant to help her over the initial stages of her loss, but somehow she'd managed to co-opt enough responsibility to make herself indispensable. Or at least provide that illusion.

"Be careful when you go into the room," she told us. "He's painting."

The room was a long rectangle lined on three walls with tall arch-top mahogany doors. The floor was tiled with glossy red ceramic squares and the ceiling rose up into a series of vaulted domes, which Burton was in the act of painting a brilliant white. He stood on a rolling scaffold and was leaning backwards in what looked like a painfully contorted position.

"Missed a spot," I called up.

"And to think what Michelangelo had to contend with."

"Had a tough client."

"Not an issue here. All I battle is sniffing from Isabella."

"Doesn't like white?"

"What is it with you men and scaffolding," said Amanda.

"I think old Mick did it all from a recumbent position," said Burton, wiping a glob of paint off his forehead.

"We should probably let you work," Amanda said.

"Not offering to help?" I asked her.

"Not unless it involves a power nailer."

"Stay put," Burton called down. "I'll order up refreshment."

Before climbing down from the scaffold Burton called Isabella on his cell phone to ask for drinks and a side of soap and water. Then he led us out one of the big doors to a slate patio furnished in wrought iron and shaded by an enormous dark green market umbrella under which were suspended tiny electric globes. As we waited for a staffer to bring refreshments, Burton dragged a garden hose out from behind a Japanese andromeda to do some preliminary rinsing. The night air was soft, but cooled by a breeze coming from the ocean, which you could hear as a low rumble washing around the neighboring estate on the shoreline side of Gin Lane, and through the privet hedge at the distant edge of the yard.

I'd lost track of Burton for a few years after I'd screwed up my job and left Abby, who'd been our common link. If you asked her, she'd say Burton belonged to her, declaring the supremacy of social parity, never noticing he actually preferred me to the empty-headed gentility that often gathered on his lawn to sip Campari and play one-upsmanship with each other. He was younger than me, now maybe forty-five or forty-six, but looked like a well-preserved older version of himself. Perpetually tan, his faced was creased and gaunt, offsetting a full head of light brown hair that fell in a French curve across his forehead.

Over the first round of drinks Amanda endured a thorough examination of the current and prospective fortunes of the New York Yankees, which led to general agreement on the inevitable four-game sweep of the World Series. Back when I had a job I'd often duck out of the office to meet Burton down in the Bronx where we'd take our chances on general admission or patronize one of the resident scalpers with whom Burton had an ongoing business relationship. It was fun, but I admit I liked basketball season better in his private box at Madison Square Garden, which looked a little like the inside of his law offices on Wall Street, complete with a full bar and a happy Romanian kid named Mihail who always made me name my drink, even though it was always the same thing.

It took a little longer to catch him up with the Eldridge thing, but at least Amanda was able to join in. I told him about Joyce Whithers and her connections to Appolonia. And about Agent Ig, with his ominous cautions and impenetrable intimations. Burton started nodding when we got to the part about Joe Sullivan and my conversation with Ross Semple, a friend of Burton's from a time years ago when they'd squared off over the case of a young black kid some people thought was getting railroaded by the Southampton DA. It all ended with the kid free, the community becalmed and only the media expressing disappointment over the expeditious resolution of the case. Burton himself managed to direct all the credit to Ross Semple, who accepted it, I always thought, as part of the deal.

"The Chief called me in the City to ask about Mr. Fleming. I told him I'd learn what I could as far as background, but any Federals investigating a car bombing were likely tied to Homeland Security and that means the proverbial black hole. I know a few folks who have access, but when it comes to that territory, one doesn't even ask."

"I wasn't thinking you should, Burt. I was only looking for an opinion. What do you think's going on?"

"Haven't a clue. Anyone care for a snack? I seem to have missed dinner."

People who worked for Burton had to get used to his indifference to conventions of time and space. You were as likely to find him reading in Battery Park in the early afternoon as you were having him show up at your apartment at three in the morning to consult on a case.

"I've got a list of Jonathan's clients, along with some notes on three we're calling the hostiles. Ivor Fleming and Joyce Whithers, along with his brother Butch Ellington, who's in a somewhat separate category. Anything you or your hundred-thousand-person investigative staff can tell me about these people would be deeply appreciated."

Burton sat back in his chair and crossed his legs, resting his drink on his knee.

"Does this mean I don't have to browbeat you into accepting my help?" he asked.

I'd inherited a keen sense of reciprocity from my father. You borrow a guy's tools, you lend him yours without hesitation. You help frame a garage, you get the same help when you build the addition off the back. This unspoken contract among working people sustained both a sense of community and self-reliance, because it was unspoken. Nobody made a big deal about it. Though it only worked if the quid pro quo was reasonably proportionate, an impossibility when you traded favors with Burton Lewis.

But I was on a program of self-improvement. I knew it would give Burton pleasure to help out, that he'd be slightly pained if I didn't let him. Allowing him the chance to express his generosity for nothing in return was in this case the less selfish thing to do.

"Only if you come up with something good," I said tossing the manila envelope toward his lap. "There're plenty of rich lawyers where you came from."

He snatched it midair and disgorged the contents.

"Since you're making it competitive."

He looked over the client list and notes, straining slightly to read without his glasses.

"I knew Walter Whithers, speaking of competition. An excellent attorney from a very wealthy family. More inclined to general corporate governance, not much in the tax game. Sat on several boards. We did his taxes. Died of a heart attack in his mid-forties. At least that was the family's story. Undoubtedly true, though eyebrows were raised."

"How come?"

"Walter was a bit of a gambler. High stakes poker, very high, with friends and associates, and even an occasional trip to the casinos, I was told. Didn't know him very well personally."

"So he blew a bunch of money and offed himself? And Joyce made it look like a heart attack. Would explain why she's so pissed at him."

"It would, except it's highly unlikely. Walter was actually quite an accomplished gambler. Consistently won more than he lost. You can do that with poker, some make their living at it. It's probably not too great a breach of ethics to tell you his tax returns always expressed a general northerly direction in his financial circumstances. Joyce came into the marriage with her own plethora of trusts and investment instruments. I wouldn't know the particulars, but a dramatic shortfall would be noticed."

"Maybe all the excitement got to him."

"It's possible. He was a very reserved person."

At that point I lost his attention to a half-wheel of Brie and a small pile of hand-sliced baguette. Amanda and I helped him wipe it out over another round of drinks. I started to sink deeper into the lush padding that softened the ornate iron recliner, feeling the sea breeze gently stir the satin summer air, now inky black and flecked with the random twinkle of lightning bugs.

"So no thoughts on Ivor Fleming," I asked him.

"As I said, no chance of any inside information if he's connected to a car bombing. But I can speculate, Governor Ridge's proscriptions notwithstanding," he said while surveying a plate of assorted fruits and crudités that suddenly appeared from out of the night as if the woman with the tray had been poised on the lawn for his cue. Probably sensed the disappearance of the last slice of cheese.

"Option one," said Burton. "The investigators know Fleming is their man, and are merely crossing every imaginable T and dotting every I in constructing a bombproof case, if you will, essentially eliminating Fleming's ability to mount a successful defense. Which is their modus operandi. Once they indict, they win, virtually every time. With no statute of limitations, and a steady, albeit constrained, flow of public financing, time is on their side. Peaches, anyone?"

"That's what you think?"

"Just a possibility. It's also possible Fleming's appearance on the client list was just a bit of bad luck for Fleming, drawing the kind of scrutiny that could yield a banquet of unrelated but delectable prosecutorial fodder. So, the Federals, and now the State it appears, could be focused entirely on these collateral opportunities, preparing to move ahead with or without a resolution of the Eldridge matter."

"Or the Sullivan matter, for that matter," I said.

"This is merely speculation."

"But it's possible they'd be satisfied with a racketeering conviction and to hell with the murder."

"You try the case you can win. It isn't always the one you want."

"It's not what I want. I could give a crap about Fleming's rackets."

Burton rummaged around for one more peach, which he took some care in selecting.

"I don't suppose you'd listen if I suggested you leave well enough alone," he said.

"I would, Burt, honest to God I would. I never wanted any part of this thing. I was only trying to have a drink with Jackie Swaitkowski. Sullivan never should have asked me. As soon as he revisits the planet I'm telling him. That's what I really want. His goddamned fault anyway."

"With a knife in the gut and a smack on the head for his trouble," said Burton.

"I'd have smacked him myself if I'd known where this was going. Take a page from Joyce Whithers."

"You know how it is with people like Ivor Fleming. Once the die is cast, the threat perceived, it's on to the death. Lacking the subtlety for a less self-destructive course, they never know how to stop."

"I know."

I was talking to Burton, but I was watching Amanda. I couldn't tell what she was thinking. Not surprising for a girl who led with her looks and knew how to keep herself to herself. Who only let you see the part of her she wanted seen and nothing more. Hunkered down within a reinforced bunker built of intelligence and effortless deceit, as much to conceal an essential goodness as to advance the cause of self-preservation. It might have been because she grew up without a father, alert and aware but unsure of where it was all going. Or the natural accumulation of experience that comes early to girls men admire, but fear to approach. In fact, she'd been knocked around pretty hard most of her forty years, though it didn't show unless you knew where to look. Maybe I saw it more than most, since I could never stop looking.

"So you won't be coming to Butch's Council Rock on the Giant Finger," she said.

"Wouldn't miss that. Art lover like me."

"Butch Ellington," she said to Burton, "he wants me to let him assemble a giant sculpture in one of the WB buildings. I told him I'd think about it."

"Do you want a lengthy speech on exposure to regulatory sanctions, property damage and the finer points of joint and several liability?" Burton asked her.

"Not particularly."

"Then say no."

"Attitudes like that are what calls for a Giant Finger," I told him.

"Then tell Mr. Ellington he's made his point, obviating the need for further implementation."

Amanda laughed a light little laugh.

"What if Michelangelo had to contend with you two," she said.

Isabella picked that moment to roll a tray out on the patio filled with serving bowls, vodka, bread and wine. I knew what Burton was doing. He wanted company and was asking us to stay. Further evidence that anyone can be lonely. Or that everyone is lonely in one way or another. He tolerated, or maybe even enjoyed, the eager flock of sycophants that usually fluttered about. But a man like Burton would starve on a steady diet of that. For some reason he hadn't found a partner he could stick with. Or more likely, one he could trust. But all in all he was a happy man. Like Amanda, content to live within a containment field of his own design, occasionally foraying out to the territories to refresh his sensibilities and re-establish affiliations, before returning gratefully to the worn enclosure of his mind—safe, free and secure.

SEVENTEEN

I WAS ABLE TO EXAMINE Burton's theories on the inexorabil-
ity of aggression a few days later at the big lumberyard. Frank
had sent over a set of plans for me to build an elaborate architectural detail for Melinda McCarthy's backyard. A pair of custom
benches, merged into a freestanding fence and gate affair that
would anchor a future flower garden. My favorite kind of job,
where I could prefab most of the pieces at the cottage, then
have a gang of Frank's guys haul the stuff to the site for me to
install. Best of all I got to work with clear cedar and mahogany,
nice smelling, straight grain stuff you can easily shape and join.

Wood like this is a specialty item, but I could usually buy
what I needed from a regular yard if I had the time to pick
through the stacks. They kept it out of the weather in a large
shed at the far end, away from the main traffic area. It was open
on one side where you could back up your truck, or in my case,
your '67 Grand Prix with a set of rusty roof racks temporarily
bolted on the top.

It was early but the sun was already heating up the air. In a few hours the lumberyard would be a cruelly hot and dusty place, filled with runners from the big construction sites sent over to resupply the crews. The yard guys knew these often weren't skilled people, more often simple haulers, Spanish speakers or somebody's drunken or nitwit nephew who knew enough to stand in line, put an order on account and drive a truck that somebody else helped load. They didn't get a lot of respect from the yard guys, whose status was only marginally greater than the runners. Which was why the yard guys were generally disrespected by the skilled tradesmen and contractors. And by their own counter guys, whose craft was plied indoors, and who therefore disrespected everybody, though most earnestly their customers.

I usually got there at opening time while it was still fairly cool and all the employees were too groggy to engage in hierarchical power plays. I'd just finished selecting and stacking a load of clear cedar on the roof and was about to tie it all down when a noisy diesel pickup backed in hard against the right side of the Grand Prix. I didn't have to look up to know who it was, so I kept uncoiling and untangling a length of clothesline I'd just pulled out of the trunk, smoothing out the twists and kinks.

"Hey, lookee here," said Ivor Fleming's skinny guy, now in a baseball cap, chewing something like tobacco or a big wad of bubble gum. "The crazy dude."

He walked around the Grand Prix and stood a few paces away from me. Without looking up I turned slightly and leaned up against the rear fender of the car, seeing in my peripheral vision to my left, as expected, the shape of the fat one, Connie. I looked over at the skinny guy.

"'Lookee here?' You from Arkansas?"

"Bed-Stuy, man."

"That explains it."

The skinny guy moved out a few more paces, filling the space between the back of my car and a stack of decking lumber.

"Interesting," he said. "Financial fucker and carpenter. You're a busy boy."

"Diversification. Ask any financial fucker."

He pointed at the lumber on my car.

"Talk about Arkansas. That looks like the Beverly Hillbillies."

"Maybe you boys could haul it for me."

That made the skinny guy smile, which was unfortunate since it partially exposed whatever it was he had in his mouth.

"So what are you here for?" I asked him. "Ivor building a new doghouse?"

"Just passing through," he said.

"Passing through? You know this is a lumberyard. You can tell from all the wood."

"I told you he's got a mouth, Ike," said Connie.

"Ike?" I laughed. "That's your name? Ike and Connie? Is that like Ike and Tina? Must be why you guys are always together. Good thing Connie's the fat one. Be tough with him on top."

"A mouth with a death wish," said Ike.

I thought about that. Conceptually anyway, he'd raised an important issue. After losing my job, my wife, most of my money and the affection of my daughter, my only child, I might not have wished for death, but I had little interest in living. Of all the loss the worst was the loss of time. I'd used up all those irreplaceable decades formulating an existence that turned out to be largely illusory. A mental construct within which I accomplished things of substance, but when the artifice became impossible to sustain, it all collapsed, every achievement and satisfaction taking its place amongst the rubble.

"Not true. Maybe at one time, but I'm over that. Death's way too permanent. Ruins any chance of catching an upswing in circumstances. Guarantees you'll miss out on things like the World Series and the Little Peconic Bay. And then there are other human beings."

Though that was always the hard part for me, the human beings. The division I ran for my company was called Technical Services and Support, which better described its heritage than its eventual raison d'etre, which was essentially research and development. The original TS&S was a maintenance and repair operation that mounted expeditions into the company's sprawling industrial infrastructure to optimize processes, troubleshoot failures and invent new systems. I liked that part of the job. They paid me to solve puzzles and crack codes. I thought at the time my skill in this derived from solid, clearheaded engineering, though in retrospect I ran almost entirely on intuition. I could see the resolution almost as a thing, an image in my brain, and then I'd reverse-engineer the steps needed to accomplish it. It was a game of physics, and chemistry and mechanical engineering, in which nobody scored more points than me. So they rewarded me by stirring people into the mix, thereby complicating the task a thousandfold with every unit of humanity introduced into the intricate, but far more predictable universe of fluid dynamics, energy and mass, cause and effect.

"Jesus, what a head job," said Ike, spitting whatever he'd been chewing on the ground.

"Come on, think about it," I said. "Once you decide you're not gonna be dead, at least for the foreseeable future, you start facing the fact that you have to live among other human beings. Some, if you aren't careful, you get to know. Get used to them hanging around. Not everybody, just certain ones. You can even start liking them. Take you guys. I feel like I'm really getting to know you."

I was still leaning against the car, but I shifted forward enough to spread my weight more evenly to the balls of my feet.

"I think he's a philosopher," said Connie. "That's what he is."

"It's rude to talk about people in the third person when they're standing right next to you," I told Connie, while keeping eye contact with Ike.

"Yeah fuck the third person, and the fourth," said Connie, settling the etiquette question, if not the grammatical.

He inched a little closer, but I stayed focused on Ike.

"Speaking of human beings, after a fashion, how's Ivor? Still concerned?"

"I can't speak for the man, but I'd say he's feeling okay," said Ike. "I'd be interested in telling him there's nothing about you that oughta be concerning. Not that he's thinkin' that much about it, but you know, it'd be nice for me to tell him that you're off the list of *potential* concerns."

"Like Joe Sullivan."

Ike frowned and glanced over at Connie.

"Don't know the man. You know him?"

"Joe Sullivan? Don't know him," said Connie.

"Really. Big blond guy. Southampton Town cop. Recently irrigated with a three-inch blade."

"Another friend of yours? Like me and Connie?"

"Yeah. He's not a concern for Ivor, and neither am I. Tell that to Ivor. I'm committed full time to building Melinda McCarthy's garden furniture. I'm retired from the financial business."

Ike actually seemed to relax a little at that. Connie took his cue and stepped back a pace, crossing his arms. I went back to messing with my clothesline.

"That's interesting information," said Ike. "I'd pass it along to Mr. Fleming if I thought he actually gave half a shit."

"You gotta make yourself useful somehow. He's got a Doberman, could probably use a pair of bird dogs."

That had less of a calming effect. Connie uncrossed his arms and moved almost all the way in. Ike looked really disappointed. He scanned the lumberyard and saw we were well away from general activity and blocked from view by the high stacks of decking timber and the side walls of the cedar shed. Which was a little disappointing to me.

"Maybe I tell him you're a crazy old fuck who's nothing but trouble," said Ike.

"That'd be unconstructive."

"Unconstructive. What the hell does that mean," said Connie.

"Unhelpful. Detrimental to achieving a positive outcome. Counterproductive. These are all English words. Not very good words, but useful in big corporations. Maybe not in your line of work. Whatever that is. We covered watch dog and bird dog. How about lap dog?"

"How'd you get to be such an old man with that kind of attitude?" Ike asked me.

"Regular exercise?"

I noticed Ike edge closer with a little shuffle of his feet. Connie had been pretending to look around the lumberyard while we talked as if to cover his own obvious intrusion into my immediate space.

"How 'bout *de*-structive. You know that word?" asked Ike.

"Oh, of course, deconstructionists. That's what you guys are. Why didn't you tell me? I gotta tell you, I hate that shit.

Sorry, but it's all such nihilistic, anti-intellectual prattle parading as cultural sensitivity. Or let's just say it's stupid and ugly. Like the two of you."

I don't think Connie took that commentary in the spirit with which it was expressed, though he did take another step toward me, which is when I stuck a left jab into his Adam's apple. This is harder to do in the ring because the glove usually won't fit under the guy's chin, but a bare knuckle will. It's a real shock to the system, especially when you have no idea it's coming. You tend to grab your throat with both hands, which Connie did, leaving me plenty of time to swivel and plant a full-out right hook on the end of his nose, the other vulnerable part of the anatomy above the shoulders. It was a good right, especially for a finesse fighter like me. It took him off his feet and into the reject pile of clear cedar I was planning to lay back on the stacks.

For a wiry guy, Ike didn't have much in the way of reflexes. Before Connie had settled into the cedar I had him by the throat. By instinct he used both hands to grab my wrist, which allowed me to get my right leg behind his calf and shove him over on his back. A little whoof of air shot out his mouth, choked off when I planted my knee in his solar plexus. I moved my hand from his throat to the collar of his shirt, pulling his head up off the dirt so I could punch it back down again with another quick jab. Blood shot out his nose. He looked terrified.

"Sorry about the temper. I'm not proud of it," I told him, cinching up my grip on his shirtfront and giving him one more shot in the face. He managed to get a forearm up over his mouth into which he gurgled something that sounded like okay, okay, okay.

"Back to Ivor," I said to him. "When you see him, tell him I have nothing to offer, nothing to sell. Tell him I'm sorry I

bothered him at his house. I really am. If I learn he had anything to do with Joe Sullivan, that's a different story. But for
now, let's just leave each other alone. And that includes all
the tough talk. I don't like it. Never did. If you agree, nod
your head."

He nodded.

"Good. That's settled."

I looked over at Connie. He wasn't moving, but I could see
him breathing wetly through his freshly broken nose. I patted around Ike's pockets and waistband before letting go of
his shirt and getting up. He rolled over and pulled himself up
onto his hands and knees, watching the blood from his nose
drip on the dusty gravel.

Connie had his eyes open by the time I had him frisked,
but wasn't ready to try standing up. While I tied off my load
I kept a steady eye on both. Connie lay there gingerly touch-
ing his nose and throat and wiping blood and tears off his
cheeks. Ike by now was just sitting on the ground, propped
up by one arm. Neither said anything or tried to move until I
was in my car driving away. I watched Ike in my rearview
stand up and help Connie to his feet. I gave the checkout guy
at the gate his copy of the receipt and left the yard like all I'd
done was load up on a bunch of expensive semi-hardwoods.
He might have been tempted to make a wisecrack about my
car, like they usually did, but I busied myself lighting a cigarette so I didn't have to work out a comeback.

I had the rest of the day to set up my outdoor shop using a
pair of folding sawhorses and some old luan hollow-core
doors. I had a flimsy shed my father built for lawnmowers,
rakes and outboard motors, where I could break down and
store everything at night. It made for extra steps, but I didn't
mind. It was nice to be out in the sun where the breeze off the
Peconic could keep the air clear of sawdust. I had a moment

when the aftereffects of excess adrenaline caused a little nausea, but it passed quickly as I applied myself to ripping and cutting a bundle of cedar to the proper dimensions, predrilling and coding for assembly according to Frank's plans.

The work was interesting but simple enough to give me a chance to brood on the preordained nature of cycles, manifest in personal habits, good and bad, forever recurring like the waves and troughs of the sea. And my discussion with Ike and Connie on the interplay between awareness of mortality and the thirst for human connectedness. Is it that one leads to the other, or are they inextricably bound together, each reinforcing the other until you surprise yourself by wanting to stay alive, and wanting to believe in the myths of kinship and love?

I didn't know, but I was new to the whole concept. Might take some getting used to.

EIGHTEEN

IT WAS DEEP IN JULY, when the air out on the East End hung like hot, wet gauze, and the sun was busy charring the epidermals of investment bankers, administrative assistants and trophy wives, and irrigation systems drew down the aquifer to convert three-acre flower gardens into simulated rain forests and maintain the water level of organically shaped gunite pools surrounded by tumbled marble pavers and teak recliners with built-in cupholders drenched in the condensate of crystal-decanted, lime-choked gin and tonics. Even then, the weather could turn capricious and redirect the jet stream to flood the atmosphere with oceans of cool, sharp, dried-out air delivered directly from the sainted upper latitudes of Canada. I think I was the only one who wasn't surprised by this. Maybe because I'd made note of the phenomenon in the past, as a bored child searching for a mystery to divine, relishing every time my secret expectation was fulfilled.

That cool morning air rushed across the bay, setting the view of the North Fork in sharp focus and sweeping stale air and insects aside as if with a casual brush of the hand. Eddie really dug it. He took summer stoically, metering his bursts of energy and visiting his water bowl more often, but it wasn't his favorite time of year. For him, the cool wind was an intoxicant. He busted out of the side door and ran the perimeter of the property like a dog possessed, stopping every few minutes to bark at me where I'd settled into the Adirondacks with a cup of hazelnut, as if insulted by my lack of appreciation for the change in meteorological circumstances.

I'd finished prefabbing the main components of Melinda McCarthy's garden extravaganza the day before, when it was still hot and humid, but that was all right. The blessed change was part of my reward—deferred compensation. I took advantage of the air to take a run over to Hodges's boat. The parallel tracks in the sand road that ran along the bay were worn down to the rocky substrate by the summer traffic heading out to the waterside cottages, and now the occasional behemoth crammed into every square inch of building envelope after the original shack had been bulldozed and carted away. I stayed on the grassy median and worried about twisting my ankle. Eddie crisscrossed in front of me, occasionally disappearing into the underbrush to flush out a bird or disrupt the tranquility of the amphibian population.

I could smell breakfast half a mile before we got there. It was the specialty of the house. Some sort of indefinable multicolored protein swirled around a cast iron grill. Though unfortunately mostly all consumed.

Instead he offered up a few chunks of fried chicken hash brought home from the Pequot and the usual bucket of wretched coffee, served in a cracked plastic mug swiped from the Chowder Pot Café, Wildwood, NJ.

"Salt and pepper are over there. Season to taste."

"Not sure the word 'taste' applies in this context."

"Drink plenty of coffee. Takes some of the sting out."

He took a handful of dog biscuits and threw them into the scrub woods on the other side of the docks, occupying Eddie and the Shih Tzus and giving me a little peace and quiet so I could eat.

After a while, I asked him.

"Say, Hodges. You know a guy named Ivor Fleming? Owns a scrap-metal business up island."

"Don't know him. Heard of him. Gangster."

"Everybody but me knows about this guy."

"Not a made guy. What we used to call a punk. Not connected but runs the same kind of deal. Got his own corner of the market. At least that's the story. Could be all talk."

"Whose talk?"

"Guys chartering boats. From up island, Nassau County. Like to chat up the tough stuff. Most of it's bullshit."

I told him about my visit to Ivor's house in Sagaponack. And the escort Ike and Connie gave me off the property. I left out our little dance at the lumberyard.

"Well, shit, Sam, that's what I'm talking about. Be careful. Guys like that always have something to prove."

I let it drop at that and concentrated on getting through the over-spiced conglomeration on my paper plate. Hodges watched me attentively.

"If I'd known you were coming I'd have saved some eggs Benedict."

"Chicken's great. You can keep your traitorous eggs."

"If you're thinking Benedict Arnold, that's a myth. It was actually a secret recipe of the Benedictines. The monks. The ones in France."

"I thought they were into brandy."

"Made it to wash down the eggs."

The northwesterly breeze, concentrated by the narrow channel that led into the marina, was strong enough to flip Hodges's baseball cap into the water, which he deftly retrieved with a dock hook. All the sailboats, laying perpendicular to the breeze, were heeled slightly to starboard. Unfettered halyards smacked against the masts, laying down a syncopated rhythm over which a low, steady whistle played through the shrouds and stays. Down in the semi-protection behind the dodger the wind cooled the sweat off my forehead and combed stylish waves into the black-and-white manes of Hodges's frantic Shih Tzus, who'd rejoined us in the cockpit. Eddie went out to the bow to stare at the water in an effort to conjure up a swan.

"I think that Polish girl's in a lot better shape," said Hodges. "She was all over that goofy secret agent."

"She's Irish. Ig's FBI."

"That's just my impression, technicalities aside."

Eddie trotted back down the deck, poking his head through the lifelines to check for infiltration along the freeboard. I tossed a hunk of chicken into the water to see if I could stir up a little action.

"She brought him around again the other night. Said it was his idea, which definitely plays in his favor."

"That's good. I'm glad."

"New customers always welcome."

"For her. You got all the trade you can handle."

"True. It's important to keep at least half the seats available at all times. In case a bus tour comes through."

The swans didn't go for the bait, but a family of Canada geese came out of nowhere, snaking along in single file, a string of furry gray-brown goslings bookended by their parents, the showy male in the lead, the female, unadorned but attentive, bringing up the rear. Eddie grumbled and snorted, but was clearly ambivalent about the prize. Like me, he fared poorly with upended expectations.

"How's her face?" I asked him.

"She's going in for another round. The last one, supposedly. Somewhere in the City." He looked at his watch. "Sometime this week if I remember right."

"Didn't tell me."

Hodges arched his oversized eyebrows at me.

"Why would she tell you?"

"I don't know. Give her a pep talk."

"Which is why she didn't tell you."

"She might even look better when it's all over with. I could tell her that."

"Yeah, that'd buck her up."

I scooped the rest of the chicken off the plate and tossed it at the Canada geese.

"How's that coffee?" he asked me.

"Still expressing its unique character."

"The secret's in the beans."

"I thought it was the presentation."

"The fishing crews really go for it. It's an important topic of conversation around the bar. I try to tell 'em the principles behind the ideal coffee bean, but I lose them somewhere between soil composition and sub-equatorial temperature oscillation."

"I can always spot a premium coffee by the inflated price. You might consider that. Goes directly to the bottom line."

Hodges pursed his lips in thought.

"I'll take it up with Dotty. She's the one who buys the shit. God knows where."

"Or consult Joyce Whithers. I can get you an introduction."

He looked mildly surprised.

"Isn't that a little uptown for you, no offense?"

"I've been helping with her fig tree."

"Figs, coffee beans, nobody knows more about food."

"Really."

"The price of a meal is about my gross take for the whole weekend, but they say it's worth it. Can't testify from personal experience."

I told him about her connection to Jonathan and Appolonia Eldridge.

"So she's a friend of Appolonia's? Hard to imagine," he said.

"How come?"

"The waitstaff calls her the Queen of Darkness. Apparently isn't much better with the customers. I'm trying to picture her as somebody's chum."

"I think it's a socioeconomic thing."

"Could be, though by my lights, a bitch is a bitch."

"So I guess a date is out of the question."

"Only if she helps out in the kitchen."

I caught him up on meeting Jonathan's brother Butch and his wife. I tried to replay the conversation, but the full sense of it resisted easy description. He listened carefully, working his teeth with a snapped-off kabob skewer to aid concentration. The wind tugged at the bunches of steel gray hair that sprung from under his baseball cap and rippled the slick white fabric of his warm-up jacket.

"I used to play cards with that artist over in Springs," he said. "They called him a genius, though to me he wasn't much more than a nasty drunk. Got so fucked up he could hardly talk. Actually, could hardly talk even when he wasn't all fucked up. Some of the guys we played with were itching to slap him upside the head, but other guys said, lay off, he's got his brains all churned up from doing art. So you had to give him a pass, something like innocent by reason of insanity. I was never in favor of slapping people upside the head, so that was fine with me. Insane or not, I just thought he was an asshole. Finally managed to wrap his car around a tree. Killed two women. And himself in the bargain, which I guess was the least he could do."

"Killing yourself is good for sales, but it puts a cap on future production."

"Sure wasn't making it playing cards. Hard to be much good when you're half-stewed all the time."

"Unlike Walter Whithers, who Burton said was a first-rate poker player."

"Way out of my league," said Hodges.

"Don't sell yourself short. That game in Springs is taught in art school."

"If you met Joyce you can understand why Whithers needed to get out of the house. Probably motivated his card skills. Which I heard were considerable."

"You did?"

"The Spoon's been open for about twenty years. Used to be a regular game there. Serious. All whales."

"As in the prince or the big fish?"

"Casino talk for high rollers. Big bet boys. At least that's what you heard from the people who worked there, parking cars, serving drinks, muscling drunks out the door. When you work in the restaurant business, nothing's private. By the way, whales aren't fish. They're mammals. Descended from herbivores. Used to walk on land. Weren't as big then."

"Still probably couldn't fit 'em in a fry pan."

I heard some rustling feet up toward the bow and looked in time to see Eddie launch into hysterics over a pair of swans who'd finally decided to glide into view. I don't know what it was about the big white birds, but they really pushed his buttons. Maybe because, unlike other victims of Eddie's belligerence toward all things feathered, swans were inclined to fight back, rearing their long necks and spitting out a deep wet hiss, which scared the crap out of me even if it didn't deter him.

Hodges's Shih Tzus joined in the clamor, Eddie's supporting cast, heedless and vocal, black-and-white balls of reckless frenzy. Hodges stood up in the cockpit and yelled something at the swans, who must have understood, because they quickly turned and slid back around the stern of the hulking houseboat next door. Eddie looked like he was about to give chase, but I told him to cool it, so he sat down on the bow of the boat and stared at the water, ready for the next encounter. The Shih Tzus fluttered back into the cockpit so Hodges could acknowledge their audacity. He had a hand for each, to scratch behind their ears.

"I was just remembering those games at the Silver Spoon. Whithers and Charlie Garmin, Edgar Rose, the producer, ah, what's-his-name, Balducci, Enrico Balducci, developer, vintner—that's another word for winemaker. Has a place on the North Fork. I don't remember who else."

"Good recall."

"I remember a lot of stuff, Sam. But only stupid stuff. It's a curse. Can't remember where I put my checkbook or whether it's Dotty's birthday or the day my wife died. But this wasn't that hard. Big topic of conversation during the late late shift. It's tough when you're a waiter or a bartender—where do you go when you're done work? The guys from the Spoon would come into the Pequot after knocking off, knowing we'd serve them as long as they wanted. I used to consider closing hours sort of an academic concept."

"A legal theory."

"Exactly."

With breakfast finished I helped Hodges clean up and get the cockpit of the boat shipshape. I was about to start jogging back to Oak Point when he suggested sailing me back, since he was planning to cruise up to Sag Harbor to relieve Dotty, who'd opened the joint and would be working through lunch. After almost breaking his neck, and succeeding with a stack of ribs, Hodges was having trouble working the eight-, ten-hour days he'd worked for forty years. He'd been lucky enough to find a kid to manage the kitchen, and the rest Dotty could handle on her own, more or less. The medical people had wanted to keep him in physical therapy, but he felt that's what sailboats were for, and since he already owned one, a cruise up across the Little Peconic, atop Noyac Bay and under Shelter Island to Sag Harbor every once in a while was therapy enough.

We cast off the dock lines and Hodges motored out of the slip and eased along the dock-lined channel and out into Hawk Pond. The light delivered by the Canadian air was hard and brittle, but would deepen as the sun burned up and swept away the morning haze. The tall grasses that filled the marshland bordering the pond swayed in the wind, and cormorants were lining up along the booms of the boats moored in the pond to dry out their wings and crap white graffiti all over the blue-and-tan sail covers. The wind was on our nose through most of the course. Then the channel made a right turn and it hit the port side hard enough to heel us over, an accomplishment given the heavy displacement of Hodges's stolid old Gulf Star. I checked the wind gauge, which showed around thirteen knots, which was high for the protected reaches of Hawk Pond. Ten minutes later we were through the cut and out into the Little Peconic, beating upwind under power through a succession of buoys that led to the deep water. The boat started to meet a stiff chop shoved up by the northwesterly, but was unperturbed. The gauge showed about fifteen knots of actual wind, which wasn't much of a challenge for the heavy sea-worn cruiser now that we were underway. Hodges stood behind the wheel and squinted into the light spray that bounced off the dodger, one hand to keep us on course, the other to finish his cup of coffee. I lit a cigarette and followed suit, savoring the bitter concoction like a crystal snifter of vintage brandy. The Shih Tzus were happily stowed below, but Eddie was still out on the bow, face to the wind, fur combed back, legs spread to compensate for the motion of the boat, watchful but otherwise composed.

Once clear of the buoys and into open water, Hodges came up into the wind and I helped him hoist the mainsail. The main halyard winch was in sore need of lubrication, and the halyard itself was bristling with frayed cords, but we got the big sail up and tight behind the mast, so Hodges could fall off toward Sag Harbor and kill the engine. This was my favorite moment, when the sounds of the tightening sails and the gentle slap of water on the hull, the creak and rattle of the rigging replace the chug and rumble of the little diesel, and the vertiginous slant of the boat as she finds her balance and accelerates up into the wind tells you the hand of nature is now engaged in your propulsion, and all pretense of human supremacy is rendered inconsequential.

Without waiting for Hodges to ask, I unfurled the jib and set it a crank or two shy of the lifelines, flattening the chaotic telltales and pulling the boat up close to her hull speed. I knew from a lifetime of plying the waters of the Little Peconic that we needed to be tight to the wind to make decent headway toward a place where he could drop me off and still have a reasonable sail up through the messy race above Jessup's Neck and on to Sag Harbor. After tightening and tailing off the jib sheets I looked back at Hodges manning the helm and he grinned, as all seaman do under a set of wind-filled sails and a sunny day. I saw him then as a young man, rough and ugly but receptive to the resonance of sun and salted air, and the cruel unpredictability of the water, the way it seduced you into numb devotion, blind to its terrors until it was too late.

"You know, in about four hours we could have this thing clear of Montauk and be on our way to France. Or the coast of Africa," he yelled over the wind.

"We could see the lions playing on the beach."

"Or stroll down the Champs Élysées."

"Fine if you're into Pernod."

"All talk and no action. Tighten down that boomvang, will you?"

Eddie worked his way back toward the cockpit down the windward side of the boat on cautious legs, casting occasional glances over the gunwale at the foam churning out from the hull. For a rejected lubber of a mutt he had great instincts for the random kick and pull of sea movement, demonstrated on both Hodges's old cruiser and Burton's elegant thoroughbred. I was poised for a leap across the deck if he got into trouble, but as always, he slalomed through the rigging and bounded nimbly into the cockpit.

"Where's the catch? I was expecting a mouthful of bass."

Instead he gave me the privilege of scratching under his chin for a few seconds before scooting down the companionway to join the Shih Tzus.

Our point of sail exposed us to the full brunt of the rising sun as it crested the top of the short ridge that ran like a leafy spine down the center of the South Fork. Along the coast were little bay-front cottages like mine, slowly but inevitably succumbing to demolition and rebirth. I'd been watching the process from the dirt side as I jogged along the coastal sand roads, but you could see it better out here on the bay. Some of the new houses were very beautiful, architectural jewels crafted by gentle, thoughtful people in cool, sophisticated studios in East Hampton, or Amagansett, or high above the tangle of city streets. Others were clumsy or idiotic derivations, prideful, foolish assertions of self-importance or blind ignorance.

As it always was, as it always will be.

"What say we haul over to Jessup's Neck, then come back around to drop you off," said Hodges. "We're doing over six knots. Gives us plenty of time."

"No argument here. All I have to do today is help stick a Giant Finger Up the Ass of Authority."

"I thought you were on a reform kick."

"Technical assistance only."

I told him what I knew about Butch Ellington's project; Amanda had left me a note that the Council Rock was in session later that afternoon. Hodges made some trenchant comment about the dynamic tension between the forces of abstract and representational art, though not quite in those words, but otherwise kept his concentration on steering the boat toward Jessup's Neck, the sandy wooded peninsula and bird refuge that defined the line between the Little Peconic and Noyac Bays. He took us just shy of the shallow water along the beach before cranking the wheel hard and bringing us about, interrupting the breezy peace with the clamor and commotion of flapping sails as we stuck the bow through the wind and retrimmed for the trip back.

"I never had what you'd call a cuddly relationship with authority myself over the years," said Hodges. "But I'm not sure I'd want to be sticking them with any fingers, assuming you could find the point of entry."

"Always the danger they'll stick you back."

"That's my thinking."

In what felt like a few minutes we were off the pebble beach at the tip of Oak Point. I furled the jib and Hodges dropped the mainsail into a loose pile between the lazy jacks, and Eddie bounded up from below to watch me drop the anchor off a roller on the bow. He knew all this activity preceded a trip to shore in the dinghy, another chance to set a bold figure at the bow of the inflatable as it shot across the water. I cinched a piece of dock line around his collar just to be safe, while Hodges manned the smelly antique outboard that drove the dinghy into shore. I'd seen my cottage, and what was once Regina's, from the water side a million times, though the sight never quite lost its novelty. The houses from a distance looked like miniatures, scale models dwarfed by the surrounding oak trees and the wooded hills beyond.

As we closed in on the beach I could see Amanda in her recliner settled in with book and bikini. Next door was another figure, sitting in one of my Adirondack chairs. Also a woman, with a flare of kinky strawberry-blond hair and a white eye patch. She looked agitated, even from several hundred yards, waving what looked like a big beige-colored envelope.

"Yeah, she's better all right," I yelled to Hodges over the snarl of the old two-cycle outboard. "God help me."

NINETEEN

EDDIE AND I waded in the last few feet so Hodges could spin the dinghy around without grounding the propeller and head back to his boat, affording Jackie the special joy of being greeted by a wet, sandy dog.

"Love you, too, Eddie, get the hell off of me. That heap of yours was in the drive, so I thought you were jogging."

She looked a lot better than the last time I'd seen her. Someone had evolved my bandage redesign into something even more elegantly discreet. And her color was back. Kind of a fleshy spotted pink.

"You were half right. Want some coffee?"

She held up the envelope, which turned out to be a manila file folder.

"Yes. And a conversation."

I really didn't need any more coffee, I just wanted to get the taste of Hodges's hand-picked beans out of my mouth. When I got back she had the folder open on her lap, with a binder clip securing the short stack of papers against the breeze coming off the water. She had a pen stuck in her mouth and a pencil behind her ear, probably forgotten there.

"The first thing to decide," she said, "is whether to burn these right away or wait until tonight when we might need the heat."

"Okay, I'm listening."

"Most of the stuff is blacked out. Understandably, given the risk he was already taking."

"Who?"

"Web."

"You did it."

"Kind of. Took a protracted game of twenty questions. More like twenty thousand. And things like, 'if I'm getting warm, hum a few bars of *La Marseillaise.*'"

"Takes persistence."

"And a little tit, per your suggestion. Though I'd have done that anyway."

"And?"

She pulled a piece of yellow legal paper out of the middle of the stack and clipped it on the top. It was covered with her handwriting. She put it up to her chest and cleared her throat.

"Where do you think Jonathan ranked in his class at the Harvard Business School?"

"Is this another twenty questions?"

"Come on. You'd do it to me."

"I don't know. First."

"Sure should've, given his performance. Though it's hard to graduate at the top of your class when you never graduate."

"Really."

"Or even matriculate. Not according to Harvard. And they're sticklers on things like admission and tuition."

"He didn't go?"

"Not officially. He somehow managed to sneak into some courses and even submitted papers that impressed his professors, until they discovered he wasn't actually enrolled in the school."

"Gosh."

"All I have is the copy of a memo from one of his professors to the Dean of Admissions. Alternately apologetic, or defensive, about getting snookered, and full of admiration for the quality of Jonathan's work. It ends with something like, 'if Mr. Eldridge ever decides to engage with the university in an appropriate fashion, assuming the absence of legal encumbrances, I fully recommend we consider his candidacy very seriously, yadda, yadda.' I think Web let me see this as a good summary of the situation. Took me about three stanzas into the French national anthem, but I got the gist."

I struggled to remember the drab little office in Riverhead. One of the few adornments was a wall partially covered with framed documents, the kind with Old English script inked in with the name Jonathan Eldridge. I thought I could visualize a diploma from Harvard, but it might have been a manufactured memory, born of another file I got from Joe Sullivan that held Jonathan's resume.

Jackie had the look of canary-fed cat.

"Okay. I bet there's more," I said to her.

"Nobody said you had to be a graduate of Harvard to be a stockbroker, or even a financial adviser. So what's the big deal, you might ask."

"Rhetorically, like they do at Harvard."

"I mean, even Alena has an NASD Series 7 broker's license, which is the basic, national thing. Jonathan would have to have at least that, and probably a Series 63, which you get from New York State. And in order to legally perform the duties of a licensed financial consultant, he'd naturally have a Series 65. Beyond that, he'd need to be registered in all the states his clients live in, not just New York, and registered with the New York Stock Exchange, since he put through trades."

The framed documents came back into my mind's eye. I tried to remember if there were any other wall decorations, but I didn't think so. They were behind his desk, which faced Alena's, so she probably had the specifics branded into her consciousness. Clients and prospects would call, she'd always be first to pick up the phone. Answer any questions, provide an overview of the firm's capabilities and credentials. Confident and reassuring, convincingly supportive of her boss's attainments and proficiency, because she was convinced herself.

"You're kidding."

"None of 'em. And I looked, trust me. Checked with the NASD, the stock exchange, state agencies, nothing. Never took the tests, much less secured the licenses."

For the first time since seeing him throw the tennis ball for his French poodle, I wanted to have a conversation with Jonathan Eldridge. Suddenly I desperately wanted to get a close look at his face, listen to his speech, test his body language. He'd always just been the guy some other guy blew up, interesting more for the lack of interest he inspired. More than a caricature, but easily categorized—the tight-assed financial wonk, the circumspect researcher, settled comfortably within his narrow forte, calibrating his own serenity as carefully as his investment recommendations. A man engaged in one of the most stressful occupations you could choose in a way that precisely established the optimum level of stress. Jonathan Eldridge, once almost two-dimensional, was now fractured into an infinity of possibilities, like the splinters of a broken window. Or rather, everything I'd thought about him up to then simply winked out of existence, and in its place a blank unknown appeared, all questions and no answers.

Like a cheap theatrical device, my brain replayed the whole thing in reverse, searching for another start point. As I once did in the face of unexpected and catastrophic systems failure, I needed a way to reset the operating assumptions.

I stood up.

"I need another cup of coffee."

Jackie held up her manila folder.

"You don't want to hear the rest?"

"Okay," I said, sitting back down.

"Alena was dead right on her hostiles list, at least for two of them, and yes I'm sorry I was mean to Alena, just don't make me apologize every time I mention her name."

"Which two?"

"Back up. Once you get past the fact that Jonathan had zero academic or regulatory sanction, he was very good at picking stocks and managing portfolios. The logistics were actually quite easy. Jonathan Eldridge Consultants had an account with Eagle Exchange, the brokerage firm. This account was divided into a string of discrete sub-accounts, all legally the same, but stand-alone in terms of what went in and out and how statements were issued. This, on the face of it, is not an uncommon practice with small securities shops, boutiques, one-man bands who don't have the infrastructure to handle all the administrative detail involved in trading, which is quite onerous and potentially devastating for the broker if he happens to mess up a transaction. Perfectly legal. They make their money, as Jonathan did, by taking a percentage of the assets under management; the brokerage house still gets its commission as it would if it was all Jonathan's personal money.

"Alena kept track of it all with her own accounting system, tied directly to the sub-accounts at the brokerage house, which were identified only by number. So, Alena had an account called Joyce Whithers that corresponded to a numbered sub-account at Eagle. Alena handled all the transactions at Jonathan's direction, and managed the working relationship with a guy at the other end of the phone. She got the statements each month from Eagle, and issued statements of her own to the individual clients. This system was already set up by Jonathan when she started working for him, though she improved on it considerably. I could start in on how it's another example of an underappreciated female assistant doing all the work and the boss getting all the credit, but he credited her just fine when you hear what she was making."

"Ig told you that?"

"I start throwing out numbers to you, and you either point up or down."

"Got it."

"The clients don't have to know all their money is getting pooled in a single account at the buy-sell end as long as their statements from Jonathan and Alena accurately reflect what they bought and sold, and the consequent proceeds. Which is what everybody got, lots of nice proceeds. All but Ivor Fleming and Joyce Whithers. No evidence, according to Mr. Doll Face, that Jonathan was skimming or misrepresenting the performance of individual portfolios. He might have made some bad calls for Joyce and Ivor, but it's all accurately accounted for, fair and square."

"He took better care of Butch."

"Splendid care. I should have such care from my broker. If I had a broker."

"But Alena called him hostile."

"Strictly personal reasons. Tense phone calls overheard in the office, nasty little notes he gave her to pass to Jonathan, family crap. She really despises him, and I can see why."

It must have been irresistible for Butch to have such an obvious target for his flavor of social rebellion so close to home, such an easy mark, yet apparently free of consequences, at least financial. But when I brought up Jonathan at the fundraiser, his regret was palpable. I didn't have a brother, but I had an understanding with my sister that neither of us ever articulated. It was the bond of a common enemy, and a shared defensive strategy. We never contended with each other, conserving our resources for the real battle. There wasn't a lot of warmth, but certainly an abiding respect for the private nature of the other. Not that any of that was obvious. What family opera is ever understandable by people watching from the outside? There's no decoding an underlying communication that even the participants aren't fully aware of.

"Unless you're packing a few more revelations, I'm going for that cup of coffee," I told Jackie.

"You drink a lot of coffee."

"Keeps me calm."

"That's all Web would let me have. And I'm serious about burning this, and you have to promise me not to give him up."

"I don't know what we're doing here, Jackie. So sure. He's safe with me."

"I don't know what we're doing, either, but I'm going to corroborate this so it looks like I dug it all up on my own. Then look brilliant. For whom, I don't know. For what reason, I don't know either."

"Okay."

She walked me back to the cottage, but I let her walk on her own to her Toyota pickup. I knew she'd seen Amanda sunning herself next door, but held back the wisecracks, either being overly distracted or suddenly afflicted with a case of good manners.

But when I heard the little truck start up something occurred to me. I ran outside and caught her at the end of the driveway.

"Say, Jackie, what about undergrad? Where did Jonathan go to college, or did he fake that, too?"

"I don't know. Though I haven't looked everywhere. I did pin down Butch's transcript. Went to BU, graduated with honors."

"Really. What'd he major in?"

"You're gonna love it."

She reached out the truck window and patted my shoulder, an uncharacteristically familiar gesture that caused an unwanted recollection of Joyce Whithers's scaly hands.

"Economics."

TWENTY

BACK INSIDE THE COTTAGE I was delighted to see it was well past noon, so I bypassed the coffee and filled up a fishing cooler with the fixings of a batch of gin and tonics and hauled it over to Amanda's recliner. Eddie popped out from one of his summer hiding places beneath the yew bushes and followed along.

"You can have a lounge of your own if you don't mind dragging it out from behind the house," said Amanda without looking up from her book. "You could have invited your lawyer friend, too. I wouldn't mind."

"Not until you get a third recliner."

Her bikini was stark white, what there was of it, contrasting brilliantly with her skin, which was deepening toward a test of the term Caucasian. I busied myself setting up the G&Ts and fetching the chaise lounge so I wouldn't be caught like a dolt just standing there looking at her.

I used to like looking at Abby. I never tired of it, actually, long after she tired of me. She wasn't an artistic girl, but the way she put herself together, the precision and care that went into preserving her body and maneuvering around the consequences of aging, showed an artistry of a sort. Amanda somehow achieved more or less the same thing, without appearing to try.

We spent the early afternoon catching her up, though I left out Ike and Connie as I had with Hodges. I didn't want her to worry, though more importantly, I was afraid of what she'd think. Maybe another echo from my long marriage. Abby took it for granted that I could protect her from physical threats, yet hated any demonstration of my ability to do so. She saw it as proof of my incorrigible brutality, a matter of breeding, that I was genetically destined to play out the baser impulses of the immigrant class.

Socking our chief corporate counsel hadn't done much to improve her outlook.

I also needed Amanda to believe that Jackie had turned up all the new information on Jonathan Eldridge on her own. Barely into my first new relationship in years and already the deceptions were piling up.

"You're not going to say anything to Butch," said Amanda, suggesting by the question that she didn't think I should.

"There'll be plenty of other distractions at the Council Rock. Do we need to prepare for this?"

"I was wondering about the dress code."

"Come as you are?" I offered.

"In my case, that might prompt revision of the code."

"Not if Butch is enforcing."

"He's harmless enough," she said.

"If it helps your planning, I'd like to leave a little early so I can stop in on Sullivan."

"How's he doing?"

"I don't know. That's why I'm stopping in. Markham told

me he was healing but still couldn't remember anything past the night before. Probably won't ever at this point."

"I won't forget it," she said, quietly.

"Bummer alert."

She laughed a sharp little laugh.

"Where did you come from again?" she asked.

"The Land of Thuggery, darling, born and raised."

———

I found Markham Fairchild seated in front of a computer at the nurses' station. He didn't look up but must have seen me in his peripheral vision.

"I be right with you. Just getting a step-by-step lesson in double amputation. You can learn anyt'ing on the Internet."

I was prepared to believe him when he said he was kidding.

"I was just checking on Jamaica Defense Force, who I'd like to amputate at the neck the way they play dis year. You looking for the officer?"

"Is he awake?"

"Oh yes. Very much on the mend. Go home in a day or two. Get him away from this germ factory we like to call a hospital. Good patient. Much more cooperative than other people we could talk about."

I'd dropped Amanda off in the Village. I knew Sullivan wouldn't like somebody he didn't know very well to see him in this situation, and anyway, she wouldn't get past the uniform at the door without getting frisked. Luckily I knew the cop already, so I got through with my modesty intact.

Sullivan was sitting up in bed watching the Mets on TV. He'd lost weight, too quickly, causing his skin to hang loosely around his neck and jaws. Always pale, a platinum blond who never saw a day at the beach, Sullivan now nearly disappeared into the starched white hospital sheets. But there was nothing lost in the vitality of his eyes, hard as a pair of light-blue marbles.

"What's the score?" I asked him.

"I don't know. Not really paying attention."

"I've heard of the Mets. Play for Queens, I think."

"Don't like baseball. But it's better than game shows."

"How you feel?"

"Like I been bashed over the head and stuck with a knife."

"That's an improvement on the last time I was here. You were sure it was a batch of bad baked ziti."

"Don't bullshit me. Everybody's bullshitting me."

"About what?"

"Who did it."

He was motionless in the bed, his hands resting atop the covers, palms raised, one holding the remote for the TV. You could see the bulge of bandages around his midsection pushing out from the hospital gown. Only his head moved as it followed me across the room to the other bed where I could sit down.

"I don't know, Joe. Nobody does."

"More bullshit."

"I'm not bullshitting. All I have is a theory."

"Ivor Fleming. The guy we talked about at the diner."

"Yeah. Ivor Fleming. More specifically, a couple of his goons. But like I said, just a theory. It'd help if you could remember something."

"Shock, loss of blood to the brain, blow to the head, natural defenses against severe trauma. All that shit wipes out the memory. Erases the disc. Cleans the slate. Nothing's left. Nada, zilch. I'm sick of explaining this to people. Ross is in here every other day asking me the same stuff. I'm ready to start making shit up just to get him to lay off."

"Sorry."

"Like I'd want to blank it all out. Motherfuckers."

I was happy to see him shut off the TV, a blessed silence, moderated only by the low whir of an air conditioner filling in for the nattering announcers.

"I know you've been going over all this with Ross, but the Chief isn't inclined to keep me in the loop. So you could get me up to speed, or use this time to yell at me some more and I'll come back tomorrow and try again."

"Ah, Christ, who's yelling," he said, then clammed up.

I just sat there on the bed and waited him out. It's a trick I learned from a shrink I once had to see in a deal with a prosecutor. Most people hate dead air, so if you make some, they'll fill it.

Sullivan lasted about five minutes.

"My shift that day is all on record," he said. "In my case book, and through all the contacts with the dispatcher. All routine stuff. I must have come home at the end of it at about three-thirty in the afternoon. Judy's still at work then, and I normally either go work out, or play softball, or screw around in the yard, making sure I get back by dinnertime, say six-thirty. Though that night she was working late, so I'm not sure about that part. I always change my clothes as soon as I get home, which I did, of course, then I took the Bronco to wherever I took it. For whatever goddamn reason."

"And no prints, hairs, anything traceable?"

"Oh, you think we shoulda checked for prints? Geez, didn't think of that."

I saw something that made me go over and take a closer look at his right hand. He pulled it away and looked at me like I'd tried to give him a kiss.

"Give me the hand," I said. "Palm down."

He did it despite himself.

"Interesting. Did Markham say anything about this?"

"What?"

"The abrasion. Been over a week and it's still healing. Must have been a good shot. Can't believe I didn't see it before."

Sullivan took a look himself, rotating his hand under the pale bedside lamp.

"It's been sore. Though not a big deal given the hole in my gut."

"You see? You got one in. Probably a couple. They had to club you or you would've beat the crap out of them. You were unarmed. Nothing you could've done."

Sullivan looked at his left hand.

"Not much on this one. Little sore, though."

"You're too much of a righty. I've seen the way you use your left. More defensive. Your right's the big one."

As we talked the climate in the room took a decided turn for the better. Clouds of humiliation cleared enough to let a little sun peek through. A little sea breeze blew away some of the fear and the unfamiliar shame of vulnerability.

"I bet I remembered to keep my shoulder up," he said.

"That's exactly what I was thinking."

There wasn't much else he could tell me. It might be that Ross was holding out on him. Though probably not. Ross had a high regard for Sullivan, trusting his basic good sense and honest cop way in the world. So I chatted some more with him about everything but getting stabbed, until the evening shift nurse showed up, which was good timing because now I was having trouble getting him to shut up so I could leave.

I was half out the door and he was about to chug a little white cup full of pain pills when another thought intercepted me.

"Joe, tell me something."

"What."

"Why didn't you have your gun?"

"I never carry it when I'm off duty. Don't believe in it."

"But if you were going to do a little off-hours, semi-official thing, like get in your civvies to pay a call on Ivor Fleming, you'd bring your gun."

"In which case, I'd be wearing my sport jacket that's cut for the holster, because yeah, sometimes there's call to wear civvies on duty. I thought about that. Don't know what it means."

"Me neither. Just interesting."

I left him to think for a few minutes before those happy pills knocked out his ability to think and then knocked him out for the night. But he'd keep chewing on it. Maybe it'd help him turn something up. There wasn't much else I could do. I really didn't know what I was thinking about any of it, except to think I wasn't really thinking properly at all. Ever since Jackie told me Jonathan Eldridge had ginned up his credentials I'd slipped my moorings and been carried off by the tide. With a central assumption destroyed, every other assumption looked devious and contorted.

Just thinking about that gave me a slight case of vertigo as I walked out of the hospital into the early evening light, the sun low on the horizon, casting the surrounding neighborhood into a shadowless glow and capping off the treetops with what looked like gold paint against the deepening blue sky. Seemed like the right time for a drink, and luckily, I'd arranged to rendezvous with Amanda at the big bar on Main Street, so my powers of judgment hadn't completely abandoned me.

TWENTY-ONE

MONTAUK HIGHWAY, the east-west artery of the South Fork, established an economic Maginot Line as it ran through Southampton. To the south you had to add a decimal point or two to the price of a house, but it also marked a horticultural divide between a hundred years of decorative landscaping and open farm country, now interrupted by strips of new construction featuring halfhearted nods to late-twentieth-century architectural detail appliquéd over standard suburban boxes, and an occasional old farmhouse accompanied by a cluster of outbuildings of the same vintage, tucked inside a grove of sugar maples or white oaks once planted by an actual farmer. When I was growing up one of these places had evolved into an auto repair and body shop specializing in foreign sports cars when the farmer's kids, Rudy and Johnny Fournier, returned from World War II thoroughly seduced by the exotica of Alfa Romeos, bathtub Porsches and T-series MGs. It was called Contemporary

Car Care. I liked to hang around there and watch the mechanics, some of whom were French and Italian imports themselves, deconstruct peculiar little engines and transmissions and restore lithe lowrider auto bodies to their original *insouciance*. Eventually they started to ask me to hold a wrench or change a tire, which led to simple repair tasks, which evolved into summer and weekend jobs managing progressively more sophisticated undertakings. It was good training for an engineering career, in some ways better than what they taught me at MIT, where the puzzles were more logical and failure had less immediate consequence.

The mechanical design of those postwar European cars was idiosyncratic at best. Parts were hard to come by, or completely unavailable. What manuals we had were usually in the car's native language, like British English, which stubbornly renamed every automotive component and included tips on driving like "when coming upon an unexpected incline, briskly engage the braking mechanism." It made working on their American counterparts, with their cavernous engine compartments and adjustment tolerances as wide as the Great Plains, seem entirely sensible and effortless.

So when Amanda gave me the directions to Butch's place, I knew exactly where it was. The big painted sign with three nesting Cs had disappeared years ago. When you live in the place where you grew up you get used to the continual destruction of familiar reference points. After the sign was gone and the jumble of sports cars in various states of disassembly and repair had vanished from around the only outbuilding visible from the road, I'd never bothered to see what had taken its place. It turned out to be Butch's Institute of the Consolidated Industrial Divine.

We pulled in the driveway and rounded the first big curve into the main area. The tall trees on the property had grown considerably, crowding the house in a leafy embrace. The house itself was almost unrecognizable. The screened-in front porch was furnished in mismatched overstuffed chairs and couches, bicycles, a refrigerator, an old streamlined gas pump that used to sit over by the repair bays, a pair of armless mannequins standing front to back, and a jumble of coffee cups, oriental vases, carved wooden statues of Dali's camel-legged elephants, hookahs, a TV set and a big scale model of a three-masted schooner. On the wall hung a large abstract painting in predominantly reds and oranges, which contrasted alarmingly with the flaky putty-gray color of the cedar siding—the result of some distant ill-advised paint job. I vaguely remembered a neat lawn, which was now full of rocks, weedy broad-leafed plants and feral perennials. Though long gone to neglect, you could discern an underlying order, suggesting the tangled remains of a Japanese garden.

I turned off the engine and was about to get out when the door of the house and the garage doors of the closest outbuilding were flung open and people in bright red jumpsuits, black ski masks and goggles poured out. They quickly surrounded the car and opened both doors, motioning with a flourish for us to step out. Amanda was saying things like, "well, hello," but I was too busy keeping an eye on everybody. They all carried some sort of tool, and two of the bigger ones were rolling a big hydraulic jack out of the garage. No one spoke, but their gestures were exaggerated, theatrical, like mimes. One motioned for us to step back from the car while the others circled it, using a lot of extra steps and movements, nodding at each other and shrugging and waving their tools in the air. The pair with the jack rolled it under the car and one dropped to the ground to set the lifting pad under a sturdy part of the chassis. At least I hoped that's what he, or she, was doing.

I made a move toward the car to make sure but Amanda gently gripped my forearm, so I stopped. Seconds later one side of the Grand Prix was up off the ground. Everyone applauded, a muffled sound since they were all wearing red leather gloves. Then one of them blew on a bosun's whistle, which prompted three of the red jumpsuits to run back into the garage, out of which came two more people, one in a white jumpsuit and red ski mask, the other in a tuxedo wearing a rubber mask that made him look a lot like Woody Woodpecker. He was carrying an old cast iron music stand, which he set up about ten feet from the front of the car and began to conduct the affair with a baton that he pulled from inside of his tuxedo.

Meanwhile, the white jumpsuit pulled out a chrome impact wrench and snapped it to the end of a blue hose that had been hidden in the long grass. Then before I fully grasped what was happening, he used the wrench to take off the two raised tires. The garage door rolled open again and the three red jumpsuits dragged out a wheel balancer. I knew that because I used to balance wheels on it when I worked for Contemporary Car Care. It came from Italy and accommodated standard hubs as well as wire wheels, which you had to tune and true-up as well as balance. A heavy machine, they'd somehow managed to get it up on an industrial grade dolly so they could roll it over the gravel drive to within a few feet of my car. Two other red jumpsuits brought over my tires and hoisted them one at a time onto the machine for balancing. I tried to remember the last time they'd been balanced, and couldn't, since I'd only driven the car on the highway once in the last five years, lessening the need.

Somewhere over my head in the trees somebody started playing a French horn. That brought my attention back to the Grand Prix, where another team was changing my oil, with one guy on a creeper under the car emptying the oil pan, the other ready to fill from above. I wondered how trustworthy the old jack was, especially given the weight of the Grand Prix, hoisted up on two wheels. I fought the urge to go find a pair of jack stands, though it wasn't long before they had all the tires balanced and all four wheels back on the ground. At this point, a pair of garden hoses appeared and the whole crew worked on washing the car, caring little about keeping the jumpsuits dry. In fact, on the final rinse, the holder of the hose turned it on the rest and the whole event degenerated (or advanced, hard to tell) into a kids' water fight, with a lot of yelling and laughter, which caused me to realize that until now it had been an entirely soundless production, except for the French horn, now silent.

One of first rifts I can remember forming between me and my daughter was after a trip to the City to go to museums, at her urging, since at about sixteen she was already considering going to art school. Allison's education and enrichment was normally Abby's task, but there was something about big museums that repelled my wife. Probably because they were filled with art and people who understood what it might all mean, raising the danger someone would ask her opinion on the subject. She had none, since she'd made no attempt to learn anything about Western civilization, except to feel that museums might be useful to her daughter. So under the pretext of improving our father-daughter relationship, already starting to fray, Abby volunteered me for the duty.

Abby thought being an engineer made me biologically incapable of knowing anything about art beyond spelling the word. Allison, building on that assumption, and flush with self-importance having had a high school art appreciation course, spent the day instructing me and expressing pity over my sad lack of comprehension. Nevertheless, I did my best to support her critical judgment as we moved from the Middle Ages through the Renaissance, and into the Romantic Period, agreeing that Leonardo was awesome and that El Greco gave us the creeps. Trouble came when we were standing before some huge piece of canvas apparently ruined by somebody who'd knocked over a can of paint. She said she loved it. I said I didn't get it. She sighed with exasperation.

"You just don't know how to like it," she said.

"No, I'm saying I don't get it."

"That's your way of saying you don't like it. You're saying you don't want to understand it."

In retrospect, I should have said something like, "You're right, honey, why don't you help me understand." Instead I let her hypothesis of my motives take root, later to combine with other grim hostilities and sad misconceptions, until it all grew into a profound alienation.

I did take the central criticism to heart, and put some effort into learning about contemporary art, and even started to like some things I'd earlier pass by. I learned to approach every artistic expression with an open mind. *Tabula rasa*. To withhold reflex judgments, and allow the underlying intentions of the artist to reveal themselves over time. Most of all, to be caring and sensitive.

"So what the fuck was that all about?" I asked Amanda, after they finally turned off the hoses, applauded each other, turned to us and did a deep bow, before walking back into one of the outbuildings, stripping off the soaked jumpsuits as they went.

"It's just Butch. Performance art is his first love."

"I'm glad he's not a deconstructionist."

"You took it well."

"I only wish he'd looked at the differential while the car was off the ground. I think it's leaking."

She took my arm and led me toward the house.

"It's how he got started as an artist, according to Dione. Doing theater, writing one-act plays. But the formalities of all that became too restraining. So he started his own thing."

"Looks like a team sport. Must like a lot of people around him."

"They do everything together. Some have been with Butch a long time. Two or three all the way back to Boston. Like Charles and Edgar."

"Really."

"That's where he started. He ran a framing shop in a loft in the North End for one of the galleries to help pay for his theater work. Turned it into a full-out artists' commune until the gallery found out and fired him. So he came down here when you could still find cheap places to crash. The rest is history, art history if you believe Butch. You should let him tell the story, though. It's hilarious."

On the way to the house I stopped to hold the bottom of a ladder stuck up into one of the maple trees for a teenage girl who was descending with a French horn under her arm.

"Hi, Evelyn," said Amanda, putting out her hand to shake. "Lovely music. Added an essential ingredient to the experience. Evelyn is Butch and Dione's daughter. Meet Sam Acquillo."

"Owner of the car. Equally essential."

She took my hand. She was tall and slim, like her father, with her mother's broad face and freckles. She wore a pair of freshly ironed khaki shorts and a white cotton shirt, her light brown hair tied back in a ponytail.

"I'm sorry about all this," she said to Amanda, brushing some bark debris off her shorts. "You know how my father is when he gets an enthusiasm."

"It was fun," said Amanda.

"Yeah," I said. "I'll be back for my five-thousand-mile checkup."

She walked with us toward the house.

"He loves to use all the stuff left over from when this was a repair shop. I don't know where the red suits came from. I don't know much about any of this stuff. The French horn was Mommy's idea. My father had to put me in the tree. So stupid."

When we got to the house we followed Evelyn through the screened-in porch past the mannequins and into what I remembered was a mudroom, now lined with shelves crammed with model trains and cars, china figurines from several different eras, Pez dispensers, salt and pepper shakers, Christmas ornaments—miniature Santas riding sleighs, skiing or offering bottles of Coke, some lit from within, others gyrating in a mechanized flat-footed dance—chrome cocktail decanters, martini glasses and an unnerving assortment of voodoo dolls, or so I surmised from the pins and grimacing faces. I rushed Amanda through to the kitchen, where Dione was leaning over a huge butcherblock center island aggressively massaging a large wad of yellowy dough. She wore a scooped neck T-shirt that exposed a string of glass beads, more like marbles, half submerged in the folds of her neck. Her hair, barely under control at the fundraiser, was now in full revolt, springing from her head at random angles, or tucked hastily into dark tortoise-shell barrettes. Sweat gleamed on her forehead and upper lip, and both cheeks glowed red, not unlike the creepy illuminated Santas.

The kitchen itself was no less claustrophobically decorated than the passageway, though the theme here was more agrarian. I had to duck to get underneath bundles of fragrant grasses twisted into manageable shapes and hung from hooks in the ceiling. The walls were also lined with open shelves that held enough copper pots, fry pans, cauldrons, double boilers, casserole dishes, woks and fondue sets to prepare Thanksgiving dinner for most of Long Island. More striking were the glass jars, the kind you seal with glass tops and wire clasps. There might have been hundreds, each filled with a different material, granular or liquid, each a different color.

"Hey, Sweetie. You did great," she said to Evelyn, who walked by without comment and disappeared through a door at the other end of the room. Dione smiled at us as if there'd just been a pleasant exchange, and dug her hands into the dough.

"Most people need love, I knead bread. That's 'K,N,E,A,D.' It's a joke," said Dione, through short puffs of exertion as she squeezed and beat the dough, occasionally lifting it off the table and slapping it back down again.

"You bake?" she asked Amanda.

"I hardly cook," she answered.

"Great exercise—for the forearms and the olfactories," she said, calling my attention to the symphony of smells that swirled around the room. Not all pleasant, including the one coming off Dione herself. But I could also pick out spices, like curry and nutmeg, cinnamon, maybe, and coffee. There must have been a loaf or two of bread in the oven, with its unmistakable aroma. My ability in the kitchen trailed Amanda's by a considerable distance, so I'm sure there were things wafting around the air that would have impressed a more cultivated nose. To me it was more like an assault my olfactories were struggling to withstand.

"So, your red jumpsuit must be at the cleaners," I said to Dione.

She smiled broadly.

"What a kick, huh? They only just worked it out today. You can blame Amanda."

Amanda put her hands out like somebody was about to swing a stick at her. She looked at me like I had the stick.

"Oh no, I had nothing to do with that."

"When Butch called you about the Council Rock you told him about Sam's big old car. That gave him the idea."

"Come over to Oak Point and we'll return the favor," I said. "Just give me time to install the lift. Don't have as big a crew."

"No, no, you can't repeat the same performance. It has to be distinctively right for the moment," said Dione as she left the center island and walked over to a large cabinet that held a stack of stereo components.

"Bach, Mingus or Green Day? What's your mood?"

"Smirnoff," I said.

Amanda frowned at me.

"Bach would be lovely," she said.

"I was getting to the drink requests. Though I thought you were an Absolut man."

"I used to be, but now I'm rethinking the gray areas."

The music blasted out from all corners of the room, causing both of us to jump a little. Dione apologized and turned it down.

"Sorry, I was trying to listen to NPR over the French horn. Need company when I'm baking bread."

When she moved away from the center island I could see she was barefoot and wore a pair of blue-jean cutoffs that struggled to contain the vaguely contoured mass of her thighs and butt. Also that she was braless, though containing those mighty globes probably wouldn't have done much to improve the situation. I doubted any undergarment could have restrained her nipples, which stuck out from her T-shirt like a pair of artillery rounds.

"And for the lady, Pinot Noir is what I remember," she said, swinging open the doors of another tall cabinet, this one stocked floor to ceiling with bottles and cans—food, wine, liquor, household cleaners, olive oil, motor oil, anything that came in a cylindrical container.

"That'd be lovely," said Amanda.

"I'm not sure about the Pinot part, but the Noir seems to suit you," said Dione, pulling the cork like a veteran sommelier.

"Noir means black, even I know that," said Amanda. "Should I be flattered?"

"No, merely impressed," said Dione, while I stood there feeling again like I was watching a Kabuki play without a libretto, or whatever you call the thing that tells you what the hell is going on. I had about thirty years in heavy industry, ten of which I ran a technology operation in support of a huge global corporation that made billions refining fundamental resources like air, iron and crude oil. I got to see a lot of things, and work my way around a lot of people, many of whom spoke a different language, prayed in mosques or performed their trades under the threat of secret police. A lot of times things were a little strange and confusing, but at least we shared a frame of reference. We were all basically trying to do the same thing, which was to squeeze the greatest return on investment out of every molecule of matter God chose to make accessible to human manipulation. It was all ostensibly about science and engineering, though I guess you could say there was considerable art in the pursuit. I was beginning to feel, however, that none of it could prepare me for artists.

On cue, Butch and his merry men burst into the kitchen, all naked, drying themselves off and joking around, shoving and snapping towels at each other's butt. They were followed by two women, young and furtive, their towels cinched up tight around their chests. Dione opened the refrigerator and dispensed Gatorade and soda as they moved through the kitchen and out another door, I assumed heading upstairs to dress, though I wouldn't have bet on anything at that point. Throughout the parade Amanda leaned unflinching against a stack of shelves, sipping her wine.

"Well," she said, after the last guy cleared the room. "I supposed that was the long and the short of it."

Dione toasted her with her wineglass and I went over to the tall cabinet to see if I could find something clear and astringent you could pour over ice cubes. Dione apologized again and dug out a liter bottle of some fruity flavored version of Absolut. I accepted it magnanimously.

"So how do you like living out on Oak Point?" Dione asked Amanda. "It must be exciting, being so close to the water. The primordial soup."

"The soup's over on the ocean side," I said. "The Little Peconic's more like a broth."

"I'm happy there," answered Amanda, ignoring me. "It's a good place to collect yourself."

"She's already joined the neighborhood watch," I said. "Which mostly involves keeping an eye on the bay."

"So I suppose you know a threat when you see one?" asked Dione, returning to strangle some more bread dough.

"I used to. Now I'm not so sure."

"More gray areas?"

"More gray hair. Getting harder to keep up."

Amanda let out a sympathetic little sound and wrapped her arms around me.

"Don't listen to him. He keeps up fine."

Dione picked up a slab of dough and slammed it down hard enough to cause a little piece to fly up and hit me on the cheek. She grinned at me and knocked it away with a swift flick of her finger.

"I don't doubt that to be true."

Butch appeared in the kitchen wearing a Hawaiian shirt, sandals and baggy off-white cotton pants that stopped at mid-calf. His wet hair was combed straight back and his face scrubbed pink. His eyes would widen occasionally, setting off the irises in a field of white. I wondered if he'd trained himself to do that, an appropriate accessory to the mania that surrounded him like static electricity.

"We're planning to gather in the Great Hall of the Ancients in about five minutes. What sort of fruit do we have? I'm thinking of a big basket, overload it like the horn of plenty."

"He means the barn," said Dione. "Will this do?" she asked Butch, pulling a soft woven bag, the kind sophisticates use to haul groceries, down off a high shelf. "I'm not sure what we have in the way of fruit."

It wasn't hard for me to imagine, given everything else in the kitchen, that she had an orchard full of apples, peaches and pears piled inside one of the towering cabinets.

"Your call, darling," he said. "I'll rally the troops. You bring the fruit and the guests, configured any way that pleases you."

"I'll carry the bag," I said.

The Great Hall of the Ancients was as Dione had said. The original barn built at the same time as the farmhouse, where the guys I used to work for kept racks and bins filled with salvaged parts, a tool crib and several oddball sports cars in various stages of restoration. All of that was gone, replaced by a wide open space, causing me to see for the first time the barn's beautiful hand-hewn post-and-beam framing. Or maybe it was always there, and I'd only had eyes for machine tools and sheet metal.

In the middle of the center bay people were finding their way to folding chairs set up in a U-shape, inside of which was a small table holding a projector and laptop computer. A screen was mounted on the opposite wall, in front of which Butch stood nervously folding and unfolding a telescoping pointer.

"Sit, sit, sit. We have a lot to cover. Arrange your chairs so you can see the screen, but keep the U-shape. Does anyone know the significance of the broken oval in ancient celestial-based iconography? The rite of the parabola?"

No one bit, preoccupied perhaps with settling into their seats.

"Come on, somebody must know. Fern, Peter, Charles? Are you serious? Amanda?" He looked out at the gathering and shook his head sadly, then popped on a wide grin. "That's good, because there isn't such a thing. I made it up. Okay, fire up the computer. Let's see what we're getting our asses into."

Without the ski masks and red jumpsuits the group looked like a normal distribution of types. I counted eleven—two girls, one of whom was black, two black men and an Asian guy, I thought Korean or Chinese, and the rest were white men in an assortment of ages and body types, though everyone in the room looked fit and bright eyed. No Evelyn.

The man named Charles worked the laptop and projector. In a moment a stylized image of a metallic finger, slightly curved in the natural way it would, appeared on the screen. It looked like the type of renderings we used to make with an airbrush, now composed on computer with enough shading and detail to look as if someone had lopped off a robot's middle finger.

"The GF-Double-A," announced Butch. "The question here before us is not if, but when and how. Or how, and then when, depending on how complicated the how is. Any questions so far?"

"We don't know how to build it, Butch," said one of the black guys. "So it's hard to have any questions yet. Maybe you could give a couple details."

Heads nodded around the U-shape. Butch looked excited.

"Of course you have questions. My God, how could you not? First some facts. Dione, how big?"

"Thirty-five and a half feet. Thirty-five feet is the height limit zoning puts on residential housing. Let's see what six inches does to their little heads."

Smiles and grunts broke out around the room.

"Dione," said Butch. "What's it made of?"

"Plate steel. Welded and riveted. Massively heavy so no one can afford to move or destroy it."

"Edgar, where does it go?

I picked out Edgar from the crowd by his uncomfortable indecision.

"Wherever we want?" he offered.

Butch slapped his pointer on his palm in the style of an impatient field general. Then he pointed it directly at me.

"Our engineering consultant, Sam Acquillo, would like to address that."

All eyes turned curiously, or maybe hostilely, in my direction. There were too many faces to pick out which was which. So I kept my eyes on Butch.

"What do you think it'll take to get this puppy up in the air?" he asked.

"More than a hydraulic jack. Though you guys make a decent pit crew."

"Imagination's more powerful than knowledge," said the Asian guy.

"Right. Einstein. He also had a lot to say about the kind of energy it takes to control mass, especially within a gravitational field, like the one we got here on earth."

"Let's start with earth," said Butch. "We'll conquer space in phase two."

Everybody seemed to like that line. Chatter broke out around the room. They had the easy way about them of a group who'd worked together for a long time. The bond of common purpose, secured by a strong leader in clear control.

It would take more than a few minutes to judge all the interplay, but it felt like they'd bought all the way into Butch, happily, if not blindly. The old hands from Boston, Charles and Edgar, closer to my age, were likely lieutenants. The Asian guy, whose name was Scott, was much younger and also spoke with confidence. The young women looked docile, or overwhelmed. But eager. The rest looked like the subcontractors who showed up on Frank's jobs. Sturdy, with strong hands and work clothes. Lots of scrapes and bruises, the telltales of tough, punishing labor. Edgar, bigger than Charles by at least thirty pounds, had a split lip sewn together with a pair of black stitches.

Butch let things roll along for a while, then pulled the group's attention back to me.

"Okay," I said. "First you need a hole at least twice the diameter of the base of the finger, and down about twelve feet, tamped level—likely be sand if you're talking about the East End. Pour a pad to about six inches above grade with high tensile strength anchor rods set to the depth of the pad. Good quality concrete with lots of rebar."

"It'll take a steel fabricator at least a year to form the plates, assuming you can supply the dimensions. Flat steel's easy, but here you'll need some precise curving. Very difficult to pull off without sophisticated CAD/CAM, though the French did it in the nineteenth century with the Statue of Liberty. You just have work out the proportionality issues. If it's going to look like a real human finger, which is almost as wide at the top as at the base, and articulated at two ascending points, you'll have to cheat the effects of gravity. The steel helps, though I'm not sure what sort of interior framing you'll need to redistribute the loads. Unless some of you have experience welding up boilers or skyscrapers, you'll have to bring them in, which raises union issues, which I'm not up on. And a crane, size depending on the weight of the individual sections. All of which assumes you've worked out costs, construction permits and catering, none of which is in my purview."

I sat back and took a sip of my drink. Butch still had the pointer in my direction, which he seemed to realize when I stopped talking. He resumed slapping it on his palm.

"So, it's basically doable, am I right?" he asked me.

"Sure, anything's doable that's been done before. I'm talking the construction, not the idea," I added quickly, reacting to another of Amanda's gentle prompts, this time with her knee.

I scanned the faces around the U-shape, hoping to express casual optimism, something that never came naturally to me, though it might have helped me with board members and senior management, who often looked at me with the same vague confusion and disappointment as those gathered in Butch's Main Hall of the Ancients.

Ever alert to the bummer factor, Dione jumped out of her seat and started distributing fruit from the big market bag. Everyone was equally appreciative of the nourishment and excuse to chatter with each other about something other than the focus of the get together. As I crunched down on an apple, I looked over at Amanda to check her mood.

"You did fine," she whispered. "They have to know. Better now."

Butch waited for the interruption to work its calming effect before re-engaging the group.

"Okay. Thoughts."

It was silent for a few minutes. Butch seemed comfortable letting the dead air sit.

"We should re-evaluate the steel," said Edgar, finally. "Too limiting in terms of placement and timing."

"We could simulate the look," somebody else said. "Make it out of something lighter."

That started a whirl of commentary around the room that Butch let run on its own.

"But then it's moveable. Destroyable."

"Has to be defiant."

"Subversive."

"That's the concept."

"Steel is a metaphor of industrial exploitation. It's like a fixed version of *Modern Times*."

"The one with Charlie Chaplin."

"Will take too long. Ruins the element of surprise."

"What about aluminum?"

"Too space age."

"No it's not. It's like early twentieth century."

"Flash Gordon."

"What about the rivets?"

"No rivets."

"Then we paint it."

"Flesh color. Like a real finger."

"Well, then, we're changing the concept."

"So what? How about plastic?"

"Still too heavy, I bet."

"It's got to be really strong. An act of resistance."

"Why not go the other way," I said. "Make it out of ice or tissue paper. Something perishable. Make it about the ephemeral nature of human achievement. The illusion of permanence beloved by authority."

That immediately killed the chatter. Though I was relieved to see Amanda nodding at me as if both surprised and impressed with my conceptual virtuosity. Not shared by the room, which slowly filled with a leaden silence. But again, Butch seemed content to let the group regain its own bearings.

"That'd really change everything," said Edgar, kicking things off again.

"Concepts are also ephemeral."

"We'd be turning an act of disaffection into a throwaway."

"A consumable."

"Temporary art."

"Isn't that what Christo does?"

"That's completely different."

That set everybody off on a trip through contemporary art theory that quickly left me in the dust. Amanda threw in an observation or two, tentatively, which I was glad no one dismissed without careful review. In fact, I found myself enjoying the flow of commentary around the room, mostly for the collegiality and respect they showed each other, even when asserting contrary points of view. It reminded me of when I'd have a team of engineers on the floor of some steaming production facility trying to root out the cause of an equipment failure, or explain why the results of a bench test were unrepeatable in full scale-up.

"Since our engineering consultant prompted this discussion," he said, redirecting the group again, "we should ask how he'd execute an ephemera strategy. Sam?"

"I think you've equated a heavy steel object with permanence, which it might be symbolically, but not physically. It'd take a long time to create, but a half-day to knock down and cart off. Any commercial demolisher could do it without breaking a sweat. If I understand your objectives right, it doesn't do the job."

Butch looked genuinely interested.

"Okay, that's cool. What're your thoughts?"

"Balloons."

"Balloons?"

"Lots of them. Not the flimsy kind you blow up for parties, or the things they make for the Macy's parade, but big like that, same size as your GF-Double-A, but made to look like a real finger. There're lots of reinforced synthetics that are relatively easy to form into whatever you want, but tough enough to withstand the environment for a long time, and take the air pressure needed to inflate into a standing position. And a lot more affordable, so you could have a bunch of them folded up in the back of pickup trucks. You'd just need a way to anchor the base, and an equal number of compressors running off generators, so you could rapidly deploy them all at the same time, strategically. Or pop them up one at a time, which would be cheaper still. So either way, it'd be a lot easier to pull off, but equally hard for whatever ass you're intending to shove these up to miss the point, metaphorically speaking of course."

The room was quiet again for a long time, only this time Butch had the same look of pensive concentration as the others. Amanda was positively beaming at me, out of admiration or relief it was hard to tell. I realized then what a risk she'd taken hauling me to the fundraiser, and then over to Butch's place. That whenever I looked at her and wondered what mysteries lay hidden beneath the citadel of her cautious reserve she was looking back at me wondering the same thing.

"Motherfucker, I fucking love it," said Butch, breaking the silence with a sharp smack of the pointer against the big white screen. Dione started clapping, which no one joined in with, but I could see a lot of nodding and grins, producing the fragrance of general agreement.

"Cool," said Scott. "I can see it."

"Sure," said Charles. "Me, too."

"And we won't need the WB building," said Butch, smiling at Amanda. "Is that why you brought him here?"

"Oh, Butch, please," she said, still too buoyant to take offense.

It took another hour to talk about various technical and logistical considerations. I told them what I could about materials and possible fabricators, and how much they could realistically execute on their own. Most of the discussion involved Edgar, Charlie and Scott, who'd clearly emerged as Butch's middle management, all of whom had considerable technical education, learned at places like Cal Tech and on the job building Butch's installations and theater sets. Edgar had even taken some of the same evening courses I'd had at MIT, raising the possibility that we'd sat next to each other in class, though neither of us could remember. I told them I wished I'd had them with me in TS&S, which made them happy, ignoring for a moment they'd have been helping me uphold one of the pillars of authority our current project was intended to defy. The air was thick with collaboration and bonhomie.

The others, all apparently artists-in-training or hangers-on, listened at a safe distance until Butch adjourned the council and invited Amanda and me to stay for dinner. The good vibes aside, I was feeling ready to make a break for it, which Amanda thwarted by immediately accepting the invitation.

"Wonderful. We'll have fresh bread," said Dione, herding us out of the Great Hall and back to the house.

In further mockery of social convention, Butch and me and the other boys settled on the screened-in porch with drinks and the women went in to put together the meal.

"You are, like, most definitely the man," Butch said to me when the others were engaged in a side conversation. "Very cool, the balloon idea."

"The least I could do for an oil change."

"You were cool about that, too. I didn't even know you used to work here. Amanda told me."

"Selling me out at every step."

"I downloaded a repair manual on your car from the Internet so we wouldn't screw anything up. I wouldn't do that to a man's car."

"That's cool," I said. "Your guys know what they're doing."

"No shit. They're my sorcerers of technology."

"Got the cred for it," I said, invoking Gabe Szwit.

"No shit. Edgar's a chem engineer, Charles took mechanical."

"You all came down from Boston?"

"Amanda tell you? Yeah. Edgar and Charlie. Scott's from the West Coast. Picked him up about ten years ago."

"Me and Osvaldo," said Scott, overhearing.

Edgar and Charles stopped their conversation to listen in.

"Hey," said Edgar, with a little bite in his voice.

Scott looked down at his drink.

"Sorry, man. We don't talk about Osvaldo."

"That's cool, Scott, no problem," said Butch. "An Italian dude, from Bologna or something. Had this political thing about art. Too bugged out even for this crowd. Got buggier by the minute."

"Brilliant dude," said Scott. "I don't know what happened."

"We shunned his ass, like the pilgrims used to do with people caught playing cards, or dancing on Sunday," said Charles.

"It wasn't like that," said Scott.

"Just kidding, man."

"He was headed someplace else," said Butch quietly. "I just told him he should go there without us slowing him down. It was all good."

I felt like it was time for Dione to announce another bummer alert, but she was in the kitchen, so I filled in as best I could.

"I'm ready for another. Anyone else?"

Spirits returned and stayed aloft throughout a giant multi-course dinner, at which all of Dione's fresh baked loaves of bread were devoured. Bottles of red and white circulated continuously and everyone but Evelyn was eager to jump in and out of the zigzag of conversation that seemed a feature of the gang's interaction. She was civil enough, but to my sorrow I easily recognized the situation. Amanda tried to engage her a few times, with some success, but it looked like her prime objective was to get some nourishment and then get the hell out of there.

In the Grand Prix on the way back Amanda entertained me with a description of how Dione prepared the meal, in succulent detail, adding to the feeling of satiation.

"So what did you men talk about out on the porch?" she asked. "I'm guessing not baseball or the stock market."

"Reliving old times in Boston."

"It's amazing to think they've been together for so long."

"Lot of ways to make a living."

"A handsome one, if you go by Butch's bank statements, which I already said I can't reveal, so don't ask."

"Then quit bringing it up."

"I guess I shouldn't be so voyeuristic about it, but it's impressive when you think how hard it is for artists to make money, much less a whole lot of money."

"So I guess Osvaldo really screwed the pooch."

"I guess so. I only met him a few times. Seemed just like the rest of them, only with a very nice Italian accent to go with a beautiful Italian face. And athletic build."

"Quit being so negative."

"You think Butch doesn't talk about him, don't even bring up the name around Dione. Unless you want to see all that kumbaya, love and brotherhood go right out the window."

"They said he got too radical politically, quite an accomplishment."

"That's what I heard, but I never saw it."

"Too distracted."

"I'd say the same about you, except for the accent. Maybe not the face either, but you are athletic."

"Tell me more about how Dione made the crème brûlée."

Eddie was over at Amanda's house when we pulled into our common drive. So much for loyalty. She made it worse by giving him another Big Dog biscuit. I might have protested, but she had a reward in mind for me as well, and being as susceptible to placation as the next guy, I acquiesced without further comment.

TWENTY-TWO

Tom split, creep. New sublet. Balcony! Hours
long, pay short. So what else is new. Tom
split, boo. Oh shit, if you really want to know.

SHE INCLUDED the address of her new place in type so tiny
I needed a magnifying glass to read it. Allison liked to do
tricky things like this with her computer, but I saw some significance in the act of diminishing the move. Or maybe I was
projecting my own anxiety on her behalf. Or maybe I'd been
overexposed lately to symbolism and metaphor.

It was a good time to go to the gym and beat on something for a while. A purification ritual for brutes.

When I got there the guy who handed out towels asked
me about Sullivan. I'd never heard him utter a sound, much
less a word before, so it almost made me jump.

"He's okay," I said. "Coming around. You'll see him in
here before you know it."

The towel guy took that in, then nodded. Satisfied with the report, a good return on the investment of breath. I just hoped I wouldn't have to talk to him now every time I needed a towel.

Several other guys ask me about Sullivan, mostly other cops, which surprised me. Partly because I didn't know anyone gave a shit about him, or that I'd be the one you'd want to ask if you did. Since I'd brought him in, it transferred to me all rights to knowledge of his well-being. Even Ronny got in on the act.

"So he's comin' around and all, gettin' back his functionality," he said to me while I was trying to work the speed bag.

"Yeah. Can't talk to all the functions, but the doc says he's basically sound. Or will be."

"What the hell happened?"

"I don't know. If Ross does, he's not reporting to me."

"Ross only reports to the Planet Zircon."

"He's okay. He's on it."

"Hasn't talked to me."

I stopped the chattering bag with my gloves.

"Does he usually?" I asked.

"No, but the bitch of it is I seen Sullie that day. Came in late to sit in the whirlpool for an hour. Said he was tired, had pulled a time and a half, and felt like crap from eating too much the night before."

"Doesn't sound like a man itching to run out and get stabbed."

"I don't know what it sounds like, but it don't mean nothin'."

Ronny had been a cop himself, first with the NYPD, then out in West Hampton Beach. You can be tempted watching cop shows to think there's not a lot of difference between police and civilians. But that would be a mistake. The only people in the world who thought like cops were cops.

"He didn't have his service revolver with him when I found him," I told Ronny. "It was still at his house."

"He wasn't big on carrying off-duty. I know that from the chumps who come in here armed to the teeth. I got a rule, check 'em at the door. Nothin' in the locker. Kids in here'll boost it faster than you can say gangsta rap."

"Or Mel Tormé."

"But he'd carry if he had to. Sullivan's a tight-ass but he's good at being a cop. It's hard to like him, but you got to respect him."

"So if it doesn't mean nothing, what does it mean?"

Ronny was also a really big man, in a tall, fleshy kind of way. Big head with a full scalp of dyed black hair. Always in a set of dark blue sweatpants and sweatshirt, though I never saw him work out or spar with anybody. Everybody just assumed since he owned the place and trained the kids that he could kick anybody's ass he wanted to. I never saw any reason to challenge the assumption.

"Got set up. Bushwhacked. Never saw it coming."

"That's what I'm thinking," I had to tell him. "You should tell Ross. He'd want to know."

"Fair enough."

"Joe got in a few rights before they knocked him on the head. Don't tell him I told you."

Ronny liked hearing that.

"Like I said, you got to respect him."

He let me go back to the bag, which I got humming like an oversized bumblebee. I was always good at the speed bag, changing up rhythms and modulating the monotonous patter. There was something hypnotic about it, the blur of brown leather as backdrop to my scruffy maroon workout gloves. And it was something I could still do as I got older. Took more style than muscle. A good way to signal the hormone-crazed kids that I'd be tougher game than I looked without having to actually demonstrate it in the ring. Anything to stay the hell out of the ring.

I don't know how long I was lost in the bag before I realized Ronny was standing there again.

"I remembered something," he said when I dropped my gloves. "Actually it was the thing I was going to tell you when I saw you come in, only I forgot it till now. I got the short-term memory of a brain-damaged gnat."

"I'm listening."

"Sullivan said his wife was planning to work late and that he'd have to figure out how to feed himself. In other words, he had to find some place that'd feed him. I made some crack about the Pequot being the right choice given his intestinal situation."

"Hodges always said whitefish has medicinal properties."

Ronny took that briefly under consideration. "He hasn't poisoned me yet. Though you got to wonder where some of those concoctions actually come from."

"Far as I know Sullivan never showed up that night at the Pequot. Hodges would have told me."

"He told me he was making a stop on the way," said Ronny. "Pick somebody up. Pequot regular."

"Regular?"

"You, actually. Said you didn't care what you ate."

"Only I was at a fundraiser. He wouldn't've known that."

"Fundraiser. Pretty uptown."

"Ross never talked to you?"

"Like I said. Lost in space."

"Tell him anyway," I said. "It's material."

"Sure, if that's what it is. Seems like it is to me. Go back to your bag," he told me, and left me there halfway through my workout and now all the way bugged out of my concentration. I went over to a bench and sat down, resting my gloves palms-up on my thighs.

There were so many things I wasn't good at that a full accounting would never be completed. But it wasn't hard to list some principal failings. I could group them around general headings, like the tendency to objectify any ugly, seemingly unsolvable problem until it almost took on mass, creating a focus for my frustration and wrath. When the data points defied organization and whirled around in a crazed Brownian motion of willful disorder it was easier to see it as a living thing. I once thought I could live without uncovering a solution if I could only comprehend the problem. But that was probably another lie. Maybe what I ultimately feared was the loss of control that comes from a failure to understand.

"Over our heads," I said. "No shit."

I closed my eyes and tried to see Jonathan standing outside his Lexus tossing the tennis ball into the harbor. But I couldn't hold the image. Sullivan kept coming in, floating like a pale manatee in the Jacuzzi at Sonny's. Bullshitting with Ronny. Heading home to change his clothes. Putzing around his yard for a while. Checking his watch. Getting in his Bronco and driving slowly, obeying every scofflaw speed limit as he drove from where he lives in Shinnecock Hills over to North Sea. Up to Oak Point. I'm not there, but he's tired and edgy and really wants to talk to somebody—really doesn't want to eat dinner on his own. Knows the door's never locked so he goes in to say hi to Eddie, who's usually outside. Sullivan doesn't let him out, having the responsible cop sense to assume I had a reason for leaving him in. Grabs some of Burton's fancy imported beer from the refrigerator. Goes out to the Adirondack chairs. Drinks the beers. Pissed off that Sam hasn't showed up yet. Stares at the Peconic. Drinks a few more beers.

I went and told Ronny that I'd call Ross for him, that he'd probably have to follow up, but I needed to talk to him right away.

"No problem here," he said. "I got a phone in my office. All he's gotta do is call."

I think he had more to say about it, but I was on my way to the shower.

———

The Town's police headquarters was in the pine scrubs north of Hampton Bays, but closer than the nearest pay phone, so I took a chance and drove over there to see if I could intercept Ross. The woman who usually commanded the little sliding window in the reception room looked like she'd been waiting all day for me to show up. She had close-cropped curly brown hair and thick glasses. Wore a starched blue shirt and a territorial attitude. I irritated her, which put me in familiar territory.

"I need to talk to Ross. He in?" I asked.

"And this is concerning?" she asked me.

"He knows me. Is he in?"

"I need your name," she said, looking at me as if to say, "if you don't tell me your name in half a second I'll have you spread-eagle on the floor."

"Sam Acquillo, Janet. The same Sam Acquillo you nod at when we bump into each other in the grocery store. You could save us both a lot of time if you just called Ross and told him I want to talk to him."

"I don't know if he's back there."

"Let's check. What can it hurt?"

She didn't like it but reached over anyway and dialed Ross's line, keeping her eyes fixed on me. I wondered if she'd done some time on the street, and then realized that of course she had. Explained why we understood each other so well. She slid the glass window shut while she talked on the phone, then hung up and slid it open again.

"You can go back," she said, buzzing me in, as if I'd just passed the initiation.

I was always struck by the universality of office environments. I'd been in hundreds around the world and every one was essentially the same. Whether your purpose was cracking hydrocarbons, producing movies or sending people to jail, the desks, phones, cubicles and feigned industry were all fundamentally the same. I snaked my way through the open task room to Ross's glass-enclosed office in the back. Ross was leaning back in his chair supported by one foot stuck in an open drawer. A cigarette smoldered in the ashtray while he pulled another from a crumpled soft pack.

"I think you offended Officer Orlovsky," he said.

"Probably. I'm good at that."

"Got to be good at something."

"How can I get through this without offending you?" I asked him.

"Easy. Can't offend me. And if you do, I'll just shoot you. Kidding."

He got the cigarette lit, so I stubbed out the one in the ashtray and pushed it across his desk so he could smoke without tilting his chair back down.

"I'm guessing forensics did a full deal on Sullivan's shirt," I said.

"Yeah, Staties up in Albany. First rate."

"And you can't tell me what they found."

"That's right. The DA has a little rule about discussing evidence with a suspect."

"Suspect? You think I stabbed Sullivan?"

"No, but I don't think you're telling me everything I need to know. So if the DA wants to like you a little, that's okay with me. Makes for kind of a bonding thing between us, legally speaking. Gives me the right to keep an eye on you."

"That's great. Thanks a lot, Ross."

"You know my old man used to fish with yours."

"No, I didn't."

"Said he was a Grade A son of a bitch."

"That'd be generous."

"But honest. Too honest. Said whatever he thought. My dad was a cop, too. Suffolk County."

"I think I knew that."

"Still alive. Has a place in the Village. He remembers you. Said you were like a weird version of your old man. Tough little shit. Never knew how to back down. We pulled your sheet after that last thing. Seems like you still don't."

"I'm over that now."

"Your old man told my old man he could never push you past a certain point. He liked that about you. Bragged about it."

That was news to me. I never thought my father even noticed I was living in the same house except when I was in the way of the TV or when he wanted me to go get a tool from the shed. I tried to imagine him talking about me to other people, but couldn't. It made me a little light-headed, so I stopped.

"What if I just asked you stuff about the shirt and you can tell me if I'm hot or cold."

I figured that worked with the FBI.

"We've been on Fleming and his people like white on rice, but haven't seen anything but Statie undercover doing the same thing. Though we did notice two of his boys were a little banged up." He cast a conspicuous glance at my hands. I held them up.

"Must have gotten into it with each other," he said.

"No honor among meatballs."

He settled his chair back down and propped his elbows on his desk, the smoke from his cigarette hanging about his face like a veil in the still air of the office.

"Burton Lewis thinks a lot of you, too. Otherwise you'd have a much bigger problem around here," he said, matter of factly.

"I don't expect you to believe me, Ross, but I got next to no interest in doing your job. What I'd really rather be doing right now is working on my addition instead of sitting here with you, no offense. I just think you oughta take a look at that forensics report and see if there's anything other than the material of the shirt mixed into that hole. Any other kind of fibers."

Ross's face stopped its endless wiggling as it momentarily formed into a scowl.

"If somebody gave that up to you I'll have his behind," he said.

"Same stuff was stuck to his other clothing. And in his hair. Unless the hospital got to him before you could brush it out. Is that it?"

"One other place, Sherlock."

"The abrasion on his right hand along the knuckles."

He extracted another cigarette from the soft pack and lit it with the one he was already smoking. He offered me one and I took it.

"Joe's not doing too good with this thing," said Ross.

"I know."

"No you don't. The Hamptons aren't exactly Fort Apache, but every cop everywhere knows there's an everyday potential of getting hurt. You're not the same after it actually happens."

"Intimations of mortality."

"*There was a time when meadow, grove and stream, the earth and every common sight, to me did seem apparelled in celestial light,*" said Ross, flatly, with little puffs of smoke punctuating every word.

"Nobody told me anything," I said. "Especially Sullivan. It was just a guess."

"Sullivan doesn't know anything. Because I haven't told him anything."

"He'll be okay. Just give him time."

"I know he will. It's you I'm not so sure about."

"Come on, Ross. I'm on your side."

"I'm not talking about me. Whoever took out Jonathan Eldridge knew what they were doing. Quite a coincidence that Joe Sullivan gets found in your front yard stuck like a pig about the time we opened the case to the whole squad. Which was about the time I find out from some lawyer over in Riverhead that you're pestering Eldridge's widow. If you think I don't know what you two were up to, you're not the brain Sullivan says you are. If Sullivan was onto something, so were you."

Throughout the conversation Ross maintained the usual unmodulated tone in his voice that always seemed out of synch with his twitchy body. Flat, but friendly. Unthreatening. Analytical. Make a fine addition to my new engineering staff. Ross, Charles, Scott and Edgar.

"What do you want to know?" I asked him.

"Who killed Jonathan Eldridge," he said without hesitation.

"I don't know."

"But you have theories."

"Not really. I wish I had," I said, with all the earnest conviction I felt.

"I thought you liked Fleming."

"I do. My favorite, but far from a slam dunk."

"Eldridge and Sullivan are connected."

"Maybe."

"Christ."

"Parallel unrelated component failure we used to call it. What looks like cause and effect is just dumb coincidence."

"Why not Fleming?"

"Can't see what's in it for him. Sure, Eldridge screwed up on his investments, but why the big bang? Seems like a statement, but what're you saying? Pick better stocks? And to whom, your other financial consultants? You think Merrill Lynch management has a memo out to all their brokers, 'please be advised in handling Ivor Fleming's account to show a positive return or take the train home.'"

"His sheet has about a half-dozen suspected homicides. Not like he's not up to it. And the State people sure seem interested. We can hardly find a place to park near his house in Sagaponack for all the plain-wrapper Fords."

"Rackets. The bombing investigation gave them something to go on. New, or supplemental, who knows, but that's their game."

"You know this."

"I do, but I can't tell you how. I'd be giving somebody up. But it's good information."

"I could make you."

"I know, but you'll wish you hadn't. Not because of me, because of the source. Talk to Burton. He can probably plug you in."

It was impossible to read Ross Semple. But I thought as we talked through everything I knew, or wanted to share, including my chat with Ronny, that he was feeling a little better about me. I wanted him to. Not only to get out from under his suspicious gaze, but to honor Sullivan and Burton's faith in me. To not let them down, even in the abstract.

When we were finished he walked me out to the reception area. Janet Orlovsky was still on duty. I noticed she was wearing her service revolver. Thought she ought to arm herself with me in the building. She buzzed me back out and Ross followed me into the parking lot.

"I hope you don't come down on Sullivan for anything that's been going on," I said. "Not that I'm saying he's done anything he shouldn't."

"He's done all kinds of things he shouldn't. But I'm okay. Just keep talking to me, or I won't be."

"Okay."

He followed me all the way to the Grand Prix and opened the door for me. Eddie jumped out so he could take a piss on the post that held up a sign that said "Visitors Only. Southampton Town Police." I thought of a way to divert Ross's attention.

"Those fibers you found on Sullivan," I said. "I got a guess."

Before I had a chance to say it he told me what it was.

"Burlap. Heavy weave. The kind the potato farmers have been using out here for years."

"I thought you were concerned about the DA," I said.

"Not when it's just you and me out here in the parking lot where nobody can hear us talk. Anyway, you guessed it already."

"What does that tell you?" I asked him.

"Somebody made the mistake of putting a burlap bag over Sullivan's head."

"Caught him sleeping in my lawn chair."

"Yeah. That's the point. Your chair. They thought he was you. Sullivan must've put up a hell of a fight."

"Probably didn't even mean to stab him. Or clobber him on the head. The situation just got away from them. When they realized they had the wrong guy, they just left him there. Might've thought he was already dead or would be soon enough."

"Like I said, him I'm not so concerned about."

As I drove out of the parking lot I looked in my rearview mirror. He was still standing there, as if waiting to be sure I was completely gone. He was watching me steadily as he rummaged around his shirt pocket for cigarettes. Nicotine addict and inscrutable fidget that he was, sent down from the Planet Zircon to serve and protect the safety of all the souls within the confines of the Town of Southampton, Long Island.

TWENTY-THREE

Mom's dating. Old fart, old money, old brain.
Me hurting. New guy, new money, new life.
Till he dumps me, same old shit. Think I'll
take up drinking, Daddy-style.

I wrote her back:

Dad's dating, too. Stick with vodka, less of a
hangover.

WITHOUT AMANDA'S HELP it took longer to lay down the
rest of the subroof, but she had a different job to do that
day, lying on her chaise lounge with only bikini bottoms
and a trade paperback as defense against the pounding
July sun, providing an incentive for frequent water breaks
and a considerable upgrade in the aesthetic character of the
neighborhood.

The addition was now a defined building, a plywood box with a roof jutting perpendicular from the ridge line of the original house. I'd waited for this stage to stand back and take it all in, deferring disappointment until it was too late to do anything about it. But it looked okay. I don't know what my father would have thought. He had no design sense as far as I knew, though I could hear him growling that I'd messed up the look of the place, even though all the angles were his angles, established by feel and eye over fifty years ago.

I wasn't sure why I'd starting building it in the first place. I'd lived with what I had for almost five years. I didn't want or need much more than the screened-in front porch with a kitchen stuck to it, and two miniature bedrooms, one that was my parents' and the other a glorified closet where my sister and I slept on bunk beds, both paneled in Masonite and lit by an assortment of randomly sized windows retrieved from surplus bins, or possibly stolen off job sites up island in the dead of night and hauled out east, old man Semple's assessment of my father's honesty notwithstanding. But there it was, a product of physical effort unencumbered by self-reflection or analysis, which I was happy to defer to some indefinite time in the future.

By the time I'd showered and climbed into clean clothes, Amanda had switched over to my Adirondacks, still lined up along the breakwater, box seats for the evening's performance in the sky. The grandiflora was coming into bloom, the leggy stems curved groundward under the weight of giant balls of tiny white petals, shaded with pink and blue hues cast off by the light show over on the horizon. The Little Peconic was rendered passive by the innervating south-southwesterlies that coasted in over the South Fork from the Atlantic Ocean, the weak trails of the African trade winds that once spent their energy sweeping in rapacious Caucasians and now merely cooled their Nivea-soaked skin as they sprawled across the Caribbean and up the East Coast. The only sailboats within view were drifting upright, their sails ballooning and collapsing as the evening zephyrs taunted with the possibility of a freshening evening breeze. Others had wisely given up the quest and were ghosting under power with bare poles to the next anchorage or back to home moorings. A yellow-and-orange cigarette boat shot across the bay, a steady streak over still waters, its rumble of exhaust tones felt as much as heard through the weathered slats of the Adirondacks, leaving behind a slim white wake that looked from a distance like a foamy contrail.

Amanda had brought a little side table with her, on which she'd stocked all the necessary provisions. She wore a white cotton beach shift and her new favorite wraparound sun-glasses. Having abandoned the book, she was calmly watch-ing the bay when I approached.

"I could see you finished the roof. I thought that called for a celebration."

"Just the ply, but who's counting."

"When do you think you'll be all finished?"

"I don't know. I've got a full hold on expectations."

"And that's news?"

"I liked your tanning outfit, what there was of it."

"So you still believe repression, avoidance and denial are effective operating strategies? Doesn't leave much to expect."

"Unavoidably."

I thought there must have been a time when all I had were expectations, probably in the form of goals and ambitions. Maybe not fully formed, more like focused impulses that thrust me through successive days and nights of compulsive determination and professional tumult. But all that was get-ting harder to remember now. Probably because I'd spent the last five years determined to repress, avoid and deny it all ever happened, which had worked to the extent that specific images and streams of anxious recollection had dissipated, now replaced by a vague hollow pain, an awareness that much had passed raucously through my consciousness, leaving only impressions of destruction, free floating and indistinct, the phantoms of experience.

"You're not asking," said Amanda, "but I'd like you to know I've adopted your strategy, at least for the time being."

"It's the air at the tip of Oak Point. Gets to everybody eventually."

Amanda had been raised by her single mother on a tight budget. Not quite poor, but lean, stuck along the fringes where my own family lived. She'd lived a comfortable life with Roy, financially anyway, but now that she'd come into her inheritance she could afford to withhold any expectations she wanted to.

"You haven't asked me what I'm going to do with Regina's house," she said.

The muscles along the back of my neck and across my shoulders stiffened in that dreary involuntary way they often did when topics arose that I'd rather avoid.

"Your house, you mean."

"I'm not going to knock it down, or even alter the exterior dimensions. In fact, for now, I'm keeping it just the way it is. If you ever come inside you'll see. Her nephew took all her furniture. I brought in just enough. Nothing I care about, strictly utilitarian. So when I leave, if I leave, I don't have to care about what's left behind."

"You'll need a new furnace. Circulating fan and heat exchanger are on their last legs."

"My, you are a champion avoider," she said.

"Just leading by example. More wine?"

I did get to see the inside of her house that night, and she was true to her word. She'd stripped out all the furniture, dug up the rugs and whitewashed the walls. I was glad for it. I didn't want to be reminded of Regina any more than I had to. The interior spaces felt like they'd doubled in size, and as she said, they were furnished in a spare and simple style that would be easy to forget. Though my mother would have thought it all decadently luxurious. An air of sanctuary mingled with one of impermanence, which likely expressed the climate of Amanda's mind. Whatever effect that had on my own mind, I couldn't tell, since my recently discussed life scheme was in full operation. I did like sitting on her own version of the screened-in porch, and wandering along circuitous and mostly meaningless conversational pathways. I liked her loose lavender translucent dress and bare feet, and noticing the beginnings of razor-thin crow's-feet beside her eyes formed solely by an occasional laugh, or a particular breed of smile I could generate with a particular style of wisecrack. Eddie, bribed into stupefaction by cheese and duck pâté, slept in a ball on a cushioned wicker chair. Out of deference to me, I'm sure, Oscar Peterson was playing somewhere in the house, and when I took the trouble to search for it I seemed to have misplaced that ugly hollow pain. Or its location inside my chest had been appropriated by something else, though in no way did I want to think about what that could be.

Trouble, I thought, as she took my hand and led me to another part of the house. I knew it the moment I first saw her car in Regina's driveway. More trouble than I'd ever be equipped to endure.

—

Jackie Swaitkowski showed up the next day for a road trip we'd been planning. The Grand Prix was all ready to go, having been thoroughly cleaned and maintained by a team of crack performance artists. Eddie was happy to live outside, using a little covert dog hatch to get in and out of the house, but I felt better having Amanda keep an eye on him, bringing him in her house if it got late. Not a hard sell given the left-over cheese and pâté.

By way of preparation I'd filled a large thermos full of freshly ground Viennese cinnamon from the coffee place on the corner and cleaned up a travel mug for Jackie, which she accepted gracefully. She had her rebellious hair throttled into a ponytail and wore a spiffy light oxford-cloth shirt and khaki shorts outfit that made her look like a recent graduate of an exclusive women's boarding school. Or a recently expelled undergraduate lobbying for readmission, a far more likely scenario.

She'd done the best she could with her eye patch and contusions. For her, the trip would end with me dropping her off at NYU Medical Center where they were supposed to put her face all the way back to the one she had before joining me for lunch on the Windsong deck. I coaxed her into letting me drive her in by describing some stops we could make along the way, and promising not to give her a pep talk or act in any way that could be construed as sensitive or nurturing.

"Stick to your strengths," she'd said to me. "Make the coffee, drive your lunatic car, offend people we meet along the way."

Inspired by her wardrobe, I picked out a pair of khakis and a blue shirt of my own.

"Team uniforms."

It was early in the morning. The sky was overcast, but bright enough to drench the scrub oak and maple of North

Sea in rich shadowless light. We drove south out to Montauk Highway where it turned into Route 27, the four-lane highway that formed a bridge to the west over which City people and tradesmen crossed the pine barrens. But only stayed there long enough to pick up Route 24 north to Riverhead, where I thought I could easily find the Sisters of Mercy home where my mother had lived out the last few years of her life, and where Gabe Szwit and Appolonia had told me Mrs. Eldridge was living out hers.

Jackie and I had debated the wisdom of getting Butch's or even Gabe's okay to see her, then decided it would be easier to explain later than get permission. Jackie gamely asserted some legal theory on why we didn't need to ask, which was good enough for me. I was more preoccupied anyway with the prospect of revisiting a place I thought I'd never have to see again. Voluntarily.

It wasn't the Sisters' fault. They ran as good a home as you could. It was the sight and sound of all that human wreckage, sick and exhausted souls waiting it out, or simply bewildered to find themselves wherever they thought they were. My mother never knew, or if she did, she was determined not to share that knowledge with me.

By the time we hit the incongruous four-lane road that passed the crotch of the Great Peconic Bay, the sun had burned off the morning haze and was now busy burning up the grasslands and vineyards of the North Fork. We followed it up to Sound Avenue, then went west until we came to a complex of three-story brick buildings with white trim, and discreet notices of the home's ecclesiastical affiliations.

I crossed myself and found a place to park.

The reception desk sat in the middle of a small foyer. An overweight white guy in a white shirt and tie with a photo ID badge clipped to his breast pocket was on duty. On the desk were a large sign-in book, a phone, a walkie-talkie and a paper plate littered with the consequences of a partially eaten corn muffin.

Jackie had done most of the prep work, so I let her take the lead.

"Hi. We're here to see Aunt Lillian," she told the guard, her face filled with an ingratiating smile. "Lillian Eldridge. I called ahead, they said this was a good time."

The guard nodded.

"Oh, yeah, they're all done with the morning routine by now. Folks're either in their rooms or out on the patio or in the open areas with the TVs. Eldridge, is it?"

"I'm her niece Lillian. They named me after her. This is my husband, Dashiell."

I smiled, too, and tried to look like the victim of a winter-summer romance. The guard called somebody on his walkie-talkie to check out our story, ignoring the phone on his desk. I would, too, I guess. More fun to say things like, "copy that."

He signed off and said, "Okay, I just need some identification."

Jackie looked at me.

"You probably left your wallet in the car again, but here's mine," she said to the guard, dropping an official-looking photo ID in front of him. He squinted to read the fine print.

"Institute of Blepharoplasty? You got your driver's license?"

She looked embarrassed.

"Sorry. It's all I brought. Dash likes to do all the driving," she said, mooning at me and slipping her arm through mine to demonstrate how safe she felt with me behind the wheel.

"I always tell you to bring your purse," I grumbled. "But what do I know."

"At this point, not a heck of a lot," she said, sprightly.

"That's okay," said the guard, seeing a way to take the side of a pretty young wife against her grouchy old husband. "This is okay. What's blepharoplasty?"

"Eyelid surgery," she said, signing the book. "I've been practicing on myself all week."

The guard gave us each passes to clip to our shirts and a map of the facilities with Lillian's room x-ed in. We walked the distance without challenge, passing rooms with open doors with white-haired wraiths in and out of the beds, and common rooms, the TVs blasting out advice from talk show hosts, the volume set to the viewers' average hearing capacity.

"Wasn't that some kind of felony you just committed back there?" I asked her.

"I don't think you can be charged with pretending to be a member of a society that doesn't actually exist. Or giving a false ID to a private security guard. I looked it up last night, sort of."

"Whatever you say, Lil."

The guard's map brought us to a nurses' station behind a high counter that protruded into the corridor. Two women were sitting in swivel desk chairs and deep in conversation. We waited for an opening.

"We're here to see Lillian Eldridge," said Jackie, waving her visitors tag.

"Isn't that nice," said the bigger of the two as she stood up. Bigger by a hundred pounds, carried unsteadily on legs shaped like inverted cones. Her face was round as a full moon and slick, with a yellowy, almost jaundiced tint, though warmed considerably by her happy smile. She established her balance with some effort, then offered her hand.

"What a nice surprise," she said. "She'll be thrilled."

"She will?" I asked, surprised myself.

"Well, it's been like forever. Nobody from the family ever seems to come, I'm sorry. And you're her niece?" she asked Jackie.

"We're from California. First chance we've had," said Jackie, looking a little guilty on behalf of her impersonation.

"So you haven't seen Butch or Jonathan?" I asked.

She thought about it.

"No, I don't think so. I don't recall the names."

"So how is she?" asked Jackie.

"Remarkably well, if you ask me," she said, forthrightly. "Very stable. Been that way for quite some time."

"So how would you describe her mental state," said Jackie. "I just want to know what to expect."

The nurse, Maryanne by her name tag, pondered the question.

"Well, she's not agitated, if that's what you mean. Might seem to you perfectly normal. Medication is a miracle, especially for people as profoundly dissociative as Lillian," she said.

"Dissociative? I'm so sorry, I don't know what that means," said Jackie.

"Too much time in California," I said. "Dissociation central."

"Doesn't know if she's here or not," said Maryanne. "Can't quite seem to get herself fixed in the world. We all drift off a little. Lillian is never able to get all the way back."

Jackie and her assumed identity thought about that.

"Will she know who I am?" she asked Maryanne. "It's been a few years. Will she remember?"

"Maybe. I'm not sure. She has a difficult time remembering who she is herself, so it's doubly hard to remember anyone else."

Jackie jerked her thumb at me. "By the way, she never met Dash," she said, and then, as if to celebrate Maryanne's professional tact, pointed to her face, adding, "It was an acci-

dent. I'm here to have some work done at NYU. Thought,
while I'm in the neighborhood . . . "

"You're a doll," said Maryanne. "Mrs. Eldridge is lucky to
have you."

"We all are," I said, giving her waist a husbandly squeeze.

Jackie returned a glowing but not entirely sincere smile.
She built on her rapport with Maryanne as we moved down
the hall toward the patio where Lillian was reportedly taking
in the late morning sun.

"I think they've done a wonderful job keeping Lillian sta-
bilized," I heard Maryanne tell Jackie. "I just wonder," she
added, turning down the volume of her voice so I could
barely hear.

"What do you mean?"

She hesitated, maybe for dramatic effect.

"I mean, Mrs. Eldridge is seventy-eight years old. At this
point, how can you tell mental pathology from simple aging?
I wonder if something different should be done. But it's not
up to me. It's really the family."

"We'll be talking to Arthur," said Jackie.

"See him tonight. Just got in from LA," I added, trying to
get in on the act.

As Maryanne escorted us to Lillian's room, I wondered if
Jackie had worked up a plan for the unlikely event we'd get
this far. Based on a sidelong glance, I guessed she hadn't.

I knew it was Lillian Eldridge before we were halfway
across the patio, the resemblance to Butch was so strong.
Slender, but a little paunchy, long narrow face and weak jaw,
curly dyed-brown hair recklessly shaped by hairpins into the
type of hairdo makeup people on movie sets conceived to
represent the mentally ill. Everything but the harelip and
manic eyes. Instead her eyes were a bland milky gray, distant
and tired. Dissociated.

She wore matching pale lavender sweatpants and sweat-shirt and clean white Nikes, cleaving to the fashion standards at the Sisters of Mercy home.

Maryanne strode up to her and put her arm over the old lady's shoulders.

"Hey, Lillian," she said, looking back at Jackie as she approached. "Do you remember Lillian?"

Mrs. Eldridge looked up at Maryanne, annoyed.

"Why of course I remember Lillian. What kind of a question is that?"

Maryanne was obviously pleased.

"Well, she's here to see you. Isn't that nice?"

Lillian was still frowning as we walked up to her. Jackie leaned down and kissed her check.

"Hi, Aunt Lillian. It's Lillian."

"Of course it is," said the old woman. "Lillian's right here. Ridiculous."

"Lillian and her husband are going to visit for a while, okay?" asked Maryanne, the way parents do with their children.

Lillian looked at me as if to say, "What the hell is that woman talking about?"

Maryanne plowed ahead.

"I'll be back in a little while," she said, still in the same sing-song voice. "You have a nice visit."

Lillian had her eyes on us intently until we pulled up a pair of chairs, at which point her gaze shifted to the rhodo-dendron bush beside her park bench. She was shaking her head.

"Sorry to bother you," said Jackie. "I really am."

She looked up at us, surprised.

"You're not bothering me. It's that idiot nurse who thinks I don't remember myself. What is wrong with these people?"

she asked, more as a genuine question than an accusation. She looked more closely at Jackie. "Do I know you?"

"No," said Jackie, moving her chair a little closer and resting her hand on the woman's shoulder. "We pretended to be your family so we could talk to you. I hope that's okay."

Lillian's attention had drifted off again by then, but Jackie moved closer to the bench to stay in her line of sight.

"Okay?" Jackie repeated.

"I've got nothing else to do," said Lillian, then laughed a self-conscious little laugh. "I've got nothing to do all day. Not bad work if you can get it."

"Can I call you Lillian?" asked Jackie.

"I don't think she'll mind."

"Who?"

"Lillian. You're sitting on her, you should know."

Jackie, who was now sitting on the park bench stroking the old lady's shoulder, involuntarily sat up part of the way.

"I am?"

"It's okay. I just keep her over there. Sometimes I keep her in the room. She's not a lot of bother." She leaned closer to Jackie. "Not terribly bright," she said, confidentially.

"You seem awfully bright."

"I do? Really. Interesting. Who's Prince Charming?" she asked, looking at me.

"A friend of mine."

"Doesn't say much."

"He would if he could think of something to say. Not terribly bright."

Lillian seemed satisfied with that.

"Not much to look at, either," she said.

"So," said Jackie. "How're you doing? Everything okay? Food okay?"

Lillian picked at her sweatpants as she thought about the question.

"I don't know. I think it's okay. I think so."

"You getting visitors? Arthur, Jonathan?"

"Jonathan's with his father," she said quickly, her attention drawn again to the fat white rhododendron petals. Jackie rubbed her arm some more, pulling her back.

"He's there now?"

"He's always with his father." She held her hands up defensively, and shook her head. "I don't argue, it's up to them."

"And where's Arthur?"

"I don't know. With his wife. He's married. You could tell him to come see me more often. I don't like to prod, but I'm not going to be around forever."

A nun in a pure white outfit rolled a cart out of the building and across the patio's brick pavers. The noise and the sight of a tall chrome coffee percolator killed my interest in the conversation. I almost broke an ankle getting out of my chair to queue up with the visitors and residents nimble and caffeine-addicted enough to make the effort. Jackie and Lillian continued their conversation while I was gone.

When I got back Lillian was saying, "I wish there were more trees. I can hardly see any from my room. I like to lie in bed in the morning and look at trees, but that's not possible if there are none."

"You had a lot of trees in Shirley?" Jackie asked.

"Arthur's father loved trees. Wept when he had to cut one down."

"Jonathan, too?"

"I don't know," she looked disturbed by the thought. "I suppose he would, being with his father."

"So, the boy's father and you were separated," said Jackie. "I'm sorry."

"They go," said Lillian. "You know that. Everything's fine, then they go. Just as you please."

"I do know," said Jackie, glowering at me, the closest representative of the offending group.

"So, Arthur stayed with you and Jonathan went with his father. That must have been hard."

Lillian let out another one of her nervous, humorless laughs.

"What're you going to do? If that's what the boy wants to do? He can be anybody, anywhere he wants, I can't help that. I think I could drink some of that coffee," she said, pointing at my cup. I got her some.

"Arthur was your husband's name, too, wasn't it?" asked Jackie.

"I don't know where he is. I haven't seen him in a while. Arthur should tell him to come see me."

She showed the first signs of agitation, so Jackie slid back and let out a contented little breath, looking out at the gathering on the patio.

"You must like to sit here. It's very pleasant," she told Lillian.

"Lillian likes it here. I don't care. I can sit in the room just as easily."

"How does Lillian feel about Arthur? Your husband," I asked her.

"Another country heard from."

"She want to see him?" Jackie asked.

"Doesn't much care for him, truth be told. He should still come and see me."

"Could bring along Jonathan," I suggested. I could sense Jackie tensing up, thinking I was about to blow her play.

"That's up to Arthur."

"Your husband."

"No, of course not. I'm talking about Arthur."

"Your son."

Lillian looked at Jackie.

"You should introduce him to the rest of the family," she whispered. "I think he's a little confused."

"Happens easily."

Maryanne came back out on to the patio. She carried a clipboard and a blood pressure gauge stuffed under her arm.

"Hello, Sweetheart. Are you having a nice visit?" she asked Lillian.

"I think so. I have some coffee."

Maryanne looked impressed.

"Well, that's a new thing. I didn't know you liked coffee." She took me by the sleeve and pulled me out of earshot. "Five years I've been here, never saw her drink coffee."

"Maybe we should stay for cocktail hour. Could start a whole new trend."

"Why not. Just have to check for adverse reactions."

"What sort of meds is she on?"

"You want to talk cocktails. Quite the mix. Mostly tranqs, a serotonin reuptake inhibitor—between the two they flatten things out a little. Not that she's bipolar, technically, but you get a lot of the same symptoms. Anhedonia, dysphoria, depression, agitation. They've been prescribing antipsychotics, but I don't know what for. She isn't delusional."

"I notice she's got another Lillian hanging around with her."

Maryanne smiled.

"Not another. *The* Lillian."

"So who're we talking to?"

"She doesn't know." She leaned into me, as best she could given her girth, and whispered, "That's why she's here."

Maryanne gave me a clinical briefing on Lillian's condition, which promptly took me out of my depth.

"She said I'm the one that's confused. She's right."

"Welcome to my wonderful world."

Jackie was still talking to her when we rejoined the two of them, sitting sideways Buddha-style on the bench. It didn't seem to matter much to Lillian that we were back. She hadn't moved and was back to picking at her clothing, though she seemed reasonably calm. I guess I would be too if I was drugged to the gills.

Jackie stood up when she saw me and Maryanne approach. She pulled me back over to where I'd just come from.

"How's the chat?" I asked her.

"Getting a little circular. And I'm getting short on things to talk about. Kind of like my blind dates. I do all the yapping while the guy answers in monosyllables and stares out into space. Not sure what else we can learn."

"Where did her husband live after he left? Arthur the first."

"Riverhead. I think. Makes sense if he raised Jonathan." She looked around the patio. "Sam, I'm getting a little paranoid."

"Must be the ambience."

"We're sort of here on false pretenses. The longer we stay, the bigger the risk."

"Is that what your research told you?"

"Not exactly research. I just tried to remember some case law before I fell asleep last night."

While we talked we walked back over to the bench to say goodbye. Maryanne caressed the top of Lillian's head and then escorted us back to the entrance. We were all quiet until we got to the security desk, where Jackie and I signed out and relinquished our passes. Maryanne took both our hands, joined them together, and then held them enclosed within her own two hands.

"I know it doesn't seem like much, but it was wonderful that you spent a little time with Lillian. I honestly think it's been over a year since I saw anybody from the family. I'm not supposed to be judgmental about the relatives, but I think it's disgraceful. The therapeutic value of your visit might be debatable, but I like to think it makes a difference. So, if only for my own sake, thank you very much."

"So, last year. Who came to visit?" I asked.

"The two of them, I think. The son Arthur and the lawyer. Funny name."

"Gabriel Szwit."

"Something like that. Funny little man. Not very pleasant."

"They were here together?"

"Usually are. Mr. Szwit handles all the paperwork for the family. He makes a pest out of himself with the administrative people while the son sits with his mother. They don't talk much, but I still think it's important to spend the time."

Even though the parking lot had the same weather as the patio within the complex of brick buildings, it seemed sunnier and the atmosphere was filled with oxygen. I took in a few hearty gulps before lighting a cigarette. Jackie was quiet, and stayed that way for about a half-hour after we got underway. That was okay with me. I didn't want to talk much myself. The whole experience might have been easier if it hadn't been the same place I'd stored my mother the last few years of her life. Where I'd neglected to see her as often as I should have, even though in the end she really didn't know who I was. Like Maryanne was trying to say, it almost doesn't matter if they know you or not, or if they seem to get anything out of seeing you sitting there in their rooms. It's just what you're supposed to do. It's how you honor all those years in the past when the same scooped-out mummies fed your face and wiped your ass and put up with your wailing selfishness.

Though this was about more than just growing old. This was a brief visit with madness, a condition that had no age preference, no discrimination between the innocent and the damned. In those rare, quiet moments of pure lucidity that come fleeting past your consciousness, you can sometimes capture insights into your true nature, and in so doing, glimpse the darker potentials of your mind. For me I'd always known, and feared, what I sensed was close proximity to genuine insanity. That my father's abiding fury was more than simple rage, that it was an indicator, a symptom of incipient pathology, that died stillborn with him on the floor of a filthy restroom at the back of a ratty bar in the Bronx, and that the same embryonic madness festers within me, darkly watchful, waiting to be born.

TWENTY-FOUR

I FELT LIKE Appolonia Eldridge when Jackie and I first rolled into Nassau County. It was only the second time in five years I'd been out of the East End and I was unprepared for the crush of traffic, chaotic zoning and neon sprawl. It was getting hot, so I also had to endure Jackie's comments on the air-conditioning inside the Grand Prix, centering on the fact that there was none. It did have some pretty big windows, which let in a lot of hot, wet and noisy Nassau County air, forcing her to pull her thickets of insubordinate hair into a ponytail again. The only compensation was our destination—the Long Island headquarters of the FBI, Web Ig's home base.

There was little chance he'd give us any more information. I only wanted to give Jackie another glimpse of him before she went back into surgery. As we closed in she gave him a ring.

"He's going to meet us for lunch," she said, snapping her

cell phone closed. "He said his boss doesn't like civilians in the office unless they're in the interrogation rooms."

"I'll pay. Haven't filed a 1040 in a few years. Least I can do for my country."

"Tax shelters?"

"Yeah, the ultimate. No income. Not enough to pay taxes, anyway."

Now that we were back to civil discourse, she reopened our favorite subject.

"Are you going to give me an opinion?"

"On tax policy?"

"On Lillian Eldridge."

"She's nuts."

"That's the kind of sensitivity I was hoping for."

"Depersonalization disorder. Marked by loss, distortion or fragmentation of the identity. Pretty rare, hard to diagnose, harder to treat, wreaks hell on people and their families. Probably, maybe, triggered in the susceptible by some traumatic event. Usually in childhood or adolescence, but not exclusively."

"You knew that?"

"I just thought about Psych 101 before going to sleep last night."

"Come on."

"Maryanne told me. At least something that sounded like that."

"How traumatic an event?"

"Usually natural disasters, war, sexual abuse—though trauma is in the mind of the traumatized. Kids kill themselves over being cut from the cheerleading squad."

"The divorce. Lost her husband and one of her kids in one fell swoop."

"Would all be in her medical records. Good luck with

that. Make the FBI look like a bunch of blabbermouths. And I don't think Maryanne would be into a game of hot and cold."

I made a turn off a four-lane boulevard that ran through what I thought was an overdeveloped retail district, only to plunge into a six-lane version of the same thing that stretched before me in a straight line all the way to the horizon. Maybe beyond. Maybe it was endless, and they'd managed to warp space-time into an infinite series of branded restaurants, home centers, bathroom fixture emporiums, dry cleaners, banks, hardware stores, self-storage units, gas stations and single-story asbestos-shingled houses with low-pitch roofs and bright red pickup trucks, decorated with scrub oak and cedars planted along chainlink fences by the random hand of the wind.

I reminded myself that inside the grids drawn by these monstrous Gomorrahs were large tracks of blessed Long Island landscape filled with serene homes settled within verdant gardens, in which kind and intelligent people raised joyful children and lived lives of thoughtfulness and reflection. Who barely noticed the vulgarity through which they traveled on the way to meaningful vocations, as doctors, engineers, professors of abnormal psychology.

"Don't underestimate me," said Jackie.

"Only an opinion. What's yours?"

"She's nuts. But not crazy. Or stupid. I think she's happy being where she is. Getting cared for, fussed over even, finding safe haven from a world that didn't work out the way she wanted. Three squares a day and all the drugs her liver can withstand. What the hell. Doesn't sound that bad."

"Maryanne thought she was lonely."

"Lillian might be lonely. The woman we talked to is all set."

"And what else?" I asked her, rhetorically. "The big news."

"It looks like Butch is the only one who paid either of them any attention. I thought he was the family brat and Jonathan Mr. Responsible."

"So did Sam," I said. "Dashiell is not surprised."

"Well, have him tell Sam to find a place where I can pee and fix up my face. I want to do it before we get there."

Agent Ig's invisible gray Ford was parked in a corner of a nearly empty parking lot surrounding a franchise restaurant called something like The Olde Mill Tavern, the name written out in eighteenth-century script in ten-foot-high neon letters, just like they did in the time of Alexander Hamilton. The facade was mostly made of fieldstone, marred only by the random placement of actual barrelheads, protruding from the walls as if they'd been shot there by a cannon.

Web met us in the foyer. He kissed Jackie and shook my hand with both of his, which I took to be an outpouring of nearly untamable emotion.

"Hey, Web. What's up?"

"I've secured us a table in the back so we can have a little privacy," he said. It occurred to me that the Olde Mill Tavern chain must be a big front for the FBI. Put them all over the country. Pick a decor all the troops could agree on. Place to have meetings, have a little lunch and stay camouflaged. Probably turned a profit. Helped defray Bureau expenses for things like plain gray Fords and in-ear communication devices.

"Awfully nice to see you both."

Jackie let him hold her arm so she could glide across the floor from the foyer to the far end of the main room. There might have been a hundred tables there, at which only a handful of people were eating. It was after one. All the early birds had flown the coop. Webster Ig's white shirt looked like it just came out of the laundry box, the sleeves billowing and buttoned tight at the wrists. I always wondered how certain guys could pull that off. If I didn't roll up my sleeves the second I took off my jacket I'd start to sweat and lose concentration.

"How's the Pequot?" he asked us when we settled in our seats. "Mr. Hodges is quite the chef."

"Hasn't killed anybody yet. Far as we know," I told him.

"I've tried to describe his special whitefish."

"Indescribable is fair enough."

He nodded enthusiastically. It occurred to me that for a stitched-up guy like Web, confined most days within a parched office cubicle, relieved only by forays into the shop-worn municipal grime of courtrooms and record repositories, spending long hours on the phone or with US Attorneys, or more likely their legal assistants, a simple lunch with a lavish oddball like Jackie Swaitkowski must seem like an epic adventure. Jackie, meanwhile, had managed to transform herself into a softer, sweeter and more accommodating version of the woman I'd been driving around all day. Made me ponder whatever Darwinian imperative underlies the aphorism that opposites attract. But only until I was attracted by the specials of the day.

"So," said Jackie, after her plain chicken and deviled egg salad arrived, "aren't you going to ask us how the investigation is going?"

"I would if I hadn't already urged, actually begged, you to abandon it," said Web. "And if even saying the name Jonathan Eldridge out loud wouldn't cost me my job and any future employment with the federal government."

"Are you completely off the case?" she asked. "You can tell us that, can't you."

"I can tell you my name and that I live in an apartment with a cat. And that's about it."

"Okay," she said, content to focus on her salad.

"Say, Web, this is not about the case, but just a general question," I said to him, probably unconvincingly. "Does the government actually keep gigantic databases on everybody, some kind of central Big Brother thing like everybody thinks they do?"

"No. Sorry to disappoint you. And all the conspiracy theorists out there. Fact is, I think they would if they could. There's just too much in the way. Inter-agency rivalries, mostly. Some of which were put there intentionally as a protection against a real Big Brother taking root. That'll probably change now, given the situation, but it'll be a long time coming, right or wrong."

"That's all irrelevant," said Jackie to me, trying to delicately shove an uncut piece of lettuce in her mouth. "I can find anything you want on the Internet."

"Anything?"

"Yeah. I can't help it if you've been living in a cave for the last five years. Tell me what you want to know, about anything, anywhere. I can dig it out."

"Jackie's maybe exaggerating a little, but you'd be surprised."

If he only knew.

"Let me ask you something else," I said to Web. "When everybody can find out anything they want about anybody and everything, will we be closer to or farther away from achieving the ultimate in human understanding?"

He sat back in his chair and folded his arms to buy a little time to think. Then he shook his head.

"Nah. It's all the same shit, just recycled," he said, smiling at his own wisdom and digging into his three-quarter-pound mound of chopped sirloin with cheddar, bacon, lettuce and tomato.

———

It once made me nervous to drive the Grand Prix into New York City, especially in the warm weather, but that was before I'd changed out the thermostat for a new aftermarket model that improved on the original in that it actually functioned as advertised. Having to keep the windows down to avoid suffocation was a new challenge as we emerged from the tunnel and slid into the cacophonous, malodorous atmosphere of midtown Manhattan. I told Jackie it made for a much more authentic street-level experience. Still afloat from her lunch with Web, she let that stand.

We turned south and headed for downtown, where we had one more stop to make before I dropped Jackie off at NYU Medical Center. The Eagle Exchange was almost on Wall Street, almost in the financial district, slightly out of the mainstream, which basically delineated its status within the hierarchy of American securities brokers. It was notable, though irrelevant to our pursuit, that Eagle was still an independent company, neither beholden to nor subsumed into some mega-conglomeration of competing financial services.

Alena had given us two names, one she marked with a star as her main man. Brad Maplewhite. Jackie had pinned him down with a cell call on the way in, so we had a clear shot at catching him at his desk. We just had to pilot the Grand Prix down the East Side, through Chinatown and into the backside of downtown where Eagle had its thirty-two-story office tower. Easier said than done.

"First time I ever saw New York cabbies afraid of another car," said Jackie.

"Nothing to worry about. All bark and no bite."

We found a parking garage within a block of our destination, though it took three tries before they came up with a guy who thought he could drive a full-sized car with a stick shift.

"I'll park it myself," I offered.

"No, no. Insurance. No good. We do it. No problem."

"You can ride the clutch all the way to LA," I told the nervous Middle Eastern kid who drew the straw. "Just be careful if you're backing her in. Can't see the end of the trunk. Too far away."

It seem to take more effort to get into the Eagle Exchange being what I thought were bona fide, legal, totally forthright visitors than it took to lie our way into the Sisters of Mercy home in Riverhead. A phalanx of very serious guys in dark blue uniforms and baseball hats, packing heavy ordnance inside bulging leather holsters, stood to either side of the reception desk and in front of a bank of elevators. All I could do, all I wanted to do, was repeat the name of the guy who'd agreed to see us and stand ready to be jacked up against the nearest wall and strip searched.

After we waited half an hour, the lead guard called us over and handed us ID badges, then told us to wait again until a person from up above came down to escort us to our destination, which she did soon after—a tall woman in a form-fitting blue skirt, pumps and blue blouse, very reminiscent of a stewardess outfit circa 1975. We followed the click of her heels across the marble floor to a bank of elevators with tall brass doors embossed with an Art Deco rendering of heroic-looking people gazing off toward a brilliant sun, presumably meant to represent the brokers upstairs spotting a hot stock pick. I didn't bother chatting it up with the woman in the blue dress as we ascended in the elevator. Way too scary.

She opened a pair of glass doors by swiping a pass card she wore around her neck, then left us without a word at an enormous curved reception desk—more like a hardwood fortress—behind which a stringy little woman sat on duty. She was very thin, African-American, about sixty, her jet-black hair straightened and formed into large waves that accentuated her narrow, finely featured face. As we approached she dropped both hands on the surface of the desk in front of her, palms up.

"Badges," she said.

We gave them up, Jackie to the right hand, me to the left. The woman, Eugenia Wilde according to the nameplate, pulled out the white inserts and wrote in the time, and her initials, EW, then handed them back for us to reassemble. She pointed to the one tiny couch a mile or two away at the far end of reception area.

"Someone will be out to get you," she said.

We took the trip to the couch and sat there for a few minutes in the pale utter silence of the room. The couch had side tables at either end, but no magazines or phones or pinball machines or anything else to keep you occupied, so I spent the time humming the chorus to *Night on Bald Mountain* until Jackie asked me to stop. Right about then, as predicted, someone came out to get us.

He was about my height—an inch under six feet—but shaped more like a cylinder, with narrow shoulders and broad hips. He wore a blue-and-white-striped dress shirt with starched white collar and French cuffs, and a deep burgundy-colored tie sprinkled with tiny fleurs-de-lis. His dark brown hair had receded to about the peak of his round head, though it fit well with his heavy horn-rimmed glasses and look of serious intent.

"Brad Maplewhite," he said, shaking our hands. "How was your trip in?"

He was probably somewhere in his mid- to late thirties, though with guys like Brad chronological age was irrelevant.

He repeated our names as we introduced ourselves while studying our faces, as if to prepare himself for the inevitable police sketch. He had a very small mouth, and when he smiled it was the only thing that moved.

"Not bad, considering we came all the way from the other end of Long Island," I said.

"It was fine," said Jackie, cutting me off. "We appreciate your seeing us. Hope it's not a bad time."

"Not at all," said Brad. "Let's go find a place to sit."

The office was an open plan honeycombed with cubicles furnished with walnut desk sets and divided by panels upholstered in a cushioned black-and-silver herringbone fabric ideal for sticking full of pushpins. Brad took us into a small conference room with a window, whiteboard and computer workstation, which he immediately sat in front of and fired up.

The building across the street had the unsettling proximity typical of downtown. The facade was ornately decorated, with moldings in Roman ogee, filigrees and pediments over the windows in alternating curved and triangular patterns. The summer sunlight was just bright enough to penetrate the canyon and cast a glare on the glass, providing some privacy for the Brads next door tapping away at their own computers.

"I'll just get all the relevant account history ready before we talk."

"I really appreciate it," said Jackie.

"Well," said Brad, "when the FBI is on the phone, you take notice."

I couldn't help an involuntary glance in Jackie's direction, which she returned with a quick twitch of her head.

"How's Alena?" asked Brad while waiting for the computer to respond.

"Fine," said Jackie. "She's back in town now." She told him the name of her new brokerage house. "Getting on with the next phase."

"Good. I liked working with her. Very colorful."

"More than you know," I said.

He tapped a few more times on the keyboard, then, satisfied, spun the screen around so we could see what he'd brought up.

"As I explained on the phone, I looked after the Eldridge Consultants account, which is fundamentally one account split into about twenty-three sub-accounts, designated by these numbers here at the back of the string—101, 102, 103, etc. Some have been dormant for a while, but they'd all show up here as long as the principal account is still open. I'd only send Alena statements on the active subs, suppressing the rest, so I wouldn't load her up with a lot of paperwork. Of course, now there's only the one main account, the original, plus the ECM."

"ECM?"

"Eagle Cash Manager. A place for cash to flow in and out as clients make deposits, securities are sold off, portfolios rebalanced, all of that. Plus you can use it like a normal bank account, write checks, have a debit card. Quite handy for everybody."

"Did you only deal with Alena?"

"Usually, but I spoke to Mr. Eldridge occasionally. Sometimes he'd ask me to make a trade, buy or sell, move things around, or perform some other task. All very routine stuff. But he always asked me to double back with Alena so she could keep her records up to date. He was very respectful of her capabilities."

"But you never met him."

"Face to face? No, never met either one of them face to face. Not unusual. No need. Especially with professional people like that. A dream account. Very large pool of assets, fair number of trades, though not too many, low maintenance, utterly fluent with the process. Knew what they wanted, but would listen to advice, not that they needed much."

"You're gonna miss them," said Jackie.

I think Brad raised his eyebrows a tiny bit at that, but I can't be sure.

"Once you folks unfroze the assets the sub-accounts were vacated by the consultancy." He used a ballpoint pen to tap down a column of numbers that coincided with the sub-accounts, all showing zero balances. "Though Mrs. Eldridge has opted to maintain the core account as it stands for now. Her attorney, Mr. Szwit, seems quite capable of carrying on with the management on her behalf, with my assistance, of course."

Appolonia's balance was anything but zero. I felt an uncomfortable surge of protectiveness toward her for no other reason than the scale of loss should she fall prey to incompetence or evil.

"I guess old Jonathan was pretty good with investments."

"Indeed he was. Played the tech thing like he had a time machine. Not a lot of frantic trading, just steady, even brilliant. Especially in retrospect. I'm an S&P type myself, like to stay away from big peaks and valleys. I've done okay for myself and my clients, but I wish I'd just followed this guy around. When I did, I was always happy."

Jackie had her manila envelope on her lap. She pulled out a Xeroxed page.

"Do me a favor, Brad, and look up the history on 115 and 123."

This time I was sure I saw his eyes brighten. Or maybe it was just a reflection off his glasses.

"I think I know what you're getting at," he said, spinning the monitor around and tapping at the keyboard. "Jonathan's players."

"Players?"

"That's my word. Every broker has them. Just can't stop messing with the portfolio. Day trader mentality. No patience, no adherence to a sound investment plan. No sense of diversification or dispersal of risk. Absolutely the wrong type of investor for an elegant adviser like Jonathan Eldridge. Here we are. Oh yes, I remember now. Some very unfortunate moves."

He spun the monitor back around for us.

"There're a lot of numbers here, but look at this column, then this one here. Note the red brackets."

"Ouch," said Jackie.

"You can lead 'em to water," said Brad.

"Do you know who these people are?" I asked.

He put his hands over his ears.

"Don't tell me. I don't want to know. I can't tell you how unhappy our compliance people were when this whole thing erupted. There's nothing improper or illegal about this approach. But our liability extends only to Jonathan Eldridge Consultants, since technically, everything in this account belongs to them. It gets grayer when you have knowledge of his client relationships upstream. I just don't want to know."

I remembered Alena saying that Jonathan worked hard to calibrate his level of stress to just the right pitch. It looked like he'd found in Brad Maplewhite the ideal partner for the downstream portion of the calibration.

I reached over and took the Xeroxed sheet from Jackie.

"What about the other side of the equation. Any luckiest of the lucky?"

CHRIS KNOPF

Brad worked at the screen for a while, occasionally cock- ing his head from side to side as he typed like a concert pianist. The chatter of keys was fleet enough to betray a true virtuoso. Something you wouldn't see much with men my age, most of whom had barely mastered the technological intricacies of IBM Selectrics before typewriters turned into television sets.

"Well, 102 and 105 have faired very well over the years. Especially in the months preceding the, ah, event. Quite a burst of activity, mostly funded out of the ECM."

"The cash pool."

"That's right. It's just a total figure here. You'll have to see Alena for the backup."

Jackie tried to read the sheet, squinting her good eye.

"Who are they?" she asked.

"Hey Brad, stick your fingers in your ears," I said, which he did with eyes shut and elbows held high. I leaned over to whisper in Jackie's ear just to be sure. A distant part of me hoped someone from his office would pick that moment to poke his head in the conference room.

"Neville St. Clair and Hugh Boone."

"All the sub-accounts have been emptied out," said Jackie. "Including 102 and 105?"

"At Alena's instructions," said Brad, unblocking his ears again. "You saw the columns."

If Brad was an S&P type, I was a passbook savings type. I hated everything relating to investments and money man- agement, and all that crap. Abby had tried to take it over, probably alarmed by my irritability over the subject, but I hadn't let her. I knew a guy who ran an investment desk for a bank in Stamford who was honest and easygoing enough to put whatever I came up with for retirement into the most conservative instruments he could find. Without argument

290

or reproach. I think in this way Abby was right about my working-class upbringing, where the distrust of banks and brokers, and anyone else who used the word "finance" when he meant "money," ran deep. Money we knew about. You got it when you worked your ass off and then spent every dime of it just getting by. All that talk about investments and portfolios was just a dangerous abstraction.

"How did it work?" I asked him. "You wrote a bunch of checks?"

"More or less. Alena did. We could have transferred each bundle of assets to another account or brokerage house if they'd been in the clients' names, but as you know, they weren't. So we sold everything and deposited the proceeds into the ECM, from which Alena drew the appropriate disbursements. Probably had some unpleasant tax implications for some, but given that their adviser had been blown to Kingdom Come, it wouldn't seem politic to carp."

"So you could identify individual investors by the names on the checks drawn against the ECM."

Brad thought about it a moment.

"I suppose you could. Of course. Not that I would. But somewhere here there's a scan of every one of those checks. Lord knows how you'd find it. You don't know the word 'labyrinthine' until you've dealt with our internal administration."

Jackie started to say something, but I put my hand on her leg to stop her. I needed a second of quiet. I closed my eyes and saw a miniature version of a bank check, a smudged-looking photostat, festooned with stamps and inked-in notations. I'd seen one once when someone had stolen my checkbook and used it to buy a set of tires. They'd copied the front and back, so you could see the endorsement was clearly a fake, not even an attempt at forgery.

"Do you have the addresses and phone numbers for all these clients?" I asked Jackie, holding up the sheet.

"Not here. In my computer with the stuff Alena gave me. But I'm sure she still has all that. I could give her a call. Nobody's given much thought to the non-hostiles. Actually none. Why are we now?"

"I feel like I know those guys. Neville and Hugh."

"You must have played darts with them at the pub."

"Yeah. Sound like Brits."

"The Oppressors."

"Don't start getting tribal."

"I'll confirm with Alena."

Brad looked like he was about to put his fingers back in his ears, so I got him back in our conversation.

"So Gabe Szwit's doing okay for Appolonia. Jonathan's wife. Far as you know."

"Yes, seems quite competent. We did some rebalancing last month. He had a plan, but was interested in what I had to say. Asked some very insightful questions. Felt like old times, though without Miss Zapata's charm. That I'll miss."

I looked for the first time to see if he had a wedding ring, which he did. Too bad. Would be another excellent test of the theorem that opposites attract.

It looked like Jackie had learned enough to start feeling paranoid again, so I took the hint and stood up, reaching out my hand to Brad. Jackie joined me.

"Thanks for all your time and information," she said "Very good of you."

The faintest suggestion of pleasure flickered across his face.

"Not at all. I like to be of help. We're basically a service organization here, so I guess it's in the DNA," he said, warmly, and I believed him.

It was pleasant to have him walk us all the way down to the lobby and help Eugenia sign us out. He paid her a crisp little compliment, something like, "Don't you look put together today, Eugenia," which caused her to toss back a bountiful smile. I thought to myself, there isn't enough genius in the world to fully divine the social subtexts of a modern American corporation. Lord knows I never could.

It was still summer when we got out to the street, only now the air was palpable, a fine concoction of heat, humidity and fetid reek of a style available exclusively on the midsummer streets of New York City.

"This clinches it," I said. "I'm spending the rest of the summer in the Hamptons."

"Pretty cruel, given where I'm going."

"Not at all. NYU's like a resort."

"That's why I picked it."

"Oh, not because they have special deals for FBI agents? Or lawyers following their disbarment for impersonating FBI agents?"

She grimaced.

"I called Brad on my cell phone last week when I was alone in Web's office. Told him to call me back on Web's land line, so he heard 'Welcome to the Nassau County office of the Federal Bureau of Investigation. If you know your party's extension, dial it now, yadda, yadda.' So technically, I never said I was with the FBI. I was going to straighten him out today, but it didn't actually quite come up, not directly, and it was going so well, I never got around to it."

"Just hope Brad and Maryanne never end up sitting together on an airplane."

It was a relatively short drive from the parking garage back up the East Side and over to First Avenue. Jackie didn't seem in the mood to talk, and that was okay with me. I needed a chance to think, something a lot of chatter wouldn't have helped. I offered to park and walk her in, but she wouldn't let me.

"Don't try babying me," she said, opening the car door and dragging her bags out of the backseat. "You won't be any good at it."

"Say, Jackie, what're the chances you can get on a computer before they operate on you?"

She closed the door and leaned in the open window.

"I don't know. Given what I've done today, I might as well just steal one."

"Don't move for a second," I said, though I made her wait for almost five minutes while I wrote out some stuff on a piece of notepaper and handed it to her. "You said you could find out anything on the Internet. See if you can answer those questions."

After reading it, she folded the paper and stuck it in her shirt pocket.

"Census data is all online. You can actually look at scans of the forms the census workers fill out. Yearbooks, I don't know. Depends on the school, but I'm guessing they only started putting that stuff online in the last five years or so. Most colleges have alumni sites. I could try that. I was already going to check into Neville and Hugh. It would help if I knew what you were getting at," she said, "though if past experience is any guide, you aren't about to tell me."

"Just see what you can find out."

"Right, and then what. You're the last person on the planet who doesn't have a computer, cell phone or answering machine. If I don't catch you at home, that's it."

"Give me the paper back."

I wrote down a phone number and email address.

"This is my daughter. Call her and ask her if you can email everything you get—I'd like to see any original documents— and have her print it out and overnight it to my house."

"Why don't you ask her yourself?"

"She'll do it as a favor to you. Better than me asking directly."

"I can't believe I'm going into the hospital for life-defining surgery and you give me a ridiculous assignment."

"You said not to baby you."

She shook her head, stuffed the paper back in her pocket and collected her bags off the sidewalk. I committed myself to at least watching her till she got through the entrance, so I saw her when she turned around and looked back. I was too far away to clearly see her expression, which had something sadly complicated going on, but I heard her say, "You do the best you can, Sam," and then something else, but by now she was too far away and I missed it as she disappeared through the entrance to the hospital.

TWENTY-FIVE

THE MIDTOWN TUNNEL was only a few blocks away so I was out of Manhattan in a few minutes, heading east. There was one more stop I had in mind, one I hadn't shared with Jackie. I'd written the address down on the top of a map of Long Island I kept stored in the console, now on the passenger seat to help me plot my course.

General Resource Recovery was located near Massapequa, a town just above the south shore of the Island. Their ad in Thomas Register promised fair prices for scrap metal of all kinds, and an assortment of high-quality, contaminant-free recycled material. There was a phone number, so I could have called ahead, but I knew Ivor Fleming was always delighted by a surprise visit.

It was getting late in the afternoon, so I hustled along as fast as the traffic on the Long Island Expressway and Wantagh Parkway would let me. I made it there by quarter to four, relieved to see an open parking lot instead of a tall chainlink fence and guard hut. A plain one-story office block fronted the lot. Behind and above you could see an elevated transport system for lifting and sorting a mountain of tangled, rusty red scrap. Somewhere out of sight a furnace was cooking up the goodies, separating elements and alloys, oxidizing and vaporizing trace materials and issuing ingots, rods and pellets of gleaming semi-molten steel.

I located the big black pickup as I approached the entrance. It was close in, but not in a reserved spot, of which there were only two. The one with the bulky black Mercedes had a sign that said, "Don't even think of parking here."

Passing through the heavy wooden entrance doors, only partly assisted by pneumatic door openers, I saw in my mind's eye a coffee-table book—*Reception Areas of Greater New York*. I could dedicate it to all the receptionists and security guards, underpaid and overlooked, who so ably administer one of the great pivot points of American commerce. Some, like Eugenia Wilde, at the helm of a stout slab of hardwood furniture. Others, like Ivor's two paunchy schlubs, relegated to a folding card table set up in a corner just inside the front door. Each guard had a uniform, a sign-in book, a Smith & Wesson, a chair and a walkie-talkie. Probably mandated by the union. There was a single black phone in the middle of the table.

I was about to approach the guards when I noticed the foyer expanded out from the entrance into a large room, at the opposite end of which was another set of double doors, and on the walls to either side a pair of huge murals. The first thing I thought of was heroic industrialism, like in 1930s Soviet art, with heavily muscled men and women, in squared-off profile, toiling with backs straight, eyes forward. But that wasn't quite it. The paintings had an abstract quality, an imprecision of form and composition that almost suggested a parody of their presumed subject. But not quite. The factories in the background were partly made of boxes and smoke stacks, but also office towers, redwoods and ancient campaniles. The colors were indescribable except to say they were dark and light, familiar and entirely out of context. But not a mishmash—there was a strong organizing sense underlying both the paintings that reminded me of Picasso. Or maybe Hieronymus Bosch.

I wished Allison was there to explain to me what I was looking at. Or better yet, the guy who painted them. Butch Ellington.

"Hey, Buddy. Over here," said one of the guards.

"Sorry," I said, walking back to their table. "Caught me by surprise."

"You get used to it. Who you here to see?"

"Ivor Fleming."

They simultaneously looked down at their respective sign-in books.

"You got an appointment? What's your name?"

"Sam Acquillo. I don't have an appointment, but he'll see me."

"Yeah, right. No appointment, no see."

They both seemed amused by the idea.

"Okay, but what if you're wrong. What if he would've seen me but you didn't let him know I was here. How would that go over?"

"There're worse things than getting fired. So if you don't mind," he said, waving me toward the door.

"How about Ike or Connie. They here?"

The mood at the guard desk took a quick turn to circumspection.

"Maybe. You got an appointment with them?"

"No. But you can probably tell them I'm here, and I guarantee they'll be out to say hello. Then, if they think Mr. Fleming'll see me, you're in the clear. How 'bout it?"

One of the two was sold enough to pick up the phone and call somebody, telling them to go find Ike and Connie and have them call the reception desk. While we waited I walked over to get another look at the murals.

One of the interesting things was the way certain images within the paintings had their own logic, telling their own little story, yet when you stood back they would collectively resolve into another coherent representation. I wondered how many levels of articulated imagery could be contained within a single work of art, like a fractal, revealing themselves layer after layer as you dove down into the painting.

Thus lost in thought, I didn't realize my two buddies were out there with me until I heard Ike clear his throat.

You couldn't say they were looking their best. Connie's nose was still swollen, maybe permanently, and Ike's lip was probably a week or two shy of full recovery.

"Hey, fellas, how's it going?"

I stuck out my hand to shake, causing them both to back up a step.

"Come on. I thought we'd cleared all that up."

"What're you doing here?" asked Ike.

"I want to see Mr. Fleming."

"And I want to see Heather Locklear in a bikini. Not happening anytime soon."

"You can be overprotective, you know, Ike. I think that's what you've been doing here."

"That's the job, asshole. Protection."

The two guards overheard the asshole part and walked over with their hands resting on their holsters. Ike smiled at me.

"You could probably use a little yourself right now," he added.

"Call up Ivor and tell him I'm out here. I've just got one thing to ask him. If he tells me to beat it, I'll beat it. And you'll never see me again."

"Not breathing," said Connie.

I pointed at him, but kept my eyes on Ike. "What'd I say about that stuff?"

Ike jerked his head at Connie and told him to back off, which he did. I walked over to the guard desk and sat down in one of their chairs.

"Go ahead, give him a call. I'll be right here."

Ike nodded at the guards, one of whom came over and made the call.

"Lois, this is Max at the front desk. I'm with Ike and Connie and we got a guy named Acquillo who's here to see Mr. Fleming. Doesn't have an appointment, but Ike thinks Mr. Fleming might want to see him anyway. Don't bother him if he's really busy with something." He paused, listening. "Okay, then I guess why not ask him. You can call me back."

From where I sat I had a good view of the mural on the right hand wall. I determined it was painted on a very smooth surface, but not directly on the wall, though that was the impression encouraged by the way it was hung. Clever. Well thought out, like everything Butch Ellington did.

The phone rang. Ike picked it up.

"He said to come on back. Let's go, hero," he said to me, ushering me into the lead, with him and Connie a close step behind. We went through the double doors and into a wide room filled with cubicles that looked a lot more like Ross's squad room than Brad Maplewhite's brokerage house. A few people looked up at us as we walked down the passageways, though not overtly. I suspected in Ivor's shop the concept of keeping your head down had some tangibility.

Ivor's office was in the corner of the open office area distinguished by walls paneled in the kind of luan ply that was popular in the fifties and sixties. Back then you could have bought dimensional mahogany for about two cents a board foot, but why do that when luan looks just as good?

A frump of a middle-aged woman, who had to be Lois, got up from her desk and planted herself just outside the office door.

"You're Mr. Acquillo," she said to me.

"I am."

"Just wait here a moment. He wants to see you alone," she said, with a firm look at Ike and Connie. It didn't seem to bother them. When she came back out to show me in, I could see why. At the far side of the room was a long leather couch, covered partway with a well-worn sheepskin mat that Cleo had deftly shaped into a comfortable bed. Ivor was at the other end behind a big wooden desk of the same vintage and aesthetic as the paneling. The walls, shelves and side tables were filled with golf memorabilia, some clearly going back decades, like a black-and-white photo of young Jack Nicklaus posing with skinny young Ivor Fleming. The present Ivor slumped down in a heavily padded green leather chair, swiveling slowly back and forth like a kid checking out his dad's office furniture.

I ignored Cleo, but sat down as swiftly as I could in one of the hot seats directly in front of the desk. Lois silently shut the door.

"You got balls, I'll give you that," said Ivor, by way of a greeting.

"More curiosity than courage, if you want to know the truth."

"I'm curious about something myself," he said. "Otherwise you wouldn't be sitting here."

"Okay."

"My boys said they were jumped by a bunch of guys they never seen before. Pulled some kind of kung fu on 'em. What do you think?"

"Must've been something like that. Nobody else would take on a pair of hard cases like Ike and Connie."

"Yeah. Sure. Nothing to do with you, then. I told them to keep an eye on you. They're not exactly Serpico when it comes to undercover work. You coulda seen 'em and called in somebody."

"Nope. Wouldn't know how, even if I was stupid enough to show that kind of disrespect to you."

He liked that. It didn't show, but I'd known a lot of Ivors over the years. They always liked that kind of thing. He slid up a little taller in his chair and pulled himself over to the desk.

"So what's with the investment deal," he asked me. "You still trying to peddle that shit?"

I glanced over at Cleo. She looked like she was asleep on the couch. A good sign.

"Doesn't look good," I told him. "Your original assessment was basically accurate. Nothing much to sell, even though most of his clients got a pretty decent return on their investment. More than decent."

That made him unhappy again. Only this time not at me.

"What a putz. I don't know why I listen to these guys."

"So he made all the calls. I mean, you followed his advice."

"What the fuck else you pay him for?"

"Some people like to lead the charge with their brokers. Like to get in the game. Like you said, a trip to the casino without the chips and slots."

"You want to know about steel? You come to me. There's nothin' I don't know about how to make it, salvage it, extract it and sell it. Then get it back, chew it up and sell it all over again. This is what I know about. Investments? I don't know shit about that stuff."

I couldn't admit it right then, but I sympathized with him. I didn't know shit about that stuff either.

"So Jonathan told you to get into art."

Ivor grinned a little at that.

"That was the only call that worked out. Those things over there on the wall? Worth five times what I paid for them."

They might have been Chagalls, or painted by somebody trying to look like Chagall. No factories or heroic workers. Rather some spindly impressionistic flowers, butterflies and starscapes. Fit right into the scrap-metal ambience of General Resource Recovery.

"Same deal?" I asked Ivor. "Jonathan told you which artists to buy?"

"Yeah. Got a bunch of stuff. All've gone up, last I looked."

"Including the big Ellingtons."

"Shit, yeah. Maybe ten times. Got 'em on the cheap. His own fault, douche bag."

"Jonathan?"

"Nah, the artist. Ellington. Professional wingnut. I'd only paid him about two-thirds of what he asked for before he got 'em hung in the reception area. I just asked him to paint some more clothes on the girls. Too much tit. Can embarrass people. He wouldn't do it, so I didn't pay him the balance. Said he'd sue me. Showed up here with this little bottle-eyed shit of a lawyer. Wouldn't let 'em in the building. Told him if he wanted the pictures back, I'd take 'em down myself. Got a factory over there full of guys who know how to use a crowbar."

That really made him happy. The happiest I'd ever seen him.

"You sure got him where you wanted him," I said.

"Yeah. I sure did. Douche bag."

I looked over at Cleo again, hoping Dobermans couldn't read minds. She looked back at me, now awake, with a blank, noncommittal stare.

"Okay," I said to Ivor. "I'm sorry again for bothering you. I really mean it this time."

I jerked my head over at Cleo.

"Can I stand up?"

"Sure. Just keep your hands out where she can see them."

I stood up and offered to shake, carefully. He took my hand.

"So that's it?" he asked. "I thought you had a question for me."

He was right. I'd lost my train of thought. Often happens when the talk turns to modern art.

"I do. I just wanted to know how you discovered Jonathan Eldridge. Who introduced you in the first place?"

"She didn't tell you? Joyce Whithers. Sold Eldridge pretty hard. I figured that's how you got on to me. Used to play cards with her. Still do, couple times a year."

"I thought her husband was the card player."

"Nah, the old lady had the brains and balls in that family. It was her game. She just brought him in so there'd be somebody around to get her a Scotch on the rocks and light her cigarettes. Smart broad. Getting me mixed up with that putz was the only thing she ever screwed me up on."

"Thanks. That's really all I wanted to know."

"Next time you got a question like that, you can try picking up the telephone. Number's in the book."

"Sorry. You're right. I will. I appreciate it," I said, making motions to leave. Then I thought of something.

"I'd really appreciate it if you cleared me with Ike and Connie. I don't want any trouble."

He waved that off.

"Nobody's lookin' for trouble," he said, although with less sincerity than I'd hoped for.

Cleo stayed put on the couch, but as I passed by she pulled back her ears and wagged her tail. When Ivor opened the door Ike and Connie could see me scratching the top of her head and cooing softly in her ear.

"Tu eres una niña hermosa. Estoy pensando que tu debes morder a esos hombres allí en el vestíbulo."

"Cute pup," I said to them as I fell into the parade back to the reception area.

———

I had an escort all the way from Ivor's scrap-metal plant to the reaches of Suffolk County. A full-sized black pickup with a clattery diesel engine. They managed to keep several car lengths between us regardless of traffic or speed limits, so every time I thought they'd abandoned the tail they showed up again. I didn't know if this was meant to convey a message, or just a signal, or even who was doing the signaling. Ivor seemed willing to let it go, but he might have been playing me the whole time. Or, Ike and Connie might have been taking a little independent initiative. Hard to tell. But it did interfere with my concentration, which was annoying, since right then I needed every bit of concentration I could muster.

I'd bypassed the traffic lights along the first leg of Sunrise Highway by going north and picking up the Southern State. From there I dropped down to Route 27 where they'd made it into a four-lane road. It was filled with cars and trucks, and local people trying to get back home to catch a little daylight savings relaxation in the outdoor furniture out on the pressure-treated deck. With a different car I might have been able to get some distance on the pickup by weaving my way through the heavy traffic, but the Grand Prix wasn't exactly engineered for nimble lane changes.

It was, however, born, raised and modified to accelerate very quickly in a straight line, hurtling its impossible mass up to a cruising speed you wouldn't want to experience in any kind of pickup truck.

I'd just passed the exit for Shirley, Butch's beloved home-town, when I noticed Ike and Connie were boxed in behind a brace of compact Japanese sedans driving side by side in tight formation. In front of me Route 27 was clear of significant traffic, a set of parallel concrete ribbons dissecting the pine barrens and disappearing into the ocean haze hanging above the South Fork.

I rolled up the windows and pushed in the clutch. I slid the Hurst shifter into third gear, brought up the RPMs, then popped out the clutch while simultaneously sticking the accelerator to the floor mat. With all four barrels opened wide, the 428-cubic-inch V8 bellowed under the hood. Just shy of the red line, I put it back into fourth, but kept the throttle open and gripped the steering wheel with both hands as the speed climbed up over a hundred miles an hour.

I started to run through a mental checklist of all the equipment failures likely triggered by the sudden torque loads and excess velocity, but quickly gave it up. Too many to count, and it wasn't going to stop me anyway.

I looked in the rearview as the speedometer pegged at 120 and the tack was flirting again with the red line. No sign of black pickups or law enforcement. I'd felt some vibrations in the suspension system as the big car accelerated up to its top end, but now everything was settled down, a tribute to Butch's skill with the wheel balancer.

I could sense the scream of the big block engine, but I couldn't hear it above the wind noise. Reality distorts a lot when you move past a hundred miles an hour. It goes by so quickly it loses definition, and takes on a jittery, smeared quality. I could feel alarm rising up in my rational brain, which was involuntarily processing the possible consequences of losing control, which at this speed could happen from nicking even the tiniest road hazard. My solution was to ignore my rational brain and keep the accelerator on the floor.

A green exit sign for Center Moriches flashed by. I eased back on the throttle until the speedometer needle came off the peg and started to move counterclockwise. A white step van appeared in the right lanc. I gave him as wide a berth as I could in case he hadn't seen me and accidentally drifted into my lane. It must have been frightening to have a gray-brown '67 Grand Prix roar by your door at 120 miles an hour. It was frightening for me to see how quickly he dropped back in my rearview. I eased up more on the accelerator, watching the speedometer mark the drop in tens—100, to 90, to 80. The Center Moriches exit ramp was suddenly there, so I had to downshift while applying steady pressure to the brakes, the most easily taxed system onboard the Grand Prix, given its extravagance of heavy-gauge sheet metal, the kind Ivor could sell to Honda to remake into a fleet of Civics.

I was almost within legal limits when I took the bend of the exit ramp. The smell of partially oxidized fuel wafted up behind me as I slowed to a halt, but I expected that from the inefficiency of rapid deceleration. At the stop sign I checked all the gauges, including oil and water temp, which looked normal. I shifted into first, pushed the buttons to lower the windows and lit a cigarette.

"Beverly Hillbillies indeed," I said aloud, feeling warmly about my preposterous car, the most puzzling legacy from my father, and the only one not encumbered by complex and hopelessly entangled associations.

———

I reached the tip of Oak Point as the last of the sunset had collapsed into a thin pink strip along the horizon. When I stopped at the mailbox Eddie came zinging over from Amanda's house, barking and spinning around in circles. He seemed honestly glad to see me, or maybe was just hedging his bets.

After filling my aluminum cocktail tumbler with Absolut and crushed ice, I shook off the wrinkled khakis and oxford-cloth-shirt and went directly to the outdoor shower. There was a lot of day to wash off. It took half the tumbler and most of the hot water to even start the job. I could pound nails and set roof rafters for twelve hours and not be half as tired. It's the mental fatigue that gets you, that clogs up the neural pathways and packs cotton behind your eyes. Proving empirically that the worst of weariness is a state of mind.

I put on a pair of clean blue jeans and a cotton shirt so threadbare you could hole it with a puff of breath and called Amanda on my rotary dial phone.

"You're back."

"How'd you like to come over and rot with me in the Adirondacks?"

"An original idea."

"An invitation. Direct and unambiguous."

"I have wine and a bowl of cherries."

"I'll be in the front yard. If I'm asleep when you get there, don't hit me on the head."

Walking barefoot across the lawn, cool and wet from the evening mist rolling in off the bay, I started feeling better.

The half tumbler of vodka had done its part, but the greater salve was being back in the company of the Little Peconic, back from those other places that weren't livable for me anymore. As it often does, the prevailing south-southwesterly had shifted all the way west, kicking up a short chop and fluttering the emerging white petals on the grandiflora. It was a dryer wind, for reasons unknown. I wished I knew more about the underlying forces that controlled the breeze crisscrossing the bay every day, or how the patterns of the prevailing winds changed with the seasons. But not that much. It was enough to keep track and stay alert for anomalies, or simply mark the familiar shifts, gusts and lulls.

"Big day, I take it," said Amanda, dropping down into the other Adirondack. Also barefoot, she wore a dress with a loud tropical print that looked two sizes too big for her. Her hair was wet, like mine, as if she'd also just taken a shower. She'd brushed it straight back so I could see the full shape of her face in the fading twilight, her prominent cheekbones and green eyes and the reddish brown of her skin, the color of a glass of fine cognac.

"It's nice to see you," I said.

She looked surprised.

"You, too. What's the occasion?"

"For what?"

"Such friendliness."

"I'm always nice."

"No, you're not. Not in the ordinary way."

"I'm not?"

"Unless you're avoiding. Is that what you're doing? You don't want to talk about the day."

"I don't. Not now. I need time to think a little. But it's still nice to see you."

Two Time

"Okay."

We sat quietly sipping our drinks and watching the evening descend into darkness, with the moon taking over, dipping the tips of the little bay waves in light blue iridescence.

"Say, Amanda."

"Yes, Sam."

"If you ever catch me expressing anything like willful pride in my ability to perceive reality, to extract the true thing even when it's cleverly hidden from view, I want you to remind me of today."

"I will if you tell me what happened."

"What is it, July 30? Just say to me, 'remember July 30.'"

"So this isn't avoidance. It's humility."

"That's right. Maybe with a little awe mixed in."

"Okay. You're humbled and awestruck. While you're at it, tag on abstruse."

I was able to deflect further questions by suggesting we go skinny-dipping.

"Your hair's already wet," I said, getting up and jumping down off the breakwater, unbuttoning my shirt and waving for her to join me.

"Is it dark enough?" she asked, as she sat down on the top of the breakwater before sliding off into the sand.

"Nobody on the point but you and me. Might as well own the whole world."

Since the wind was coming out of the west I knew the water would be warm. I had a theory that the wind scooped up the sun-warmed water from the surface of the shallow Great Peconic, then slid it over here, where it was captured and pooled against Jessup's Neck. A ridiculous notion, I'm sure, but I didn't care. There was nobody around to tell me it wasn't true. There was only Amanda, slender and supple, laughing naked in my arms after we'd dashed across the

311

painfully knobby pebble beach and dove recklessly into the
water, breaking through the surface into the fresh moon-
light. Humbled, or awed, or simply grateful and surprised, it
was easy at that moment to let all forms of thought dissolve
into the sacred waters of the Little Peconic Bay, carrying
away my manifold fears and indecisions, my uncertainties
and confusion.

There'd be time enough to gather all that up again tomorrow.

TWENTY-SIX

LIKE JONATHAN ELDRIDGE'S, Gabe Szwit's office was above a storefront. The only difference being the view, which for Gabe included the east end of Main Street and halfway down Job's Lane in Southampton Village. And the store was a little different, since it sold $10,000-a-whack couture instead of $3.95 meatball grinders, unless you wanted a salad, which would add another $1.85.

It was early and few people were on the street. The shops wouldn't open until about ten, so the sidewalks were mostly given over to early risers grabbing the *Times* at the cheese place, or couples walking their his-and-hers dogs down to the corner for breakfast and coffee. The light was diffused by the morning mist, and the angle of the sun as it tried to clear the trees and rooftops of the shops, offices and restaurants that lined the street.

As far as I could tell, you reached the office by an outside run of stairs at the back of the building, which also had a small private parking lot. I had to assume Gabe would come in this way, though I didn't know for sure, or even if he would show up for work that day. For all I knew, he only worked every other day. Or just kept the office for show, while spending the days cruising in his Jag and hanging out with grief-stricken widows.

I had the biggest size cup of coffee you could get from the place on the corner, and a fresh pack of cigarettes. WLIU promised to play jazz all morning, and the Grand Prix was the closest thing you could have to a rolling living room, so the wait didn't promise to be that hard.

Still, after about three hours I was ready for Gabe to make an appearance. I could usually busy myself noodling out construction plans for the addition, or writing postcards to Allison, or casting about for ways to divert my mind from the litany of worries and regrets it would chew on if left to its own devices. It gets harder when all you're looking at is the back end of a building, a Dumpster and a flight of rickety wooden stairs.

I gave myself to twelve noon, which is about the time Gabe pulled his Jag into the reserved parking lot, got out and locked the car, then plodded up the stairs, wearing a tan summer suit, his attaché held to his chest like a heavy bag of groceries. I waited until he was through the door at the top of the stairs before following him. The door had a translucent pane of glass in the top panel. It let in light, but you couldn't see through it. I tried the doorknob, but it was locked. I recognized the door hardware—you could open it with a key, and it would still lock behind you. Made sense for Gabe Szwit.

I bumped the door with my shoulder to test its mettle. Its mettle was more than up to the task, so I went back down to the Grand Prix and got my little three-pound sledge and a cat's paw that had a hardened wedge at the other end. I wrapped a piece of terry cloth around the cat's paw, stuck the wedge in the door next to the doorknob and gave it a hearty smack.

The door gave it up on the second hit, swinging into a dark passageway that led to another door with a translucent panel. As I walked down the hall the inside door swung open and Gabe was standing there, his suit coat off and mouth agape.

"Oh dear God," he said, looking at the sledge in my hand.

I came at him quickly, holding the hammer at eye level.

"Shut up and get back in there."

He almost leaped back into the office as I followed him, shutting the door and throwing the deadbolt. We were in a tiny waiting room and Gabe was trying to punch a number into a black office phone that was on a side table next to a stack of *Fortune* magazines. I swung my right arm and brought the sledge straight down into the middle of the phone. Gabe made some kind of groaning animal sound in his throat and cringed back against the wall, staring stupidly at the phone receiver in his hand, now dangling a disconnected cord. I used the hammer to wave him through the next door.

"Come on, keep going."

He went through and I followed him. It was a standard lawyer's office—sturdy walnut-veneered desk in the center of the room, shelves lined with law books, expensive carpet, Currier & Ives prints on the wall and the faint smell of cigars. There were two Hitchcock chairs in front of the desk with the seal of his alma mater, Boston University, stamped on the backrests. A desktop computer was on a work surface perpendicular to the desk, and a large credenza lined the wall behind, the surface of which was decorated with a pair of small aquariums. To the left, under a large bay window, was a red chesterfield. I pointed to it.

"Sit over there."

"Have you lost your mind?" he asked.

"Yes. I have. You're going to help me get it back."

He kept his eyes on me as he backed into the couch and sat down. His face, usually tinted a faint green, had gone solid white.

"You're going to jail," he said as he sat down.

I pulled over one of the Hitchcock chairs.

"One of us is."

He looked like he didn't know whether to scream, clam up or pass out.

"You mind if I smoke?"

"Yes, I do."

I took out a cigarette and lit it, leaning back in the Hitchcock and snatching a piece of pottery off the bookshelf to use as an ashtray.

"That's a McCoy," he said. "I'm calling the police."

"Go ahead. While you're doing that, I'll call Appolonia."

He stayed put on the couch, fear and fury in his eyes.

"What do you want?" he asked.

"To talk a minute."

"You expect me to talk to you when you're threatening me with a cudgel?"

I looked at the hammer.

"It's a three-pound sledge. Here. You can have it."

I tossed it in his lap. Half standing, he grabbed it with both hands and flung it to other side of the couch, as if I'd just popped it out of a kiln.

"Settle down," I told him. "I just want to talk."

"You could have made an appointment."

"I just did. Does Appolonia know?"

"Know what?"

"Any of it."

"I don't know what you mean."

"You lied about Butch Ellington. You said you never met him. You've known him all along."

He sat a little straighter on the couch as he regained some of his professional poise.

"Who I know, or don't know, is my concern."

"Fair enough. I'll just fill in the blanks myself and check it out directly with Appolonia."

He didn't like that.

"She loathes her brother-in-law," he said. "I didn't want her trust in me clouded by that association."

"Nothing like a big lie to build trust."

"Jonathan never found it necessary to reveal such a trivial thing. I presumed that was his wish and have merely honored it. And no one cared more about Appolonia's well-being than him."

"How about Belinda? She in on it, too?"

"Heavens no. And what difference could it possibly make? Is that all this is about? You break into my office, threaten and assault me, simply because I've preserved a client confidence?"

"Watch the allegations, Gabe. If I'm going down for assault anyway, I might as well bash you on the head and make it worth it."

Whatever color had found its way back into his face drained off again.

"And all that legal crap doesn't work with me. Part of my engineering training."

"Crap?"

"Yeah, you're already making your case. Won't work with Appolonia either since it won't change the fact you're hiding your relationship with Butch. Which I can prove, so don't waste our time practicing jury summations. You're busted. Concentrate on what you want to do about it."

"Do about it?" he asked, his voice getting hoarse, as if his throat was starting to constrict.

"Answer my questions or I'm leaving now and heading directly to Appolonia's."

"If I do, will you leave her alone?"

"You've know Butch since college. BU. Maybe before. When did you meet Jonathan?"

He looked away.

"About the same time."

"Butch is the one who had the mother committed. Needed you for the legalities. Still does."

"The parents split up when they were young. Butch lived with the mother, so he knew how troubled she was, how she'd never function safely on her own. That she belonged where she is now. Jonathan didn't like it, but he acquiesced. Jonathan hardly knew her. He was raised by his father. Didn't know enough to contest the decision. But he liked me administering the details. Didn't trust Butch to do it properly."

"Who pays the bills?" I asked.

"The bills?"

"Who pays the Sisters of Mercy?"

He looked reluctant to answer the question, thinking about it longer than he should have.

"Arthur. Butch. He always sent the checks. I didn't question it. No need."

"No. I suppose not. As long as she was looked after. Butch was more her kid, if you think about it. Whatever happened to Arthur Senior?"

"Their father? I don't know."

"The cops think he's dead."

"Then I suppose he is. They should know."

"Where'd they live, Jonathan and his father?"

Gabe finally let himself sit back in the sofa, looking a little less braced for an imminent blow.

"What difference does it make?" he asked.

"I don't know. Just curious."

"I think mostly around Riverhead and the North Fork. The father was an accountant. Commuted to somewhere up island. Put in long hours. Jonathan was on his own a lot. Made him very self-reliant, he claimed. Toughened him up. Although you probably know that already. You seem to know a lot."

"I know my name is Sam and I live in a house with a dog."

"That's really about all you know," said Gabe, suddenly getting up a head of steam. "You're just fishing. Trying to bully everything out of me. It's pathetic."

"Did Jonathan know you were in love with his wife?"

That got his color back. Should've thanked me for asking him.

"Don't be ridiculous."

"Come on, Gabe, you think it's that hard to tell? He must've seen it, too."

"I'm not listening to this."

"Probably part of his calculation. He knew you'd do anything to protect her, keep her safe and secure. He'd known you for years. Knew you were a good administrator, could handle things. He spent a lot of time on the road. Needed a professional go-to guy back at the ranch. Gave you a lot of face time with Appolonia. Enough to get in deeper and deeper. But also enough to know you hadn't a prayer of getting what you really wanted. She was completely devoted to Jonathan and he knew it. Didn't have to worry. Must've made you feel extra special, if you ever let yourself think about it."

Gabe was probably a pretty good lawyer. Had the poker face for it. But if you shook him up a little and looked closely, you could see it written into his countenance. The frustration and anger. Bitterness and resentment, or maybe desperation. The curse of an intelligent man who wanted to live with a delusion, but his intelligence wouldn't let him.

"Must be nice now to have her all to yourself," I said.

"Kind of."

He looked about to answer that, but stopped himself. Instead he just stared, occasionally darting his eyes over toward the phone on his desk.

"Nothing's really changed," I said. "You still got plenty of face time, but you're no closer to the prize. Was it worth it?"

"You're not suggesting?"

"Should I be?"

He actually smiled and wagged a finger at me.

"Now you're really overreaching, Mr. Acquillo."

"How come you didn't sue Ivor Fleming after he stiffed Butch? You had a good case. Did you work out a deal?"

"Now who's making false allegations? Not going to work," he said.

"We could try it out on Ross Semple. See what he thinks."

What was left of Gabe's smile faded away.

"He'll want to talk to Appolonia," he said. "You promised to leave her out of it."

"I didn't, but I will. For now."

I stood up and picked my sledge up off the couch, making him blanch again.

"Not leaving it here," I said. "Might need it again."

"It won't do you any good. You're a fool if you think it will."

"What do you mean?"

He pointed at me.

"That's what I mean. You have no idea what you're doing. And no amount of brutality will change that."

Looking down on him sitting in the couch he looked small, but defiant, assuming a posture he'd likely learned in childhood, fighting with his parents over finishing his carrots and peas. I'd pushed him as far as he could be pushed, at least for now. I knew that about smaller, physically weaker men, especially the smart ones, who'd had a lot trouble in the schoolyard. They usually had a reservoir of indignation, compensated for by a panoply of intellectual weaponry, not the least being a particularly vicious form of subterfuge. A penchant for the sneak attack, the shiv in the back.

"You should repair my door," he said. "But I'd prefer if you didn't come back again."

I left him in his office, alone again to think thoughts I wished I could read, though only from a safe distance.

TWENTY-SEVEN

ISABELLA TOLD ME over the intercom speaker at the front gate that Burton was over at the Gracefield Tennis Club having lunch. She said if I wanted to talk to him I'd have to wait till he got back, since non-members weren't allowed to say the word "Gracefield" much less eat lunch there.

"Maybe I'll join," I said.

"You got the hundred thousand a year and proof your ancestors come over on the Mayflower, you maybe got a chance."

"If they'd take me I wouldn't want to join," I said, invoking Groucho.

"Lucky for you. Save you a hundred grand."

I went over there anyway and drove right up the long entrance. To either side were grass courts on which lithe figures in white cotton played tennis under the hot sun while generating no noticeable sweat. I thought, wow, that is some breeding.

I found a parking space where I could squeeze the Grand Prix between two full-sized luxury SUVs. I felt like I was in a black canyon. The reflections in the black side panels were bright enough to use as a mirror, which I did to tuck in my shirt and put some semblance of a part in my hair.

The main clubhouse was a fat old shingle-style place that looked like most of the older homes lining the shore between the ocean and Gin Lane. The cedar shakes were a dark gray, split and curled in many places, which made the bright blue-and-white-striped awnings look all the more fresh and sporty. I trotted up onto the huge porch—carpeted with woven jute and furnished in white wicker—where it was easily ten degrees cooler. A scattering of people in and out of tennis outfits were having drinks and picking melons and strawberries out of pewter baskets. As I hoped, there was a reception area just inside the main door.

"Burton Lewis, please," I said to the guy standing there in a pink shirt and white bow tie, sleeves rolled up to the middle of his forearms.

"I'm sorry?"

"I'm here to have lunch with Burton Lewis."

He looked down at the book on his maitre d' stand.

"Your name?"

"Sam Acquillo. He might've forgotten."

He looked at me as if to say, "Mr. Lewis never forgets."

I looked at my watch, then felt immediately idiotic because I wasn't wearing one. The host saw the dumb move, too. Condescension began to creep into his expression.

"He's waiting for me. Why don't you just tell him I'm here," I said.

"We don't disturb our members at lunch. And if you're not a member," he paused to look me up and down, so we could silently agree I wasn't, "you aren't permitted to remain on the premises."

I wondered if once, just once, I'd be able to enter a building and just get to see the person I wanted to see without having to manipulate, cajole, bribe, threaten or sock some mistrustful gatekeeper in the nose.

"You're guessing that Burton wouldn't want to see me."

"I escort Mr. Lewis to his private dining room every Thursday. I'm afraid he would have mentioned it to me."

"Okay, but what if you're wrong. What if he would've seen me but you didn't let him know I was here. How would that go over?"

That almost worked with Ivor Fleming's security guards, for whom the wrong call could conceivably be a matter of life and death. Granted, the Gracefield standards were probably more strictly enforced.

He wavered.

"All you have to do is go to where he's eating and tell him Sam Acquillo is downstairs. If he says 'who the heck is that?' you're in the clear. How bad could that be?"

I was grateful that he bought the concept. I didn't want to have sock him in the nose, which I was prepared to do right at that moment, something else I'd have to regret for the rest of my life.

He was gone just a few minutes. When he reappeared in the reception area he snuck in behind a small bar and grabbed a leather-bound menu. He handed it to me.

"The specials are inside," he said, formally, as he led me down the hall. "The duck confit seems to be the most popular item."

"Excellent," I said. "I love duck. My dog'll sometimes snatch one out of the lagoon. Fry it right up."

We went up two flights of stairs, down a hallway lined

with oil paintings of seascapes, gaff-rigged racing yachts and Atlantic waterfowl and into a large, brilliantly lit room. An octagon, with windows on every side. I recognized it as the building's tower, from a glimpse of the club you could catch over the hedges when you drove down Gin Lane. I'd been catching that glimpse my whole life. It was remarkably strange to be looking at it from the inside out.

Burton was sitting alone at a round table, carving some meager little mound of oiled foliage on his plate, an ice bucket with an open bottle of white at his right elbow.

"Sam," said Burton, getting up from the table and warmly shaking my hand, "what a pleasure."

I had to hand it to the guy in the white bow tie. He stood calmly at attention, ready to take it like a man.

I jerked my thumb at him.

"This guy's good, Burt. Really looks after the place. Tell management he's a keeper."

The guy gave a neat little bow.

"And you should know, Sam. A man of your worldliness."

"You people have Absolut?" I asked the guy. "On the rocks. No fruit. Just a swizzle stick." He nodded a brisk little nod and gratefully took the opportunity to spin on his heel and beat it out of there.

"This is delightful," said Burton. "The food here is really quite good, for a club. Just stay clear of the duck. Too fatty."

"I'm sorry to bother you," I said. "We just need to catch up."

He was chewing, so he twirled his fork in the air as a way of saying, "Forget about it."

"You know this Jonathan Eldridge thing," I said to him. "It's messing me up."

He nodded eagerly.

"I have some information for you," he said. "I called you,

but you weren't there, and of course you don't have an answering machine. Or email."

"That's what they tell me."

"I was about to drive over there. Meant to do it today, actually."

He shoved the salad out of the way and took the silver cover off a plate filled with pasta, vegetables and what looked like chunks of lobster and crab.

"Here," he said, scooping a mound of the stuff on to a dinner plate, "take this. I'll eat off the serving dish."

I didn't argue with him.

"Thanks. Looks great."

The guy in the white bow tie reappeared with my drink. Burton told him to bring another plate of what we were eating and shooed him out of the room.

"So what do you got?" I asked him.

"You can't repeat this, but Mr. Fleming is a week or two away from a full-scale racketeering indictment. I think my theory was correct. Whatever information the State investigators pulled from Jonathan Eldridge's computer has provided the basis for the action. They're quite happy about it. I know it's not your principal concern. Nothing new on the car bombing."

"Anything come up about his relationship with Jonathan Eldridge, or his brother Butch?"

"You told us to focus on your hostiles, as you put it. Found more evidence to the contrary regarding the brother."

"Jonathan took good care of him. I know that."

"Oh, yes. To a fault. At least in the eyes of the State investigation."

Burton grinned at me over the top of his pasta.

"Really."

"You really can't repeat this. In fact, we aren't even having this conversation. Not for my sake, for the chap who spilled it to me."

"I'm cool, Burt, you know that."

He nodded emphatically.

"I do," he said. "It seems the forensic accountants, going through Jonathan's financial records, determined that a few days before he was killed he used substantial assets from his cash reserves at Eagle to take positions within three sub-accounts."

"Substantial?"

"Seven figures substantial. Given that there was no other accounting irregularity, this stuck out. Apparently, Jonathan was scrupulous in his bookkeeping. Had a very straightforward, conservative methodology. Left little room for shenanigans. So, this big transfer stuck out."

I struggled to remember Jackie's explanation of Jonathan's system, trying to visualize the structure in my mind.

"The cash account was a just a big pool that held all the money that flowed in and out of the sub-accounts. Just a holding tank. As long as the in and out is tracked and accounted for, doesn't mean a thing."

"That's right."

"So this big transfer could have been a routine occurrence. He was just caught between moves. If he hadn't been killed, he would have reconciled everything. Nothing illegal in that."

"Not at all. Especially when you consider that a sizeable percentage of that cash account belonged to Jonathan himself. With his wife. More than enough to cover the transfer to Butch. It was his money, theoretically. Could do anything he wanted with it."

"So why did the forensic accountants think it was important?"

Burton shrugged.

"He'd never done it before. At least never with numbers that large. That's what they look for. Anomalies. Deviations from patterns. Hiccups in the system. This was a very big one."

"Who owned the three sub-accounts?"

"Butch Ellington for one. That I remember. The other two names are in a file back at the house."

"Neville St. Clair and Hugh Boone."

"Something like that. Interesting names."

I started getting the feeling I used to get when trouble-shooting process systems, that I'd solved the problem but didn't know it yet. That my unconscious had already drawn the conclusion, and was now just hanging around waiting for the cognitive department to catch up. I drank some of the vodka to hasten the transition.

"Why?" I asked.

"Why indeed."

"The Feds have released all those assets. Who picked up the shortfall?" I asked.

"Jonathan's estate. As I said, he had more than enough to cover the delta."

Some time during the conversation another mounded plate of pasta and seafood appeared in front of me. I only noticed it when I caught myself pulling on the edge of the tablecloth so hard I was dragging everything across the table.

"Who authorized that?" I asked, though I already knew.

"The lawyer for the estate. Szwit. Gabriel Szwit. Has an office in the Village. A good litigator, they say. He's done some pro bono for this little effort I set up with the public defenders office in Suffolk County."

I got up from the table and walked over to the window that faced the ocean. A warm damp sea breeze was drifting in through the screens. The ocean looked docile, with only tiny breakers staggering in to shore. A good day to be on the beach. Comatose in a lounge chair, under an umbrella, mind blank, heart at rest.

I asked him what else he had, and we went through some complicated machinations the investigators had used to look for other blips in Jonathan's behavior patterns, only to come away admiring his skill and honesty.

"Accounting involves a lot more gray area than most people would want to think. There're conservative and aggressive ways to go about things. Jonathan was very clever, but completely honest."

"Or would have been if he hadn't been a complete fraud."

"Precisely. Completely baffled the investigators."

I went back to the table and sat down.

"There's something else I find interesting," said Burton, "but I'm not sure why."

"Okay."

"Do you know how an Internet search works?"

"Not exactly."

"It's very useful, but somewhat random. Odd items pop up, simply because the word or words you're searching for appear in an online database."

"I'm already lost."

"If you do a search on Arthur Eldridge, the brother, you'll see he was a witness in an open court proceeding, duly recorded and logged on the court's website. It was a bail hearing involving an Italian national."

"Osvaldo."

Burton looked pleased.

"That's exactly right. I have the file at the house, but as I remember his full name is Osvaldo Allegre. At issue was a complaint that Mr. Allegre had molested a teenage girl. Arthur and Dione Eldridge were listed as witnesses, though all testimony was sealed, given the girl's age. But you can surmise it was good enough to charge the Italian, because the judge set a trial date. Which never happened, because about a week before the trial Allegre jumped bail and disappeared. The case was referred to the INS, but that was the end of that."

I got up again and went back over to the window. The ocean was still there, still calm. The few clouds that had been over the horizon had dissolved away.

"You find that interesting, too," said Burton. "Or else you've been drinking too much coffee."

"You can't drink too much coffee, Burt," I said, still looking out the window. Then I asked him, "Didn't you once tell me, 'just because you think it's true doesn't mean it isn't'?"

"Yes. Quoted from a former law professor."

"What if everything you think is true, isn't? Is that the corollary? What if everything you thought was wrong?"

"At least you'd be consistent."

I hung out with him until we finished lunch. By then the conversation had moved off Jonathan Eldridge and on to baseball. Neither one of us would watch a game on television, so we agreed on the need to go to Yankee Stadium to see for ourselves the performance capabilities of some recent trades we'd read about in the *Times*. Burton said he'd call me with some options on dates and match-ups.

"I'll keep my calendar clear," I said.

"Splendid."

We walked out together and I dropped him off at his car, a white, early 1980s Ford Country Squire with fake wood paneling. The rear seats were folded down and the back was filled with garden tools, bags of topsoil and a tray of red and yellow chrysanthemums that Burton was apparently going to plant in some remote corner of the estate reachable only by station wagon.

"I hope I was helpful," he said as he climbed into the car.

"You always are, Burt," I said. "At the very least you keep me fed."

"You seem better, in general, than you've been," he said, squinting against the bright sun, "but specifically out of sorts."

I leaned on the door panel.

"I've been on a program of self-improvement."

"Has anything improved?"

"Just my appreciation for the stupidity of self-improvement programs."

"So there you are. Progress."

———

I waited until he was all the way off the grounds and onto Gin Lane before going back into the clubhouse to call Joe Sullivan. They'd released him from the hospital to convalesce at home, but I knew there was an odds-on chance I'd catch him at his desk at police headquarters.

"So, how're you feeling?" I asked when he answered the phone.

"I'm breathing."

"You working regular hours?"

"Ross said I could do half days. Still putting in a whole shift."

"So you could leave anytime you want? You could say you felt crappy and needed to go home?"

"Is that what I'm going to do?"

"Instead of going home, meet me at my place. It'll take me about a half-hour to get there."

"Anything else you want to tell me?"

"Are you allowed to carry?"

"No reason why I shouldn't," he said, defensively.

"Bring it," I said, then hung up on him so he wouldn't keep asking me questions.

On the way home I drove through the parking lot behind Gabe's office, but his Jag was gone. I went up the stairs to double-check, but the outside door was secured with a hasp and a beefy combination lock. I couldn't see through the glazed window pane, so I left.

Probably halfway to Argentina by now.

I stopped at the corner place to get some hazelnut coffee to counteract the two Absoluts I'd had with Burton. The shop was full as it always was that time of year with graceful young women in translucent sarongs and distracted-looking middle aged couples fresh off the beach, eating a late lunch or scanning the real-estate flyers for hopes and dreams. It took me a while to get to the counter.

The tiny Central American lady who'd been serving me for over five years asked how I was doing. A first. I guess she was feeling a little homesick for the off season. I answered her in Spanish which made her perk up even more. I apologized for my lousy grammar. She said I spoke like they did in Madrid, only not as well.

"*Es sólo importante tratar,*" she said, handing me my change.

"It is," I agreed, "and that's what I'm going to do."

———

Joe and Eddie were waiting for me out in the Adirondacks when I got to the cottage. Sullivan was drinking one of my beers in more or less the same position I'd found him in the last time, only less bloody and apparently wide awake.

I stopped in the kitchen to get a beer of my own. Leaning against the screen door was an envelope from an overnight delivery service. I brought it out with me to the Adirondacks.

"I didn't know they delivered all the way out here," said Sullivan, nodding at the envelope.

"Yeah. Causes quite a stir in the neighborhood."

I pulled out a stack of papers with a postcard on top.

> Your lawyer is sweet. How did that
> happen? What's up with this stuff? You owe
> me big time. I'm cashing in next week. Tell
> Eddie to get the hell off my pillow.

Jackie's search had produced more material than I needed, so I had to shuffle through a lot of extraneous paper until I found what I was looking for.

"What's all that?" Sullivan finally asked, his patience wearing thin.

"Census data. They collect it in big surveys once every decade. Mandated by the Constitution."

"So that's why I'm over here? You gonna survey me?"

"Drink your beer and give me a minute."

At the top of one of the census reports was a note from Jackie via Allison:

> Alena gave me addresses and phone numbers.
> The addresses are post-office boxes. The phone
> numbers go to answering machines. Alena said
> they conducted business entirely through back-
> and-forth messages. I see what you're getting
> at. It pisses me off when you don't share any-
> thing until after the fact. By the time you get
> this I'll be heavily sedated. Don't wake me up.

There was more in the envelope that might have been interesting, but I had enough. I had what I wanted.

I put my hand on Sullivan's forearm.

"Can you just stay put for a few minutes while I go talk to Amanda? I'll get you another beer."

He frowned at me.

"I can get my own damn beer. Go ahead. I'll still be here. Especially if somebody stabs me again."

"You have a cell phone?" I asked him.

"Who doesn't?"

"What's the number?"

I whistled for Eddie to follow me over to Amanda's house. Her car was in the driveway, but she wasn't out on her chaise. I rang the bell and she answered wearing a terry cloth bathrobe.

"Well, hello," she said. "I was about to get dressed. Should I not bother?"

"Not in front of the dog," I said, walking past her into the house. "Actually, what I'd like is for you to take the dog and drive directly to Burton's house. Stay there until I call. Tell him I'm with Sullivan and to keep you safe until he hears from me."

"You're frightening me," she said.

"Sorry. Just a precaution."

"Where are you going?"

"To test a theory."

"That clears that up."

"Can you go?"

"I guess. Just don't wait too long to call. Burton'll be worried. I'll be worried. I'm worried now."

I put my arm around her shoulders and gave a squeeze.

"What's to worry?" I asked.

"I know the risks you take."

"I've got Sullivan with me. Nobody's stupid enough to mess with a cop."

I left her and Eddie and went to retrieve Sullivan before Burton's expensive beer put him to sleep. Though first I had to stop at my house to make a phone call.

A man answered the phone.

"Neville St. Clair?" I asked.

It was quiet on the other end of the line for what seemed a long time.

"Or do you prefer Hugh Boone?" I asked.

"Who is this?"

"Sam Acquillo."

There was some more silence.

"What do you want?" he said, flatly.

"To meet. Talk about it."

"Tell me now."

"You'll have to meet me."

"Where?"

I told him to go to Appolonia's. He didn't need directions.

"Why now?" he asked.

"Sorry, but it's a one-time offer. Now or never."

It was silent again for a moment.

"So you're saying I haven't a choice."

"Not really."

He hung up the phone. I didn't know what that meant, so I let it go at that and went out to get Sullivan. I was able to pile him into the Grand Prix and get underway before I had to tell him where we were going.

"To see the spooky lady who's afraid of the whole world. Appolonia Eldridge."

"Now I know why I needed the piece."

"Not for her, it's the housekeeper you have to worry about."

I had an approximation of a plan, though I didn't think it would work. Way too many variables dependent on luck. And timing I couldn't control. Very incompatible with an engineer's precise calculations. Though it didn't have to work all the way. No matter what, something would happen. The fuse was already lit.

The day was getting hotter; the breeze had died off and it felt like vapor was rising from the scorched ground. Sullivan was coming to grips with the Grand Prix's lack of air-conditioning. Luckily there was so much wind noise inside the car I didn't have to listen to him bitch about it.

We went out to Route 27, then up Route 24 past the big white duck, the pride of Flanders, then on to the incongruous four-lane road whose original purpose was probably lost in the misty legends of the Department of Transportation. From there over to Appolonia's barren, treeless neighborhood. We were the first to get there, assuming anyone else would show up. At least I could be reasonably sure Appolonia was there, so we'd have somebody to talk to. Before we rang the doorbell I gave Sullivan a five-minute version of what I thought could happen, and why.

"You're telling me this now?" he asked.

"I could have left you out. I thought you should be here."

"I'm supposed to thank you."

"Unless I got it wrong, in which case, you're here to arrest me, so it won't be a total waste of time."

"Jesus Christ," he said, hauling his sore gut out of the Grand Prix.

Belinda answered the door, peering at us under the security chain.

"You didn't call," she said.

"Sorry. But we need to see Mrs. Eldridge."

"You can't come in unless you call."

Sullivan held up his badge and ID.

"I'm a police officer, ma'am. We're here to see Mrs. Eldridge. It's important. May we come in?"

That had an impact on her, but she wasn't ready to cave. "I need to talk to the lawyer."

"No, you don't," I said, in a voice loud enough to hear in downtown Riverhead. "You need to tell Mrs. Eldridge that we're here, and you need to do it now."

"Belinda, for pity's sake, let them in," I heard Appolonia call from the living room.

The door shut, then reopened with the chain off. Belinda backed in as she opened the door. I kept Sullivan between us. He had the gun.

Appolonia was where I'd last seen her, perched more than seated in the high-backed stuffed chair, a book open in her lap. She was wearing a light coral cashmere sweater, clasped at the neck with a tiny silver chain, and black slacks. Her feet were tucked up under her butt.

"Mr. Acquillo. And?"

"Officer Joe Sullivan. Southampton Town Police."

She shook his outreached hand.

"Nice to meet you," said Sullivan. "Thanks for letting us in. Nice house."

"Sam told me about you. Said I'd like you."

"You have a good memory," I told her.

"Not hard when it's so little taxed. What's the occasion?"

"I'm sorry to just bust in on you like this, but there're some things we have to talk about."

"Sounds rather grave. Does that explain the reinforcements? Come, sit."

Sullivan looked like he'd have been a lot happier standing, but sat anyway on the edge of the Victorian love seat. I took the other high-backed chair.

"I don't have a lot of time to get into long explanations, not now anyway," I said to her. "I'm sorry for that."

If this was alarming her, it didn't show, beyond the simple

gesture of closing her book, after carefully marking her place with a slip of paper, and putting it on a side table.

"Very well. Should Gabe be here?" she asked.

"Well, that's the first thing. You're going to have to fire him."

"Really. How so?"

"He's been defrauding you and misrepresenting himself. For starters."

"You know this?"

I looked over at Sullivan. He nodded convincingly.

"Yes, ma'am. I'm afraid so."

"Dammit."

You couldn't get any whiter than Appolonia, so she wasn't turning white. But maybe a little pink was creeping up into her cheeks. Probably good for her.

"You have worse news than that?" she asked.

"I don't know if 'worse' is the word. Different."

She put her fingertips up to her mouth.

"You know who killed Jonathan."

"I have a theory."

"Yes, of course. You're the scientist."

"But I need your help to prove it out."

I realized that Belinda was in the room with us. Had likely been there all along, only now she was close enough to hear the conversation. I pointed to her with my thumb.

"Belinda should be out of the room, and out of the foyer. Another person should be arriving shortly. Officer Sullivan needs to answer the door."

"Who on earth would that be?" asked Appolonia.

By now she'd realigned herself on her chair, leaning forward, her bare feet side by side on the Chinese rug. I saw her as a young girl, self-conscious and withdrawn, but aware of the world. Amusing herself with an internal monologue, satirizing and excoriating people she knew—teachers, aunts and uncles, nannies—people unaware of her gift for insight, her busy contemplative mind. They wouldn't know because she'd never allow them to. For Appolonia, thought by definition must be private. Contained and secure within a sealed chamber. A safe haven where both the fruits of perception and passion could be allowed full expression.

Her parents' death may have been the deciding event in condemning her to complete isolation, but only in hastening the inevitable. Serving up a ghastly, but welcome rationale. An objective, identifiable cause for the foregone effect.

Because Appolonia gloried in the ice castle of her mind. A luminous, precisely organized mind that should have been able to recognize that no one can separate themselves entirely, and forever, from the hot and messy, chaotic reality just outside those castle walls.

"Jonathan Eldridge. Your husband."

Appolonia clamped a hand across her mouth and lurched back into her chair, drawing her feet up off the floor as if the rug had just burst into flames. Her eyes opened to the whites. I sat quietly, waiting for her to catch her breath. She slapped her hand down to her lap.

"You are very cruel. How dare you say such a thing."

"You didn't know," I said, not as a question, but as an answer.

"He was killed."

"Lots of people were killed. And one was damaged in a way that she'll never fully recover from, even after they put her face back as close as they can to what it used to look like."

And somebody else would never be the same. Me, as it turns out. I'd have to live with the sight of the orange flames consuming the interior of that black Lexus with its desperate and agonized human cargo, and the jolt of horror when my somnambulant brain finally processed what was happening, the desperate hope clutching my heart as I threw Jackie across the big table, and the regret later that maybe I'd saved her life, but that was all I could save. Only her, and not the four innocent people who were only having a pleasant cocktail on an outdoor deck, and the waitress whose only thought was keeping our drinks filled and picking out which of us was most likely to leave a decent tip. And the manager of the place, counting the till, trying to calculate the size of the impending dinner crowd. All those people who were atomized and sprayed across the harbor shore because I only had time to save a single person.

And myself.

Appolonia nearly jumped out of her chair when the doorbell rang. Sullivan stood up quickly and pulled his Smith & Wesson out of the holster under his arm. He took Belinda by the elbow and propelled her out to the foyer and into the kitchen. I stood up, too, between the door and where Appolonia was sitting. I could hear her behind me, making little breathing sounds and whispering words I couldn't make out. Sullivan opened the door with his right hand, stepping back and covering the entrance with the gun held in his left.

"Hands where I can see them," said Sullivan. "Step forward slowly. Don't do anything stupid."

"I never do anything stupid," said Butch Ellington as he walked into the living room. "Insane, maybe, but never stupid."

TWENTY-EIGHT

APPOLONIA SHOT ME a bewildered and angry look.

"It's him," I said, grabbing him by the neck and using my thumb to smear back his moustache, revealing the scarred lip. "Look familiar?"

He tried to pull back, but I dug in my grip and brought my mouth up to his ear.

"Tell her," I said.

His antic eyes were darting around the room, as if searching for a way out, an escape hatch into another dimension.

"Tell her," I said again and let go of his head. His eyes abruptly stopped their search and focused on me. His face lit into a smile and he made a small bow.

"*Signore Aquila*. The eagle has landed."

"Enough of that crap," I said to him. "Say it."

He made another little bow and turned toward Appolonia.

"It's me, darling," he said, in a softly modulated version of his voice. "You know that it is. Your Jonathan."

Appolonia had her hand back up to her mouth and was trying to disappear into her chair. Belinda barreled into the room, pushed passed Sullivan and me and knelt at Appolonia's feet. Sullivan moved around in front of me and gestured slightly with his revolver, forcing Butch to move back a step. Sullivan patted him down, then took his shoulder and pushed him gently into the love seat while taking out his cell phone and dialing a number.

"Keep your hands flat on the cushions where I can see them. You come with anybody? Anybody outside?" He raised the revolver up to Butch's eye level to help him remember.

"Why don't you ask *Signore Aquila*? He's apparently omniscient."

"Keep your insults to yourself," said Sullivan.

I went over to the window and slipped the edge of my hand between the curtains, just enough to see out. There was an old Jeep Cherokee parked behind the Grand Prix. Charles and Edgar were leaning against the side of the truck, looking relaxed, but focused on the front door. I described the scene to Sullivan, who had the cell phone at his ear.

"Okey-dokey, dude," he said to Eldridge. "Not a twitch, not a wink, not a nod." Then into the phone, "Hiya, Janet. Got a little situation here. Need you to radio the Riverhead station."

He went on with a string of code numbers and a description of the neighborhood and the present dispersal of Butch's crew. Appolonia was now crying, in a steady, forceful way, full and unrestrained. Belinda stroked her arm and spoke to her in soothing tones, telling her everything would be all right, that she would take care of her, that she would not let anything bad happen to her, ignoring the fact that something very bad just had.

"Too elegant to pass up, wasn't it," I said to Butch. "The chance to kill two birds with one stone. Jonathan and Osvaldo."

Butch grinned at me.

"The man was sleeping with my daughter. Starting when she was twelve years old. She refused to testify at the trial. She said it was our fault for letting him in our house. Maybe the hearing was too much for her, I don't know. The worst betrayal imaginable and I could do nothing about it."

"He didn't know that," I said. "And neither did the DA. The trial was still on. You told Osvaldo you were ready to work out a deal, but he had to meet you. Alone. The arrangements were wacky, but not to Osvaldo. That's just the way you did things. Everything's performance art. He was given Jonathan's Lexus and told to drive over to the Windsong parking lot, get out of the car and play with the dog—you wanted to make sure there were witnesses. And to wait for a call. On the cell phone that came with the car, the obvious way to trigger the firebomb. Only you or someone else was stupid enough to load the bomb that came after with about five times the necessary C-4. Or maybe not so stupid. The fire might not have burned him up enough to destroy his DNA. He had to be vaporized."

As I spoke I started to lose Butch's attention. He was watching Appolonia, his eyes filled with their usual gleam of brilliant curiosity.

Sullivan finished his call and clicked the phone shut.

"It's gonna take a few minutes for backup to get here. What did you tell your boys to do?" he asked Butch.

"To improvise, of course. We're famous for improv."

"They armed?" Sullivan asked. "They supposed to bust in here if you don't give them a high sign?"

"I should tell you everything? Please, some imagination."

Sullivan leaned down and pulled Butch to his feet.

"Grab a lamp cord," he said to me.

He used it to tie Butch's hands behind his back. Then shoved him back down on the couch. He took my spot at the window, delicately pulling back a sliver of curtain. I dragged an ottoman over next to Butch and sat down.

"It was getting too hot to sustain, wasn't it?" I asked him. "You'd finally screwed up by losing your temper at Joyce Whithers after she insulted you at her restaurant. The subtle mockery of the Schnauzer painting wasn't enough. You had to screw her in the markets. Just like you did to Ivor Fleming when he cheated you and dared suggest you alter your paintings. Joyce wasn't as easy a mark. She went ballistic, threatened a lawsuit. Your phony gig could never withstand that kind of legal scrutiny. And she knew Fleming. They'd surely compare notes. And far worse than any of that, she knew Appolonia. It was time to bail. But in a way so dramatic all the attention would be on the perpetrators of the crime, away from the victim."

"I love you, darling," he said to Appolonia, in the same soothing voice he'd used before. "I always did. You know I made you happy."

"While she made you rich."

I lowered my voice, hoping she wouldn't hear me from across the room, but I couldn't stop myself from saying what I said.

"What a godsend. A wealthy, needy, orphaned agoraphobic. You had the prescience to introduce yourself as your old alter ego. Things flowed nicely from there. You told her you were at the Harvard B School. Even took a few courses to beef up your story. Married her and moved her down here from Boston, isolating her from her old friends, while you continued your life as an artistic impresario, complete with entourage. Got Gabe involved to help keep an eye on her when you couldn't be around. You had a whole team dedicated to sustaining the illusion. At least Charles and Edgar, in on it from the beginning. And why not? You literally owned the goose that laid the golden egg, and there were plenty of eggs to go around."

"I took splendid care of you, darling," said Butch to Appolonia. "You're richer than ever."

If that was meant to make her feel better, it didn't work. Her sobs deepened, causing Belinda to almost climb into the chair with her as she gathered a tighter hold. I made him look back at me.

"You did. And yourself as well. And your buddies. Pretty good investment manager for an artist," I said. "Or is it the other way around? Do you even know anymore?"

"There's no art in failure. If I were to become you, I'd be the most successful Sam Acquillo that could ever be. I'd be the eagle you wish you were. Flying high above the earth, seeing all below with perfect clarity."

Before I could grapple with that image I had a new thought.

"What about Dione? She had to know, too. You met her after you came back to Long Island. Sold her on the idea that Jonathan and his life was the greatest work of performance art in history. Did she know you fricasseed the Italian?"

He stared at me, not ready to give that up.

"Of course she did," I said. "Might've been her idea."

"You're welcome to burn in hell yourself, *Signore Aquila*," he said.

"I don't think that's what Appolonia's Jonathan would have said."

Sullivan grunted.

"Hey, Sam. I've got some movement out there."

I stood up next to him and peeked out the seam in the curtains. Charles had moved away from the truck and was standing out on the lawn, directly in front of the door. His arms were folded, but he was frowning.

"We should make a move while we can still surprise these guys," said Sullivan.

He told me what he had in mind. I pulled Butch up on his feet, collected the back of his collar in my right hand and gripped his elbow with my left. I shook him a little so he'd register the fact that he couldn't break free.

"For what it's worth," I told him, "I really liked your paintings, the ones at Ivor's."

"I've renamed them *Pearls before Philistines*."

"How about *The Wages of Ego*. If you'd had better control of yours, you might've pulled it off."

I pushed him into the foyer and waited until Sullivan could reach around us and open the front door. As the door swung into the foyer I walked Butch out onto the stoop. Sullivan came right up behind us and rested his arm on Eldridge's shoulder, pointing the revolver at Charles, and then Edgar, then back again.

"On your bellies," he yelled. "First guy to take a step this way takes a bullet."

Neither moved. They stood and stared, incomprehension and indecision playing across their faces. Time slowed and the world stood motionless but for Sullivan's arm, pivoting between the two men, now looking at each other, trying to hear each other's thoughts.

Butch started to quietly hum *Semper Fidelis* by John Philip Sousa. I snugged up my grip on his shirt enough to choke it off.

"He isn't worth it," I said to them, as calmly as I could. "Not anymore."

"Last chance," yelled Sullivan. "Do it."

And they did. Charles first, then Edgar, dropping down to their hands and knees, then lying face down on the ground, arms and legs spread. I did the old schoolyard trick of unlocking Eldridge's knees from behind, causing him to crumple to a kneeling position, from where I shoved him forward onto his face, hitting the ground hard enough to force out a grunt. I held him there until we saw bright strobe lights reflected off the neighboring houses from a small fleet of patrol cars silently descending on and forever altering Jonathan and Appolonia's cherished sanctuary.

"You wanted to explore a giant finger up the ass," I said to him, taking my knee off his back as I stood up to make way for the Riverhead cops. "I think you'll be getting your wish."

I went back into the house. Belinda was sitting on the arm of the high-backed chair, cradling Appolonia and stroking her jet-black hair. I expected to be laid waste by the older woman's expression, but she only looked stricken by grief and uncertainty.

"We have some medicine," she said to me, "for the especially bad days. She can have a little of that."

"Can I call anybody?" I asked.

"We have a person we can call. In a minute," she said to Appolonia. "We can call her in a minute."

I wanted to tell Appolonia I was sorry, but it wasn't the right time. And "sorry" felt like too meager a word. So I left them and went back out to join Sullivan.

A swarm of uniformed officers were busy handcuffing Eldridge and his boys, going through their wallets, jotting information down in notebooks and on clipboards and talking on radio receivers tethered by coil cords to their patrol cars. Sullivan was talking to a lieutenant, as designated by an arm patch sewed on her uniform.

"What're we charging these guys with again?" he asked as I approached.

"That's a question for Ross, but for now try the murder of Osvaldo Allegre and six other people at the Windsong

Restaurant, investment fraud, bigamy and Christ knows how many counts of identity theft, falsifying records, illegal impersonations, and oh, assaulting a police officer," I said, putting my hand on Sullivan's shoulder.

"You're shitting me."

"Not intentionally. They thought they were assaulting a design engineer. That's almost legal."

He looked over to where the uniforms were talking to Edgar and Charles.

"Now I wish I'd shot 'em."

"You'd had a big day, you were tired, and full of Burton's beer. You nodded off in my Adirondacks. They came up behind you and dumped a burlap sack over your head. I doubt Butch was there. He would've known it wasn't me. Anyway, you didn't go down easy. Like I told you, you got in a few of those rights, might've got a grip on one of them through the burlap. Somebody panicked and stuck you with a knife—maybe had one on hand to cut the burlap, or a rope, or both. I don't know what they had in mind for me, but you were screwing it all up. So they smacked you on the head, peeled off the burlap and left you there."

"What the hell for?"

"You gotta know artists, Joe. Everything has to say something. Once the original concept was upended, they improvised."

He looked past me at the uniforms leading Edgar and Charles toward separate cruisers.

"Some freaking artists. Whatever happened to watercolors?"

The Riverhead cops had secured Butch, Charles and Edgar in separate cars. A police van pulled up filled with plain-clothesmen who began stringing yellow tape and taking photographs of the scene. I didn't think Appolonia wanted to see much more of me, and I couldn't get to Butch, so I said to Sullivan that I knew I'd be spending time with Ross, but needed to stop off at Burton's on the way to check on Amanda. I asked him to call on his cell to tell them everything was okay.

"It's not on the way," he said, but didn't want to push it. He was happy just to be in the moment, in control again, faith restored in himself and his view of the world as a place where things could turn out the way you wanted if you only took a little trouble to make sure of it. A view of the world I didn't really believe in, but liked that somebody did.

While I waited for the Riverhead cops to move the Cherokee out of the way I stared at the person sitting in the back of the police cruiser. Looking at him, all I saw was Butch, so that's who he was in my mind. I hadn't known Jonathan, not directly, though I might have liked him better. Not that I didn't like Butch. Probably one of his gifts. He could make you like him. He knew instinctively how to control your perception of him, to trick your senses with distractions and diversions, like a magician, playing emotional sleights of hand. Even now, knowing what he'd done, I couldn't look at him without feeling the urge to talk to him, to watch him perform and play the rhetorical master of ceremonies.

But moving closer that's not what I saw. His head was bobbing up and down, and side to side, and his mouth was moving, and though I couldn't hear it clearly, I could tell he was talking to himself, alone in the car, now essentially alone in the world.

I was assaulted by an unwanted vision of Butch and Jonathan having a conversation with each other. It wasn't the last time I would see him, but it formed an image I could never fully eradicate from my mind.

—

Isabella let me through the gate at the head of Burton's quarter-mile driveway without much of a fight. Probably on direct orders. The white pebble drive ran in a straight line between two tall privet hedges that hid the house from view until you made a sharp right turn and were suddenly confronted by a three-story porch and balcony-laden facade. At this point the drive became an oval, inside of which was a natural garden of indigenous wild shrubs and vines entangling pergolas and curved trellises. And strategically placed teak benches, on one of which sat Amanda.

"Eddie's inside watching Burton paint," she said when I walked over and sat down next to her.

"Good. Maybe he'll pick up better work habits."

"Joe said everything was okay, but that's all he'd say."

"He's big on need-to-know."

"I need to know what happened."

"I need a drink, and a place to sit, and Burton Lewis in the audience."

"Okay. But only after I tell you I'm glad you're okay. Your well-being never seems to matter to you, but it matters to me. That makes you uncomfortable, doesn't it?"

"A little."

"Why?"

"Not sure."

"You can still tell me you appreciate it."

"I do."

"Okay. Let's go find Burton."

Soon after that Isabella had us set up in lawn chairs, way out on the lawn as it turns out, with a trolley full of refreshments and a stainless steel bowl for Eddie to drink water out of. Burton still wore a paint-spattered madras shirt and white cotton shorts, but looked grateful to be diverted from his task. I was more than grateful for the Absolut on the rocks.

"Ross Semple called here before you arrived," said Burton. "He wants you there in about two hours. You're meeting at the DA's office, with the East Hampton investigators, people from the State and two FBI agents. I'm coming along, too."

"You are?"

"To look after you. As Ms. Swaitkowski's proxy."

"Thanks, Burt. I appreciate it."

"He told me a few other remarkable things, but I'd rather hear your version."

"So who killed Jonathan?" Amanda asked.

It took a few minutes to explain that it wasn't Jonathan Eldridge who got blown up in the Lexus, but an Italian named Osvaldo Allegre. And then about an hour to explain that the killer was Jonathan Eldridge himself. Sort of.

"A split personality. Like Sybil," said Amanda.

"No, people like her are unaware of their multiple selves. Eldridge was not only conscious of Butch and Jonathan, he reveled in his creations."

All children pretend they're imagined characters at one time or another. For about a year my daughter wanted us to call her Madame Pele, a character out of Hawaiian folklore that for some reason had captivated her. It was almost pre-destined that a brilliant and inventive child like Butch would be moved to create entirely different personas to fit the con-trasting lives he led, simultaneously pleasing his accountant father while protecting his growing psyche from the conse-quences of his mother's illness. An illness that ebbed and flowed, but ultimately overwhelmed her, taking permanent hold. By then, his father was gone, and with Lillian safely ensconced with the Sisters of Mercy, there was nothing to thwart the development of Butch's parallel personalities.

As time passed, the dual lives became more entrenched. In perfect contrast to the dutiful, tidy young man who spent peaceful nights with the erudite Appolonia, his other self also flourished—the wildly clever, charismatic, artistically courageous self. The alter ego that was allowed to become the bigger ego, allowed to be protean and abundant, evolving further as Butch Ellington, even more grand and audacious, but also darkly treacherous. And devoted to his mad mother, who reinforced by her very nature the seductive possibilities of a dissociated identity.

Her behavioral, and likely genetic, legacy to her son.

"Being two people allowed him to live at both ends of the personality scale at the same time," said Burton.

"Impulsive, creative, sensual and charismatic at one end. Compulsive, professional, coolly detached and analytical on the other. Eldridge got to act out both extremes of human behavior."

"Each complete with a wife," said Amanda.

"The ultimate two-timer."

I threw a chunk of ice as far as I could so Eddie would have something to chase. I hoped he'd find it before it melted. Otherwise I'd never get him back in the car. Persistence was an Oak Point affliction.

"You owe Ivor Fleming an apology," said Burton.

"I wish I could say I knew that all along, but I didn't. I only started doubting when I talked to Ike and Connie. They aren't smart enough to lie convincingly. And they knew what I looked like. They wouldn't have jumped Sullivan, even if they hadn't known he was a cop. No reason to. It had all the markings of an amateur screw-up. Butch's place had been a potato farm, even when the family who owned it before had diversified into auto repair. The barns were always full of bundles of burlap. But old, half rotten. Not that hard for

Sullivan to punch his way through. I thought of all that, but even after Burt told me about Osvaldo's legal trouble, I couldn't quite believe it. To paraphrase Burton's professor, 'just because you think it's true doesn't mean you aren't full of crap.'

"It wasn't until Allison got me all the stuff Jackie had pulled off the Internet, including census data showing only one kid living with either Eldridge parent at any given time, and a copy of Butch's senior picture from BU, with his black, straight, neatly combed hair, that I knew it had to be."

"You owe me one, too," said Amanda. "For scaring me half to death."

"Sorry. It was all I could think of at the time. I was afraid I might have already tipped off Butch when I went after Gabe Szwit. As it is, I'd burned up a lot of time after leaving him at his office. Stupid of me."

"He may or may not have alerted Butch," said Burton. "It doesn't explain why he agreed to meet you at Appolonia's. He must have known it was a trap."

"He came because he knew I had him. Neville St. Clair and Hugh Boone were characters in a Sherlock Holmes story. Both the same man, one a distinguished gentleman, the other an ugly beggar with a talent for street theater. Butch told me he'd studied Conan Doyle. When he needed client names for two phantom accounts he'd set up to suck money out of Jonathan's consulting business he couldn't resist the temptation, the parallels were too compelling."

"*The Man with the Twisted Lip*," said Burton.

"That was the other thing Jackie had in the package. She came across the story on the Internet after doing a search on the names. This whole thing would've been solved a long time ago if me or the FBI were more conversant with the inventions of the twentieth century."

I was glad for that time I spent with Burton and Amanda. I knew I'd need it before going in for the grilling later that night. I'd been through similar things before, and this one was no better. Though one saving grace was seeing Webster Ig again. He'd spoken to Jackie's nurses, who said she was doing well, that the plastic surgeons were sure she'd come out as good as new.

And it was nice to have Burton along. Helped keep the discussion on a civil plane. Ross's mood also helped things along. Joe Sullivan, and consequently the Southampton Town police force, would get credit for the collars. If high-profile arrests are the coin of the realm in law enforcement, Southampton had discovered El Dorado.

It was well after midnight when I finally got to sleep. Out on the screened-in front porch with Amanda in the bed and Eddie on the braided rug. They were both breathing steadily by the time I drifted off, my mind strangely blank, and feeling something akin to peace for the first time since deciding on that second drink on the Windsong deck.

TWENTY-NINE

IT WAS STILL DARK when I woke up and decided to take a run. I left Amanda sleeping and crept out on the front lawn carrying my running shoes, shorts and T-shirt. Eddie heard me and came out to see what was up. He yawned, stretching his front paws forward and sticking his butt in the air. I hadn't looked at the clock on my way out, but it was probably a little after five judging by the faint glow forming along the eastern horizon.

I took my northern route that started behind Amanda's house and followed the shore of the Oak Point Lagoon, on which launches, fishing boats and shoal draft sailboats drifted languorously in the calm water at the end of bulky mooring lines.

I wasn't looking to make a big run of it. I just wanted to get as far as a sandy bluff I knew where a chunk of glacial rock stuck out partway down the hill, giving you a good place to sit and watch the sun slowly light up the bay as it rose over your left shoulder.

Eddie was always a little iffy about the whole thing, reluctant to make the short slide from the edge of the bluff down to the outcrop of stone, but he always did it anyway. And always landed where he was supposed to, though a clean miss would have been far from fatal. Might even like it. Climb back up the hill and do it again.

I just needed a place to think. Where distractions were at a minimum. Where you could do little but brood and brace yourself against an unplanned tumble down the sandbank to the bay shore. When I had a job troubleshooting engineered systems I picked out a few of these places within a short driving distance from the office in White Plains. Parks, coffee shops, bars, congenial habitats where you could be anonymous and unmolested for a brief period, enough to sketch out an answer to a puzzle on a yellow legal pad, or simply tick through all the points of contention.

I took it as a matter of faith that any problem could be solved eventually if you only put the right amount of thought into it, if you only had the time and mental capacity to focus on a solution. I was wrong about that. Startlingly wrong, but I didn't know that then.

Like most serious joggers, I brought a pack of cigarettes along with me to assist in the focusing process. I lit one and leaned up against the sandbank. I missed the adjoining cup of coffee, but there's only so much you can haul in a pair of nylon jogging shorts.

I slid further down the bank until I could look up at the blue sky emerging from the silver-gray of early morning. I waited for enlightenment to drift effortlessly into my mind, but all that happened was the urge to go back to sleep. I don't know what I thought I should be thinking about, only that there was an unresolved issue floating freely somewhere inside my consciousness, one that had been obscured by the clamorous thoughts of the last few weeks, and was now asserting itself.

I waited for more inspiration until the sun had the Little Peconic bathed in a pale new light and Eddie, uncharacteristically, began to whine with impatience.

"All right, all right," I said to him, carrying him back up the sandbank and dropping him down on the trail so we could jog back. I took an extended route, though it was still early when I got back to the cottage to find Amanda, wrapped in a blanket, out in the Adirondacks drinking coffee. I swung by my kitchen to pour a cup for myself and joined her.

"You must be tired," she said. "You didn't get much sleep."

"Sometimes tiredness will do that to you."

We sat quietly for a while, sipping the coffee and watching big seabirds skim along barely a foot above the still water, searching for breakfast.

"I'm moving out in a few days," said Amanda.

"Really."

"I'm thinking I might even leave the area. I've been here for a long time. And now I can be anywhere I want."

"That's true."

Another silence settled in for a while. As I cooled down from the run I realized the air was not as warm as it had been, and drier, so you could easily see the houses on Nassau Point across the bay. Yet the winds were calm. That wasn't a typical combination, and I wondered what it meant.

"How come?" I asked.

"How come what?"

"You want to leave?"

"I'm not sure it's what I want. I just don't want to go through it again."

"Through what?"

She'd been looking out at the bay the whole time, but now she rolled up on her shoulder so she could look at me.

"Now that there's nothing forcing you into the world, you'll head back into hibernation. That's where you'd prefer to be. Alone with yourself. You did it before, you'll do it again."

"I had a reason."

"What, because I damaged you? You thought no more damage was possible, and just like that, it happened anyway."

I thought about that.

"It's more than that."

She didn't say anything, waiting for me.

"You hate this, don't you?" she said, finally.

"I hate the fact that there's something I'm suppose to say that will cause you to change your mind, but I'm not sure what it is."

"You would if you truly wanted me to change my mind," she said, rolling back in the chair so she could refocus on the bay.

This was exactly the thing I was trying to noodle out that morning by running over to the rock stuck in the sandbank. It was what I first started to contemplate that day in the lumberyard during my discussion with Ike and Connie. It had something to do with the awful possibility that first choosing to live, and then choosing to live among people, exposed you to more than the danger you'd actually become attached to some of them.

If you weren't careful, you might even start to love somebody. Worse than that, you could love somebody you'd never be able to trust. Not completely. Not ever. No amount of denial, repression or avoidance would ever change that.

Amanda started to get up from her chair.

"If I tell you I love you will you sit back down?" I asked.
She sat back down.
"Yes."
"Good. Now try to stay put while I get some more coffee."

ACKNOWLEDGEMENTS

Eternal thanks to Literary Agent Mary Jack Wald, and Judy and Marty Shepard, without whom I'd be writing this in my imagination. Bob Willemin for investment management advice—if I got any of it wrong, trust me, it's my fault. My brother Whit and sister-in-law Adele for Spanish translations. Treasured reader Randy Costello for advice in English and Español. Rich Orr on legal affairs. Editorial wisdom from Anne Collins at Random House, Canada. Meagan Longcore, who can make anybody look good, literally. Mary Farrell for everything.